To
Lisa

keep on
swinging!

D1596280

The
DEVIL
in the
DIAMOND

For information, contact: henrygraypub2022@gmail.com

Publisher's Cataloging-in-Publication Data:

Name: Cioffi, Gregory, 1987 -.
Title: The devil in the diamond / Gregory Cioffi.
Description: Granada Hills, CA : Henry Gray Publishing, 2023.
Identifiers: LCCN 2023911079 | ISBN 9781960415066 (pbk.)|
ISBN 9781960415073 (ebook)
Subjects: LCSH: World War, 1939-1945—Campaigns—Pacific
Area—Fiction. | Baseball—Fiction. | Prisoners of War—Japan—
Ficion. | Race relations—Fiction. | Friendship—Fiction. | Shrijō
(Naha-Shi, Japan)—Fiction. New York (N.Y.)—Fiction. |BISAC:
FICTION / Historical / 20th Century / World War II. | FICTION
/ Sports
Classification: LCC 3603.154 D48 2023 | DDC 813 C56—dc23
LC record available at https://lccn.loc.gov/2023911079

Made in the United States of America.

Published by Henry Gray Publishing
P.O. Box 33832, Granada Hills, California 91394

For more information or to join our mailing list, visit
HenryGrayPublishing.com

The
DEVIL
in the
DIAMOND

Gregory Cioffi

HENRY GRAY
HG
PUBLISHING

Granada Hills, CA
"Select books for selective readers"

To My Parents

who encouraged this

not-so-great little leaguer

to blossom into the writer

he always wanted to be

"Love is the most important thing
in the world, but baseball
is pretty good, too."

— *Yogi Berra*

Prologue

The Morning of May 25th, 1945

Spectacular. That was the only word that came to Yuujin's mind as he admired the flaming crimson-coral that gleamed brilliance, now slightly above the horizon. Although it ascended and descended daily, Yuujin wondered why today of all days he appreciated it the most. It reminded him of the vibrancy of a rose with the robustness of a wine. It continued to gradually escalate and a glorious red hue dispersed over to the East and onto the land and nearby ocean. It was a moment frozen in time, or so he wished.

Yuujin also felt more attuned with nature as he marveled at the Luchu pine and Tiger's Claw, thorny deciduous trees that contained dense clusters of scarlet flowers and black seeds. He recollected how his mother used to warn him how the seeds were poisonous. When cooked, however, they were quite delicious. His father would often take the raw seeds and feed them to fish to benumb them, making them easier to catch.

Suddenly, a dark brown woodpecker with red-tipped feathers sprinkled with white spots soared past him and rose upward. Its head was a paler brown than its body and was topped with a dark red crown. Yuujin expected the creature to chirp as it often did but today it let out a raucous screech. The bird glided through the air, silhouetted as it positioned itself against the backdrop of the rising sun.

Yuujin turned to look at what he, along with many others, was protecting: Shuri Castle. Although the dazzling and elegant dwelling had been neglected in recent years, it was once the palace of the Ryukyu Kingdom. Being one who appreciated history, Yuujin recalled from his studies how this kingdom once thrived in the golden age of maritime trade.

The red tiles of the crimson castle that stood atop the hill provided a strategically sound headquarters for the Imperial Japanese Army. Yuujin, however, wasn't overly concerned with public spirit; his true dream was for this war to cease so he could go back to his hobbies and pleasurable pastimes.

Yuujin grabbed the base of his rifle and wrapped both of his hands around its butt. Imagining a small sphere with twine-covered cork covered by stitched horsehide, he gently swung the rifle while conceiving of the fanciful and extravagant notion of connecting so squarely that the hypothetical ball sailed deep into the air, towering so tall that it too became silhouetted in sunrise.

An outburst echoed in the morning breeze. Yuujin turned towards the discord and for a few moments detected nothing. Abruptly, however, a deafening detonation erupted in the not so far off distance. Yuujin could see other soldiers stirring about. One came jogging up to him.

"We are being shelled by a battleship off the coast!"

Yuujin gazed at the cardinal symbol of strength; he suspected his kin would wish to fight at Shuri to the death, as it would not be in the best traditions of the Japanese Army to withdraw.

Another blast of artillery fire fulminated, this time a little closer than the last. Yuujin knew this was only the beginning of a full-scale bombardment. He also knew that the loss of the remaining positions on the east and south of Conical Hill made the defense of Shuri extremely difficult and perhaps it even tipped the scales of battle.

Private Yuujin Miyano grasped his rifle in a more traditional manner and hoped the words of his brethren proved true and that the ghosts of his warlike ancestors would enter his heart and guide his hands in battle. He wondered if such an inheritance of honor was even possible before beholding the sunrise one last time.

Chapter 1

Clash for the Crest

Sugar Loaf Hill
The Morning of May 15th 1945

Private First Class Eugene Durante sat crouched atop the crest of Sugar Loaf Hill. The night before had been a horrific ordeal to say the least, as forty-four good men climbed upwards, towards the top of the hill, constantly hurling grenades into the nearby caves. Once they reached the top, they could hear the grunts of the Japanese as they too flung their explosive hand-weapons. A speedy preemptive strike allowed the Americans to, for the moment, remain atop the crest. Their commander had warned them if they didn't take the hill last night, the Japanese would drive them away in the morning. Morning had sprung and fifteen soldiers remained.

Eugene did not sleep a wink as mortars and sniper fire cut into the night, and his compatriots.

His heart had pounded rapidly before, but what he experienced the night prior was different. He never imagined an organ could palpitate so fast for so long without full-scale cardiovascular failure. Eugene suspected this was the new normal. For a moment, at some point in the night, his heartbeat lowered to a normal rate; it felt as if his heart ceased beating all together. This distress, within itself, caused his heart to once again vigorously ramp up. Eugene wondered which was worse.

About a month ago, Eugene received word that the troops of the 96th Infantry Division and the 763rd Tank Battalion had captured Conical Hill, an eastern anchor of the island. He was currently on the opposite coast and understood the importance of holding his position as these two locations exposed the Japanese around Shuri on both sides.

A small rock caught Eugene's eye. He picked it up, feeling the weight of it in his palm. He imagined how far he could throw it and with what velocity. Eugene thought up a scenario of utmost excitement.

The bases were loaded. He was on the mound facing the batter, his feet on the rubber. It was a full count. He took a step back with his right foot, his right shoulder pointing towards home plate. He lifted his front leg, bending at the knee, before tossing the round object to the catcher, his foot making an explosive step forward in the process. He released the ball.

You're out!

He could hear the cheers.

And then all he heard was silence. Of course he never really threw the pebble. Nor did he wind up. He just sat looking at the inanimate object, wondering what sort of sport could be had if this were all a very different situation.

He let the stone slip out of his hands. It clattered back onto the craggy terrain.

Eugene took a deep breath, in through his nose and out through his mouth. The pit of his stomach knew nothing was over. Any second, any minute, or any hour, all hell would break loose once more. He surmised it was the waiting that was the worst part.

That's when he heard it. The word resonated in the morning air, piercing the peace that was so short lived.

"Counterattack!"

Eugene had thought too soon.

Japanese combatants came storming up the hill; grenades began bursting immediately.

Through the intermittent blasts he heard someone yell, "Hold this position!"

Eugene began shooting down the hillside, somehow surprised at the number of enemy soldiers heading towards him.

The private first class sent a scattering of bullets from his submachine gun into the bodies of numerous attackers. Those he hit quickly lost their balance and went tumbling down the hill.

When his 30-round magazine expired, he grabbed a hand grenade, pulled the pin, and rolled it down the ridge. Before it could even blow, he reached for another. With a precision that became almost automated, Eugene repeated this seemingly mechanical process relentlessly.

One by one the pineapple-style weapons staggered down, rotating randomly towards the scaling men. Explosion after explosion halted the Japanese for what seemed like a mere moment before they were replaced with new men in the same spots.

"You could have been a grenadier!" he heard someone yell out.

Eugene could not feign a smile although he would have liked to; a chuckle, even a fictitious one, could be invaluable to morale.

An enemy soldier leaped up, almost making it onto the peak of the hill. Instinctively, Durante grabbed a grenade, pulled its pin, and gripped it with his index and middle finger like they were set on a line. He placed his thumb directly underneath the grenade as if it rested on smooth leather. He clutched the grenade hard and hurled it directly towards the upcoming aggressor. The Americans protectively threw their heads down as the explosive weapon struck the soldier directly in his chest, which was precisely where Eugene had aimed. His accuracy had not failed him.

Eugene looked away as the charge did its job. He could feel the aftermath splatter on him, as the soldier had been dangerously close.

His heart skipped a beat, which he quickly attributed to the fact that it couldn't possibly pulse faster so that was the only next logical course.

The momentary lapse had allowed more of the Japanese to gain ground.

Durante reached to find another grenade. This time, however, there were none left to be seized.

He speedily reloaded his weapon as he could hear the yells of nearing danger. Japanese soldiers began climbing onto the peak of Sugar Loaf Hill.

Eugene, having just replaced the .45 ACP cartridge, looked up to see an adversary practically on top of him. As his barrel collided with a stomach, he fired immediately. The weight of the now-deceased body coming down over his weapon knocked Eugene to the ground. His gun inadvertently cemented itself within the clutch of the man it had just killed.

Hordes of the Japanese fighters were uniting atop the hill.

Eugene stood, foregoing the fastened gun; it would be of no use in close-quarter combat.

In an instant he could hear the ceasing of all firearms. For that brief period of time, there existed a peaceful sound, a millisecond of serenity. It was the flash of calm before what would surely be a very bloody storm.

Eugene grabbed his combat knife as bayonets came jabbing at him. The long knives were fitted on the end of the Japanese rifles, making them extremely deadly when close.

Durante grabbed the wrist of an attacker and pulled him away, avoiding the blade, while striking down with his own.

He turned to see a familiar face, a corporal, who was ramming a number of enemy soldiers, like a defensive lineman, all the way to the edge of the hill. With a forceful groan, he knocked a hand-full of them straight off; sending them tumbling onto their backs, down the ridge.

"Still got it!" he called out.

A punch interrupted the corporal's ceremony and sent him staggering back a few steps. The opponent was in for a rude awakening, however, as the corporal soon sent him flying over the bluff too.

Eugene continued to slash as an onslaught of sharp edges came narrowly close to penetrating him. He noticed his ground on the hill was inevitably being pushed farther and farther back. Judging from the numbers, he knew he would not be standing on the highland for much longer.

A bayonet jabbed him in the leg. His knee buckled for a moment before he overcame the pain and stabbed the trooper in the neck. As the unfamiliar man went down, Eugene couldn't dislodge his knife.

Durante swung his fists valiantly, hitting and kicking everyone he came across. He felt a stabbing sensation again, this time in his lower back. He looked to his rear to see a rifle coming towards his face. He sidestepped and grabbed it, throwing it out of the hands of the man wielding it. The infantryman countered by unsheathing a sword out of a painted wooden scabbard.

Fierce strikes sent Eugene back even more until he found himself on a precipice. Not knowing exactly how to defend himself against the sword-wielding soldier, he froze at cliff's edge.

As his foe charged, the corporal that had moments before manhandled those numerous men, came surging in and barreled into the Japanese serviceman. Eugene, relieved for just a moment, gasped for air.

That's when he heard it. A single shot from a pistol.

An instant later, he felt it.

Eugene had been shot in his shoulder, the impact forcibly pushing him backwards. There was, however, no more ground for him to step on.

Private First Class Eugene Durante violently tumbled down the side of Sugar Loaf Hill. When he hit the base, he let out an emphatic cry. Supine, he looked up to see his brothers on the side of the slope, retreating back down.

He tried to move but could only let out a painful shriek. He closed his eyes, convincing himself a wound to the shoulder was not terminal. The stabs from the bayonets were not deeply pierced. At the moment, he believed he had no life-threatening injuries.

Eugene mustered up the strength to get up. He stumbled on the attempt but nonetheless stood his ground. There were other Marines at the hill's base.

He heard one scream, "Stem the attack!"

Eugene knew a stand would be made, here, on the Marine lines. He could also see there were men pinned down on the side of Sugar Loaf. Instincts took over and he proceeded onwards.

"Where are you going!?" one American yelled out.

"Back up that damn hill!" Durante retorted without looking at the soldier who asked.

Eugene reached for his pistol. As he began to head upwards, he aimed towards the crest and fired a series of shots.

He sprinted up the side of the hill as best he could. Every few steps he stopped to let off a couple rounds above him, as if to provide himself cover.

He continued to trek until a small nearby explosion caused Eugene to halt. He looked up. The Japanese were rolling grenades down the slope.

Eugene continued his ascent, visually dodging the spherical assassins and their outbursts. Adding to the cacophony, he could hear gunfire erupt; the Marines at the hill's base were no doubt trying to keep the Japanese at bay at the top of the cliff and the enemy was returning fire.

Durante suddenly felt something against the tip of his boot. It felt different than a rock or a stone. He looked down. It was precisely what he feared it to be; it was a grenade.

Eugene froze up like a deer in harm's way, his eyes transfixed on the bulbous bomb. Similar to the hoofed mammal, he did not know what to do so he simply did nothing.

Durante knew he could not stand upright forever. He was either going to get picked off with a rifle any second or the hazard under his foot would activate. He deduced the only logical course of action was to assume the grenade was defective.

Eugene slowly lifted his foot. The device nudged, signaling that it was going to trickle downwards immediately after clearing his leg. He let out a sigh and completely revoked his foot.

He watched the grenade languidly rotate beyond his foot and down the hill. When it was a good fifty feet away from him, it exploded.

Dozens of small metal fragments launched in every direction.

A razor sharp piece of shrapnel grazed Eugene's leg. His footing promptly gave out and the private first class went down hard, his head striking down upon a large rounded worn boulder.

His body convulsed to its side and then, somehow, he found himself on his back once again.

Looking up, Eugene could hear all the sounds of war. He couldn't, however, move. He noted that the sky was particularly blue that morning. Soon, however, the beautiful blues turned into deep purples before being overtaken entirely by complete and utter blackness.

Private First Class Eugene Durante awoke as his eyes gently opened. His first sight was not unlike his last. Darkness surrounded him. He could, however, make out white specks amongst the obscurity. After a few seconds, he came to realize those specks were stars in the sky. It was nighttime.

His head tilted to see his corporal comrade only a few feet away. He was on his side looking directly towards Eugene. Durante was about to attempt to move when he noticed the corporal's eyes. His optics sent a silent but chilling message. It was the look of imminent danger.

It was then that Eugene realized he was still on the lateral surface of Sugar Loaf Hill. It was also then that he heard them: a sequence of footsteps all around him.

Eugene tensed up. He noticed the corporal purposely close his eyes and he did the same.

Blinded, Eugene sought to go over the situation in his mind. They were out of contact with the rest of the Marines. The Japanese were currently swarming all sides of the hill.

He recalled how earlier in the day he felt like a deer. Now he was playing possum. Perhaps one day he would feel like a human again.

Durante wondered how long they could fool the Japanese. He imagined they would shoot all of the bodies as a precaution.

He shook his thoughts, attempting to only think of productive ideas.

For whatever reason, his father popped into his head. He wondered if he too faced a similar challenge while in the First World War. He didn't talk about it much, which Eugene finally comprehended. He was born seven years after his father returned from battle and by that time he had adequately shoved the whale of war down to a place of containment. In that moment, Eugene hoped he would have the opportunity to do the same.

Thinking of his father provided an inkling of contentment. A small impulsive smile crossed his face.

A Japanese boot landed on the edge of Eugene's face. He did his best not to breathe.

Eugene's hand was being grabbed. He felt a loosening of some sort before he realized what was happening. His wristwatch was being removed. The wristwatch his father had given him.

He could hear his dad now, screaming at him to let the damn trinket go.

He obeyed. He had no choice.

Eugene could hear the soldier put the wristwatch in a pouch. Suddenly, he felt his jacket pocket being touched. The hand of the Japanese officer was searching for valuables.

Eugene anguished over the very real possibility that the soldier was about to feel his pounding heart if he couldn't already hear it.

The hand traveled upwards.

The Japanese soldier abruptly snapped back without grabbing anything.

Eugene's mind raced on what to do. Should he open his eyes and attack, take as many out until his certain death? Or should he continue laying still and hope it was not his heart that the Japanese man felt?

Eugene fully expected a bullet to penetrate him at any moment.

He heard the soldier take a few steps back and grunt in disgust. He was walking away.

Eugene opened his eyes to see the back of the enemy soldier. He was angrily flicking blood off of his fingers.

The gunshot wound from his shoulder and the red bodily fluid it generated had momentarily saved his life.

Eugene knew the battle for Sugar Loaf was far from over, as the Marine line would eventually reach them. He, and his corporal friend, just had to stay calm and motionless until that happened.

The sky painstakingly transitioned from total darkness to the blood orange of a sunrise, and this time Eugene was conscious for all of it. He could feel the warmth on his face. He was content to allow this feeling, the heated glow of the sun, to be his last. He could currently imagine no greater sensation from which to exit this very complicated life. It even felt like an appropriate departure from the nightmarish inferno of Okinawa. A day had passed and absolutely no cavalry had arrived.

It was then that the private first class remembered the brother that lay beside him. Perhaps he hated the radiation that was beaming upon their faces. Maybe he desired a very different exit strategy. Eugene hadn't checked if the corporal was still alive, as his eyes hadn't opened in many hours. He could nevertheless feel his presence, looking over him. Eugene just hoped that it was indeed the corporal and not Death incarnate, scythe at the ready, prepared to carry him away.

A couple of hours later, Eugene reminisced about a time he was playing catch with his father. He ascertained that he was about five years old. It wasn't the catch itself that kept lingering in his memory but the brief conversation that followed.

Eugene had asked his father why he liked baseball so much.

His father answered, "Baseball is great because it's unusual. Most sports have time boundaries. Baseball doesn't. You can be out there all day and all night. You're never truly sure when it's all going to end. The only sudden death comes in extra innings but even then only once both teams have had a crack at batting. It's a game of strategy and inches. It's beautiful really."

Durante could recall the breeze that day and the lemonade he had after his father's explanation. He would give anything for a glass of lemonade right now.

Eugene longed to see anything of beauty in his current state—a butterfly, a hot meal, the face of the girl he left back home. The mental mirages of these things provided him the slightest fraction of satisfaction in comparison to their palpable real-world counterparts.

With his eyes closed, the private first class clandestinely breathed in, something he was forced to do every now and again. It became a time of deep stress on each and every occasion; dead soldiers don't breathe.

As Eugene surreptitiously exhaled, an abundance of shooting swiftly transpired. He could hear yelling and screaming, and not just those of the Japanese. He heard Americans.

His eyes jolted open. He was but bedrock amidst a full-scale assault. He looked around and saw a pistol. It was an arm's length away.

Eugene gathered up the energy he needed to obtain the weapon. He grabbed the loaded gun and reverted back to his position.

He turned to view the corporal whose eyes were still sealed shut.

Durante lifted his head; he could see a line of distant troops wearing familiar fatigues.

To his left, a Japanese soldier fired round after round towards the incoming 22nd Regiment. Eugene lifted the pistol up and aimed.

The soldier, as if feeling the presence of death, turned to face him. As the enemy swung his weapon around, Durante fired. And then fired again.

The first shot nailed him in the abdomen, the second in the chest.

The combatant fell to the ground.

Eugene looked up once more and his eyes interlocked with an American in the distance. He could see the soldier pointing and yelling something to the others.

His head crashed back down onto the crag as the deafening barrage continued.

Private First Class Durante wasn't sure how long he had been lying there on that jagged hillside when he felt a tetrad of arms lifting him up. He was being placed on a medical stretcher.

"I can still fight," Eugene sluggishly exclaimed.

"No doubt," the combat medic responded. "You'll be right back out there once we patch you up, don't you worry. We got it from here."

Durante could feel his muscles relax for the first time in what felt like forever. He felt safe within the olive canvas cocoon.

Right before he was about to fall asleep out of pure exhaustion, he remembered.

"The corporal! A corporal was next to me!"

The combat medic smiled, looked down at Durante and responded, "We got him too. He's going to be just fine."

Chapter 2

Seizing Shuri

May 29th, 1945

Yuujin stood steadfast in front of the once ornate stronghold. A stronghold now completely abandoned, excluding the small group of soldiers left behind as a rearguard. Their mission was simple: to deter the American troops for as long as possible while their companions made the escape they had already started.

As for the castle itself, an American battleship, the USS Mississippi, had uninterruptedly shelled it for three days straight. Yuujin could only watch as the refined palace was set ablaze by the unending bombardment, setting in motion the 32nd Japanese Army's southern retreat into the night.

Yuujin now stood in front of ruined rubble, remnants of what once was. The symbol of strength had collapsed and so too did the private's resolve.

There was no beauty in destruction, he thought.

Still, he had values and great expectations to uphold; he had a duty to assist, respect, and support his leaders. That is what his father did and thus what he was going to do. At least, that's what he kept telling himself.

Yuujin's eyes were fixed forward as he readied himself for any sign of the enemy who, unbeknownst to him, had already entered Shuri through a gap in the covering forces caused by confusion amidst the Japanese retreat. It wouldn't be long at all before the Americans established a perimeter in the south of Shuri.

Heavy machine-gun and 47-mm anti-tank fire a few hundred yards north of the castle kept the Americans at bay throughout the day.

Yuujin peered through his binoculars to see, through compressed clouds, supplies dropping from American aircraft. This proved worrisome to the private as the enemy was being, at least somewhat, replenished with much-needed food and water, and surely ammunition. Yuujin was counting on American exhaustion to play a role in the upcoming fight. He would now have to count on something else. What that would be, however, he had no idea.

As nightfall loomed, the Japanese soldier wondered if this would be when the Americans made their move. He gleaned that it was not. If he were in command he would order his men to get a good night's sleep while the enemy stayed awake all through the night, burdened by the possibility of attack.

His stomach was hungry and slumber was a good way to avoid the grumblings. Yuujin closed his eyes and decided to rest, much to the surprise and dismay of those around him. He deemed the least he could do was be as prepared as possible for what he predicted the next day would be.

Yuujin calmly breathed in and out while sitting on a pile of edificial remains. He dozed off into a peaceful and calming sleep.

His prediction proved perilously correct as the next day Private Miyano found himself in the castle's courtyard, pinned down against a towering dilapidated structure that just days before stood bright and tall. A massive wall still remained, however, and Yuujin used it to peer out. He returned fire when he could see the Americans inch closer.

He could hear the unmusical blasts of mortars and viewed a small group of Japanese soldiers swarm the Americans with a banzai charge.

In succession they yelled, *"Tennōheika Banzai!"*

Long Live His Majesty the Emperor.

Yuujin shook his head; the tactic was suicide. He, at one point, had even read a handout that romanticized the attack by likening it to Bushido, the codes of honor and ideals.

As he watched the men get cut down, he questioned how that action proved to be an honorable death. The participants of the charge almost always suffered great losses while inflicting little damage.

His superiors had told them that war was purifying and that death was duty. Yuujin understood his role as a soldier, but after seeing so many civilians join the fight, he wholeheartedly believed his country's decree, *ichioku gyokusai,* that if it were necessary they were willing to sacrifice the entire Japanese population to continue resisting the opposition.

The private fired his weapon towards the American attackers. He killed one, sending a bullet to a forehead. They were nevertheless gaining ground. Yuujin knew it was time to fall back. The problem being, there weren't many places to fall back to.

Yuujin darted across the large open field and slid to secure cover behind another ravaged courtyard building. He could hear the swishing of sniper fire expediting towards the assailants.

He sprayed the courtyard with ammunition as the fury of fighting was reaching its boiling point.

Fellow Japanese soldiers tossed their grooved, segmented-bodied grenades before succumbing to the lethal hail from American firepower.

Yuujin looked around to see no Japanese soldiers standing.

He aimed his rifle towards the creeping Americans, his presence for the moment still unknown.

Dozens of scenarios began playing out in the private's head, almost all of which ended in the exact same outcome. Silent sleep and surrender were both deemed unsatisfactory by the young soldier. In all of Shuri there was perhaps one place that could still act as a holdout.

Yuujin lowered his weapon and moved stealthily to avoid detection. He propelled himself in a semicircular fashion, traveling back around the enemy to eventually reach the debris of Shuri Castle.

In 1879 the Empire of Japan annexed the Ryukyu Kingdom and Shuri Castle. It became a barracks for the army. The garrison withdrew in 1896, but before they did, they created a series of tunnels and caverns below the castle.

This subterranean sanctuary acted as the headquarters for the 32nd Japanese Army throughout the battle in Okinawa.

Yuujin entered the darkened command caves. Numerous papers were scattered on the floor next to kicked-out wooden chairs.

It was in this very place that General Ushijima, just nine days prior, called a night conference to discuss the future of the Japanese in Shuri. Yuujin, of course, was not invited—only the division and brigade commanders attended the meeting. The private nevertheless deduced the only three possible courses of action were discussed: a final stand at the castle, a withdrawal to the Chinen Peninsula, or a withdrawal to the south. Never did he think the general would acknowledge the concluding two options. He ascertained that his superiors must not have viewed this as a defeat but a vehicle to prolong the battle while wearing down the American forces. They evidently viewed a last stand as a quicker defeat for the Japanese Army.

Yuujin continued down the underground base and recalled watching Shuri Castle burn.

His eyes reflected the dancing orange flares upon the red surfaces. It was as if the blaze itself was on fire. He stood in a humbled dispirit until word came of the retreat. If Yuujin was being honest with himself, he felt marginally relieved upon hearing the news. A withdrawal meant a greater chance of survival. As he was experiencing this minimal peace of mind, his commanding officer came up to him to inform the private he had been assigned the rearguard.

The memory came to an abrupt halt as Yuujin walked into a den with numerous Japanese soldiers. They instinctively aimed their weapons, but seeing it was one of their own, they lowered them, clearly on edge.

The soldiers said nothing to the private. Neither did they speak amongst themselves. They simply stood dejected, awaiting the demise that seemed at hand.

Yuujin, not knowing what to do, thought to say something that might provide them with a sense of purpose. "We need to hold this position. No American gets in."

He saw a succession of nods, which provided Yuujin with a strange confidence. Perhaps it was his function to provide these men with dignity in death. The private appreciated the proposition's irony.

The Japanese blockaded the entrance, with the men rotating watches. They placed their only infantry gun at the mouth of the obstructed passageway and waited.

The soldiers found a small bundle of field rations and passed them out to one another. They opened the containers and indulged in the rice and barley that they feared would be their final meal.

They ate slowly and in silence, their heads never ascending to look at one another. Yuujin was, of course, the exception. He couldn't stop staring at his comrades in arms and their understandably devastated countenances.

Yuujin savored each and every small bite he took; he was grateful, at this point, for any food at all. The private looked down at the empty can after his last nibble and placed it on the table.

The infantry gun suddenly boomed.

"They're here!" Yuujin affirmed as he turned to search for his rifle, which he had placed against a wall.

He grabbed it and headed towards the cavernous corridor leading to the entryway. Behind him, Yuujin heard a synchronized metal melody. He turned back to see all of the soldiers had unsheathed their guntō swords. They each took a seat on the floor.

"What are you doing!?" Yuujin demanded.

"Now we will die," a soldier responded while plunging his blade into his belly, drawing it from left to right.

The remaining soldiers simultaneously engaged in the ritual suicide by disembowelment known as seppuku.

As the last body limped forward, the roaring sound from the infantry gun swiftly ceased.

Yuujin Miyano surmised he was the only living Japanese soldier left in the cave under the castle. He had mere moments left. The private threw down his rifle and looked down by his side, where his own guntō dangled. He unsheathed it.

The sounds of American troops could be heard; they had entered the Imperial Army's former headquarters.

Yuujin lifted the sword over his left shoulder with the blade curving downward. He was prepared for battle, but he was also prepared to die, albeit his way.

The boot-thumps neared.

Yuujin couldn't help but think how he was never traditionally trained in swordsmanship. A fact currently bearing very little significance, he concluded.

His feet grew restless and anticipatory as they yearned to be put in motion.

The thumps came to a hush; the private knew they were right outside the room.

Yuujin noticed the tip of a boot enter the doorframe and lunged, his sword striking as his adversary stepped into the private's line of sight.

The blade pushed over the allied serviceman's left shoulder without a pierce. The American contorted upwards and to his left as the sword narrowly missed. He instinctively sent the butt of his rifle, which was raised from the soldier twisting in such a manner, directly into the forehead of the Japanese private.

Yuujin was knocked backwards and hit the floor with great force. He was immediately unconscious.

Private First Class Durante aimed his weapon at the paralyzed attacker as a surplus of Marines flooded the room.

He placed himself directly on top of Yuujin, his barrel pointed directly at the face of the senseless soldier.

If Yuujin would have so much as twitched, Eugene would have pulled the trigger.

"Clear," a soldier declared.

There was no longer a threat, especially not from Yuujin; Eugene withdrew his weapon.

Chapter 3

Over the Parapets

Yuujin awoke, his eyes barely opening. His hazy vision made the private unaware of his surroundings. The last thing he remembered was charging an American soldier.

He suddenly became aware of two Marines carrying him. His arms were draped over their shoulders.

A bright light blinded Yuujin as he realized he was being removed from the cave. He also realized what all of this meant: he was a prisoner of war.

Upon setting foot outside, Miyano's eyes took time to adjust. His hand instinctively went to shield his eyes.

"Looks like this one's up," he could hear a soldier say.

"Perfect timing! Look!"

Yuujin saw the second soldier pointing towards something nearby. With his eyes finally adapted, the private could see the sight come into focus.

An American Lieutenant Colonel was, while enduring heavy sniper fire from afar, planting the American flag over the parapets of Shuri Castle. After some fiddling, the flag was snug and waved triumphantly in the Okinawa air.

"That Ross is one crazy son of a bitch," the first soldier remarked.

The second looked back at Yuujin, "You see that? You Japs aren't as tough as you thought, huh? I guess you're the smart one. All your buddies around here committed suicide. You're the only POW we got in the last two days."

"Sit over there," instructed the first soldier while pointing to the ground.

Yuujin obeyed and sat with his legs crossed. The more aggressive of the two Marines leaned into his ear.

"My brother died in that cowardly attack of yours on Pearl Harbor. If it was up to me, I'd kill every last one of you."

The Marine walked away and barked, "Durante—you want to watch him?"

Eugene Durante turned around and asked, "Why the hell would I want to do that?"

"Because it's an order. Don't worry, if he runs you can shoot him this time. In the meantime, give him something good to read."

The first Marine, who helped carry Yuujin, threw a leaflet down at the feet of the Japanese soldier.

Yuujin picked up the small flat sheet of printed-paper. On it he viewed the exaggerated illustration of an enormous American bomber heading towards homeland Japan. He turned it over. On the back was a message written in his native tongue:

> **Since our new giant bombers began their frequent air raids against Japan proper in June and our Navy and Marines captured Saipan, Tinian, and Guam, your leaders at home have been fearful lest Japan itself be invaded and seized. In a radio broadcast, for example, one of your leaders stated: 'Our forces on the coast must keep watch and prevent the landing within our defenses by enemy paratroops.'**

Resistance on your part is futile. You cannot withstand the overwhelming force of our men, ships, planes, tanks, and various other weapons of war. You cannot match our amazing industrial strength. For Japan the war is already lost.

Yuujin decorously placed the propaganda leaflet down on the ground. He looked up to see Durante and another guard engaging in small talk. He attempted to listen raptly.

"Hey, Loughran, you hear about Pete Gray?" asked Eugene.

"No. Who is that?"

"An amputee that made his major league debut last month with the Browns."

"Saint Louis signed an amputee?"

"That's right."

"Is he a veteran?" asked Loughran while lighting up a cigarette and passing one to Eugene.

"Nah. Lost it in a childhood accident."

"Damn. I hope he's not a pitcher."

They both chuckled until Durante responded, through the vocal muffling from the lit smoke, "Outfielder."

"How does he do that?"

"I don't know. I hear he's not bad though."

"God bless. He must be superhuman, like you."

"Like me?"

"That's right."

"How do you figure?"

"No one heals as quick as you. Shot in the shoulder, stabbed, sliced by shrapnel; thrown down a hill. Next thing you know, reassigned and on the front line. You're insane."

"The punctures were just grazes. I rolled down the hill as best I could. I have to admit, though, the bullet was a bitch."

"I imagined as much. Hey, you hear about the All-American Girls Professional Baseball League?"

"That started when I was still home," Eugene said.

"Any good?"

Actually, yeah, pretty damn good. Who knows, they might give us a run for our money one day."

Loughran nodded in amusement and added, "I heard it rained just as hard at home last week as it's been raining here. Goddamn monsoons have been killing us both medically and tactically. Some of the old timers said it's like the First World War battlefield all over again. I saw a guy the other day so covered in mud I thought he was the goddamn Werewolf of London."

They shared another laugh.

Eugene added, "I heard about the rain at home. Four days straight. Every American League game was postponed because of it."

"No shit? Where do you get your Intel?"

"I have my sources," Eugene answered, smiling.

Yuujin, in perfect English, chimed in, "You like baseball?"

The two Marines looked up at the captive in disbelief, their cigarettes hanging out of their mouths.

"Well I'll be," remarked Loughran. "He speaks English."

Eugene took a few steps forward towards Yuujin and asked, "You like baseball?"

"Very much," Yuujin answered.

In his excitement the Japanese private gracelessly attempted to stand. Loughran, seeing this, immediately raised his weapon. Eugene put his hand out to stop the anxious Marine.

"It's okay. Let him stand," Durante insisted.

Yuujin finally got to his feet and Eugene was now standing toe to toe with him. Eugene took a final big drag from the cigarette.

"What do you know about baseball?" Eugene asked interrogatively while tossing his finished smoke.

"Everything."

"Everything?"

"Everything."

"Okay. What's a balk?"

"Lots of things could constitute a balk."

Loughran, still a few feet away, said, "Did he just use the word constitute?"

Unsatisfied, Eugene continued, "What is it?"

"When the pitcher deceives the hitter or a runner. It could be a flinch on the mound, you could drop the ball after you set, many things."

"Dropping the ball is a balk?" asked Loughran from afar.

"Yes," Yuujin and Eugene answered simultaneously.

Durante shot the hostage a dirty look.

"How do you grip a curveball?" pressed Eugene.

"When you hold the ball you place your middle finger along the bottom seam with your index finger next to it. Your thumb goes on the back seam."

"How do you throw it?"

"The thumb rotates upwards and the middle finger snaps downwards."

Durante was dumbfounded. He looked back at his companion. Loughran simply shrugged his shoulders in response.

Yuujin was beaming when Eugene turned back to him.

"What the hell are you smiling for? You're a prisoner of war."

"I like baseball."

"I see that. Who's your favorite player?"

"Eiji Sawamura."

"Favorite team?"

"Tokyo Kyojin."

"What does that mean?"

"Giants. Tokyo Giants."

"Oh yeah? We have our own Giants. They play in the Polo Grounds and I bet you anything they would kick the ever loving shit out of the Tokyo Giants."

"Yes, New York Giants, very good team."

"Durante, maybe you shouldn't be talking to him like this," warned Loughran.

"Give me a minute! I haven't had a conversation about baseball like this in forever and I could be dead tomorrow."

Eugene looked Yuujin in the eye.

"Like the New York Giants do you?"

"Yes, but they are not my favorite American team."

"Who is?"

"The Boston Red Sox."

Eugene punched Yuujin square in the jaw.

The captive fell back, landing ungracefully. Durante stood over him, a look of anger engulfing his face. Loughran burst out in laughter as he approached the fallen prisoner, saying, "A word of advice: never tell a Yankee fan you like the Red Sox."

Yuujin confusingly looked back up at Eugene, who continued to smolder.

About twenty minutes of silence went by as Yuujin continued to sit perplexed over the incident. Meanwhile, Private First Class Durante paced back and forth amidst the broken bits of Shuri Castle, clearly disconcerted. Finally, he headed towards the docile prisoner.

"What the hell do you like about the Red Sox?" Eugene inquired.

"Ted Williams. Very good player."

"Ted Williams hates Boston. He said it himself! Called his salary peanuts. In 1940 he said the only fun he had all season was when he pitched the last two innings of a blowout."

"Still a great player."

"That may be true. Who knows, maybe he'll come to New York after the war. I doubt he'll play his entire career over there. The reporters despise him just as much as he despises them."

"Joe DiMaggio is also a great player."

"Now you're talkin'! 56-game hitting streak, greatest accomplishment in all of baseball."

"Do you think it will ever be broken?"

"Never."

"Never?"

"Never."

"It would be very hard."

"Impossible. Even if baseball lasts forever, DiMaggio's record will hold."

"They say nothing lasts forever."

The two looked at one another. The statement struck an emotional chord for each of them.

"This war sure as hell ain't gonna last forever. Not with Shuri in our grasp."

"What will happen to me now?" asked Yuujin, candidly concerned.

"You're awaiting transport."

"To where?"

"A makeshift prison camp. You'll be joining your kind behind barbed wire. But don't worry, unlike your people, when it comes to POWs, we don't engage in mass killings, torture, forced labor, or the execution of captured soldiers."

"What about Chenogne?"

Eugene did not expect him to know about the incident where American captors had massacred eighty German prisoners of war earlier that year. It was said that they were assembled in a field and shot with machine guns.

"A response to the Malmedy Massacre during the Battle of the Bulge. You heard of that one, where a German Waffen-SS unit killed eighty-four American prisoners of war?"

"Yes. Now you see why I am wary. Germans mistreat Americans, Americans mistreat Germans. Japanese mistreat Americans…"

Durante could see that Yuujin's worry was genuine; he backed off. "You'll be fine."

Yuujin nodded his head, blatantly discontented.

An awkward silence fell between the two enemies.

Not knowing what to say, but wishing to end the excruciating silence, Eugene asked, "You smoke?"

Yuujin looked at him curiously.

"I can get you a cigarette."

The Japanese private shook his head and responded, "No, thank you."

Eugene nodded. The two men returned to a cumbersome silence.

Yuujin looked around at the American stronghold. He picked up some rubble from the battered ground and let the ashlike remains slowly slip out of his clutch and back onto the earth.

"This used to be a very beautiful place, you know," Yuujin remarked.

"I can imagine." After contemplating whether or not he should end the conversation, Eugene asked, "Are you from here? Born in Okinawa?"

"I was born in Tokyo. But we had family here on the island. I would visit as a child."

"Seems like it could be a peaceful place when bombs aren't going off every second of the day."

"It was very peaceful. My father taught me how to fish here."

"Any good?"

"At catching fish? No. Not good at all."

Durante snickered at the comment.

"Where are you from?" asked Yuujin.

"Hell's Kitchen."

"Hell's Kitchen?" Yuujin repeated, attempting to clarify the odd name.

"It's a neighborhood in Manhattan."

"Manhattan, New York."

"You got it."

"I always wanted to go there."

"Well, you're not dead, so you might just get that chance once all this is over."

"Have you ever been to Tokyo?"

"No."

"Do you wish to?"

"Not particularly."

Eugene felt firm about this and would have normally answered in a harsher manner. But, for whatever reason, he did not wish to further distress the captive. Durante could hear his father's voice—you don't kick a man when he's down.

"I see. When I come to New York, perhaps you shall take me to Yankee Stadium."

Eugene stared at him as if insulted. He surmised that perhaps his father was wrong about some things.

"Maybe you got the wrong idea about me talking to you," Durante explained with the firmness of a vice's grip. "I'm not your friend. If you tried to run to safety I wouldn't hesitate putting a bullet in the back of your Jap head. Do you understand?"

"Yes."

"Good. What we're doing here is killing time."

"Time killing?"

"We're passing the time, trying to make it go by quicker."

"Ah. I see."

"I don't think you're a bad person but you are nevertheless my enemy. Yes?"

"Yes."

"Good. Now that we have an understanding, how the hell do you speak such good English?"

"My grandfather traveled to the United States. He worked there before coming back to Japan. He picked up the language, among other things, and passed it down to my father who in turn passed it down to me."

"I see. What were the 'among other things'?"

Yuujin smiled. "Baseball."

"So that's why you're so well versed in the sport."

"Baseball is in my blood."

Eugene looked around, somewhat regretting the harshness he unleashed upon the soldier just moments before.

"Listen, it's going to be a little while before you leave and we head out. We have time. Why don't you tell me about how baseball is supposedly in your blood?"

Yuujin gazed at the American soldier; an olive branch in a war torn terrain had just been extended. The private, for the first time in quite some time, felt a modicum of hope.

"I suppose I should start with my grandfather then."

Chapter 4

The Legend of Jin Miyano

In 1871, my grandfather Jin Miyano stepped off a charter boat and onto the port of San Francisco.

He was sixteen years old and was not in the United States on his own accord. You see, the end of Japan's diplomatic seclusion presented an opportunity for the Japanese families who were looking to get rid of, what you might call, the black sheep of the household. It was my grandfather's father's opinion that Jin would never do well in life. And so, he was shipped off to school in America. His father was a minor aristocrat and so he had connections. He also had exasperations because Jin had behavioral issues. Being a privileged person, my great-grandfather had contacts and used them to place his unruly son on a U.S.-bound government mission.

As my grandfather left, his father told him, "You are Jin Miyano. It is a good name. Enmeshed in a name is one's reputation. And reputation, Jin, is the only true immortal part of one's self."

When Jin landed in The Golden City, he walked until he came across a most spectacular sight: train tracks. He put his belongings on the ground and simply stood across from the railway, waiting. Eventually he heard it, the whisper of a whistle followed by a chugging echo. His anticipation grew until the iron giant finally came into view. Jin marveled at the moving train; it was the first time he had ever seen one in person. As the moving mechanical vehicle bellowed past him, Jin felt purpose and opportunity collide. He believed he had just witnessed the potent symbol of civilization and progress itself. He was intrigued by engineering and the secrets that were hidden behind those levers, springs, axles, and beams.

San Francisco was not Jin's destination. He was to attend high school in Boston and his mode of transportation was the railroad.

As Jin journeyed towards Oakland Long Wharf, the west coast terminus of the First Transcontinental Railroad along the east shore of San Francisco Bay, he was amazed that he could travel from one side of a nation to the other in under a week. To him, this was the most astonishing feat humanity had yet to offer.

He had heard of the train luxuries by reading about them in magazines back home. He recalled the descriptions of beautifully appointed cars with plush velvet seats. They were even said to convert into sleeping berths. Passengers would receive steam heat, fresh linens daily, and they would have attentive porters to cater to their every whim. He read that for only an extra $4 one could experience world-renowned dining.

Of course, when Jin arrived he soon found out those descriptions were true for first-class passengers only; Jin's father saw no reason to purchase amenities for his spoiled child.

Jin's car was fitted with rows of narrow wooden benches and was cramped, boisterous, and uncomfortable. Furthermore, the railroad often attached coach cars to freight cars that were consistently diverted aside to make way for the luxurious express trains. Jin's third-class journey east took ten additional days than those of the first class trains.

Still, Jin did not complain. He felt privileged to even be on the iron horse and motivated to make his mark so that he could one day travel in the plush velvet seats.

A friendly face leaned in towards Jin and said, "This trip would have taken me six months on the Oregon Trail!"

The stranger smiled and Jin smiled back, thinking about how he was heading to Boston to receive an education.

Of course, being disobedient, defiant, and disregardful didn't bode well in the American school, especially when it came from a foreigner. Within no time, Jin quit high school and landed himself a locomotive apprenticeship.

Jin found himself in the Bell in Hand Tavern. He noted that the patrons all looked nothing like him. He proceeded nonetheless and sat at the bar.

A jolly man came up to Jin from behind the wooden bar and asked, "What can I get for ya?"

Jin shrugged his shoulders, clearly unsure of where to even begin.

"Thirsty?" the bartender asked.

"Yes," Jin responded.

"I got just the thing."

The bartender poured the immigrant a dark heavy malt beverage, the foam pouring down the sides of the large glass.

He placed it down and said, "Here we are. Smith's Philadelphia Cream Ale. Try that."

Jin took a sip, the foam leaving him whitely bearded. He swallowed and felt his thirst quenched. He nodded his head.

"Very good!"

The bartender smiled and responded, "You don't have to tell me. I know it. You hungry?"

Jin nodded again.

"You sit tight. We'll put some food in that belly of yours."

The bartender walked off. Jin looked around. Most people were sitting at shabby tables. There was one person, however, sitting at the bar, just a few stools down. He appeared a few years older and sported a formidable mustache. His parted hair was wavy but neat. He too was drinking cream ale. The young man caught the outsider looking at him and Jin embarrassingly dropped his head.

The slender man stood up and walked over. He stretched out his hand.

"Hey there. You must be new here. My name is Albert Goodwill Spalding."

Jin reciprocated and shook the stranger's hand while responding, "Jin Miyano."

"Good to meet ya, Jin."

Spalding took a seat near Jin, just two stools down, as he moved his drink closer.

"Where are you from originally?"

"Japan."

"I gathered. I was trying to get a little more specific."

"Tokyo."

"I hear it's a big city."

"Very big."

"Maybe one day I'll play there. Me, I'm from Byron, Illinois. Ever heard of it?"

"No."

"No, of course not. Why would you? Nothing or no one has ever come out of good old Byron. Except for me of course. Well, there is the soldier's monument. It's quite nice. Heard and Lindsley built it. Ever heard of them? Probably not. There's a nice little twelve-foot spire and an eagle atop the point. I don't know about you, Jin, but I ain't no soldier. You don't look like one neither. You look like you're still in high school—is that right?"

Before Jin could answer, Spalding cut him off; he was the fastest talker he had ever come across.

"Myself, I went to school. Rockford Central High School in Rockford—you guessed it—Illinois. Why did you pick Boston to study?

"Actually I—"

"—Being as this is an urban city, schools are in session eleven months of the year. Back where I'm from we only went to school for six months. Gotta love the harvests. Hey, I suppose that makes you smarter than me!"

Spalding slapped Jin's shoulder, which Jin only assumed was some sort of friendly tradition.

"This is my first year here too. So I guess we're both outsiders."

"I am an apprentice."

"Really!? To what?"

"Locomotive apprentice."

"A railroad man! I have a bone to pick with you people but we'll save it for another time. Good for you, kid. Hey, I wouldn't want to spend over two hundred and forty days in a classroom either. Good choice."

"What brings you here?" Jin asked, echoing the phrasing he heard just moments ago.

"I'm a pitcher. You know what that is?"

Jin shook his head.

"I play baseball. Ever heard of baseball?"

Jin once again shook his head.

"I'll be. Baseball is a sport. As a matter of fact, this year is the inaugural year for the National Association of Professional Base Ball Players. It's a damn good game. Here's how it works. There are two teams and they play against each other."

"Only two teams in total?"

"Yes. Well, no. I mean there are a lot of teams but only two play each other at any one time. Does that make sense?"

"Yes."

"Good. Now, the teams take turns batting and fielding. A player on the fielding team called a pitcher, that's me, throws a ball and a player on the batting team has to try and hit it with a bat. The object for the batting team is to hit the ball and round the bases."

"What are bases?"

"Good question. Well, they are sort of like checkpoints. Here—let me show you."

Spalding grabbed a napkin.

"You're an engineer, you got a pencil on ya?"

Jin did and handed it to the strange but charismatic American. He started drawing a diamond on the small square paper.

"There are four of them—first base, second base, third base—"

"Fourth base!"

"No, that would be ridiculous. Home plate. The fourth base is called home plate. Now the bases form a diamond, as you can see, starting with home plate. Third base is to its left, first base to its right, and second base is in the middle between first and third. A batter wants to go from first base all the way around and when he makes it to home plate he scores. That team gets a run. Other games may call that a point. Here, it's a run. The team that scores the most runs by the end of a game is the team that wins. See, simple."

Spalding slid the napkin, along with the pencil, over to the young newcomer.

"This game, where do I see it?"

"South End Grounds right here in Boston."

"What is your team called?"

"The Boston Red Stockings."

"Boston Red Stockings. South End Grounds," Jin repeated as if to chisel the words into memory.

"Tell you what, kid. Your first game is on me."

"What does that mean?"

"It means you're clearly broke as hell and I want you to see a damn baseball game. I'll take care of the money."

He tossed the kid a couple of coins.

"Thank you," Jin responded with excitement. He lowered his head in gratitude.

"My pleasure," Spalding answered as he sprang up from his stool. "I come in this place pretty often. I'll see you around."

"Goodbye. Where do you go now?"

Spalding began rotating his arm and answered, "I have to go get ready for a ballgame."

Spalding threw some money down for his beverage and exited the tavern.

As Jin looked back at the first person with whom he'd shared a real conversation, the bartender placed a hot plate in front of him and said, "I see you met Al. Good kid. Doesn't shut the hell up though."

"Is he good?"

"At baseball?" clarified the bartender. "Yea. He's the best pitcher on the team."

Jin looked back again as if to catch a glimpse of the best pitcher on the team.

"Don't let your food get cold. It's best hot."

Jin turned back and looked at his meal. "What is it?"

"Mutton! You'll love it!"

The South End Grounds was packed as Jin maneuvered his way between the thousands of bustling Bostonians. The rectangular stands were small and the field itself reminded Jin of a bathtub. Left field was 250 feet from home plate while right field was 255. Centerfield, however, was 450 feet back, making it a prime space to either dump a hit in front of the center fielder or launch one behind him.

The main grandstand was boxy and contained twenty-five rows of seats under the cover of an overhanging roof, which was held up by six supports. In front of the grandstand, and behind a three-foot wooden fence, were four rows of box seats and a smaller wooden bleacher section made for cheaper seats, exactly half the price.

Jin took a seat and marveled at the stadium. For many others, this structure might simply have been a field of recreation, but to Jin it was a palace.

The locomotive apprentice was given a scorecard with a picture of Harry Wright on the front. He was told that each home game featured a different player so that fans could continually collect them and eventually amass the full set of Red Stocking players by the time the season concluded. Jin wondered if this trend would catch on.

He looked past right field to see residences and other tall buildings. A Providence and Boston Railroad roundhouse was located to the north of the field but it wasn't until the game started that Jin understood the full magnitude of that circumstance.

Albert Spalding was on the mound. He stood in a box and threw balls and strikes to the catcher, who stood several feet behind home plate; attempting to catch the pitches on their first bounce.

His pitches were like fireballs, zooming to the batter so quickly that Jin had trouble even seeing the ball. After watching one inning, Jin realized this was a somewhat dangerous game.

He was amazed how no one thought it might be a good idea for the catcher to wear some sort of mask or for the fielders in general to have some sort of glove to protect themselves from hard hit balls. He surmised that his thinking was cowardly; these were Americans, people who prided themselves on grit and fortitude.

In the third inning, as Jin had been watching studiously, a passing train down-poured smoke and cinders onto him and everyone else in the section on the third base side. Not only that, but the field itself was deluged with the train's aftermath.

Jin looked to the umpire, an unpaid volunteer who was chosen by the home team after being given a list of five names provided by the visiting club to be the enforcer of the rules of the game. The great arbiter of authority waved his hands in the air.

The game appeared halted and players trotted off the field as a thick haze, produced by the train, enveloped South End Grounds.

Jin could hear a nearby child ask his father, "Does this happen all the time?"

The father answered, "When the winds are right and the traffic is heavy, yes, son, it does."

After an involuntary intermission, the players took the field once again, propelled by the cheers of the patrons in the stands, Jin included.

Soon thereafter, he noticed the catcher had come out of the game. A few fans pointed and chuckled. Jin was not sure why.

A couple innings later, the second catcher began flapping his hands in anguish. The player-manager, Harry Wright, who Jin recognized from the scorecard, came out and met with his core players. Jin watched as Wright relieved his ballplayer.

It turned out that Spalding had to stop pitching because both of the catchers developed sore hands from his fast pitching. Jin was amazed.

The Red Stockings beat Rockford Forest Citys 21-12 that day and as the spectators were dispersing, Jin felt as if he participated in a ceremonial rite of passage, a customary observance that granted him, perhaps unofficially, a membership into this society. He was honored to participate, even as a patron, in the sport.

He also felt that he knew a celebrity. He had shared a drink and a conversation with Spalding, whom the crowd cheered enthusiastically. Jin had no idea that he was so superior at the game he played.

This single game certainly did not prove to be a fluke for Spalding either. By the end of the season, he accumulated 19 wins and 0 losses in 31 games while posting a 3.36 ERA, the average of earned runs given up by a pitcher per nine innings pitched. He was practically a local hero. And Jin was his friend.

The integrated foreigner loved fielding his own position at the railroad too. He loved it as much as he did baseball. His dream of becoming a locomotive engineer was only exacerbated by the public's perspective of the profession. It was akin to a captain and his boat sailing the high seas. But here, the high seas were miles upon miles of ground, from farmlands to plains to mountains and deserts. The engineers and conductors were men of great authority; children and adults respected them and treated them accordingly. In this way, Jin expected that perhaps his path wouldn't be unlike Spalding's.

Jin started out as a brakeman and quickly learned that if he were to indeed climb the ranks, it would only be through hazardously hard work.

Jin sat in the caboose, the last car in the train built with the intention to allow the crew to easily apply the brakes. The train was awaiting departure.

A portly fellow entered the train car and asked, "How's it going today?"

"Good, thank you," Jin responded. "How are you?"

"Can't complain! I have the first two cars today. You hear about Charlie Gould yesterday?"

"First player to ever hit a home run with the bases loaded. You think the Red Stockings will win it all?"

The fellow brakeman laughed and answered, "I hope so! That would make my year. I think you're good luck; you come along as this whole baseball thing is starting. I hope it doesn't leave when you do!" He went to exit the car but then turned and asked, "Hey, you like this job, don't you?"

"I do. It's fun."

"Ha! If dangerous be fun, then fun it is."

"I take pride in the craft and I like the idea of helping to build up the country."

"I feel the same way. My father followed a mule and plow his entire life and my brother works in a factory. What they don't understand is that I have a well paying job for life. Everyone else works on a daily basis or endures famine. We got it made! It's not so bad seeing different parts of the country, either. Am I right?"

"You are."

"All you have to do is serve faithfully, take care of your own safety on the rails, and follow the rules. Hey, it kinda sounds like the army doesn't it? You don't strike me much for a soldier though, I must say."

"I've been told."

"I bet. I suppose following the rules would be hardest for you. I heard you were a bit of a rebel."

"I quit school because they couldn't teach me anything I didn't know."

"And arrogant to boot."

"I want to do this. I want to be an engineer. Here for us, rules mean life or death. I welcome them."

"Glad to hear it. Okay, I'm going to the front. We should be leaving pretty soon. Go Red Stockings."

As the brakeman exited the car, Jin climbed the small set of stairs and took his place on the top of the train.

"Go Red Stockings," he mumbled to himself.

A few months later, that very same portly brakeman fell off the top of a train and died instantly. Jin forever regretted not speaking to him more often as he always proved to be a bright spot in a dark and lonesome occupation.

1871 proved not to be the year for the Red Stockings as The Athletics of Philadelphia defeated the Chicago White Stockings to clinch the first professional baseball championship on October 30th. Despite this, Al Spalding did lead the league in wins, notching nineteen of them.

Along the way, however, Jin witnessed many milestones. Esteban Enrique Bellán became the first Hispanic player in Major League Baseball history. The first game between a black team and a white team was played on July 6th as the black Uniques defeated the white Alerts 17–16 in Chicago. And in true New York fashion, the Brooklyn police drew their firearms to stop a crowd from attacking the Troy Haymakers following several altercations between players from the Haymakers and the New York Mutuals. Baseball was born.

A year passed and Jin continued to soak up technological knowledge. But one day, in 1872, his roots came calling.

He was cleaning the engine spaces and machinery, assisting the engineers as directed, when he heard his name being called. It was his boss, Colm O'Brien.

"Jin!"

"Yes, sir?"

"You obviously speak Japanese, don't ya?"

"I do."

"Good. Get down to City Hall. 45 School Street, along the Freedom Trail between the Old South Meeting House and King's Chapel. The Japanese embassy is arriving and the officials, God bless 'em, just realized they don't have an interpreter. You've been summoned!"

Jin, processing this very unexpected request, appeared flustered.

"Well don't just stand there! Get a move on!"

Jin's mental fog cleared. He threw down his cleaning materials and started to run.

Jin could see a group of American government types standing outside City Hall. Out of breath he arrived, to the horror of the delegates, in his soiled and sweat-stained work attire. The American officials looked at one another with troubled faces.

"They're coming!" someone called out from up the street.

"Do we have an extra suit!?" a senator asked.

"Not one so small," another answered.

"Great. Our first meeting with the Iwakura Embassy and one of their own looks like a sweatshop worker."

A series of horse-drawn carriages pulled up in front of City Hall. The embassy officials exited the vehicles. A series of bows and handshakes ensued along with greetings.

"Hello."

"Hajimemashite."

"Pleased to meet your acquaintance."

"Konnichiwa."

The Americans turned to bring Jin to the forefront.

"Introduce yourself, young man."

Jin, in Japanese, said, "My name is Jin. Excuse my attire. It only just dawned on these men that they would require an interpreter. I ran here as fast as I could, just moments before you arrived."

The Japanese ambassadors stoically looked at one another. Their American counterparts did the same. Suddenly, the Japanese men began laughing. The Americans followed suit though they were not sure why.

"What is your name?" asked one of the Japanese men.

"Jin Miyano."

Another member of the embassy stated, "I know you! Your father is an aristocrat. You were sent here to get an American education. What better interpreter could we possibly have?"

The embassy all nodded in an enthusiastic agreement.

"Actually I dropped out of school and became a locomotive apprentice," Jin gleefully corrected. "I'm learning far more there."

The Japanese delegates looked disapprovingly at Jin.

"What are they asking you, Jin?" an American politely asked.

"About school. I told them I dropped out and joined the railroad. Why are they here, anyway?"

He answered aghast; with a forced smile, "They are interested in observing schools and learning more about the excellent educational policy here in Boston."

A look of dumbfounded fright immediately emerged across the face of Jin.

He swiveled back to the embassy and assured, "I have grown to enjoy this city very much and I am hoping you will as well."

An American extended his hand to invite the commission in.

The group sat in chairs as Jin translated. Iwakura Tomomi held the role of extraordinary and plenipotentiary ambassador. He spoke strictly and quickly.

Jin translated, "Our mission is simple in nature. Complicated in execution. We are here to begin preliminary renegotiation of the unequal treaties with the dominant world powers; this obviously includes you. While we are on this international diplomatic voyage, we are also to make a comprehensive study of modern industrial, political, military and educational systems. Since America is said to be at the forefront of modern education, we thought this meeting could lean heavily in that direction."

An American official nodded courteously and looked to Jin to answer, "It is an honor to have you, along with your leading statesmen and scholars, in our home. The Office of Shinto Worship and the sovereign ideas that you are embracing encourage us. I hear the office ranks above even the Council of State. Although I cannot guarantee the renegotiation of the existing treaties, whatever help we can be, I pledge to you that we will try our best to reach a mutual understanding. In the meantime, in anticipation of your request, we have set up tours of our schools, universities, and industrial locations."

Needless to say, Jin was not enthused about going back to school.

He did, however, win over his brethren through his candor and benevolence. In addition, after that initial day, the American delegates purchased Jin a proper suit. The party set sail for the United Kingdom in August of that year, unsuccessful in their main mission to renegotiate the treaties.

The next few years were kind to Jin. He continued to gain the respect and admiration of his peers. Recreationally, things were at an all time high; the Boston Red Stockings won three straight national championships between 1872 and 1874. Al Spalding had a particularly good run. In 1872 Spalding led the league in both wins and ERA, with 38 victories and a 1.98 earned run average. He subsequently led the league in wins in 1873 with 41, and then again in 1874 with 52.

On September 6th of 1875, The Boston Red Stockings won their fourth-straight pennant. This came about six weeks sooner than the previous clinches of their last three seasons. As a matter of fact, Boston secured their position with sixteen games still left to play on their schedule. The city of Boston had a cause to celebrate.

The tavern was packed with ballplayers and fans alike. People played music, drinks were poured, and chants were recited.

Jin was there too, holding up a beer to the immortalized players. He had become an accepted member of the society and there were few who didn't call him friend.

Al weaved his way through the crowd, spotting his familiar friend. His clothes were disheveled and he spilled a little bit of his drink with every step he took.

When he reached his destination, he put his hand on his companion's shoulder and declared, "I need a smoke. Join me?"

The late summer air contained wisps of briskness as the seasonal change had begun its annual metamorphosis. Spalding lit a cigarette and offered one to Jin, who had continually declined every such offer. Tonight, however, felt different.

"Good for you," remarked Spalding as he handed over his rolled finely cut tobacco.

Al provided a light for the novice and awaited the inevitable. To neither man's surprise, the smoking amateur began coughing incessantly.

"There ya go," Spalding smirked. "You can be my tobacco apprentice if you're looking for more work."

"I'll get used to it," responded Jin, still expelling air with sound.

"I need to tell you something."

"What?"

Spalding took a drag, as if needing to prepare himself to say it out loud, before admitting, "It's going to leak soon in the press. I want you to hear it from me first."

"Okay," Jin said cautiously.

"I'm leaving Boston. I'm leaving the Red Stockings."

Miyano, shocked by this news, naturally asked, "Why? You're leading the National Association in wins and ERA again! You are a part of a dynasty. Three straight championships, and it looks like you guys could win again this year!"

Al half-smiled and responded, "That's the funny thing about a dynasty isn't it? They never do last. It all ends sooner or later. Me leaving is not all. I'm taking Deacon White, Ross Barnes and Cal McVey with me."

"Where are you going?"

"Chicago."

"The White Stockings?"

"I know, ironic. Can't get away from damn stockings."

"Does Harry Wright know?"

"He does. We told him in July."

"July!? You've known for this long?"

"Yea."

"How does he feel about it?"

"You didn't hear? The Chicago Tribune reported in late July that he's going to return to Cincinnati to start a new team."

"It really is the end of an era then."

"That it is. Who knows, maybe a better one will come along. I don't think the National Association is going to last, to be honest with you."

"What do you mean?"

"Funny thing is, our dominance may have played a factor. It's not fun for the other cities if a single team is winning everything. There's also a general instability for a lot of these franchises. Many were placed in cities way too small to financially support baseball as a professional sport. Add to that there's no real central authority in the game, and as I'm sure you've heard, gambling has become a bit of an issue."

"So what happens? How are you going to Chicago if the association will be disbanded?"

"The guy who owns the White Stockings, William Hulbert, decided to create a new organization. He's calling it the National League of Baseball Clubs. The White Stockings will be playing in that division."

Jin was beside himself. He could only think to say, "At least you can go back to your mid-western roots."

"That was certainly part of it. Don't get me wrong; I do love it here. But that doesn't make it home, does it?"

He looked at Jin as if he, more than anyone, would understand.

"It does not," Jin answered.

"Anyway, I figure the fans aren't gonna take it too well. Probably start cussing at us in our own damn ballpark."

"I won't be."

"Thanks, kid. How much longer do you have here?"

"About a year and a half."

"Then back off to Japan."

"That's right."

"Well, you know how to write in English now. You can stay in touch."

"That would be nice."

All sound seemingly subsided as the two men stood amidst the light breeze. It was at that moment that Jin suspected, for whatever far-sighted reason, that this was goodbye. He looked forward, trying to gather the words to say. He decided to tell his friend how much he had meant to him, how he helped him during his time in Boston. He was going to say how much he appreciated him, the ballgame, and their kinship. But when Jin turned, Al was gone.

Jin looked down to see the still-smoking cigarette on the ground. He observed the last breath of embers gasping for oxygen before the inescapable disintegration of its ash. The entrancing experience was like staring into the pit of hell as small fiery fissures unfolded, allowing one to see into the depths of existence itself.

Jin looked back up. He wasn't sure if Spalding had gone back inside or drifted into the magic of the Boston night. Nor did he want to.

Al's prediction proved prophetic as news of the signings leaked to the press before the season ended. The Boston fans did not take the news lightly as the players thereafter faced both verbal harassment and physical threats on a daily basis. Spalding was not seen at any bars or restaurants during this time, much to Jin's dismay.

Despite this, the Boston Red Stockings ranked first and finished the season with 71 wins and just 8 losses. They went on to win their fourth-straight championship on October 30th by defeating the Hartford Dark Blues 7-4. The victory proved to be the very final game in the history of the National Association.

Twenty days prior, on October 10th, at a meeting of Chicago White Stockings stockholders, William Hulbert named Albert Spalding as Secretary of his team.

In his final season with Boston, Spalding once again led the league in wins and ERA. A local paper published his statistics, documenting his time in Boston.

Year	Age	Tm	W	L	W/L%	ERA	G	GS	CG	IP	H	ER	BB	HR	SO
1871	20	Bos	19	10	.655	3.36	31	31	22	257.1	333	96	39	2	23
1872	21	Bos	38	8	.826	1.85	48	48	41	404.2	417	83	27	0	28
1873	22	Bos	41	14	.745	2.99	60	54	46	496.2	643	165	36	5	50
1874	23	Bos	52	16	.765	1.92	71	69	65	617.1	755	132	19	1	31
1875	24	Bos	54	5	.916	1.59	72	62	52	570.2	573	101	18	1	75

1876 was an odd year for both Jin and baseball. With his friend gone, there existed a fragmentary void in his life. The Red Stockings changed their name to the Red Caps to avoid confusion with the Cincinnati Red Stockings and joined the newly established National League.

Before the season even started, Spalding made the announcement that he was going to open a sporting goods retail store in Chicago. He seemed to have secured his future and Jin was happy for him.

Boston had the honor of playing the first ever National League game and they defeated the Philadelphia Athletics by a score of 6-5. From there, however, the season was uninspiring and the team finished with a lackluster record of 39-31. To no ones surprise, the Chicago White Stockings finished with the best record in baseball, making them the default National League champions as playoffs did not yet exist.

Boston fans took some delight, however, in the unofficial five-game square-off for a title dubbed "Champions of the West" between Chicago and the St. Louis Brown Stockings after a clear rivalry had been established. The Brown Stockings won the series.

To Jin, however, baseball had lost a part of its supernatural power. He considered himself lucky nonetheless to have borne witness to the true emergence of the game. He would forever hold that memory of his first visit to the South End Grounds as one of his most treasured.

By 1876, Jin had gained an enormous amount of engineering knowledge, made honest friends, enveloped himself in an foreign culture that included Smith's Philadelphia Cream Ale and cream pie, learned everything there was to know about baseball, and cultivated connections with Japan's political elites while acting as an interpreter. Yet, there was still one feat that Jin sought to accomplish. It was a terrifying and intimidating feat, one filled with strain and stress. Jin wanted to woo a woman.

Jin approached the young beauty carefully. He knew he couldn't be too aggressive while simultaneously he knew he couldn't be too meek. He had to be confident like Al was. He had to make her realize, through his charm, he had something to offer.

He sleekly asked, while being very aware of his physicality and the tenacity it attempted to imbue, "Would you like to have dinner with me?"

The woman smiled and looked at Jin directly in the eyes while assuredly responding, "No."

That was pretty much how it went for the better half of the year.

Jin had stopped frequenting the Bell in Hand Tavern as he oddly felt that he had outgrown the establishment, possibly because ale was the hardest thing they served.

He started patronizing The Green Dragon Tavern; admittedly the name reminded him of his childhood. His mother would often recite mythology and in such stories dragons were the protectors of mankind, benefactors to the Japanese people. Green ones in particular were associated with nature. Jin wondered if Americans viewed dragons in the same light. He daydreamed how he would do anything for even a small, little dragon that could provide some sort of companionship.

Jin sipped from his glass of Jameson, the triple distilled Irish whiskey. His head was down, as he appeared engrossed in the drink.

"Why haven't you asked me?" a voice pointedly challenged.

Jin looked up, not even sure if the inquiry was directed at him. It took only a matter of seconds for him to realize that it most certainly was as an almond-eyed woman guided her gaze directly into his startled eyes.

She had full, luscious hair and smooth unmarred silken skin that glimmered with an olive hue. She glowed in the most natural way.

"I'm sorry?" Jin stuttered.

"You've asked out nearly every woman who comes to this bar except the one that might actually say yes."

Jin looked around nervously. He awkwardly pointed at her.

"Yes. Me."

"With—" Jin, somehow even more awkwardly, pointed at himself.

"Yes. You."

She walked up to him with conviction and held her hand out.

"My name is Sana."

Jin shook her hand and responded, "Jin."

"You're new at this," she concluded.

Jin nodded like an unworthy mortal interacting with a goddess and answered, "It's true what they say. Women are the paragon of paradoxes."

Sana laughed at the precept and continued, "I am new at this as well. We already have something in common. Tonight. The Public Garden. The Suspension Bridge. Seven o'clock."

"I'll be there," Jin resolved.

And just like that, Jin's final puzzle piece had found its place.

His belly full of butterflies, Jin entered the garden through the western entrance. It was there that he saw a towering statue of George Washington upon a horse. He did recall that bit of history from school. It was one of the few stories that amazed him in his studies. Jin found Washington to be bold and distinctive, at least that's the way he was taught.

He remembered learning how Washington took control of the Continental Army just before the Siege of Boston. He thought it exciting when, under the cover of darkness, the eventual first president bombarded the British ships in Boston harbor. Soon enough the chaotic ten-day evacuation of Boston by the British was underway.

He could only imagine what it must have been like to live in that time, the dawn of a new era. Jin supposed that perhaps people never really know when they are in the midst of such change; they only look back and wonder how they didn't notice the transition.

The bronze horse really caught his eye. The large solid-hoofed creature seemed to have a personality. Its ears were thrown back and its eyes were fixated on something near. Perhaps they were being attacked. While Washington seemed attentive he also seemed relatively at ease. Perhaps this was the point. To display great resolve in the face of uncertainty. Jin admired heroism. Of course, he also understood one man's hero is often another man's tyrant.

He progressed deeper into the park, now illuminated by gas lamps.

Jin found his way to the pedestrian bridge; there was no one on it. He lackadaisically traversed to the center of the overpass for the best vantage point and looked out.

The fall foliage blazed across the city as the tapestry of autumnal colors captivated the young man. For whatever reason, Jin never appreciated this time of year in the United States as much as he did in that moment. The night conjured a harmonious breeze while the park itself remained quiet. The water under the bridge was placid and peaceful. Jin enjoyed the moment.

Something caught the corner of his eye and Jin's head, not so much unlike the bronze equestrian he recently observed, darted to observe a leaf rotating along the footpath. He could tell it was vibrant yellow not so long ago but now had browned, stiffened, and crumbled. The wind tried to elevate it into the night air but every time it lifted just a morsel off the ground, it crashed back down onto the cold, hard platform like it had some sort of organic outgrowth of an anchor attached to it. It was as if the leaf didn't want to ascend at all but rather just wanted the gusts to let it be. He supposed it had its reasons.

"You're early," remarked a mollifying voice.

Jin turned to see Sana on the far end of the suspended bridge. She was walking towards him.

"Punctuality was drilled into me from an early age," Jin said.

"I see we have something else in common. Usually I'm the first to arrive."

When she reached him, she looked out at the city from his viewpoint.

"It's beautiful isn't it?"

"Yes," Jin answered. "I've never been here before."

"You've been missing out."

"Thank you for showing it to me."

"Let's walk, shall we?"

The two strolled side-by-side—though at an arm's length—through the dazzling growth and greenness of the park.

"Have you always lived in Boston?" asked Jin.

She smiled and answered, "Most people ask the same question differently. They ask—what are you? Or, where do you come from? Your way sounds more human. Thank you. I was born in Mount Lebanon. In 1860 a civil war broke out in my homeland. The result was a massacre of thousands upon thousands of Christians."

"Why?"

"My family are Maronites. Do you know that term?"

Jin shook his head.

"A Christian group whose members adhere to the Syriac Maronite Church. We settled in the Druze regions on the Mount. The Druze saw this as a threat to their power. As usual when such a clash happens, war and death followed."

"I'm sorry."

"It is not of your doing. This is life. My family wasn't interested in the bloodshed. We came here immediately. I was seven."

"I haven't noticed many Arab immigrants around. Your family must have been one of the few."

"We are. Although my family still believes more will come soon due to the silk industry failing and agriculture dying. The Ottoman Empire will tax its people out of their own home."

"How many of your family members are here?"

"Just my parents and myself."

"That must have been hard."

"It was that or death. But it's been a welcome change. It must have been harder for you, not knowing a single soul."

"How did you know that?"

"I see you around," she answered with a smile. Sana stopped to examine a particularly comely crimson-colored tree. "It's gorgeous," she declared.

"Do you know what it is?"

"No."

"Japanese maple."

"Really?"

"They were my mother's favorite. She enjoyed the spectacular colors."

They both observed the bright woody plant, unknowingly inching closer to one another.

"Do you miss your parents?"

"The longer I'm here, the more I miss them."

"Will you be returning home?"

"Yes. Shortly."

"And how do you feel about that?"

"I'm ready. I didn't think I would be. But things are changing here; people leave, pastimes shift. Such things make me feel less at home. Of course Japan hasn't been home for years. I wonder if I'll even recognize it."

"I understand that."

"Do you ever think you'll go back?" Jin asked curiously.

"I doubt that very much. Can I ask you something?"

"Of course."

"If you're leaving soon, why were you so persistent on courtship?"

"When I first came here I was told American women do not think of Asian men as romantically desirable. I was told a lot of things, most of which I succeeded in disproving. This one still remains."

"I see. Too bad I'm not an American woman."

Jin turned away from the ornamental tree, looked directly at Sana, and announced, "You're better."

With boundless courage and unforeseen assurance, Jin kissed Sana. It was as all first kisses are, imperfectly wonderful.

When he pulled away, he felt as if he had consummated all of life's desires. He knew he had such a feeling not because he had finally kissed someone but because of whom he kissed.

Sana's eyes were enlarged and one of her eyebrow's darted upwards.

"I did not expect that."

"If you do not expect the unexpected you will not find it, for it is not to be reached by search or trail."

"Are you quoting Greek philosophy to me?"

"Yes. Heraclitus."

"Impressive."

They both fell quiet, staring into each other's eyes, closing them as their lips met again. The two persisted, their spirited passions combusting in front of that fiery tree with red-hot leaves.

Jin had a feeling that when he would one day think back on his American days, this would often be the first memory to surface. Needless to say, he would be proved right many a time.

When they eventually pulled away from one another, Jin self-confessed, "I do not want this moment to end."

Sana smiled and placed her smooth hand upon his eager cheek. She kissed him once more although this kiss was different. It was not a kiss of fervor but rather one of remembrance. It lasted longer than Jin expected and yet severely shorter than he yearned. But in that moment the two strangers, once newcomers to this place, and now to each other, endured in a bubble of abiding bliss. Until, of course, it forever popped with the receding lips of the admired woman.

Sana took a step back to gaze upon Jin.

She smiled one final smile and recited, "But at the laste, as every thing hath ende, She took hir leve, and nedes wolde wende."

Sana slowly changed course, her last impression permanently chiseled in memory. She walked away from Jin as unswervingly as she walked up to him. He attempted to keep her in his vision for as long as possible but her backside soon evaporated into darkness. Jin stared helplessly as she too expired into the enchanting and uncanny obscurity of blackness that encompassed the Boston night.

Chapter 5

The Legend of Jin Miyano Part II

Jin returned to his childhood home of Japan in 1877, now a young man. He entered his household with his luggage in hand as he could hear his mother trample downstairs. When she saw him, she stopped in her tracks and gasped. The two grinned at each other from ear to ear before she hurled herself into his arms. The grip was tight and felt mutually incredible.

She pulled back and grabbed the cheeks of her forever baby boy.

"You lost your baby fat," she gleamed.

Jin laughed as he looked at his mother's face. She had aged. Not terribly, Jin thought, but naturally. It had been six years; anyone would look a little older after such time.

"Yua," said a strong, vigorous voice.

Jin looked up to see his father over his mother's shoulder.

"Let me see my boy."

Yua moved aside, still beaming, as the two men came face to face. Instinctively, Jin put his hand out to initiate a handshake. His father looked down curiously.

"It's called a handshake. It is a symbol of greeting. You grip it and shake it."

Still decidedly looking down, his father asked, "You greet in the same manner you take a piss?"

Jin did not know what was coming next. Would his father berate him for assimilating to the Western world? Or would he perhaps simply walk away in that holier than thou fashion Jin so often remembered?

Jin's father extended his hand and gripped his son's.

"It is good to have you home," he declared.

Jin's room was precisely how he remembered it. He placed his luggage upon his bed and unzipped the bag. He lifted the top section up and over to view his belongings. On top of his messily packed clothes laid a series of baseballs. He reached into a side compartment and slid out a beautiful wooden bat. And just like that, the West had come to the East.

They each sat on a cushion placed on a tatami-matted floor around the low dinner table as Jin marveled at the feast his mother prepared. Before him were plates of *niku dōfu*, prepared with beef, tofu, onions, shiitake and enoki mushrooms, *kiriboshi daikon,* dried radish, carrot and deep-fried tofu, miso soup with potatoes and onions, rice, shrimp dumplings and a pitcher of jasmine tea. It was as if Jin had been transported into the past.

They raised their glasses and in unison uttered the drinking salute, *"Kampai!"*

"I bet they don't have this food in America," his mother asserted.

"They most certainly do not. Not yet anyway."

They dove in with their chopsticks and spoons as Jin moaned in glee from the deliciousness of the food.

"This is perfect. Thank you."

"You deserve it," Yua said.

"Obviously, I was not pleased when I received word that you dropped out of school."

"He was furious," Yua added.

"Nonetheless, I am happy you received an education, albeit an informal one. What will you do for work now that you are home?"

"I am to work for the Shinbashi Railroad Bureau," Jin answered.

"How will you do that?" asked his mother. "That is considered one of the most glamorous jobs a young man could have."

"I already have it. Forty-five yen a month. Itō Hirobumi saw to it."

"Itō Hirobumi?" his father questioned. "The Minister of Public Works?"

"Yes, although I hear he refers to it as The Ministry of Engineering."

"How do you know him?" his father questioned.

"He was sent on the Iwakura Mission around the world as vice-envoy extraordinary. When he came to Boston, the Americans needed an interpreter."

"And you were the only Japanese person around," his father continued.

"Correct."

"You cultivated a good connection, Jin," his mother applauded.

Jin's father stared at his son as if not recognizing him. He subtly nodded.

"I'm proud of you," he said, his head immediately descending back down towards his food.

Both Jin and his mother looked up, surprised. His father continued to eat as if he said nothing. Jin smirked and continued to dotingly devour his dinner.

The job at the railroad bureau paid well but lacked the excitement needed to quench Jin's unscathed youthful playfulness. He had no intention of quitting, however. He had a different idea altogether.

Jin walked up to the agency's managerial staff as they sat for lunch one afternoon.

"May I?" Miyano asked, referring to the empty seat at the table.

They all nodded or held their hand out and Jin sat.

"Beautiful day," remarked Jin.

"Yes, it is" one answered.

"What do you guys do for fun around here?"

The managerial staff looked at him awkwardly.

"After hours, I mean," Jin amended.

"I go home to my family," one answered.

"Sometimes we play the poem game," another said.

"The poem game?" Jin questioned.

"Yes. You don't know it? There are two hundred cards. They are stored in a decorated box, sometimes metal, sometimes lacquer. Half the cards show a portrait of one of the well-known Hundred Poets and the beginning of one of their poems. The other half, the other 100 cards, contains the endings to the poems. Players have to match the two cards that belong together."

The managers murmured with delight at the memory of the game.

"That sounds like fun," Jin said. "But what about outdoor activities?"

They once again looked oddly at the young employee.

"You're the one that just came back from America, aren't you?"

"Yes," Jin responded.

"The country of masculine prowess and bravado."

Ignoring the comments, Jin continued, "Do you engage in no outdoor games? Exercise?"

There was no answer.

Jin pounced, "Have you heard of baseball?"

They looked at one another until one said, "Base ball. America's game?"

"Yes! America's game," Jin responded excitedly.

"I think some of the kids are playing it now. America's game should stay in America, no?" one commented.

"We don't have the tools for the game anyway," another remarked.

"Yes, we do," retorted Jin with a smile. "And I notice there's a lot of empty space outside, in this very compound."

The next day Jin brought his baseball bat and balls to work. The managerial staff appeared surprised as if they didn't believe yesterday's words.

"Today. After work. We learn baseball."

It began with a simple catch. Jin would throw each of them the ball and they would persistently drop it or miss it all together. Then they would attempt to throw the ball back to Jin, which usually entailed him having to track it down, as it was typically thrown nowhere near him.

Batting was even more entertaining.

"Keep your eye on the ball," ordered Jin as he threw it to the batter, who astutely observed the round object pass by.

"That was good. But you forgot to swing."

The batter nodded with the assurance that he understood. On the next pitch he did indeed swing and the bat went flying towards the rail tracks.

"Good! But you're supposed to hold on to the bat. The ball is the thing that should go flying."

As another staffer grabbed the bat, Jin said, "Swing through the ball."

"Impossible!" the staffer disputed. "Or do the physical laws that govern energy and matter not exist in America!?"

"I just mean instead of swinging the bat just far enough to make contact with the ball, wait until you have actually hit it before you stop adding force to your swing. I have also heard people call this 'following through'. You want to hit the ball when your swing is most forceful."

The argumentative batter scowled at the young engineer. When he swung, he neither followed through nor made contact. He threw the bat down in anger.

Jin could only think to say, "Yes! Passion is good! This is a game of passion!"

A different colleague attempted to bat but stood clumsily at the makeshift plate.

"Your head should be right in the middle of your feet," Jin instructed.

His colleague dropped down to the ground, sat with his legs bent and literally placed his head in the middle of his feet.

"Okay. I wasn't expecting that," Jin remarked to himself.

"This was good. Tomorrow we will try again. It's a lot of fun once you get used to it, I promise!"

Jin watched as the destitute managerial staff of the Shinbashi Railroad Bureau meekly walked away.

He sighed, feeling as though he had failed miserably in his attempt to show them baseball.

That evening's meal was not as bountiful as the feast upon Jin's return but just as delicious. Nevertheless, Jin ate his soba in deep thought.

"Is everything okay?" asked Yua.

"I noticed you took your play toys to work today," his father chimed in.

"I attempted to teach my coworkers a game I learned in America. It did not go as planned."

His father chuckled and said, "I can picture it now—a bunch of engineers trying to play a sport of physical skill. They are not typically known for their athleticism, you know."

Jin inhaled some buckwheat noodles as his mother commented, "I don't know, engineers are not exactly scientists. Scientists are cerebral; engineers are more willing to get their hands dirty. I'm sure if you keep trying, you will succeed. It's not exactly Newtonian physics."

Jin's head popped up. "That's it."

"What's it?" his father curiously asked.

"Newton. Classical mechanics. I'm going to teach them baseball through science."

The managerial staff huddled around Jin.

"Okay. We are simply going to do what we do. We are engineers, which means we apply the knowledge of science to the real world. Now, we're going to apply it to baseball."

The agency members appeared skeptical.

"Newton's Laws of Motion. The first law, the law of inertia, states that an object at rest will stay at rest and an object in motion will stay in motion with the same speed and direction unless acted upon by unbalanced force. So we know once a train gets going its inertia—its resistance to changes in motion—keeps our train moving forward. We also know that centripetal force helps us in that the force on the train is what allows it to follow a curved path around a bend. So to bring it full circle, the tracks are designed to provide enough outside force, centripetal force, on the train so that it turns against its natural direction, straight ahead, and instead makes those turns around the bend with no issue.

"What does this have to do with baseball?" someone eagerly asked.

"When a pitcher throws, he sets the ball in motion. What happens before it makes it to the catcher? Air pressure acts upon the surface of the spinning ball. So what if we use that to our advantage? What if we put a lateral spin on the pitch? What happens? The ball should move several inches sideways as it crosses home plate. This makes it extremely difficult to hit."

"Why? A batter can calculate the trajectory and act accordingly, no?"

"He can try. I did these calculations last night. They are very rough and impossible to gauge perfectly but the estimations speak volumes. After a baseball leaves the hand of a pitcher, it takes approximately one-hundredth of a second for a hitter to locate the ball. At this moment that ball has already traveled twelve feet. Our batter needs to calculate the speed of the ball, the spin of the ball, and the trajectory. This takes seven hundredths of a second. The ball has trekked another ten feet at this point. It will take a hitter less than two-hundredths of a second for the brain to send signals to the body so that the individual can implement a swing. In other words, the hitter has about nine-hundredths of a second to determine if he wants to swing or let it go. Any hesitation, even if that hesitation lasts for a thousandth of a second, will cause the batter to miss the pitch or at best foul it off. That is the mathematics of baseball."

The employees were captivated; he was speaking their language.

"You mentioned spin," one remarked. "Different pitches can have different spin?"

"Precisely," Jin answered excitedly. "There are other pitches besides a fastball. Curveballs and sliders are attempts to throw a batter off-balance. When you throw a curveball, you do so with a downward spin. We know spin allows air to pass on only one side of the ball because the ball is not smooth. You can see the stitches on it. So as the ball is thrown, the air passes the ball faster on one side than the other. Thus, there is an area of reduced air pressure on the side of the ball where the air passes quicker. The result is the curve because the ball is essentially dragged to the side with the lower air pressure. The preservation of angular momentum guarantees this. Newton himself described this over two hundred years ago when he observed tennis players at Cambridge. Pitching is basically Bernoulli's principle; I know you all read his 1738 masterpiece *Hydrodynamica.*"

They nodded as if that was an absolute given, still enthralled.

"I'll keep going then. So, a batter's job is fundamentally to stop the inertia of the baseball by swinging and making contact, so they too are implementing Newton's first law by setting their bats in motion."

Jin took a deep breath as if preparing himself for what was to come next.

"Now, on to Newton's second law, the law of force and acceleration. Acceleration happens when a force acts upon a mass or object. When the net force increases, acceleration increases. The more mass something has, the less it accelerates. I think we all remember this example: if one train hits another train of equal force and speed, they will both go the same distance and will feel the same force. However, if the first train is hooked to a second, the single train will go twice the distance of the double train and will feel twice the force. Newton's second law in action. Back to baseball, what is a hitter trying to do? Make contact! That moment of contact is, as we know, equal to the combined mass and acceleration of both the bat and the ball. Enter strategy. What batters should be doing is attempting to swing more calmly with the aim of getting a hit by dropping the ball between the infielders and outfielders.

"What I'm about to tell you next is a matter of controversy. It is a concept called bunting. The Red Stockings' player-manager Harry Wright claimed to have invented it when playing in Cincinnati but no one can say for sure. Bunting is a technique where the batter holds the bat over home plate and attempts to tap the ball onto the field. The weak contact is strategic in nature, as it forces infielders to make hard defensive plays. It is not common. When I was in America, there was an article in the Boston Globe that called bunting the 'black game' because it meant, in their opinion, that the batter was too weak to hit the ball far. Talk about American bravado. I think it skillful and scientific hitting. How is it scientific? When a batter bunts, the mass of the bat is not in motion, which means the mass acceleration Newton talked about is only provided by the ball. If we, as hitters, were to be smart about this, we would use these mass-acceleration factors to our advantage at the very moment of making contact by having the barrel of the bat react ever so slightly to the intense force caused by the baseball. It would surely make for the most effective bunts."

"Do Americans think in this way?" someone asked.

"From what I remember, I don't believe the ballplayers do. Who knows, through the power of science we may be able to become better ballplayers than them."

The courageous and fearless comment put confidence into the group.

"Lastly, Newton's third law: for every action there is an equal and opposite reaction. This is the very reason trains are able to move at all! The force the locomotive puts on the rails enables it to accelerate the cars. The force exerted by the locomotive on the train and the force of the train on the locomotive are the same in magnitude and opposite in direction. That's how it works. Now, its relationship to baseball!"

Jin took a ball and threw it upwards, directly over his head. They all watched studiously as it soared up towards the sun before it made its unavoidable plunge back down. It landed in front of the employees.

"A ball that goes up must come down. When we are running the bases, we make a calculation about a ball thrown by a player on the other team who is trying to get us out. We compute how long it's going to reach its destination and we determine whether or not we can make it to the next base. When we are in the outfield and a player on the opposite team hits a fly ball, we gauge the distance of that ball before it reaches the height of its arc. The better fielders are the ones who can make those computations quickest. They make an estimation the moment the ball is hit. They take into account their location and the arc of the baseball and they do their best to go after the zooming ball and make the catch."

Jin centered himself in front of his stimulated colleagues like a general before his army.

"So, as you can see—baseball is simply science. Science is about knowing. Engineering is about doing. We are the engineers that will apply this knowledge to win. And have fun. It is a game, after all."

The managerial staff trained and played everyday after work with Jin. They learned to catch. They learned to throw. And they learned to hit. They started playing scrimmage games using Jin's one bat and the few baseballs he had. Eventually, of course, after about a year's time they grew tired of constantly playing against one another. They longed for competition.

Jin seemed distracted as he placed sashimi in his mouth.

"What's going on in that head of yours?" his mother asked.

"I am thinking about starting Japan's first private baseball club."

His father looked at him and commented, "This is turning into more than just a hobby, isn't it?"

"Maybe. Regardless, the guys at work are intrigued and want more. I think people, in general, will be intrigued when they see us playing in uniforms."

"Uniforms?" his mother questioned. "Uniforms are for the military, police, and the fire brigade."

"And ballplayers," Jin corrected with a grin.

"My instinct says this is a waste of time and possibly even a little dangerous," his father proclaimed. "But my instincts have always been wrong when it comes to you. I thought you would never do well for yourself. Now, you work for the railroad. You make a good living. You understand things about the West I could never truly comprehend. Whatever decision you make, I am confident you will succeed."

"Thank you," Jin responded. It was in that moment that Jin perceived his father for who he always truly was.

"Where will you play?" his mother chimed in, breaking the thought.

"The Shinbashi Railroad Bureau gave me permission to turn part of the compound into a playing field." His parents gave him a look of astonishment as he continued, "We will imitate what I saw in Boston. We will enforce the regimen of upkeep. We will roll the ground every Saturday. People will be captivated to see men in uniforms they do not recognize. They will want to watch."

"It sounds like you have this entire thing planned out," remarked Yua.

Jin chewed on the sliced raw fish. Upon swallowing, he said, "All except the equipment. There's nothing quite like a baseball here. And I hear players are starting to wear gloves in America now. I think catchers are even wearing masks for protection. We will somehow need to address the equipment issue."

His father thought for a moment before asking, "What are these baseballs made out of?"

"It's a rubber core wrapped in yarn and leather."

"We're going on a mission tomorrow," his father declared. "The first stop will be to Yokohama."

"What's there?" asked Jin.

"An athletic club."

"I doubt they play baseball there," Jin remarked.

"They do not. They play cricket."

"Cricket? What does cricket have to do with anything?" Yua asked.

"The ball used in that game is cork centered. It is wrapped tightly with string and encased in leather with a raised sewn seam of stitches by, what the British call, the equator of the ball. They owe me a favor. Perhaps it is time to allow them to repay it. "

"That's a great idea," remarked Yua. "They will give you all the balls you need."

"For free?" inquired Jin.

"They will if they still wish to continue enjoying the 120-acre plot they play their matches on."

Jin's eyes lit up.

His father started to chuckle and Yua asked, "What is it?"

"When I was a very small child, my grandmother would scold me for crying. She used to say, 'what a coward you are to cry over such miniscule pain. What will you do when your limb is cut off in battle?' She did this to prepare me for the world. Today I vowed to help my son procure balls for a possibly lucrative sporting game. How luxurious. I can just hear my grandmother now. She would say something like, 'Luxury is the menace to manhood.' Times are changing indeed."

The father and son duo arrived at the club. Jin noted that it had a very different feel from the rest of the city.

His father leaned into his ear and said, "Just so you know, the man with whom we are about to speak with is a little, shall we say, eccentric."

Jin nodded and anticipated the man while simultaneously having no idea what to expect.

Eventually, a genial face emerged. The man sported a white mustache to match the hoariness of the hair he had on his head. He walked cheerfully over.

"Good afternoon, gentlemen! Is this your son?"

"Good to see you again, James," Jin's father said. "And yes, it is."

"A fellow cricketer in the making do we have here?" he asked in his thick Scottish accent.

"I think not. We have come to ask for a favor."

"A favor?" James questioned falteringly. He regained his composure and continued, "Of course! What can we do for ya!? You know, they keep trying to push us out but we're still standing aren't we!?"

"You are indeed, James."

"Me, I've always kept my head about it. Do you remember Charles? Poor bastard." He turned to Jin to ask, "Have you heard of the Richardson Affair?"

"We call it the Namamugi Incident," his father chimed in.

"Well, whatever you call it, about fifteen years ago there was panic among non-Japanese citizens here. Why? Because an English merchant by the name of Charles Lennox Richardson, who was visiting from Shanghai, was slashed to death by samurai on the Tōkaidō road while riding to Yokohama to visit the big shrine in Kawasaki."

"A tragedy, no doubt. But may I ask why we are reliving this specific memory?"

"Because of the result! Pressure was put on the government in London to protect us! Warships and troops were sent! And do you know what happened, lad!?"

"What?" asked Jin.

"A surge in cricket! The British military loved cricket! And guess who used that to his advantage!? Whenever we got wind of a possible samurai attack, we invited the soldiers for a game of cricket! With their rifles about, no samurai would dare try to cross us. Being a man of business, it only made sense to later create this place, the Yokohama Cricket Club! And, by the way, the Japanese started to gain an interest in what we were doing. They were impressed by our dedication, enthusiasm, and skills and they came to watch. It has since become a haven for our expatriate communities. A taste of home, if you will. And here we are!"

"Here we are indeed," echoed Jin's father.

James put his hand on Jin's father's shoulder, which he took notice of, and began walking with him while he vigorously said, "Now! About that favor! What can I do for ya?"

Jin and his father stood in the workshop of a shoemaker.

"Did you bring it, Jin?"

"Yes, like you asked," he responded while pulling out one of his baseballs.

His father took it and presented it to the shoemaker.

"This is an American baseball. We need something like it here. We're using cricket balls in the meantime but it's not the same."

The shoemaker grabbed the ball and curiously looked at it before stating, "I'm going to have to take it apart."

Jin disconcertingly looked at his father.

"It's okay. It will be worth it," were his father's words. He then turned back to the shoemaker and said, "Do it."

Jin next found himself in a dojo in Kurumazaka. Two opponents battled competitively in the center of the school hall, each wielding a shinai. Their attacks were swift and nimble; concentration as well as discipline seemed to be the true underpinnings of the activity.

A short, self-effacing man approached Jin and his father. He bowed; they returned the greeting.

"What can I do for you?" asked the man.

"It's good to see you again, Sakakibara. I have a question about the kendo stick," he said as he pointed towards the dueling competitors.

"What about them?"

"I was thinking the Japanese bamboo might make a good transition to masks."

"Masks?" questioned Sakakibara.

"Yes. One a player trying to protect his face from a speeding ball might wear."

Jin rounded out the equipment matter by taking upholstered railroad car material and repurposing it for protective gear. They created the field on the compound and dubbed it *Hokenjo*, Health Field. They had uniforms as one of the engineers had a seamstress for a wife. Upon completion, a photographer came and took a group photo of the team. And just like that, the nation's first private baseball club was born.

Soon after its introduction in Japan, baseball began catching on. People flocked to watch, intrigued at the game and the uniforms. Jin and his father's social standing only helped matters as many former feudal domain leaders, who had retained their social status after the Meiji Restoration, started to attend the games. Their presence gave credibility to the sport.

Jin was munching on his unagi as his parents did the same.

"That was some game yesterday," remarked Yua. "What was that called when you got two men out at the same time?"

"A double play," Jin answered.

"Very impressive," his father chimed in.

"I have something even more impressive," Jin noted after swallowing a piece of grilled eel.

His parents looked up.

"Some of those former feudal leaders who have been coming to games approached me with a proposition."

"What do they want?" his mother asked.

"To teach them and their families the language of the future. They want to learn English from a certain recent returnee."

His parents were shocked.

"Will you accept the offer?" asked Yua.

Jin added, "I will. And after some foundational lessons, I will teach them the language of baseball. That way they will be able to speak of and spread the knowledge of the game."

His father surprisingly looked at Yua, wondering how they produced such a cunning son.

A middle-aged woman whose attire and demeanor still had the quality of a patrician let Jin into the Takahashi household.

"Greetings," said Jin. "Are you Kayda? The one I am to tutor?"

The woman smiled and responded, "No. Kayda is my daughter. She is waiting in the next room. You may find her there."

Jin bowed and turned to the room where his pupil waited. He walked into a large space with numerous bookshelves. In the middle of the room was Kayda, sitting. Jin halted in his tracks upon seeing her. She stood up, clearly also nervous.

"Hello," she said in English. In Japanese, she continued, "That's all I know."

"That's quite alright," Jin reassured while petrified by the beauty of the young woman. "I can teach you."

Kayda smiled. Jin smiled. In his transfixed state, he had forgotten how to walk, or that he should walk, or that he had to walk to approach his student to teach her.

Kayda's mother suddenly stood behind the paralyzed tutor and gave him a tame push forward. Jin awoke from his bewitchment and clumsily headed towards Kayda as her mother disappeared once more. He placed his belongings on a table.

"Where do we start?" she asked.

"What's the first word you want to know?" he enthusiastically asked.

She looked in his eyes and vehemently answered, "Sekkusu!"

"Kayda!" her mother immediately roared from the other room.

Jin was out of sorts; he wasn't expecting any of the last five minutes to ever occur. He regained his composure and looked back at the flaming eyes of Kayda.

He whispered, "That one is pronounced sex."

Jin went on to marry Kayda and often remarked that she was the fire that lit his beacon. Her small stature was a deception as she was highly combustible and loved with a love best described as burning.

Baseball too continued in Japan. And in 1884, at the age of 29, Jin Miyano wrote a seemingly commonplace letter that would have repercussions no one could have imagined.

Jin took a copy of the photograph that had been taken at the inception of his ball club and placed it in an envelope along with a letter.

Dear A.G.,

How are you? I heard the most preposterous notion the other day. I heard that towards the end of your career you started to wear a baseball glove! Could this be true? Not only that, I heard you inspired others to take up a mitt as well. Do tell.

I'm sure life has sent you on exciting adventures—I can't wait to hear about them.

I have some exciting news. I have started a baseball club here in Japan. At first it was met with aversion, perhaps even hostility but six years later, we are still playing. People are enthusiastic. Admittedly, we lost our first ever game but went on to win the vast majority of the rest. The equipment isn't the same but we make do with substitutions and makeshift supplies. Unfortunately the deficiency of our materials often result in the rampant injuries of our players.

I am including a picture of our team. I hope it brings a smile to your face.

I wanted to thank you for befriending me all those years ago. It meant a lot to a kid who knew no one, or nothing of a culture. And most of all, I wanted to thank you for introducing me to baseball. It was the greatest gift I could have ever received. Here's one for the home team.

With Sincere Regard,

Jin

A few months later, Jin received a response.

Jin!

How are you my friend? Firstly, let me clarify—it is absolutely true that I used a glove. Everyone does now! And that's great news. You know why? Because I made the glove! It's more equipment for me to sell! I retired from playing a good six years ago and have been focused on my sporting goods business.

Do you remember in 1874 when Harry Wright sent a team to the British Isles to preach the belief of baseball? I've been thinking of doing something similar myself. It would take a good amount of planning but I think I could pull it off in the next few years. I'm thinking Hawaii, Australia, Ceylon, Egypt, Italy, France, the Netherlands, and I suppose back to the British Isles to see if they progressed any with it. Since reading your letter I was thinking about adding Japan to the list but the logistics of ocean passenger transport don't look too positive. Perhaps one day. Hey, you think Rome will let us play in the Coliseum!? Ha!

Your picture brought me great joy and indeed put a smile on my face. Perhaps I can use it to my advantage in convincing others baseball is worth investing in as even distant Asia is participating in the contemporary activities of the day!

I joke but I think baseball truly is important. And that's not just because I want to make money off the equipment, which I most assuredly do. The point of the tour would absolutely be to extend my sporting goods business to a new quarter of the globe and create a market for the goods there and everywhere. But in all honesty, this is also about something more. This is about a commitment to the American values of virility. It's a commitment to the social equality that exists in the game.

I say that well aware of the history of social equality, or lack thereof, in this country but just this year the Toledo Blue Stockings have black siblings on their team—Moss Fleetwood Walker and his brother Wendy Walker. Lord knows they don't have it easy.

As a matter of fact, while we're on the subject, five years ago there was a player by the name of William Edward White. He played one game for the Providence Grays and was never heard from again. No one made a big deal of it because he looked just like everyone else. But White was very ironically black. And no one knew! His light skin made him pass as Caucasian. Someone told me he was the son of a plantation owner and a slave, but I don't know if that's true. If it were he would probably be the first and only baseball player ever to have also been a former slave. Jesus. Imagine that. That's more than a story—that's a legend. And legends, while true or not, inspire us. I was even thinking of telling other countries in this tour how Abraham Lincoln adored the game of baseball after General Abner Doubleday, you know, the guy who fired the first shot in defense of Fort Sumter which opened up the Civil War, was actually the one who invented baseball in 1839. Legends.

I am sure having three black baseball players will inspire countless others. The number of such athletes will only increase, mark my words. Why some people see them as devils I will never understand– and I'm from Illinois!

So sure, this tour is about business. But it's also about patriotism. It's about the idealism of America and what it can be. The two need not be mutually exclusive. The future is ours to mold.

With that, I am going to help mold yours. I am going to provide you with access to American modernity. I am shipping, free of cost to you, balls, bats, gloves, and protective masks from Spalding and Brothers!

This, as you can gather, is good for my business. I will even send additional supplies free of charge in the future to help continue the promotion of baseball in Japan.

Congratulations on starting Japan's first baseball team. You should be proud. I truly hope that Japanese baseball, along with your nation's civilization, will rise like the sun.

Respectfully,

Albert Goodwill Spalding

Jin put the letter down, amazed at the words he had just read. Al sounded different, like a true businessman. He supposed he always was one. Perhaps this was what maturity sounded like.

Not long thereafter his old friend made good on his word. Shipments of equipment came with the name ***Spalding*** boldly imprinted on pretty much everything. Japanese players saw this not as a sign of exuberance but viewed it instead as a social privilege to play with America's machinery. Along with this came enclosed catalogues and promotional literature for Spalding and Brothers' sporting goods. Among these were copies of *The Official Baseball Guide* and *The Official Rules Guide for Baseball*. Both were published by Spalding himself and explicitly stated that only Spalding balls could be used if one wanted to truly play real baseball.

Baseball in Japan had just become that much more legitimate.

Spalding's prediction, however, proved erroneous as just three years after his letter and shipment, in 1887, professional baseball in America segregated, banning the signing of new contracts with black players. American racism had, for the first time in the history of baseball, drawn a color line.

My grandfather continued to play and manage until he and Kayda brought new life into the world, a decade after receiving that bountiful bundle from Spalding; he knew all too well baseball would go on without him. The child, my father, was named Keishi and he was born on July 25th, 1894. In a manner of happenstance Japan's climate was about to drastically change as also on that very date, the First Sino-Japanese War had begun.

Chapter 6

Hell on Heaven

"No shit?"

"No shit," echoed Yuujin with a smile.

"You're telling me your grandfather was one of the people responsible for bringing baseball to Japan?"

"Yes."

"I'll be. And he really knew Spalding?"

"Yes. They were good friends."

"I don't know about good. But I suppose they were friends."

Eugene looked out at Okinawa. For the first time since arriving on the island, he could see past the carnage and slaughter. For just a moment he saw the beauty that existed before war arrived. He opened his mouth to take in the air.

He saw symmetry and smelled serenity. He heard harmony. He tasted tenderness. Best of all, he felt if he touched anything it would be as if he were touching tranquility itself.

"It was beautiful once," Yuujin remarked. "Before the seas were red with blood they were as clear as a newborn's conscience."

Eugene chuckled.

"What?" asked Yuujin.

"It's just funny, that's all. My people believe babies are born with sin."

"Americans?"

"Catholics."

"Why is this?"

"From the original sin of Adam and Eve; childbirth and thorns and thistles and all that. Our punishment for disobedience."

"I hardly think those are the worst things to befall humanity from that story."

"Easy for you to say, you don't have to push one of those suckers out."

"True. Though Adam and Eve gave you something far worse than physical plights."

"Oh yea? What's that?"

"The sense of shame."

"Shame?"

"When they ate the fruit and realized they were naked, they felt shame, yes?"

"Yeah."

"Shame is far more wicked and severe than any ailment of the flesh."

"How very Japanese of you."

"Do you believe this? We are born with sin?"

Still looking out at the Japanese island, the allure of it all quickly dissipated as the very same image somehow superimposed with emotion; the identical landscape had a much different feel. He saw slaying and subjugation. He smelled subversion. He heard havoc. He tasted termination; worst of all, he felt if he touched anything it would be as if he were touching torment itself.

Eugene lit a cigarette, took a drag, and eventually responded, "Sounds about right. We never really had a chance to begin with."

"Your religion has heaven and hell, yes?"

"That's right."

"I find them funny concepts."

"Funny?" Eugene barked.

"Not laughing funny. More like ironic. There were Japanese men in my unit who waited their entire lives for this moment, for battle."

Eugene looked at his commanding officer and added, "I know a few like that."

"For them, this was heaven. It was their nirvana, the freedom from the endless cycle. This arena of Armageddon was their abode of righteousness. For me, however, this is hell. It is the place I wish to be farthest away from. This abyss of war is void of meaning for me; there is no purpose at its bottom."

"What are you? The Japanese Socrates? What's your point?"

"One man's heaven is another man's hell."

There was silence as the two considered the weight of the words.

Yuujin broke the lull with poignancy. "Which is this place to you?"

"I'm no philosopher."

"You think."

"Therefore I am?"

They cracked and let out a simultaneous cackle.

Eugene continued, "If this war has taught me anything it's that perhaps heaven and hell are the exact same place."

"How so?"

"If this is heaven for some and hell for others, and a nice boring life washing clothes and perking coffee is also heaven for some while being a hell for others, it only makes sense that the two places, heaven and hell, can never truly be mutually exclusive."

Yuujin grinned. "You are a philosopher after all."

"Must have missed my calling."

"It makes me think, this talk of heaven and hell. If they are the same place, how can we differentiate between who the angels are and who the demons are?"

"The demons are the ones who surprise people with preemptive military strikes with a complete lack of any formal warning, especially when peace negotiations are going on."

Yuujin could see his question triggered the American soldier.

Eugene continued, "What does heaven and hell matter to you anyway? You guys don't believe in them."

"The Japanese?"

"Buddhists."

Yuujin waited until Eugene realized his question was asked in jest. The American sent him a look.

"I get it," grunted Eugene. "Just because someone is wearing a different uniform doesn't necessarily make them evil. Am I right? Is that your point?"

"Yes. Our uniforms are just costumes in this theater of war."

"Maybe so. But the final curtain is about to come down on you guys real soon."

"What will happen will happen."

"How very poetic."

A lieutenant came walking up to the duo; his battle-hardened face was the first thing they both noticed.

"You need a break? You want me to watch Tojo for a while?"

Durante looked down at the captive, who looked up at him. The bruise on his face was starting to set in and puff.

"Thank you, sir, but I have the Nip under control for now."

The lieutenant said nothing; he just nodded, giving Yuujin a death stare before walking away.

"Thank you," Yuujin said.

"Must have been my better angels."

"Did he really think I was General Hideki Tojo?"

"No, I'm pretty sure he knows you're not the Japanese prime minister. It's just something we've been calling the Japanese."

"And what you said? Nip. Slur as well?"

"Yea. Short for Nippon."

"The Japanese word for Japan."

"You got it."

"You were very convincing."

"What do you mean?" asked Eugene.

"You made him believe you hate me."

"I do hate you."

"No you don't."

"I most assuredly do."

"You could have been an actor."

"Stop talking."

"Theatre of War," Yuujin remarked with a grin.

"Jesus. If I just shot you when you tried to kill me I wouldn't have to listen to your constant blather."

"Thank you."

"For what?"

"Not killing me."

Eugene peered into the eyes of pure sincerity.

"You're welcome."

"I'm going to talk less now. You talk more."

"I'm not much of a talker."

"Tell me your story."

"Nothing to tell."

"The story of your family then."

Eugene scratched his head and said, "Truth is, I'm not really sure what's true or not when it comes to my family's history. My father never knew his parents; I only heard tales of my grandparents. You wouldn't believe me if I told you, anyway. Not after your story. I'm not even sure I believe it."

"What do you mean?"

"I mean just that. You would think I'm lying to you, making it all up from the top of my head."

"I would not."

"You would so."

"I give you my word."

Yuujin looked him in the eye when he said it. Eugene believed him once again.

"Fine."

Yuujin seemed excited at the notion of whatever the private first class was about to tell him.

"I was named after my grandfather. But everyone called him Gene."

"What do people call you?"

"They call me by my name."

"Gene?"

"No. Eugene. My name is Eugene. My grandfather's name was also Eugene but people called him Gene for short."

"It is a pleasure to meet you, Eugene. My name is—"

"I don't care what your name is. Do you want to hear the story or not?"

"Yes. Please. Sorry."

"Okay. Now, my grandfather was born in the state of Massachusetts in the mid-1800s."

"What year?"

"I don't know exactly and if you interrupt me one more time I'm going to call that lieutenant back over here and have him watch you for the rest of the time. Would you prefer that?"

"No. Sorry. No more interruptions."

Chapter 7

The Tale of Gene Durante

My grandfather, Gene Durante, was supposedly an interesting combination of his parents. His mother Shannon, who was born in Ireland, craved for an education that would make her as intellectually savvy as any male of the day.

While researching higher education establishments, she came across Elena Cornaro Piscopia, a woman who earned a doctorate of philosophy at the University of Padua in 1678. The college seemed progressive in its approach. She learned the Italian language and when she became of age, she was accepted into the college.

While there, Shannon visited Padua's famed anatomical theatre where students and curious travelers alike were allowed to study the human body during public dissections. The attendees tended to be either artists or scientists; she had declared herself a scientist.

It was here, in this funnel-shaped ceremonial theatre where students looked down into the deepest bowels of human anatomy while standing within seven elevated rings reminiscent only of Dante's pits of Hell, that she met the man who would turn out to be the other half of Gene's eventual procreation.

Gene's existence was not established until after graduation. His father accepted a job at Padua University while his mother accepted one at Bradford Academy, an all-girls school in Massachusetts. They amicably agreed to go their separate ways with Gene poised to be born and educated in America, raised by a single mother.

Gene's mother picked an American name, Eugene, to help him assimilate. She bequeathed him his father's last name as the one single thread left to that part of his heritage in case he one day wished to explore his ancestry.

Although he could not attend Bradford Academy, Gene received an informal education like no other as his immigrant mother had befriended many teachers and often associated with them. By the time he was ready for formal schooling, he was quite advanced.

The unquenchable thirst for knowledge had been passed down from mother to son; Gene loved to learn and felt most at home in schools and libraries. He looked up to his mother and her friends and declared at an early age that he too wished to be a teacher.

This desire remained steadfast as Gene completed high school and much to his and his mother's delight, Gene was accepted to Rutgers College.

"Rutgers is a good school," Shannon stated. "Good history too; it was the eighth of nine colleges established during the American colonial period. Just a few years ago they became the land-grant college of New Jersey and created a nice scientific school. You should look into the departments of chemistry, agriculture, and engineering."

"I know all this. We've talked about it. What's wrong?" Gene asked while looking intently at his mother.

"Wrong? What's wrong? Why do you say there is something wrong?"

"Because I'm looking at you and can tell when something is bothering you."

"What's bothering me is that I'm going to be here in Massachusetts and you're going to be all the way in New Jersey!"

"It's not that far. I'll be back home for holidays before you know it! Plus, this coming from you is a bit humorous, no?"

"I beg your pardon?" she yipped while removing a strand of nettlesome red hair from her face.

"You left Ireland and went to Italy. That's over a thousand miles. From here to New Jersey is probably two hundred miles."

"Two hundred seventy-eight thank you very much. And there's no comparison. There was nothing for me back home. I was not close with my family nor did they appreciate me."

"Well there will always be something for me here. I appreciate the way you raised me and I appreciate the way you constantly taught me, sometimes without me even realizing I was being taught. I suppose that's the earmark of a great teacher. But now it's time that I go on my next adventure."

"Oh, I know it," she said as she grasped onto her son.

The embrace was tight and lengthy; it was the hug of devotion and tenderness. Of allegiance and cherishment. It was a hug of expected longing and predicted forlornness. It was the hug that marked the end of an era.

Gene arrived at Rutgers College looking to make a name for himself while making his mother proud; he wouldn't have had the benefit to attend if she had not borne down on him so hard. He would not squander the opportunity.

He placidly placed his bags down in the simple and small room that was his dormitory. A single window in the middle of the farthest wall provided a decent amount of light. Gene meandered his way over to the framework and peered out. He thought to himself, on the other side of that glass the outside world would continue to churn. But on his side, within these four walls, he would remain diligent and thoughtful. The world out there was industrious. He would mirror this with his scholarly studies. Gene surmised that when he needed a brief break to catch his academic breath, he would come here to this spot and look out these panes. It was, after all, the perfect place to be reflective.

The door jolted open and a brawny young man barreled into the room. Gene turned, almost frightened at the commotion, and saw the strapping student. Looking at the two twin-size beds, he realized he would not be alone and had a roommate to contend with.

"Hey!" the sinewy student said while holding out his hand. "I'm John!"

Gene shook his hand and responded, "Gene. Pleasure to meet you."

John threw his bags forcefully onto one of the beds and said, "I'm going to take this one if you don't mind. It just feels right."

"Sure."

Gene looked back at the window. Perhaps things were not going to go as he originally projected after all. Perhaps he would need to look out that window more than he initially expected.

Durante entered a local public library as a means to change his scenery. It was more crowded than he had imagined as he took a seat at the only vacant table. He put his texts on the table and set up his notebook. He looked around. Everyone seemed to know at least someone as he noticed he was the only one sitting alone. He shrugged it off. Companionship was the furthest thing from his mind.

"Do you mind if I sit here?"

Gene looked up to see a light-haired young woman with glasses peering down at him. Her smile was infuriatingly gratifying, her eyes amiable and engaging.

"Of course not," he responded.

"You took the best seat left in the house."

"What makes it the best seat?" Gene asked in hushed tones.

She sat across from him and answered, "There's no one else here."

Gene smiled at this and added, "Yeah, I try to always get away from people. Not you obviously," he fumbled. "All the other people."

"I'm the same way. I enjoy my solitude."

"Do you want me to leave?" asked Gene in a hurried befuddlement.

She looked at him curiously and responded, "No, of course not. Why? Would you prefer it if I left?"

"No!" he said way louder than he should have.

They both looked around to see if they were in trouble.

"Great," she concluded while opening her book.

A lull ensued, making Gene uncomfortable.

"What are you reading?" he asked.

She peered over the book and looked down, making it clear the title of the book was on display.

"Ah. *The Mechanism of Action.*"

"Pharmacy," she added.

"Why are you interested in pharmacy?" he asked.

She looked at his book and asked, "Why are you interested in chemistry?"

"I attend Rutgers College."

"Must be nice," she vexed.

"What do you mean?"

"It must be nice to be of the sex allowed to go to college."

"My mother went to college," he countered.

"Not in New Jersey she didn't."

It then dawned on Gene that there were no colleges in the entire state for women.

"No, she didn't," he admitted. "But you can leave. Go elsewhere."

"I plan to. One day. My mother is sick. I'm taking care of her. My father can't adequately do so with his travels."

She went back to her book, leaving Gene disquieted. He picked up his own text and began reading. He found himself hopelessly distracted.

"I'm sorry," he said softly.

She peered back up.

"For what?"

"It was rude of me. I was not properly educated in the matter."

"You sound educated to me. It's not your fault. I took my frustration out on you; it has nothing to do with you. Sorry."

"Have you always been interested in medicine?"

"My mother was a combat nurse in the Civil War and my father is a physician. I don't think I ever had a chance."

"That's quite impressive. Will you be a physician as well?"

She looked at him intently as if probing him before answering, "Maybe."

Gene nodded and the attentive young woman went back to her book. He tried to do the same but once again he could not focus. She felt his jitters.

"Valerie," she said with no context.

He wasn't going to botch this one.

"Gene."

"I come here every Saturday around this time."

"Maybe I'll see you again then," he said happily.

She remained astute and in her work. Gene took one last look at Valerie before focusing his attention on his book.

The next Saturday Gene once again frequented the library. He entered the nearly unoccupied room to find but a single inhabitant: Valerie. She was in the seat he occupied the week before. She turned with a magnetic smirk that made Gene's blood boil in the most furiously charming way imaginable.

He approached the seat across from her, where she sat last time.

"Do you mind if I sit here?"

Valerie's tone turned to stone. "There are numerous tables available and you want the one next to the only person in the room?"

Gene was immediately flummoxed. He jerked back up as he had already begun to sit. He stumbled on the chair and began looking around for a seat more suitable.

Valerie let out a muffled laugh until she couldn't hold it in anymore. She laughed hard with a series of snorts to match.

Gene looked at her, confused, as she struggled to fix her glasses. She slid the chair out with her foot.

"You think I want to torture anyone else while I'm here?"

Gene sat and she continued to chuckle. He thought he should feel ashamed or embarrassed; his palms were balmy enough, but rather he found himself utterly elated.

"You're cute when you have absolutely no idea what's going on," she said softly.

"First time I've heard that one. Usually I feel very relaxed around women."

"Why is that?"

"I grew up with a single mother who taught at an all-girls school."

"I meant why don't you feel relaxed around me?"

He knew this was a test. And if it wasn't a test, it was a booby trap.

Gene, playing it safe, simply said, "I'm not sure." He thought it best to circumvent it back to her. "You seem very composed when it comes to men."

"Man is a strong self-description but I see your point. I attended Centenary, a coeducational preparatory school."

"I see. So you have a long history of teasing the opposite sex," Gene hypothesized while taking his books out.

"Only the ones worth teasing."

"And by what criteria does one qualify for such teasing?"

"Good question. I would have to say that I tend to tease only those who I want to continue to talk to. And to rectify your previous assumption, it's been a rather short list."

Gene seemed surprised. She allowed herself a certain degree of vulnerability. He figured he should do the same.

"I find the best lists tend to be shorter lists."

"I would have to concur."

"And to expand upon my previous statement, I would have to speculate that the reason why I am now so unusually anxious must be solely attributed to the fact that I have never encountered such incomparable and unprecedented exquisiteness."

The second that last word left his mouth he looked directly into her eyes to gauge her reaction.

"Did you just call me the most beautiful girl you have ever seen?"

"I think so."

"You think so?"

"I did."

Gene's nerves reached an apex he didn't know existed.

"Hm. I knew I liked you," she said serenely while retreating back into her book.

Gene sat aghast.

Then, from behind the safeguarded shelter of her published text, Valerie proclaimed, "I'll be here again next week."

Gene very quickly, and completely involuntarily, met all of John's new friends. He was amazed that none of them knew each other just a few weeks prior. Most of them were like John—muscular and very athletic looking. They were also all quite kind despite being loud and a bit unruly. John would often invite Gene out with them but he always politely declined. He pronounced that he had too much work to do, which was true. In reality, however, Gene cherished the quiet time and took full advantage of it by gazing out his window, often reflecting upon his puerile feelings for his yellow-haired head turner of a friend. His mother had warned him of this, telling him to be weary of feelings that resembled the adoring worshipful affection one feels for a puppy. The analogy seemed apt. Worse than that, however, Gene felt more like a Cocker Spaniel than any of the other bigger and more impressive dogs. He had no bite. Yet, he still felt more at ease with Valerie than he did with John. But being at ease was not the same as acting upon one's impulses. That, Gene thought, was a much harder affair.

"I don't get this!" bellowed John as he slammed his hand down on his small desk in the dormitory.

"What is it?" Gene asked, peering over a textbook.

"I feel like I don't understand a damn word being taught to me."

"What are you studying?"

"Agriculture."

"And what about agriculture are you currently trying to read?"

"Horticulture."

Horticulture?" echoed Gene.

"Yea, it's the study of—"

"—It's the agriculture of plants, I just didn't think you were the agricultural type."

"My father says if I learn this stuff I will revolutionize the farm back home. I think he thinks too highly of me."

"Nonsense. You can do it," Gene assured. "You just need to immerse yourself."

"It's just these words. I mean, what the hell is pomology?"

"The study and cultivation of fruit."

John looked at Gene bizarrely. "Are you studying agriculture too?"

"No."

"Then how the hell did you know what that meant?"

"I read a book called *The Fruits and Fruit Trees of America* by Andrew Jackson Downing. It was very informative, I highly recommend it."

"Why did you read that if you're not studying agriculture?"

"For fun," Gene answered as seriously as one could.

"You read about bushes and vegetables for fun?"

"Sometimes."

"That's fun?"

"It is if you're interested in it. What do you do for fun?"

"Shooting and fishing. Boxing. Horse racing. Hey, I can teach you those things if you help me with this!"

Gene pondered the offer. On one hand, he could use skills that were not strictly mental. On the other hand, he found very little interest in these options. It was the desperation in John's eyes, however, that made Gene knew he was about to agree to the deal.

Before he could say anything, John dispiritedly added, "The only other thing I'm good at is getting women to like me. And I'm not sure how interested you are in those skills."

Gene's eyes widened as he met John's gaze from above the rim of his book.

Gene agreed to help John that day with all of his agricultural studies. It was the next day that John was to impart his laws of allurement onto the naïve boy.

"Okay," John said confidently. "It's time. Up you go."

Gene stood from his bed.

"Now, given our height and anatomy I will play the boy and you will play the girl."

"Okay," Gene reluctantly agreed.

"Now, look the person you like directly in the eyes." John demonstrated. "Like this. Allow your eyes to do the talking."

"What should my eyes be telling her? How beautiful she is?"

"No, nothing like that. Your eyes should be saying dominating things like, 'You're mine!' and 'I know you want me, too.'"

"That sounds incorrect," Gene hastily remarked.

"And then you grab her shoulders like this!" John forcefully grabbed Gene's shoulders. "It's important to not break eye contact just yet. Her eyes will tell you the next move. If she looks at you scared or angry you messed up. Hands come off. But that won't happen because you are a man of courage and poise. When she looks at you like she's been waiting for you to grab her shoulders for days, that's when you go in for the kiss."

John removed his hands from Gene and with a big smile concluded, "And that's about it."

John sat down at his desk and got back to work, leaving Gene more confused now than when they started.

"That's it?" Gene asked.

John turned back around and casually responded, "Yeah. Works for me every time!"

Gene crashed face-first onto his bed, feeling hopeless.

John yet again turned around and enthusiastically added, "You should take her to one of our sporting events! I'm playing! There will be plenty of people around so she will feel safe. You won't have the pressure to perform, that's on me! You'll also be witnessing history as we're going to play a brand new game! You smart types love history. It's perfect!"

It was freezing. The game was held outside on a field on College Avenue in New Brunswick on November 6th, 1869. Gene estimated about one hundred people were there to bear witness to the first season of college football. Valerie was the only female.

Gene heard a nearby spectator remark, "I heard the rules governing play are based on the London Football Association's 1863 rules."

"What's that mean?" his friend asked.

"You're not allowed to throw the ball."

Gene turned to Valerie, who was shivering.

"A bit nippy, isn't it?" she remarked.

Gene contemplated putting his arm around her. But then he thought perhaps he should take his jacket off and put that around her instead. Which was less invasive? Which was more personal? Romantic?

Valerie placed her shoulder against his and leaned her head upon his. Gene could feel his legs weaken.

The game began swiftly as fifty players engaged one another. John played for the Rutgers Queensmen, who wore scarlet-colored turbans and handkerchiefs to differentiate themselves from their opponent, the New Jersey Tigers.

Gene leaned in towards Valerie and said, "Well, this is different."

"It sure is," she answered.

The crowd cheered, as Rutgers was the first to score after a player favorably kicked the ball across the Tigers' goal. Gene imitated the congregation by clapping loudly. Valerie did the same.

She looked up at him, knowing they both felt like imposters. Gene made a funny face, as he telepathically understood precisely what she was thinking. Valerie grabbed his cheek and kissed him. The warmth between their lips heated the entirety of their bodies and in that moment Gene's very soul sweltered. She pulled away, smiling as she did. Gene felt confused yet happy.

The crowd erupted in applause once more but the two admirers had eyes only for one another.

Rutgers won the best of ten games by a score of 6 to 4. As soon as it concluded, the winning Rutgers students literally ran their competitors off the field while threatening violence. The crowd soon followed, all except for Gene and Valerie. The Tiger players jumped into their carriages with their tails between their legs and scurried off back to the College of New Jersey.

Gene and Valerie stood alone alongside the playing field, still littered with leaves.

"Fascinating game," remarked Gene.

"It sure is."

"What did you think?"

She looked up at him entrancingly and answered, "I think I can develop a liking to sports."

The next day Gene barged into his dormitory, nearly scaring John off of his seat. The enamored college student made one simple demand.

"Teach me sports."

John smiled and said, "You kissed her, didn't you?"

"She kissed me!"

"She kissed you!? Huh. That's a new one for me. Good for you!"

"I think she's interested in sports now. I need to learn something. Definitely not the game I saw yesterday; I'll be broken in two. What game is athletic but also graceful and beautiful?"

John thought for a moment before a light bulb went off in his head.

"Golf!"

"Golf? What's provocative about a man who plays golf?"

"He knows how to find the hole?"

"Hilarious. No. Something else."

"Hey, what about baseball? It's not a contact sport. It takes skill and athleticism. Plus, I hear Rutgers is going to establish a baseball team next year. I can teach you the basics. You'll have a head start!"

Gene nodded in fearful excitement; he was going to learn how to play baseball.

John kept his word as nearly every day after classes, the two would go outside and learn to throw, catch, and hit. Batting proved to be Gene's strong suit as his hand-eye coordination was better than John could have imagined. His throwing, however, was not as impressive; he had problems even reaching John and when he did there was neither accuracy nor velocity.

Academically, Gene had been succeeding. He would often write letters to his mother, giving thanks to the head start he felt she had provided for him.

Romantically, Gene and Valerie had not stopped coveting one another. Gene had garnered confidence since their first kiss turned into hundreds if not thousands. There was, of course, another great worry.

John entered their room as Gene looked out the window.

"Hey, there," John said.

There was no response. John looked over to his friend's bed and noticed new books. *Memoirs of a Woman of Pleasure, The Carnal Prayer Mat,* and The Marquis de Sade's *Justine* were all opened and spread out over his sheets.

"Jesus," he uttered.

Gene turned around, his face perplexed. "How do you have sex?" he asked.

John scratched his head and answered, "Well, I have no idea."

"You have no idea?"

"Not a clue!"

"You're—"

"—Yup!"

Gene sighed and mumbled, "This is going to be more complicated than I thought."

Gene and Valerie next met at a coffee shop. Any onlooker could infer their unofficial relationship simply by the way they looked at each other; the smiles they constantly drew out from one another, and the aimed gazes that never seemed to waver.

"I live with my parents. Great for asking questions and learning but poor when you want to have some privacy and a social life."

"I understand that. I don't seem to have the privacy I imagined either. John is very nice but not very quiet. Neither are his friends."

He noticed a disappointed look on her face.

"Of course, he would always let me have the room if I needed it. For private matters."

"Private matters? Such as?"

He balked, "Matters requiring privacy?"

"Like studying?"

"Perhaps. No. Not studying. We can study together. Or, you know, if we wanted to use the room for more exclusive matters."

"Exclusive you say! Are you, Gene Durante, running a secret society from your dorm room?"

"I want to make love to you."

There, he said it. He looked at her astonished face.

Gene quickly said, "I'm sorry. That was very direct and I know we—"

"—Yes."

"Yes?"

"Yes. I would like that, too."

"Really?"

"Don't talk yourself out of it."

"Right."

"I like when you're direct. You should do it more often."

"I will then!" Gene declared in an ultra direct tone.

Valerie slapped her palm to her face. Gene chuckled as he wrapped his hands around the hot mug. He lifted it and took a sip. It was warm and creamy and sweet, just the way he enjoyed it. Valerie arose in thought.

"What is it?"

"Huh?" she uttered as if breaking out of a trance.

"You had your thinking face on. And then you did the smirk you do when you think of something you feel you shouldn't have thought about."

"Since when did you know me this well?"

He wasn't going to let this one get away.

"So what is it? The idea."

Valerie turned to both sides, looked behind her, then leaned across the table. She whispered, "I always wanted to see a college lecture hall."

"Okay?" Gene responded while attempting to pull more information from her.

"Maybe you can take me there? At night, when no one is around? Since privacy seems to be an issue anyway…"

Gene caught on.

"Oh. Yes. YES. I can definitely do that."

Gene's heart was pounding and at this juncture, it wasn't from the coffee.

The corridors were blackened as the companions snuck into the building through the one door that Gene realized was never locked. He had been running that experiment for days.

They very carefully made sure the door closed quietly behind them before tiptoeing through the halls.

Suddenly, they heard the thuds of boots accompanied by the light of a lantern; it was the guard making his rounds.

Gene took Valerie and concealed them both in an impression in the wall. They could feel each other's hearts racing. They waited until the sentry disappeared into another part of the building. Then they snuck back out and trekked further.

When they reached the room, they crouched as Gene reached for the knob. He turned it. Locked.

"You're up," he whispered.

Valerie took out a lock pick set from inside her coat.

"Good thing my uncle is a blacksmith," she noted while placing one of the tools inside the lock.

After some tweaking and twisting, the door unlocked. They scurried in and softly shut the door behind them.

A small window allowed a modicum of moonlight in the otherwise pitch-black room. Valerie stood up and gazed at the sight. It was larger than she thought it would be. Gene kissed her clothed shoulder.

"Quite the sight," she remarked.

"You're telling me."

She turned to notice he was looking straight at her. They embraced, kissing each other from their necks to their lips.

Valerie pulled away and Gene could tell she had her thinking face on again.

She walked down the descending stairs and hopped onto the raised platform where professors would teach their class. Gene walked up to the lip of the stage and peered up.

She undressed and Gene tensely beheld the sight. When the last of her clothes hit the floor, she turned so as he could view all of her in the dim light.

"Your turn," she whispered.

Gene climbed up and gazed upon her beauty, the fullness of her breasts were illuminated by the soft moonlight. He took off his shirt and then his trousers. As he grabbed ahold of his undergarment, he felt very aware that he was about to be completely nude in front of a woman for the first time in his life. He imagined this was how Adam and Eve felt after eating the forbidden fruit from the Tree of Knowledge. He also assumed they were happy they did so, for the feelings he currently felt, coupled with the vision he currently viewed, surely marked the greatest moment of his young adult life.

He removed his undergarment and stood bare for his world to see. They inched closer to one another, their nervous systems physically reacting, until their hands clasped like magnets at a perfect distance. They stood a mere inch apart and kissed the first uncovered kiss of their lives. Valerie gently placed her hand on his bottom and pulled him closer, all of him now touching all of her. The discourse between their physiques required no words; their bodies engaged in all the spoken communication needed. Their studies of the material world failed neither of them; friction was proving itself fruitful. The development of their sexual experiment, like any good research, was purely and simply uplifting, and for good measure.

As the two paramours thrust life's predicaments away in the large, wide-open space, they both knew only one thing was certain: more testing would need to be done.

Gene entered his dormitory seemingly standing a little taller. His step had an extra bounce and his face beamed.

"What happened to you!?" John asked, perplexed.

Gene looked at his friend and said, "I hit my first career home run."

Gene went on to hit many home runs, and not just in the ballpark of passion. He made Rutgers' inaugural baseball team in 1870 and proved to be a worthwhile first baseman. He was a slick fielder and the position required very little throwing. The experience also allowed him to make friends, forging male ca-maraderie for the first time in his life.

There was a knock at the door as Shannon was setting the table. She excitedly scurried over and opened the obsta-cle between herself and her son. Gene ecstatically stood in the doorway as it opened. Shannon threw herself around her son and subsequently grabbed his face and kissed his forehead.

"It is so good to see you! I've missed you! Come in!"

She went to turn back but noticed Gene didn't budge.

"What is it?" she asked.

A silken face with flaxen hair peeked out from behind Gene.

"Well, what's this pretty thing?" Shannon inquired.

"This is Valerie," Gene answered. "I hope you don't mind. I wanted you to meet her."

His mother knew what this meant; Gene had never introduced her to a girl before. She kindly made her way back over.

"Of course. You know what we say in this house. When the world out there forgets about us, a smart, witty woman is always allowed here. I just don't know if we've ever had such a beautiful one though! Come here!"

Gene watched as the two women he cared most for hugged. It was a moment he had never conjured.

Gene was outmatched of course; two strong-willed, independent, educated women were always quite formidable. They laughed and traded stories.

"You saw the famous anatomical theatre at Padua?"

"Oh yes. I was in it! To this day, I find it to be the most beautiful sight I've ever seen on a college campus. But I'm sure as more colleges are opening and more opportunities become available to women, you will see something far surpassing that in your eventual studies."

Valerie blushed and responded, "I hope so. But I doubt it."

"Why do you say that?" Shannon questioned.

"Part of the beauty of Europe is its history. That theatre was constructed in the late 1500s. Something here might be visually exquisite but it will not have that mystical energy of the past."

"I don't hear many doctors use the word mystical," Gene chimed in.

"Oh, don't be so surprised!" Shannon retorted. "There has always been something magical about healers. People to this day use the word miracle to describe a doctor's work. I see it as no surprise. I suppose you find your goals daunting at times?"

"I do," responded Valerie, nearly crestfallen.

"Good. This is your greatest asset. When you succeed you will feel a triumph most cannot imagine. Telling someone they cannot do something provides people like us with the impetus to do just that. It is the other side of the struggle that is most rewarding. You will have your day. Mark my words."

Valerie believed every wise word.

"Thank you," she said in genuine goodwill. "That means a lot." Valerie sighed. "May I use your restroom?"

"Surely. Down that little hall and to the right," Shannon replied.

"Thank you," she responded as she stood up and made her way to the bathroom.

"Well you're awfully quiet over there," Shannon remarked.

"I enjoy listening to the two of you carry on."

"She's a good one, I must admit. Why didn't you tell me you were bringing home such a charming smart young woman?"

"I suppose it was spur-of-the-moment."

"Picked up spontaneity at college did you?"

"I suppose I did."

"How are your studies?"

"They're going very well."

"Anything newly fascinating?"

"I would say animal husbandry. But I still have my eye on teaching as always. Perhaps English actually. I've been enjoying literature more and more each semester."

"You did always say that. But perhaps there is more money in something like science?"

"Perhaps," he responded with a coy smile.

Valerie re-entered the room.

"Thank you for a lovely meal," she said as she sat.

"My pleasure. If my boy told me you were coming I would have come up with something better than that!"

"It was perfect, mom."

"Now what's this I hear about you being an athlete? I must say I didn't see that one coming."

"Neither did I," Valerie jested under her breath.

"Believe me, I'm more surprised than the both of you. It's a really enchanting game. There's such dignity and refinement in its simplicity."

"Are we still speaking about a sport?" his mother bantered.

"Yes! Truly. I am not even that bad at it. I hit pretty well. Play the field pretty well. I can't seem to throw very well though."

"The others tease him and tell him I could probably throw better" Valerie interjected.

"You probably can," Gene concluded.

Shannon seemed pensive for a moment before finally saying, "That's because you were born left-handed."

Gene looked up at his mother in pure shock. "What?"

"It is one of my biggest regrets actually. I dissuaded you from using your dominant hand as a child. I thought it would make life easier for you, being as how most machinery is constructed without a single thought in mind for our left-handed brethren. Back home where I come from, left-footers was a derogatory term used to describe Protestants by Catholics. Unsure if such slow-wittedness would be the same here, I tried to shield you from the dumbness of that superstition. I apologize. However, when you go back to school, you just try throwing that ball with your left hand and see what happens."

Gene straddled first base with a runner on third. A coach stood at home plate and tossed a baseball into the air while gripping the bat. As the ball came down, he connected and sent a ground ball to first base. Gene slickly fielded the ball as the runner broke for home.

When this happened last season, Gene would take the sure out at first, something he was initially berated for until all of his attempts to throw home proved futile. But this was practice and Gene had a nagging curiosity.

He fired the ball towards home plate. His throw was both accurate and speedy. The ball landed into the snug hands of the catcher and the tag was made on the runner.

Everyone stopped and peculiarly looked at Gene. Even the catcher stood in disbelief. The coach cocked his head at the anomaly.

Feeling the numerous eyes on him, Gene just shrugged his shoulders and yelled out, "I think I'm a lefty."

That season saw a tremendous improvement in Gene's overall game. He could always field, but his sudden gift for throwing made him one of the best defenders on the team. He was also innovative. Gene noticed he struggled more against right-handed pitchers than he did against left-handed pitchers. He observed this to be true for the majority of players who batted on the right side of the plate. And so he started batting left-handed against righties, much to the surprise of his teammates. They all concurred they had never seen anything quite like it. Gene's batting average skyrocketed as a result and the players started calling him Ambidextrous Gene; he was deceptive to players who knew not of his multi-talents. The team's coach once told him a nickname is the highest honor one could achieve in baseball.

Much to the delight of his mother, Gene's extracurricular activities never impeded his studies. Nor did his grades suffer from the few days he did not attend classes when he chose instead to console Valerie after the unfortunate passing of her mother.

He entered his last year at Rutgers College towards the very top of his class and remained that way as gradation neared. Despite enjoying it, Gene never considered or desired to play baseball outside of the college experience as his aims were more academic in nature; he spent much of that year applying to numerous positions and various opportunities.

"Fancy meeting you here," Gene said with a smile as he stood above Valerie in the library.

He kissed her and sat down across from her while adding, "Did you hear The Metropolitan Museum on Art opened a building of Fifth Avenue in New York not too long ago?"

Silence. Gene peered up to see introspection.

"What's wrong?"

Valerie looked up.

"What is it?"

She slid a piece of paper forward that she had been previously holding in her hands. Gene picked it up and began to read. Valerie had been accepted to the Woman's Medical College of Pennsylvania.

"This is fantastic! Congratulations! Why do you look so sad?"

"I'm nervous."

Gene placed his hand on top of hers and said, "There is no one more qualified, ready, or more deserving than you entering that program. You were meant to do this. Your mother would be so proud."

Valerie smiled and added, "It's not going to be easy."

"It's not supposed to be. That's what makes it all the more rewarding at the end of the journey."

"Thank you. I have never been at ease regarding the things yet to come. The unfamiliarity of the future has always frightened me. I don't know what to expect academically. I don't know how my father will be alone. And lastly I don't know what to do about you."

This was a conversation Gene knew was inevitable despite being afraid of having it. He also knew it was time to have it.

"If it makes you feel any better I haven't known what to do about me for a long time."

He had made her crack, just a little.

"I'm going to Pennsylvania. I doubt you're going to stay in New Jersey. Have you gotten any offers yet?"

"Just one. But I'm not going to take it."

"What is it?"

"Japan."

"Japan?"

"Yea. Their School of Ordinance set forth universal education for the first time in the country's history. There's a state-driven modernization program in Tokyo. They're looking to recruit teaching experts in various fields."

"Fascinating! That would certainly be a shock to your cultural senses."

"I know. Perhaps too much of a shock."

"I'm sure other offers will come in."

"My fingers remain crossed," he confirmed.

"So what do we do?"

"About us?"

"Yes."

"There are options."

"Go on."

"The traditional one would be marriage."

He studied her reaction closely.

"I've never been one for tradition. And marriage seems hardly the appropriate thing to think about when I'm about to embark on—"

"—I know. You don't have to explain yourself."

"I do love you."

"I love you, too."

"So what else is on the table?"

"Long distance."

"We don't even know how long of a distance since we don't know where you'll be."

"This is true. But Pennsylvania isn't so far from Massachusetts. You know I never go too long without visiting."

"You are good at visiting."

She was clearly in her head.

Gene continued, "And, of course, there's the third distressing option we have been evading."

They gazed at each other. In their heart of hearts they knew this alternative was more probable than they wanted it to be.

"What do you think?" she asked.

"I think you're looking for a way to alleviate the agony of it all. I don't know if that's possible, let alone preferable. I think you've searched your mind and soul and came to the conclusion that this is the choice that makes most sense. It's bizarre, isn't it? The one that makes the most sense is the same one to create the most aches. It's one big contradiction. I suppose that's what they mean by the absurdity of love."

"I think you've been thinking about this as much as I have."

He gently nodded and replied, "I have."

"This doesn't mean we can't find each other later in life."

Gene smirked. "Of course it doesn't."

"Was that cliché?"

"Terribly."

The first laugh in what seemed like forever ensued.

Valerie pondered, "If the right decision for your heart and the right decision for your brain are contradictory, what hope do we truly have for a complete life?"

"Hope is the thing with feathers that perches in the soul and sings the tune without the words and never stops at all."

"Shakespeare?"

"Emily Dickinson."

"I think you're enjoying that literature class."

"I am. I cherish it. Creativity and hope are not such distant relatives I think."

"Please—deliberate."

"Hope is a mystifying puzzle. To have such optimism appears ill-informed at times. And yet I have seen hope give rise to seemingly impossible outcomes. Perhaps, at the end of the day, hope is simply the belief that you can instigate change."

"You should have been a poet."

"Too late I suppose. Poetry is a young man's game."

"Nonsense. Anyone who has the ability to appreciate poetry never grows old."

They appreciated one another exceedingly in that moment.

"Have a drink with me tonight," Gene said.

The two sat at a small table in a dimly lit tavern. A single candle illuminated their eager bodies. Gene held a beer in his hand while a straight-up whiskey was clutched in Valerie's. The two raised their drinks.

"To a complete life," Valerie acclaimed.

"To a complete life indeed."

They clinked their glasses and allowed the consumption to begin.

They talked and drank throughout the night as neither wanted to leave the other's company. Eventually, the bar closed and they were forced to take the walk home.

The night air was still and warm as Gene and Valerie wobbled down the street hand in hand.

"I don't want this to end," Gene said.

"The night? Or us?"

Gene longingly pierced her eyes and asked, "Is there really a difference?"

They both stopped in their tracks. It was a thought that both had banished to the back of their minds earlier that day but the unrestricted inhibitions alcohol provided allowed that truth to come roaring back up to the prominent forefront of conversation.

No words came out, as words were suddenly inefficient.

Valerie seized the back of Gene's head and kissed him. It was the kiss of passion and intensity. Of joy and rage. It was a kiss of anticipated loneliness and assured heartache. It was the kiss that marked the end of an era.

Gene packed up his belongings into boxes as the time to graduate had arrived. "Ready to go back to the farm?" he asked John.

"Believe it or not, Ambidextrous Gene, I am! I'm going to turn that land upside down. Ready for no one to call you Ambidextrous Gene anymore?"

"I don't know. I suppose it had a nice ring to it," he jested.

"You were lucky to get a teaching position in Massachusetts."

"I know. I'm looking forward to going back home for a bit. Excuse me, the bathroom calls one last time."

Gene exited the room as John continued to pack up. A few moments later, there was a knock on the door. John meandered over and opened it.

"Your mail is here."

"Thank you," replied John as he took the three envelopes. "One last time, huh?"

The deliverer went off to the next room as John shut the door. He opened the top envelope and read a note from his last year lover. In it, she told him she would miss him dearly and that in order for him to remember her, she sent a separate envelope with racy pictures he wouldn't want anyone else to behold. She explained that she sent them separately in case someone else opened the envelope, this way they couldn't be traced back to her.

John excitedly ripped out the very next envelope. He pulled out a sheet of formal looking paper. Confused as to its contents, he turned the envelope over; he had opened his roommate's letter by accident.

Gene walked in and immediately noticed John. His face was flushed and his eyes were damp.

"What's wrong?"

John peered up and replied, "I opened your mail by mistake."

"Jesus. You had me worried. You looked like you had just seen a ghost. It's completely all right, I think you know everything about my life at this point anyway."

He went back to his box, committed to finishing.

"Gene-"

The way he said it promptly put a pit in Gene's stomach. He turned around; John's hand was outstretched, the letter dangling in his digits. Gene hesitantly walked over and took the paper.

Eugene Durante,

It is with great regret that I must inform you of the untimely passing of your mother, Shannon McCarthy.

There was more to it but the letter slipped out of Gene's hand and quietly drifted to the floor.

He slowly turned and faced the window that had provided him years of solace in troublesome times. It provided him with the proof that there was always something on the other side. But this time, it provided nothing; Gene was currently incapable of reflection. He appeared to enter a comatose state.

John grabbed his friend and hugged him hard. The two remained situated in this way for more time than seemingly possible. Gene did not know it, and perhaps years later he wished he did, but this would prove to be the last time these friends ever saw each other in the flesh.

Gene consequently turned down the teaching position in Massachusetts as he felt there was nothing left for him there. Those who knew him suspected it was more hurt than emptiness that kept him away.

Valerie went on to Pennsylvania and although they planned to correspond through letters, he could feel the strings of that idea slip away with each passing day. Eventually, the urge for exchanges ceased all together.

Having turned most of his offers down when he initially accepted the teaching position in Massachusetts, Gene found himself with few options. As a matter of fact, all the other propositions were rescinded as the positions had been filled. All except one. It was the one Gene ended up accepting; it was the only option he had left. Gene was to be an English instructor in a technical school in Tokyo.

In 1873 Gene Durante took the newly completed transcontinental railroad cross-country and landed in the Japanese Consular Office in San Francisco. He carried two large bags of luggage, as his contract was a rather lengthy three-year agreement.

Gene checked in and was instructed to go to the pier where his passage to Asia awaited.

The walk was only ten minutes or so but Gene instantly regretted packing essentially all of his belongings. Unfortunately he had no place to keep them.

The sun beamed down and warmed Gene's face as a breeze lightly caressed it. The sounds of the water crashing up against the sea wall could be heard as the traveler neared the pier.

Gene had yet to take the time to truly reflect on all the life-changing events of the last year. For him, it was a pill too bitter to swallow. The vagaries of Valerie lingered in the back of his mind as the last thread he had to his country. The loss of his mother he had yet to truly process. He had buried her in Bradford, gathered his belongings, dealt with the legalities and economics of it all, and hopped on the train. To say the death was fresh would be an understatement.

As Gene stood in front of the massive ship, it suddenly dawned on him that he had never been on a boat before.

The waters were calm as the solidary migrant looked out at a disappearing shoreline. This was his goodbye for now.

"Beautiful, isn't it?"

Gene turned to see a plump man with an unkempt beard. He approached the side of the boat with a labored, jerky movement.

"It is," Gene responded.

"Are you a fellow *oyatoi?*"

"That's the Japanese word for foreign employee, is it not?"

"It is!"

"I am. I take it you are as well?"

"Indeed. Ever been to Japan?"

"I've never even been on a boat."

The portly gentleman laughed and said, "My suggestion then would be to stay below deck when the waters get rough."

"Noted. What will you be teaching?"

"I am to design a college level curriculum in the natural sciences. I'll be teaching at Tokyo's South College, *Kaiseiko.*"

"I will be in Tokyo as well. At *Kaitakushi Karigakko.* Teaching English."

"Then perhaps we'll run into each other again! The name's William!"

He held out his hand and Durante responded, "Gene."

"Pleasure to make your acquaintance. Are you traveling alone?"

"I am."

"Treasure it. You're on an adventure! The hero's journey awaits you."

"That makes two of us, no?"

"No. I have my wife and kids with me. It's a bit of a different experience. Of course, I wouldn't have it any other way. I did all the adventuring needed already. Fought in the war. Being a Civil War veteran has left me with a bum knee, hence the weight gain."

"I'm sorry to hear that. But I'm very glad you are here now. And that you have a family."

"As am I! Are you leaving loved ones behind?"

Gene looked out at the professedly endless sea. He sighed, exhaling the very truth he had been suppressing.

"No," he answered honestly. "Unfortunately not. There's nothing there for me back home."

Chapter 8

The Tale of Gene Durante Part II

Gene spent nearly a month at sea and used the time to learn as much of the Japanese language as he could. Without distraction, he accomplished a great deal. He also brought along books and pamphlets that might help him culturally adjust.

William and his family were very kind to him during the excursion. He sensed that William had told his wife that Gene was a man of great sorrow. They dined together often and practiced their Japanese on one another.

It turned out they had something else in common as well; they were both fans of baseball and had brought balls and bats along with them. William repeatedly reported his belief that it was the Civil War itself that had expunged the upper-class patronage of baseball.

"That's when the game spread beyond just the urban Northeast," he would often say.

William and Gene spent a number of afternoons playing catch on the boat and they were both proud of the fact that neither one of their arms had failed them; they lost no baseballs overboard.

"We'll be arriving tomorrow," said William, peering out into the obscurity of the nighttime ocean.

Gene looked up to see a canopy of stars burning bright. William took notice.

"Interested in the heavens, are we?"

"I am curious, I will admit."

"There are eight of us out there, you know."

"We?"

"Planets. The last one, Neptune, was discovered in '46."

"And how does one discover a planet?"

"A scientist calculated the position and size of the planet from the effects of its gravitational pull on the orbit of Uranus."

"Amazing," Gene remarked. "You think there are others?"

William gazed out and said, "I suppose. Don't know why there wouldn't be."

"Do you think there are other people on them?"

"Can't say. But if there are, I bet they don't play baseball!"

William nudged Gene's shoulder in jest.

"Then what good are they?" retorted Gene.

The travelers focused their attention back to the darkened ocean. They listened to the maritime churning caused from the constant crashing waves breaking against the ship's sides as the boat unceasingly sliced through the sea.

"You think you'll ever go back?" asked William.

"To America? I don't see why I wouldn't."

"Who knows what you will find in Japan. Who knows who you will find." He patted Gene's shoulder and concluded, "I'm going to bed, my friend. You should, too, soon. Tomorrow is going to be the first day of a whole new exciting chapter of your life."

"Thanks. Good night, Will."

William drifted away, leaving Gene alone with his thoughts. He hadn't given much consideration as to his future beyond the three contracted years. What was to follow? Were the possibilities endless? Could he find authentic happiness abroad? Why did he even expect an eventual return to the states? These were all the questions that swarmed and teemed in his mind.

It was then that he heard a wispy warning from a siren of the wind. It was the alleviating voice of his mother.

"One step at a time. Don't let the uncertainties of the future prevent you from enjoying the present."

It was a most appreciated reminder. Gene wondered if the message had come from the frosty depths of the deep uncharted ocean or from the scorching unknowns of the faraway cosmic frontier. Either way, he was grateful.

Gene Durante found himself in the heart of Tokyo. His plan was to delve straight into the sudden exposure of the very different Japanese culture. His first stop was the Uchiyamashita Museum, located directly southeast of the Imperial Palace.

The museum was a temporary display as its belongings were gathered a year prior for the Yushima Seido Exhibition in order to prepare for Vienna's World Fair. It had since moved to this compound at Uchiyamashita-chō.

As he strolled along, Gene found himself excited to explore the imperial artwork and scientific specimens curated by the Ministry of Education.

He observed, with keen interest, native instruments, ceramics, dyed works and lacquer-ware. He marveled at Japanese paintings, their displays of calligraphy, their various golden items, and their collections of coral. In another part of the museum stuffed specimens and skeletal preparations of animals adorned walls and shelves. He even saw a papier-mâché version of the Kamakura Buddha.

There must have been nearly six hundred items presented. One piece in particular, however, caught Gene's eye. Perhaps it was the size. Or maybe it was due to the fact that it appeared to be made out of pure gold. It was a large ornament encased in glass labeled as a *shachi*. It appeared to have the head of a tiger with the body of a carp. A drawing he saw earlier in the exhibit showed this decorative treasure atop a castle. He thus likened it to the gargoyle, a protector of a castle. It was a glorious talisman. He thought it brilliant.

Next up on his cultural expedition was Sensō-ji, an ancient temple located in Asakusa. The area preceding the temple was open and filled with small tables where people sat, ate, and enjoyed the weather. Massive trees guarded each side of the temple.

Gene walked past two symmetrical freestanding lantern statues and continued on the path up to the temple. He walked under The Kaminarimon, an eight-pillared entrance gate originally built in 941 before being reconstructed numerous times after damaging fires. A large low-hanging lantern hovered above him as he continued. This Thunder Gate was but the outer of two entrance gates.

Next was The Hōzōmon. Two intimidating and frightening statues guarded the two-story structure, each on either side of the gate's face. Gene recognized these devilish creatures from his studies. They were known as *Niō,* the burly and wrathful sentries that were said, in Japanese tradition, to have travelled with Gautama Buddha himself, to protect him. Despite being a predominately pacifist religion, the ferocity of these two creatures proved justifiable in their use of physical force when guarding against evil.

Gene entered the temple itself as wafting incense smoked over his body, seeming to enter every pore. He took a deep breath in and strangely felt stronger, as if he were healthier.

He noticed, on display, the severed heads of the Shinto gods Fūjin and Raijin, which were once sculptures in the Kaminarimon until they were severely damaged by a fire in 1865.

Then, from the outer sanctum of the main hall, he saw it: the enshrinement. Many people prayed towards it; their hands clasped in front of their chests.

A monk noticed the curiosity of Gene and walked over.

"Englishman?" the monk asked.

"American, yes."

"You seem intrigued."

"I am. It's all so beautiful."

"Would you like to know the story behind this place?"

"I would love that. Thank you."

"Many years ago, in 628 B.C., two brothers caught a golden statue in today's Sumida River. The fishermen attempted to throw the statue back in the water numerous times but each time it curiously came back to them. The fishermen suddenly recognized the statue was of Kannon, the goddess of compassion and benevolence. Upon returning home to Asakusa, the chief of their village saw sanctity in the statue and reconditioned his house into a small temple so that the statue could be worshipped. And here we are, in the former home of Hajino Nakamoto himself."

"Magnificent," Gene remarked as he wondered what other marvels Japan had to offer.

He'd heard of sushi but never tried it before, nor had he ever actually seen it in person. He looked as curious at the vinegared rice circumscribing seafood and vegetables as he imagined the fishermen looked at that statue. He took hold of the chopsticks. Although this was his first time using a pair, he had looked at pictures in an instructional manual.

Gene used his right hand to inform his left, which held the utensils. He pushed his middle finger under one stick and placed his thumb over the other. He moved his index finger rhythmically with his thumb and went to pick up a piece of sushi. He successfully clasped it. He raised his hand to bring the captured cuisine towards his mouth. It fell and landed back on his plate. He tried again. It fell again.

Gene rearranged his posture, attempting to will the Japanese dish to do as he pleased. He would try again. And again.

Eventually, he lowered his head, placing himself very much near the serving dish. He quickly snatched up a piece and flung it into his mouth.

Success! He took his time chewing, savoring every last bite; he had worked hard for his food. He, of course, realized the ridiculousness of such a sentiment. Still, it was rewarding. He looked down at the rest of his meal.

Gene spent much of that afternoon wrestling with both the food and the chopsticks. By the end of the meal, however, he was relatively comfortable with his new utensils and therefore one step closer to harmonizing with his surroundings, or at the very least, not looking so much like a buffoon.

His students were said to be the best and brightest, recruited from across the country. This advertisement did not prove false, as Gene was very often surprised by how well his students picked up the often-times confounding language. Gene created a lot of visuals to teach and aimed to keep directions as straightforward as possible. He used simple vocabulary and did not move on to the more complex rules of grammar until he fully believed his students understood the fundamentals. As it turned out, however, his students learned the basics of English faster than he could learn the basics of Japanese. Still, much like the sushi and chopstick catastrophe, he was determined.

"How is it teaching?" asked William as he took a sip of his miso soup.

"I'm stunned how easy it feels sometimes. They're extremely intelligent young men."

"Aren't they?"

"How is your family?"

"The young one is having the time of his life. The wife, I think, will be looking forward to home when the time comes. How has your transition been?"

"Other than the language barrier, smooth. These people are on the verge of industrialization. You can feel it."

"Agreed. They're crafty. They turned to the British to teach them engineering, the Prussians for economics, medicine, and statecraft, and us Americans for education, agriculture, and animal husbandry. But perhaps their most canny move yet was to have the French and the British battle it out to prove who is better for the overhaul of their military. It cracks me up just thinking about it."

They chuckled at the thought.

Gene noted, "Modernization will soon be upon them."

"Yes. And I wonder what they'll do with us then."

The comment sobered the mood as they continued to have their soup. Gene looked to alleviate the situation.

"Anything exciting? What have you been doing for fun?"

"Actually, I started showing my students baseball," he answered with a grin.

"You have? They took to it?"

"Well it was confusing to them at first, perhaps more confusing than the sciences. But I think they're having fun with it. We're not playing games or anything like that, no competition, but we have catches and things like that. Hey, I didn't bring my equipment for nothing!"

Gene leaned back in his chair; inspiration had struck.

"How do you feel about learning baseball?"

The students' faces were blank.

"By a show of hands, how many of you have heard of baseball?"

The room consisted of a group of boys, none of whom had their hands up.

"Baseball is a sport. A game. It's also exercise and great fun. It's American, obviously. I brought some equipment with me from when I played in college for reasons I do not know. But I have them, if you ever wish to learn."

Gene turned towards the chalkboard.

"You played sports?" asked a student.

Gene turned back and responded, "Yes. Why? Is that so hard to believe?"

"Physical exertion for its own sake?" another confusedly asked.

Yet another said, "Usually those that work with their bodies for sport and those who work with their mind are not one and the same," another answered.

Gene thought about this.

"That makes sense. Where I come from, we could engage in sport while studying in school even if our aim was not to play professionally. It keeps both the mind and body sharp."

The students looked at one another; clearly an interest was piqued.

Gene aimed to teach his class the very basics of baseball. It started with the mere catches and drills he learned while in school. Eventually, they wielded the bat and hit and even took to pitching. Their eager young malleable minds made the learning experience quite fluent.

"Good for you!" William boasted with delight. "Are they taking to it?"

"They are."

"And enjoying it?"

"So far!"

"Fantastic!"

William and Gene walked through Ueno Park, one of four parks newly established in Japan. William now brandished a walking cane.

"How's the leg?"

"Can't complain. Can still walk."

"You look like a proper professor now," Gene jested.

"That's what the wife said. Although she didn't sound as enthusiastic about it as you did!"

The two gazed at the trees and other plant life. October in Japan was as beautiful as they envisioned.

"It's amazing isn't it," remarked William. "We're foreign employees from the West who haven't been in this country very long but we can already see societal shifts. This place is a perfect example. Japan just founded these parks this year following a Western example. The assimilation of a culture. An interesting concept, no?"

"Are you worried they're becoming too advanced too fast?"

"No. I wouldn't say I'm worried. I would simply say that as the Japanese borrow parts of other cultures, I hope they also retain the things that make their own culture unique."

"So you don't wish to see forks and knives at a restaurant when you sit down to eat here?" Gene asked, laughing.

"Certainly not!"

"Agreed. In a way, on a personal level, a lot of this feels more like a cultural exchange than assimilation."

"Indeed. It certainly isn't colonialism, I'll tell you that."

"I've learned so many things in such a short amount of time. I'm thankful for it."

"Well said. And who knows, they might very well improve upon the things we do best."

"What are you thinking? Education itself?"

"Possibly. But I'm more worried about bourbon. Japan is awfully far to go for good bourbon. But I do require the best bourbon. You see my dilemma."

"Very clearly."

"I suppose time will tell."

"Do you think we've made an ally for life?"

"Nothing is for life, my friend. An ally for the foreseeable future? It seems like it. An ally for one lifetime? Perhaps. But never say never and avoid assumptions when possible. I've seen friends turn on friends, brothers on fathers, and our own country on itself. Nothing ceases to surprise me at this point in my life."

"Point taken."

"It's a good viewpoint to have though, I think. It makes one prepared for anything because one knows anything can happen, at any time."

"I certainly wouldn't have guessed that I'd be teaching the Japanese youth to play baseball."

"Same here! Although I suspect my students are becoming somewhat bored by it."

The words came out before Gene could even process them as he said, "Perhaps we should have a game, then."

William stopped in his tracks and looked at his friend. He tilted his head, thinking about the proposition.

"A game," William repeated. "That would be interesting."

"Certainly a nice change of pace," Gene encouraged.

"I think it might be. Of course, you couldn't play."

"Why not!?" Gene howled as he had seen this as a fine opportunity to slip on his old mitt.

"Because I can't play!" William retorted.

"You can catch!"

"I will do no such thing! I was a center fielder in my heyday! Besides, you're missing the whole point of your own suggestion! This is an opportunity for the students. If you and I play, I will be the best player on the field and you will be the second best. What sort of encouragement or confidence would that supply? Would it not be far more culturally exciting to see the Japanese play amongst themselves without our interference!?"

Gene despised how right William was but respected his ability to use humor in regard to his player comparison.

William continued, "We'll manage each of our prospective teams. What do you say?"

Gene nodded and said, "You have yourself a friendly competition, then."

It was a cool day for baseball as the weather reflected a championship climate. The atmosphere amongst the players, however, was not so as smiles and laughter encompassed the playing field. Even Gene and William were not the battle-hardened managers they predicted themselves to be.

Gene walked over to his next hitter and instructed, "Listen, he's going to throw it and you're just going to stand there. He's going to throw a fastball and you're just going to hit it right back at him. Hard. Smooth swing! Like we talked about!"

The first baseman for *Kaitakushi Karigakko* walked up to the plate, a hunk of rubber, with his bat in hand. He took a couple of practice swings, looking at Gene for approval.

"That's right, take your time," yelled Gene from the sidelines.

He set himself and awaited the pitch, keeping in mind what Gene had said.

The pitcher wound up and released the ball, throwing it as hard as he could. The pitch sped in over the inside half of home plate and the batter swung. The connection was loud as the ball buzzed over the pitcher's head, causing him to duck. It landed in the outfield and was eventually grabbed and thrown back in. The players cheered for their teammate who had just recorded the first base hit of his life.

"That's it!" Gene cheered as he clapped. "That's how it's done!"

The player reached first base with a smile Gene had never seen before. He took a few steps off the bag when the pitcher retrieved the ball.

The *Kaiseiko* players looked confused at the maneuver and began pointing in confusion at the runner.

William took notice and shouted out to the other side of the field, "Gene! I haven't taught them about leading or stealing yet!"

"Okay!" responded Gene. He looked towards the base runner and said, "Stay on first! We're not going to be taking a lead or stealing today!"

The runner did as he was told as William strolled out to the mound to talk to his pitcher. "Okay, remember how we talked about the double play?"

"Yes," the pitcher responded.

"We're going to try and make that happen right here, right now. When you throw, try to aim at the batter's kneecaps."

"You want me to hit him?"

"No!" William corrected. "I want you to throw it over the plate but aligned with the batter's knees. If you throw it low there is more of a chance the batter will hit it into the ground and we can get a double play and get out of this thing. How does that sound?"

"I will do it!" the pitcher said enthusiastically.

"Great!"

William walked off the field and the game commenced again. *Kaiseiko's* pitcher wound up and threw. The ball sailed wildly over the batter's head.

"I apologize!" the pitcher yelled towards his coach.

"No need to apologize, son! Just try again!" William reassured.

When the pitcher got the ball back, he set himself and threw. It was low, more or less even with the batter's knees, and the batter swung, driving the ball into the ground.

"Turn two!" William screamed in excitement.

"Run it out!" Gene retorted.

The ball found its way to the shortstop, who caught it but then dropped it.

"Stay with it!" William yelled.

The shortstop picked the ball back up and tossed it to the second baseman, who had been running towards the base. The fielder caught it with his foot on the second base.

"That's one," William uttered under his breath.

The second baseman threw the ball to the first baseman as the runner made his way down the line. The runner's foot hit the base as the baseball was securely caught by the first baseman.

"Safe!" shouted Gene.

"Out!" shouted William.

The players seemed confused. It didn't help that there was no official umpire.

"What happens if it's a tie?" a player asked.

William and Gene, at the same exact time, lamented, "There are no ties!"

The colder weather of Japan's fall and winter arrived and although they were certainly not as frigid as back home, it nonetheless put a damper on athletics.

Gene occasionally met up with William and his family but found himself indoors the majority of the time awaiting the return of spring.

When the warm weather reappeared, there was a clear uptick in Gene's enthusiasm, especially as he found his students playing baseball during their recess, a sight that provided him great glee.

"Perhaps we can combine our studies with our interests today," persuaded Gene as he stood in front of the classroom. "I want you all to write an essay reflecting upon your experience thus far with the game of baseball. Feel free to use last year's game as an example. How has this sport impacted or altered, if it has, your day-to-day life?"

Suddenly, a student came sprinting in.

"You're late. I thought punctuality was your specialty."

"I found out big news," the student excitedly said.

"Big news, you say? Would you mind sharing it with all of us, then?"

"There's a game being put together: *oyatoi* teachers against other *oyatoi* teachers. My friend from Yokohama just told me in a letter."

"It seems the thrill of baseball has spread beyond our two schools. Very intriguing. Now, back to—"

"—You're going to play, right, Mr. Durante?"

Gene turned around to see a sea of expectant faces. "Me? I don't know."

The students erupted with encouraging cheers that echoed in the room. It was the most disorderly and disobedient Gene had ever seen his students. The things baseball could do…

Succumbing, he said, "Fine. I'll play."

Two teams of American players had been selected from the foreign settlements in Yokohama and Tokyo. The game was held nearly two weeks after Gene had heard of it. Gene imagined it would be a weekend to remember, as he had not played a competitive game of baseball in some time. He constantly punched the inside of his mitt as if to warm it up. The weather was just right, a prime day to play. Students from all over gathered to watch the Americans play their game, providing a palpable buzz in the air.

William was chosen as one of the coaches and Gene made sure he found his way to his friend's team.

"So, are you actually any good?" asked William.

"Not too bad," reassured Gene.

"I have to make a lineup. Where do you belong? You're one of the younger guys so I figure you belong at the top, probably still have some wheels on ya."

"Wherever is fine."

"Or should I put you at the bottom, you know, to avoid favoritism?"

"I don't think this is as big of a deal as you're making it," derided Gene.

"You're right," William agreed. "Second. You'll hit second."

He walked away shaking his head while attempting to round out the lineup. Gene chuckled at his friend and tied his shoelaces.

"Mr. Durante!" a multitude of voices reverberated. Gene looked over to see his students. "We root for you!"

"Thank you! I'll try my best," he answered. They scurried to get a good view. It was then that Gene felt a tinge of pressure. He couldn't embarrass himself in front of the very students to whom he'd taught this game; that would be humiliating.

Gene's team was considered the away team, which meant they were up to bat first. After a few warm-up pitches, the game commenced.

As their leadoff hitter dug into the batter's box, Gene strolled to the on-deck spot, an area designated in foul territory where a batter could prepare himself.

The pitcher was right-handed, so Gene exercised his left-handed swing.

The pitcher wound up and fired a strike right down the middle.

"Strike one!"

It was a decent fastball, although Gene had seen quicker in college.

The second pitch was another fastball. This time the leadoff hitter connected weakly, sending it foul.

Gene noticed no increase in velocity.

The third and fourth pitches were high, attempts to get the hitter to chase to no avail. With the count at two balls and two strikes, the fifth pitch was high again, but this time the batter swung, popping it up in the infield.

The third baseman called, "I got it!" and the ball soon landed safely in his glove.

The crowd cheered as the opponents threw the ball around the diamond for practice.

Gene walked up to the plate, his heart pounding for reasons he could not truly comprehend. He had formed a plan; he was guessing the pitcher was going to try and get ahead of the count again by throwing a first pitch strike. Gene was going to jump on it, the element of surprise he often employed during his college years.

Gene swung back and forth, a ritual he had created for himself to calm his nerves. The pitcher glared at the catcher and nodded his head. He wound up. Gene's clutch on the bat tightened. The pitcher's arm reared back. Gene's focus did not waver. The pitcher released the ball. Gene saw it clearly and lifted his front foot while his back foot pivoted. He swung ferociously.

The pitcher threw a curveball. Gene swung and missed badly, way out in front of the off-speed pitch. He could hear snickering from the fans.

"Goddammit," Gene muttered to himself as the catcher threw the ball back to the pitcher. It wasn't even a great curveball, Gene thought. He was tricked, pure and simple.

"That's okay!" roared William. "You know he has that now. Readjust!"

Gene was thankful he'd been humble and hadn't told any of the other players he'd played in college. He'd embarrassed himself on the very first pitch. Shake it off, he told himself.

He got back in the batter's box. He set himself. The pitcher had a chip on his shoulder and a grin on his face.

The second pitch was a fastball. Gene was taking all the way. It was just outside.

"One ball, one strike," the umpire, an older gentleman with a clear love for the game, announced.

Gene was ready. He had gauged the pitcher's fastball. He had seen his curveball. His game plan was simple: if it was a fastball, he was swinging, if it was a curveball, he was taking.

The pitcher wound up. Gene kept his focus on the ball in the pitcher's hand. It was released. Gene noticed a rotation on the ball directly after it left the pitcher's hand. He kept his bat back.

The pitch bounced on home plate, falling short of its target.

"Ball. Two balls, one strike," the umpire reminded.

Gene's confidence soared; he felt he had him. His practice swings became increasingly fierce, his body language more bold.

The pitcher took notice. Gene surmised he was a man of pride and would thus surely throw a fastball.

An overhand delivery placed the pitcher's arm motion parallel with his body as he came over the top of his shoulder when he threw the ball.

It was a fastball. Gene was ready for it. He swung. He connected.

The noise of the barrel meeting the ball rang out as the small spherical object sailed off into the azure sky.

The onlookers stood in bewilderment. Gene stood too, in momentary disbelief. If there had been a fence, it would have gone over it, to the other side.

The pitcher followed the ball until he couldn't even see it anymore. At that point he just turned around to look at Gene, who had just blasted his best pitch into oblivion.

Gene started trotting and eventually picked up speed as he rounded the bases. The outfielders ran after the ball but had such a long distance to go that Gene was in no danger of being caught. He casually made his way home as the spectators cheered for him. He touched home plate and jogged over to his team's bench.

His teammates all congratulated him by patting his head or his shoulders. At the end of the commendation line stood William.

"Why the hell didn't you tell me? You let me bat you second with power like that!? What's wrong with you!?" He was pointing now. "If we ever play again you're batting third or fourth!"

William scuttled off as Gene grinned from ear to ear.

When he walked into the classroom on Monday morning, Gene was met with applause. He was also greeted with a request.

"We want to play a game like that."

"Not just for fun."

"A game with real competition."

Gene looked at his eager students. Something had taken hold here that Gene could not have predicted.

And so Gene Durante began preparing his students for games. William did the same for his students as did some other schools taught by *oyatoi* instructors. There was nothing planned immediately and sometimes William's students would play Gene's for practice. At times they even switched out players for fun and to level the playing field. Gene garnered great gratification from coaching and viewed it as an extension of teaching. Even when they played competitively it was still informal.

"Your contract is coming to an end," remarked William. "Did they offer you an extension?"

"They did. You?"

"They did. What are you thinking?"

Gene sat back on the bench; this time the duo had met at Asukayama Park. "I see no reason not to stay. I've enjoyed my time here. There's fulfillment in my work."

"Good!" bellowed William. "I'm glad to hear it. You'll most likely be accepting another three year deal, then?"

"Yes, I think so. What about you?"

"I would stay but I must admit, I have been hearing the luring call of home as of late. My wife and I miss the rest of our family. I did think about staying by myself and sending my son and wife home. You know, to keep anyone from batting you second in another game. But the simple truth of it is that I would miss them too much. Besides, there are many instructors just as qualified as I waiting in the wings."

"So this is it, then?"

"It is, for now. But I'm sure you'll eventually make your way back home. We shall reconvene then! Hopefully I won't be too old to have a simple catch with you!"

Gene feigned laughter. He had never contemplated what William had become in his life. His friend was indeed a connective tissue, an anchor in a world adrift. William was a mentor in many ways and a friendly reminder that he was not alone. His absence would leave a void not easily filled.

William's comment also spurred another related thought. Did Gene now view this place as home? Would it still be home without William or would it feel just as America felt—removed? Gene did not think about when he would return, whether he would return, or perhaps most importantly, when he would know the time was right to depart. Would that time ever come? Had he been disregarding his country of origin?

Gene distilled his numerous queries down to: would there ever be a place where he truly felt at home?

Gene signed on for another three years of teaching the future elite of the Japanese while William and his family sailed back to America.

William found tensions at home, however, were less than ideal. In 1875, America passed The Page Act, which prohibited the entry of any female of East Asian descent into the United States. It was especially aimed at Chinese women as the act, among other things, aimed to curb prostitution. The law also disallowed any person who aimed to immigrate to be a forced laborer and all people considered to be convicts in their own country were barred from entering. Horace F. Page, who sponsored the act, said the purpose of it was to, "end the danger of cheap Chinese labor and immoral Chinese women." The ban on East Asian females, however, was the only aspect of the law heavily enforced.

In 1876 a formal game of baseball was announced where Gene's students could finally compete. *Kaiseiko* was to have its own team. The biggest worry was the limited supply of bats and balls. But as destiny would have it, that too would soon work itself out.

Gene sipped hot green tea while reading Jules Verne's *Twenty Thousand Leagues Under the Sea*. He had purchased a copy before graduating but had never gotten around to reading it. He was highly invested in the exploratory themes and narrative and much like Captain Nemo tells his men, he felt as if he, too, was traveling through a wonderland of sorts in his actual life.

A young man spotted the instructor sitting at the outside table. He walked up to him. "Excuse me."

Gene looked above his book to see a slender individual.

The stranger asked, "Are you the instructor at *Kaiseiko?*"

"I am," Gene answered. "Can I help you?"

"My name is Rikuto."

"You speak impeccable English, Rikuto."

"Thank you. I have just returned from Massachusetts."

Gene's interest was piqued as his eyebrow darted upward. "Massachusetts? That's the state I was born in. What part of Massachusetts?"

"Amherst. I studied at the Massachusetts Agricultural College. My parents wished me to be trained there."

"You don't say! I have a very good friend who studied agriculture. I always found it an interesting topic."

"Yes. Very fascinating."

"I'm sorry, but how did you know who I was?"

"You are the baseball instructor."

Gene chuckled and responded, "No, no. I think you have the wrong guy."

"They say you hit a home run that traveled hundreds of feet. This is not you?"

After a sigh, he answered, "Yes, that was me but I do not teach baseball. I only coach my students as a recreational activity for some exercise."

"They say the school has a baseball team now."

"Well, it's not really official in that sense. But we are going to play a few games. What's your interest?"

"I want to play baseball!"

Taken aback by his excitement, Gene asked, "You were exposed to baseball in America, I gather?"

"Yes."

"Boston fan?"

"Yes! I saw them once! At the South End Grounds."

"Exciting! When I was in college I was very fond of The Resolutes, a baseball team out of Elizabeth, New Jersey. I attended school in that state. They played in Waverly Fairgrounds."

"Were they good?"

"God, no. In 1873, the one year they were a part of the National Association of Professional Base Ball Players, they had two wins and twenty-one losses. I hoped they would improve so I could see them, but," Gene sighed, "they disbanded after that season and I left anyway."

"I'm sure there will be another New Jersey team."

"We shall see. Anyway, I'm glad you have taken a liking to the sport but I do not teach it outside of school unfortunately."

"You should start a professional baseball club!"

Gene laughed and immediately said, "No, I don't think so. Organizing is not my strong suit. Perhaps if one were to come into existence I would manage, but I'd rather not deal with the logistics of it all. I'll tell you what, though—I could use a coach for Kaiseiko. Any interest?"

Rikuto beamed and answered, "I would be honored to."

"Good. I can pay you a very small allowance for your work. It's not much and it's not agriculture but it might just quench your thirst."

"You have a deal."

Rikuto held out his hand. Gene realized it had been a while since he'd engaged in the gesture other than with William. He shook hands while wondering if the act was some sort of officiating transition. Had he just taken William's place as mentor as he once predicted? Time would tell.

"Oh, and another thing," added Rikuto. "I have plenty of balls and bats. I brought them from America."

Gene's eyes lit up; Rikuto had answered his prayers.

Kaiseiko soon opened a brand new playing ground and every Saturday they were set to play a game.

"I would like to thank you for this opportunity," Gene said to the school principal. "It means a great deal to the boys."

"They deserve it. What was once a game of American pride can now also be one of Japanese pride."

"I look forward to our games. Do you know what school we will play in our inaugural game?"

"No school," the principal answered without feeling.

"I'm sorry. I don't understand."

"You will play against a team of Americans assembled from the residents of the foreign settlement in Yokohama and American *oyatoi* teachers here in Tokyo."

"We're playing against Americans?" Gene questioned with a hint of anger in his tone.

"Yes. We will show our people we are just as good as they are."

"With all due respect, they have far more experience."

"I understand. But the students have you, the one who hit Japan's first home run, to lead them. I am not expecting a win. I am expecting to compete. Give them a run for their money, as you say."

The principal turned and walked away. Gene, flustered, knew only that he had his work cut out for him.

"It's unfair," Gene said to Rikuto. "They're not ready for that."

"We will do our best."

"We need a secret weapon."

"Do you have one in mind?"

Gene pondered before asking, "Ever hear of Bobby Matthews?"

"No."

"He's a player in America who started pitching for the Fort Wayne Kekiongas when I was in college. He's the first pitcher to throw a pitch that broke away from hitters. He also threw something really unusual that was hard to hit—a pitch that just slipped out of his fingers without the usual spin a pitch tends to have."

"How did he do that?"

"He spit on it," answered Gene. "Get our players. It's time to experiment."

Gene and Rikuto held a special training session for their hurlers and explored different pitching options. They tried different grips, different delivery points, and different flicks of the wrist. They spent the entire afternoon testing their arms.

One student, Kosuke, discovered something quite interesting. He was one of the hardest-throwing pitchers on the team and was very intrigued with research and development. He started releasing the ball just above the ground, as his torso bent and his shoulders tilted and rotated.

"I don't think you can legally throw like that," remarked Rikuto.

"Technically he's not pitching underhand or overhand," responded Gene. "It's more of a, I don't know what you would call it. The pitch starts down and then goes up instead of the other way around."

"Like a submarine emerging from the ocean," added Rikuto.

"Something like that," said Gene, paying little attention to the comment. "I think it's legal." He turned to Kosuke. "Pitch to me in this way."

The students seemed surprised; they had never squared off against their own manager before.

Gene stood in the batter's box and shouted, "Okay! Let's see how this thing works!"

Kosuke took the mound and delivered. Gene took the pitch to study it. The upside down release was disorienting.

Despite being way outside, Gene said, "You might be onto something here! If you can throw it for a strike, this can be an interesting weapon of deception."

Kosuke nodded and tried again. And again. The pitching delivery seemed unnatural and thus took much concentration and experimentation. Eventually, however, Kosuke started throwing strikes, consistently.

Gene found it difficult to time and guess the trajectory of the pitch. Ultimately, though, he acclimated and started hitting the unorthodox pitching.

"You think you can throw a curveball like that?" asked Gene.

Kosuke attempted. As he flicked his wrist at the end, the ball sputtered out of his hand and didn't even come close to reaching the plate.

"That doesn't feel right," he remarked.

"It doesn't look right, either. What about gripping your fastball in that other way we tried, the one where your index and middle fingers are along the seams?"

Kosuke gripped the ball accordingly and gave it a try. Gene saw the fastball approaching. He lifted his forward leg up for power and swung. As the ball traveled closer, it darted downwards. Gene swung over the pitch, missing it completely.

Everyone looked at one another in astonishment.

"Can you do that again!?" asked Gene.

"I can try," Kosuke answered.

He threw it again. Gene swung and missed again. He had never been so happy after missing so badly.

"Good! Now let's try mixing in your first fastball with your new fastball!"

The remainder of the practice was used to hone Kosuke's newfound talents. The entire team took turns batting as Kosuke kept tweaking to maximize proficiency.

Gene and Rikuto watched from the side.

"You know what makes this so infuriating for batters?" asked Gene.

"What?"

"When he throws his regular fastball from this new delivery, it looks as if the pitch is rising as it approaches you. When he throws his second pitch, the ball drops even though you're expecting it to rise because of the way it's thrown. The deceit will throw off both the balance and timing of the hitter."

Rikuto gleamed and with a tone of promise said, "Maybe then we do have a chance."

An abundance of spectators gathered as Gene's team of Japanese students was set to play against the Americans.

Jack, the opponents' player-manager, walked up to Gene as the players warmed up. He sported a uniform, the only player on the field to do so. Gene recognized the blue and white colors: it was the uniform of a New York Knickerbocker. They were the first team to ever wear a baseball uniform and he was proudly showing it off.

"Hey! I think you can still play for us and manage them at the same time!"

Gene had heard of Jack before despite having never met him. Jack was a former captain of the Union Army who constructed his second career teaching math in rural Japan. Gene heard he was strict and handled his new occupation with the same seasoned toughness that made him a valued soldier. He was well-respected and demanded deference.

"I don't know. Might be a conflict of interest," Gene jested. "Nice uniform."

They shook hands.

"Thanks. I played briefly with the Knickerbockers in the early 50s."

"You're a part of history, then."

"I suppose I always have been. When I was still a little too young to play, I saw them in '46 at Elysian Fields in Hoboken.

That's when things first started to get organized. They got the crap kicked out of them that day by the New York Nine. It was exciting though, I'll tell you that much. I knew I needed to be a part of it."

"Good for you. You've seen it all."

"Between the war and baseball, you got that right. Hey, I suppose we're not exactly playing New York style today?"

New York style baseball referred to the Knickerbocker rules, a formalization of the game made in 1845 that laid the groundwork for the standards of the sport. There were other variants as well, such as the Massachusetts Game and Philadelphia town ball.

"It's a bit of a combination. Most of the New York rules are there but we're sticking with the Massachusetts Game when it comes to pitching. The ball must be thrown, not pitched or tossed."

In the New York style, pitchers had to throw underhand.

"Seems a bit counterproductive, no?" asked Jack, his voice ever guttural. "They should just pick one and have at it."

Gene had heard stories about the Union Army playing baseball to pass the time during the boring days of camp life between the fighting. The game found its way through different corps, regiments, brigades and other units. Soon enough, it was a game many knew and understood.

"It is what it is," Gene answered.

"It reminds me of back in the day when individual clubs privately deliberated the rules of the game. Hey, I heard you were just as surprised as us at the matchup."

"You can say that again."

Jack leaned in, coming critically close to his ear.

"Listen, we'll try not to embarrass your kids. But if we see there's even the chance of a comeback we're going have to squash these bastards. You understand."

It was poignant that those last two words were not phrased as a question.

Gene simply smiled and said, "We'll see what happens."

Jack smirked and turned back towards his team.

"Son of a bitch," Gene muttered under his breath. He walked up to Kosuke and said, "When you warm up, throw overhand like you used to. Then on the first official pitch of the game, let him have it."

Kosuke nodded.

Kosuke took the mound; the game was ready to commence. He did precisely as he was told, throwing overhand to warm up. He didn't even throw that hard to give the illusion his velocity was slower than it really was. He noticed the Americans studying his pitches from their side of foul territory.

Their leadoff hitter settled in. Kosuke turned to Gene who offered a nimble nod. Kosuke set himself. His front leg kicked up. His body twisted, his shoulders rotating at a nearly horizontal axis. His arm came down, his knuckles hovering just above the mound. The ball left his hand with dash a hope.

"Strike one!"

The Americans turned to one another as the onlookers did the same. Chatter erupted from all sides.

Kosuke tuned out the various voices and immediately prepared himself for another pitch. He threw another fastball. The batter took again, trying to determine the exactness of the delivery.

"Strike two!"

The batter took a few practice swings, his body language clear that he was up for the challenge.

Kosuke wound up. The pitch did exactly as he intended, descending upon crossing the plate. The hitter swung and missed, striking out in the process.

The American batter walked off, confused, as Kosuke circled the mound before returning to it.

The same course of events transpired over the next two batters as Kosuke struck out the side.

"It's rising," the third batter remarked as he walked off.

"Pitches can't rise," another American responded.

Gene could feel the burning glare of Jack from the other side of the diamond; it gave him great pleasure.

The American pitcher proved just as devastating, albeit without the unconventional delivery.

The two teams seemed destined to be locked in a pitcher's duel. The Americans had never encountered such pitching trickery before and the Japanese had never experienced the overwhelming power of a pitcher with great mechanics and an annihilating curveball to match.

As a matter of fact, Gene and the American pitcher were the only two people there that day with college-level playing experience. Their hurler had attended Williams College in Massachusetts and had no problem throwing underhand or overhand. The Americans' first baseman and left fielder both played amateur ball in the early 1860's with the National Association of Base Ball Players. And of course, there was Jack who forebodingly patrolled right field. The rest of the American players were comprised of those who played games with their friends on the farms or in the fields. None of them had ever played in an organized league. Gene hoped this would be to his advantage.

Kosuke walked a batter in the second inning and gave up his first hit in the third. Despite these blemishes, he pitched five scoreless innings.

"Good! You're doing great! All of you are! But we can't outpitch them forever with no runs!" encouraged Gene. "We need to get creative!"

"What the hell is going on out there!?" roared Jack. "Hey, I understand we're not professional players here, but we're still American! Now don't get me wrong, we're doing a tremendous service by being here and these are great people. But this is still America's game! Let's go out there and prove it!"

Kaiseiko's shortstop led off the inning. He was the speediest member of the team and had great control of the bat. He stood with a plan.

As the ball discharged from the pitcher's grip, the batter slid his top hand to where the bat began to thicken into the barrel. He turned his back foot towards the pitcher as he squared up.

"Bunt!" screamed Jack from the outfield.

The Japanese shortstop angled his bat towards third base but the pitch was far lower than expected. He bent his knees and dropped his bat to the ball, pulling back ever slightly before connection was eminent. He made contact with the ball on the lower part of the barrel as he was taught, sending the ball down into the ground.

He exploded out of the box, running as fast as he could towards first base as the ball trickled down the third base side of the infield, bypassing the pitcher. The American third baseman charged the ball but by the time he grabbed it, a throw was futile. *Kaiseiko* recorded their first hit.

"You gotta be kidding me!" screamed Jack.

Gene knew this was an opportunity. Speed was an integral part of the game.

The Japanese base runner had a guess to make. He knew the pitcher threw first pitch fastballs often to get ahead of the count. If he were to steal, he would have to try and go when he predicted a curveball would be thrown.

The first pitch to *Kaiseiko's* center fielder was indeed a fastball, and a strike.

The pitcher wound up as the Japanese shortstop led off of first base. He tried to look at the pitcher's grip inside of his glove. The pitcher fast-pitched to home and the runner hesitated and consequently chose not to run.

"Strike two!"

It was another fastball. The runner didn't think he would throw three in a row. He would run on the next pitch.

The pitcher wound up and entered his motion. The runner took off. The pitch was high and outside, but another fastball. The catcher caught it easily and then flung the ball over the pitcher's head, towards second base. The American shortstop moved to preside over second base as the ball neared.

The catcher's throw was offline, sending the shortstop scurrying over to keep the ball from entering the outfield.

Second base had successfully been stolen.

The crowd cheered.

"There we go!" shouted Gene.

The next pitch was a curveball. The hitter took it as it landed low. The runner, now brimming with confidence, acted as if he was about to steal third before returning back. He had the pitcher's attention.

The next pitch was a fastball. The batter hit a weak ground ball to the first baseman. As the fielder caught the ball and tapped on the base with his foot for the out, the runner who had been on second safely reached third base.

With one out and a runner on third, the American pitcher threw three straight curveballs to the next batter. Two of them were strikes.

With the count 1-2, the hitter took a practice swing. His aim was simple: put the ball in play to give his team a chance to score. He couldn't imagine a fourth straight curveball. Gene had told him that when he expected a certain type of pitch the term used was sitting on that pitch. And so that's what he aimed to do; he was going to sit on a fastball. He settled in. The pitcher wound up.

The fourth pitch was indeed a fastball. He swung and connected, hard. The ball sailed into the outfield. Jack, however, ambled under the high fly ball and settled underneath it.

"Tag up!" yelled Gene.

The runner remained on third base, his foot clearly resting on it. He was waiting.

As soon as the ball landed in Jack's glove, the Japanese runner left the bag in a jiffy as he broke towards home plate. Jack fired the ball towards the catcher but it was short; the runner scored standing up.

The crowd cheered as the Japanese youths had manufactured a run and took the lead from the imposing American players.

The Japanese shortstop was greeted with pats and embraces as he rejoined his side.

"Let's keep focused," instructed Gene. "We have a long way to go."

The American pitcher struck the next batter out using just three pitches. The players switched sides as *Kaiseiko* once again manned the field as they entered the top of the sixth inning. Kosuke retook the mound with a razor-sharp focus and once again hurled a swift inning. As did his counterpart in the bottom of the inning.

Jack led off the top of the seventh inning but didn't immediately step up to the plate. Instead, he held his bat in his hand and unflappably glared at the Japanese pitcher. Kosuke was unsure of what to do and simply waited. Jack slowly trotted up to the plate, never taking his eyes off the pitcher.

"Don't let him intimidate you," ordered Gene. "This is your game."

Kosuke led off with his sinking fastball. Jack didn't bite.

"Ball one," the umpire declared.

Jack meandered away from the plate again as he took a practice swing, his eyes ever fixed on Kosuke. Before making his way back, he forcefully spit. His spew discharged in the direction of the pitcher as was intended. He threateningly walked back to the plate.

"Don't fall for it," muttered Gene to himself.

Kosuke wound up. Jack's eye's squinted in focus. The Japanese pitcher threw the ball as fast as he humanly could. It was a rebuttal, a challenge, and an answer to the disrespectful spittle. It was a pitch of principle and integrity, of dignity and recognition. It was also precisely what Jack wanted.

Jack swung with all of the might he had left in him. The barrel of his bat met the heater in the sweetest of spots. Kosuke watched as the ball blasted off the bat and sped directly towards him. It had left quicker than it arrived and he wasn't quick enough to get out of the way.

It shot like a cannon directly into Kosuke's kneecap. The budding pitcher went down as Jack ran to first.

Gene ran out as the umpire declared timeout. Kosuke held his leg in anguish.

"It's okay," Gene assured. "You're going to be okay."

The players helped carry their ace off the field. Spectators who knew the boy offered to take him to a doctor.

"Was that on purpose?" asked Rikuto.

"Not even Jack has that kind of bat control. But he baited him to throw a straight fastball. He was ready for it. Can you play?"

"Me?" questioned Rikuto.

"That's right. You have your chance."

"Ready to resume?" the umpire asked.

"Yes," said Gene. "We're going to make a couple of changes. My right fielder is going to come in and pitch and my bench player here is going to go to right."

"Sounds good."

Gene waved in the right fielder as Rikuto jogged out.

From first base, Jack said, "It wasn't on purpose, you know."

Gene spewed back, "We know, Jack. You're not good enough for that kind of aim."

Jack appeared surprised by the volatility as Gene greeted Katsumi, his new pitcher.

"Listen, you're a great pitcher and you have nothing to worry about."

"Am I going to get hit like that, too?"

"No. That's a freak accident. It rarely happens. Remember everything we talked about. Strategy and control."

"Strategy and control," Katsumi repeated.

Gene walked off the field.

Katsumi did not throw as hard as Kosuke, nor was his delivery as deceptive. His strength, however, was his control. He could place his pitches where he wanted and Gene had taught him to move the ball around to each quadrant to keep hitters off balance.

Katsumi did just that on the very first pitch as he precisely placed the ball on the lower inside corner. The batter swung and hit a sharp ground ball to the shortstop.

"Double play!" Gene called out.

The shortstop tossed it over to the second baseman, who tapped the bag for the first out. As he turned, he surprisingly saw Jack sliding fiercely into second base. Avoiding being taken down, the second baseman jumped in the air and attempted to throw to first as his legs separated into a split while Jack tunneled under them.

The acrobatics employed took much of the velocity off the throw and the runner beat it out.

Jack jolted up, despite his aged body, and winked at the second baseman before trotting off.

"Good job! We got one!" Gene yelled.

Katsumi wound up and fired off his next pitch. It was high and away but the batter went after it, smashing the ball into right field.

Rikuto had to move, and quick, as the ball seemed to be picking up speed and getting away from the outfielder. Still, Rikuto dashed after it, his legs moving with incredible speed. The ball headed for the gap between Rikuto and the center fielder. Knowing it was going to be close, Rikuto held out his glove while still speeding. He could feel the ball make contact with his leather. He then felt it ricochet off of it. He tumbled onto the ground from moving so fast and somersaulted through the grass. The ball dribbled away but was picked up by the center fielder. One run scored as the hitter rounded second base and headed for third. The center fielder tossed it in but the runner easily reached third base. The game was tied.

Rikuto slowly rose as the center fielder held his hand out.

"I'm sorry."

"Don't be. Most of us could have never even reached it. That alone was spectacular."

This brought a smile to Rikuto's face as he clasped his newly found friend's hand and stood up.

The next batter grounded out to the second baseman, allowing the runner on third to score. Katsumi forced the next hitter to fly out to the left fielder, ending the inning. But the Americans were winning 2-1.

Kaiseiko did not score in their half of the seventh or eighth but the American instructors tagged on another run in the ninth, making the score 3 to 1 as they entered the last frame.

Gene took the opportunity for one last pep talk.

"Guys! It's three to one! No one expected that! We have one more chance. Winning is not out of our grasp. Their pitcher is getting tired. Be patient. Wait for the pitch you like. Then put a good swing on it! We can do this!"

Kaiseiko led off with Katsumi. He took a deep breath before setting in his stance.

The pitcher flung the ball towards the plate. Katsumi went to swing but noticed the ball was too outside and held back.

"Ball one."

The next pitch was low but Katsumi swung. The ball arched over the third baseman's head as it was served into the outfield.

Katsumi sped to first base, took a big turn towards second, and retreated back safely.

Kaiseiko's catcher swung at the first pitch he saw and lined a single over second base.

"Yes!" yelled Gene.

The American pitcher sighed as he shook his head in displeasure.

Suddenly, Jack came trotting into the infield.

"You must be tired," the player-manager said.

"Haven't pitched nine innings in a while."

"Want me to close it out?" asked Jack.

"If you feel up to it."

Jack nodded and took the ball as the pitcher jogged into the outfield.

"Let's see if I still got it," Jack called out to no one in particular.

"Be patient," Gene reminded his team.

Jack threw a couple of warm-up pitches and declared himself ready.

The Japanese third baseman made his way to the plate.

Jack's first pitch was a powerful strike as everyone in attendance could hear the reverberating pop of the catcher's mitt.

"I ain't gonna try to trick ya. Fastball every pitch," Jack asserted, almost tauntingly.

The next pitch was high but the batter swung without contact.

Jack grinned as he wound up.

The pitch was directly down the middle of the plate. He swung and barely tipped it. He looked back to see the catcher had caught the ball.

"Strike three!" the umpire shouted.

With runners on first and second and one out, Rikuto came up to the plate.

"Redeem yourself," he whispered to himself.

"Come on, Rikuto!" Gene clamored.

The first pitch was a strike, straight and hard as was expected.

The second pitch was equally hard but steered high.

"One ball, one strike."

Jack fired another pitch down the middle.

Rikuto connected on what Gene called the sweet spot of the bat. The ball advanced high and far as the onlookers stood. It was way over the outfielder's head as it continued to sail but was twisting. Unsure if it would land fair or foul, Rikuto started running.

The ball finally landed as the umpire screamed, "Fair ball!"

Rikuto was halfway to second base when the left fielder approached the rolling ball.

One run scored.

"Yes!" Gene cried out.

The outfielder picked up the ball.

The second run scored.

"Keep going!" Gene hollered.

Rikuto reached third and rounded the base; he was heading home.

The throw from the outfielder was cut off by the shortstop. He secured the ball and subsequently threw it to the catcher.

The only thing every person watching knew was that the play was going to be close.

The catcher grasped onto the ball as Rikuto slid. The American backstop tossed himself, glove first, towards the runner. A cloud of dust surfaced from the accelerated skid.

Complete silence enveloped the field as everyone looked to the umpire. Through the hazy dirt, the official arbitrator drew out his elbows and then rapidly extended his arms fully to each side.

He accompanied this motion with a loud, "Safe!"

The *Kaiseiko* players rushed Rikuto and piled onto home plate.

Jack walked off the field grinning. He took his hat off and saluted it to Gene, who nodded in reciprocation.

Kaiseiko had achieved the impossible—they had beaten the Americans at their own game.

They celebrated for days on end and became a legendary local team. They continued to play and—most importantly to their instructor—they continued to have fun.

In 1877, Gene took his students on a field trip to a far more rural part of Japan. Or perhaps it would better be said that his students took him on a field trip, as they knew the lands better than their instructor.

They read American poetry and short stories and Gene introduced them to English folklore by campfire. He read them Washington Irving's *The Legend of Sleepy Hollow*. The Japanese students taught Gene their culture's oral customs as well. They told him the fables of Kintarō the superhuman Golden Boy, Momotarō the oni-slaying Peach Boy, and the Tale of the Bamboo Cutter.

Cultural differences made for such unique stories as Gene realized an English-language ghost story needed to be accompanied by an explanation of heaven or an afterlife, something not conceptualized in the same way in their culture as thoughts on death in Japan traditionally came from Buddhism, which had no compatible afterlife myth. They were fascinated to say the least.

"You are an American instructor, can you make up an English folklore?" one student asked.

"Yea! And make it scary!"

"A ghost story!"

"You can't just make up a folktale!" Gene retorted.

"Then how are they created?" the first student asked.

"Good point," Gene admitted. "Okay," he thought. "Here we go."

The fire roared, partially illuminating everyone's faces amongst the darkness. All were eager to hear what was about to transpire.

"There were two boys. They were the best of friends and both loved baseball. As a matter of fact they played baseball for their school!"

Gene could see smiling faces.

"One of the boys was a pitcher, the other a catcher. This bond made them extra close as they relied on each other more so than any other two positioned players. One day the catcher asked the pitcher, 'Do you think there's baseball in the afterlife?' The pitcher shrugged and said, 'I don't know. But I'll tell you what. The one who gets there first should let the other one know somehow.' The boys agreed; it was a deal. Well, as it turned out the catcher got there first. The pitcher was saddened by this but held hope that he would see his friend again as they had agreed. He waited patiently. One day, as the pitcher was alone on a baseball field, practicing, throwing to no one, the catcher appeared. The pitcher was overjoyed. 'What is it like up there!?' he asked. 'Is there baseball?' The catcher responded, 'I have good news and I have bad news. The good news is: there is baseball up there. We have many good teams. I catch on mine.' 'That's great,' said the pitcher. 'So what's the bad news?" The catcher took a long pause before saying, 'The bad news is: you're scheduled to pitch tomorrow.'"

The students leapt back and let out a series of shrieks. Gene smiled at the thought of participating in the creation of oral tradition. He doubted anyone would ever tell the tale again, but still, he held out hope.

The next year was scheduled to be Gene's last and he refused to think too much about the future. He would avoid it until he couldn't. This included evading the fact that Japan's Ministry of Education had offered him another three-year extension.

"Well," urged Rikuto, "What are you going to do?"

"I don't know," Gene answered.

Rikuto and Gene sat on a bench in Shiba Park, overlooking the Shinto shrine, *Shiba Tōshō-gū*.

"We still need you," pleaded Rikuto.

Gene smiled and said, "I haven't decided yet. We'll see. What about you? Your father can't be too happy you've been making little use of your agricultural studies. You should be changing the world."

"That's what we're doing," he answered, not looking Gene.

"Maybe."

"You just need to meet a woman," blurted out Rikuto. "Is that why you wish to leave? Is there someone waiting for you at home?"

Gene couldn't help think of Valerie before answering, "No. There's no one for me at home."

"Do you not find Japanese women to your liking?"

Gene laughed and said, "They're very much to my liking. I just haven't met anyone."

"Because you spend too much time with your students between teaching and baseball."

"That's my job. I find great joy in it. What about you? I don't see you courting many women."

"My parents have arranged an *omiai*."

"What's that?"

"It means looking at one another. It is a formal introduction where couples meet with the intention of choosing a spouse."

"Seems fast moving. Do you know anything about her?"

"I am told she is very beautiful," he answered solemnly.

"You don't seem excited."

Rikuto looked up at the sky and stayed quiet for quite some time before responding, "I am," but then he trailed off and stopped speaking.

Gene, sensing his friend's frustration, pressed, "What is it?"

Rikuto placed his attention on the giant ginkgo tree before him. Finally he said, "To put it in our language, in terms of attraction between men and women, I hit for the other team."

Gene thought about this for a moment before he realized its meaning. He leaned back on the bench.

"Eh, the other team," he struggled for something witty but kind to say but could only come up with, "has better catchers anyway."

They both laughed; that ice was broken.

"I suppose it works to my advantage that here love is thought to be inessential to marriage."

Gene peered out and thought about these words. He had loved before and would very much like to do it again.

In 1878, Japan's first private baseball club was formed, led by an ambitious young Japanese man who learned engineering in America. Since *Kaiseiko's* students had been practicing and playing baseball for a number of years, their graduates created their own team as well. They were scheduled to face off in the inaugural match.

Gene and Rikuto ate lunch together in the cafeteria.

"A new era of baseball in about to begin in this country," Gene remarked.

"I know," Rikuto responded enthusiastically. "I am grateful to be a part of it."

"The team is going to need a manager."

"Did they ask you?"

"They did."

"You're accepting! When I met you, you said if a league was created you would manage a team!"

"I said perhaps!" he reminded.

"So? What did you say?"

"I declined."

Rikuto seemed shocked. "Why?"

"Precisely because it is a new era. Fresh faces seem obligatory. Plus they found a manager just as good."

"Who!?"

Gene took a sip of soup before looking up and answering, "You."

"Me?"

"Yes. You."

"They haven't asked me."

"I'm asking you on their behalf. You are just as much a part of *Kaiseiko* as anyone. You are the one who defeated the Americans in the bottom of the 9th inning. You are storied. It only makes sense for someone with such credentials to lead his peers as a player-manager. What do you say?"

Rikuto abruptly stood, an uncommon act at a cafeteria, and stated, "I would be honored."

Gene smirked as he said, "Good. You're going to be a great leader."

Rikuto sat back down and asked, "What will you do?"

Gene sighed and slowly answered, "I've decided to go home."

Chapter 9

The Tale of Gene Durante Part III

Rikuto led his team to a victory and Gene Durante sailed back to America, unsure if he would recognize the place he once called his own.

He arrived back at the same San Francisco pier with no plan. Gene had always been orderly and reliant and dependable. He valued those things. Yet, he felt his adventure had not ended but rather just begun. His move to Japan was in many ways a last resort, one that he was most grateful for. And now, he found himself at a fork in the road. He had, for the first time in his life, real choice. He was designed to go to school, some might even say destined to it. But there was nothing preordained left; life was his for the taking. He felt an overpowering urge to do something rash, impulsive, and out of character.

Gene Durante booked passage to the Kingdom of Hawaii.

He landed and settled in Oahu, finding more English speakers than he imagined. Still, he set off right away to learn the native tongue, as well.

Gene spent the first few weeks of his journey touring the island. He was intrigued by the capital of Honolulu and impressed by the many beaches on the coasts. His favorite spot, however, was Waimea Valley.

Located on the North shore of Oahu, the elongated depression between uplands was home to the most beautiful natural sights Gene had ever laid eyes on.

He explored stone terraces and walls, marveled at the Polynesian plants, and all of the greenery that surrounded him.

The scene that spoke to him most however was at the valley's hind end. It was a section of landscape that could best be described as something out of a written work about untouched lands. He felt like Robinson Crusoe on the Island of Caliban as written by Thomas Moore after Odysseus visited it.

As he pulled back the shrubbery, he entered a secret garden. A small waterfall spilled its liquid gently into the shimmering swimming hole below. The sounds of chirping birds and wind-rustled shrubbery provided a paradisiacal audio that seemed all too unreal.

Gene sat beside the water and allowed the sunlight to warm his face. In such moments, Gene could forget everything about the outside world. Nothing else existed when one's mind was truly cleared.

"Beautiful, isn't it?"

The voice came from behind him. He had heard those words before, on the boat as he departed for Japan. They were words spoken by a stranger that would become a friend.

Gene swiftly turned to see a plump man with a long white beard. It wasn't William. But there was certainly a familiarity.

"I didn't mean to startle or disturb you," the man said.

"It's fine."

"I see you discovered this Eden, too."

"It's glorious."

"My favorite spot on the island. I try to visit it when I can. Are you new here?"

"I am."

"Welcome. This is a special place with special people. This valley here is considered to have great spiritual significance."

"Oh?"

"It is said that ancient Hawaiians partook in many religious ceremonies here."

"Did that include sacrifice?"

The question came out more forceful than Gene intended. He supposed it was a result of the disturbance.

The man chuckled and surmised, "Well, you can't have a sacred mythology without a little sacrifice."

Gene giggled and stood up.

"I'm Gene."

They shook hands as the man said, "Alexander."

"Pleasure."

"Are you here alone? On the island, I mean?"

"Yes. I just came back from Japan."

"Japan!? What were you doing there?"

"Teaching English to their students. And spreading the sport of baseball."

Alexander's interest was suddenly piqued. "What did you say?"

"I taught English in Japan."

"No, the other part."

"I taught baseball. No big deal, I can assure you. But we got the school to have a baseball team. By the time I left they formed their own first professional league. Then my contract was up and I came here."

The bearded man hung on every word. "Fascinating. Say, since you're unaccompanied and new to these parts and I'm a fellow countryman, what do you say to a little lunch this weekend at my place? It's not much but I think you will enjoy it, a little socialization. What do you say?"

Gene looked at the man, supposing he was sincere. "That would be lovely. Thank you."

Alexander gave him foolproof directions to his home and concluded with, "And now I shall leave you to your wonderland."

"Thank you again."

Alexander began to leave, taking a step into the brush before looking back and stating, "Oh. The last name is Cartwright, by the way. In case you need it."

"Cartwright. Got it!"

Alexander disappeared into the green and Gene sat back down, placing his feet into the water. He was about to lift his head back up so the sun could do what it does best when it suddenly clicked. He gasped. Alexander Cartwright was a founding member of the New York Knickerbockers. Alexander Cartwright was said to be the father of baseball.

The weekend could not come soon enough for Gene. When it did, he arrived promptly at the doorstep of Cartwright's home. He knocked nervously.

A woman answered the door. "You must be Gene."

"Yes, I see I've arrived at the right house."

"My name is Eliza. Please, come in."

Alexander was waiting in a section of the modest house best described as their drawing room. "Gene! Good to see you again!" He stood up and greeted his guest.

"Thank you for inviting me."

"Can I get you something to drink? Eliza has a delicious batch of homemade tea. It's cold and refreshing."

"That would be great."

"You sit, and I'll get our drinks."

Gene sat and observed the cozy room. The chairs were cushioned and comfortable. Portraits adorned the walls. Alexander came back in with two drinks as Gene graciously stood to receive the glass.

They sat, Cartwright letting out a very audible sigh. He raised his glass. "To baseball."

Gene added, "And to the man who helped make it."

Cartwright smiled before taking a sip. "I was hoping you might figure that out. Been a baseball fan since you were a child?"

"Actually, no. It was in my college years."

"Ah! An educated man."

"I played for Rutgers' baseball team."

"Rutgers has a baseball team now?"

"They do. I was part of the founding team in 1870."

"It seems I have an historic figure in my presence," Alexander chuckled.

"Funny, I was thinking the same."

"I'll tell you what. You have around thirty minutes to tell me your story."

"And then?"

"And then the real fun begins."

Gene told him of his college days and his subsequent teachings in Japan. Cartwright listened with delight and captivation. About thirty minutes later there was a knock on the door. Two men, around Alexander's age, soon entered the room.

"Gene, may I introduce you to The Nestor of Ball Players, Daniel Lucius Adams; by the way, that title is official as it was given to him on a scroll, although you may know him better by his moniker Doc Adams. And this lovely gentleman next to him is William Wheaton, another innovator of the game who I suppose we should mention was a founding member and vice president of the Knickerbocker Base Ball Club in 1845. He was just recently appointed, by President Grant himself, the Register of the General Land Office of the United States."

Gene recognized the names. Before him were arguably the three most important pioneers of the game.

"Lovely meeting you," both men said concurrently.

"Pleased to meet you," said Gene. "It's truly an honor."

"Gene here was an essential member of bringing baseball to Japan," Cartwright added.

"I wouldn't say that," Gene corrected.

"Oh, just say it!" Alexander persuaded.

"I see you haven't changed a bit," Adams said. "Old Cartwright here would have you believe he created the game in its modern form all by himself."

"I wouldn't say that! Although I would say it's close."

They all laughed as Doc Adams and Wheaton took a seat.

Adams continued, "I'll have you know, Gene, that of the three of us, my name was the only one in the lineup on that summer day in Hoboken. That was 1846."

Cartwright quickly countered, "And I'll have you know, Gene, that one year prior to that, in the summer of '85, William and I, along with Duncan Curry, were the ones to form the Knickerbocker club! I will also have it known that ten years prior to all of that, I was in the streets of Manhattan playing bat-and-ball games with volunteer firefighters!"

Wheaton turned to Gene and declared, "Sometimes I wonder why I even bother to visit."

Laughter erupted again.

Adams intervened, "Wheaton here drafted the first written rules for the Gotham Base Ball Club in '37.'"

"I doubt you heard of that one, Gene, because it split to form the Knickerbocker Club," Wheaton educated. "As Alexander said, the three of us broke free from our old club and formed the team that would go on to last longer than any of us imagined. It only recently died out, earlier this decade."

"It seems fitting that as it passes we are soon to follow," Cartwright mused.

Adams interjected, "Speak for yourself, Alexander. I plan to keep it up for a while. I want to make sure we don't sell William short either. He was then one half of the two-man Committee on By-Laws to form the Knickerbocker rules. Who was the other man again?"

"The treasurer, William H. Tucker!" Wheaton answered.

"Yes! Good old Tucker! The tobacconist. Say, do you remember Louis F. Wadsworth!?"

"He was a drunk!" asserted Cartwright.

"He was charmingly tempestuous," Adams corrected.

"He was a damn good first baseman for both the Gotham Club and our Knickerbocker team," Wheaton chimed in.

Cartwright added, "I always preferred you, Wheaton." He turned to Gene and added, "He was also one of the first umpires back in those days."

"The game was in its infancy then," Wheaton began. "We didn't play exhibition or match games. Often, our families would come over and look on with much enjoyment. We would have dinner in the middle of the day together. We did this twice a week and on those glorious days we would spend the entire afternoon in ball play. We were all mature men and in business, but we didn't have too much of it as they do nowadays. There was none of that hurry and worry so characteristic of the present New York. We enjoyed life and didn't wear out so fast."

"I haven't the foggiest idea what he's talking about; he looks plenty worn out to me!" Cartwright poked.

"Oh shush," Adams reprimanded. "You should write that down, William. It's very poetic. Perhaps *The San Francisco Daily Examiner* would be obliged to put it in print."

"Perhaps," Wheaton answered. "Gene, did you know Adams here was the one responsible for creating the shortstop position?"

Before Gene could even answer, Adams said, "Yes, apparently that's always more impressive than the fact that I am a graduate of Yale University and Harvard Medical School."

Cartwright butted in, "He was our team's president six times, and our vice president, treasurer, or director in six other years."

Gene took it all in. It was dizzying and surreal to be the fourth person in this gathering. He didn't know what to say half the time nor did he even feel the need to speak. He instead wished to act like a sponge and soak up what these trailblazers were saying. "Those are quite the accomplishments," he remarked.

"Oh that's nothing," assured Wheaton. "Adams literally authored The Laws of Base Ball."

"Those were just logistics," Adams said. "Things like bat and ball sizes, a ban on betting by players and umpires...you know, things of that nature."

"He's being modest," Wheaton pointed out. "It's because of Adams here that we have nine-man teams and nine-inning games. He finally got rid of that awful bound rule that allowed for balls to be caught after one bounce and be recorded as outs. He was, by the way, the one who put the field's bases ninety feet apart from one another."

"The dimensions are still ninety feet apart," said Gene, rather enthusiastically.

"To think," said Adams. "All this started from a simple desire to get some exercise. Amazing isn't it?"

"Don't let these men fool you, Gene," Cartwright added. "They get all the credit for the 1857 Laws of Base Ball that established the rules of the game but that is simply because I had already moved here and could not partake in the festivities!"

"Would a little trip back home have hurt so much?" jabbed Adams.

"I'll have you know that during that time I was serving as the fire chief of Honolulu!"

"An important position, no doubt," said Wheaton calmingly.

"What position did you play in college, Gene?" Adams asked.

"Mostly first base."

"I played a little first as well, "Adams said. "Actually the only position I never attempted was pitcher."

"As a lawyer and politician I can only surmise that he didn't want to be held responsible for every pitch," Wheaton prodded.

"Is there any baseball here? In Hawaii?" Gene asked, turning to Cartwright.

Alexander fixed himself in his chair and answered, "1860. The Punahou Boys faced off against the Town Boys on Sheriff Brown's property. It reminded me of our younger years actually. They were a bunch of merchants and clerks."

"Was that the first game of baseball played here?" asked Wheaton.

"Who knows? One thing the game is good at is infiltrating itself between the cracks."

"Did you set that game up?" asked Gene.

"God no! I already don't get enough credit in New York, you think I'm going to do it all over again here!?"

They all snickered as Adams shook his head. Gene leaned back in his chair, taking in their antics. He made sure to take a mental snapshot of the moment, as he perceived it to be a once-in-a-lifetime opportunity.

As, indeed, it was.

Durante stayed in Hawaii for a bit, some say a couple of years but one can't be too sure. It was even said Cartwright helped him get a job at a local fire department during his stay. Not much is known regarding what happened during this period but it is known that in the 1880's, Gene returned to the United States and settled in New York. He accepted a job at Columbia University under the condition that he would be the head coach of their baseball team. Gene often suspected they wanted his baseball experience far more than his teaching abilities, a possibility that never bothered him in the least.

It was during this time that Gene witnessed the founding of teams like the New York Giants, who for their first two years went by the classic name New York Gothams, and the Brooklyn Dodgers. The National League was founded in February of 1876 in Manhattan and Gene considered himself to be in the epicenter of modern baseball.

Gene's knowledge and experiences were invaluable assets to his young American players. His run got off to a promising start but by 1888, Columbia's baseball team went 7-12-1. The tie came when they played against Wesleyan—neither team scored.

Still, the name Gene Durante became known amongst like-minded circles. In April of 1889 he was invited to the biggest affair of his life.

The banquet took place at Delmonico's, a restaurant on Fifth Avenue and 26th street that was considered one of New York's most elegant establishments. The cause for celebration:

to honor a group of ballplayers just returning from a world tour that took them to the Sandwich Islands of Hawaii, Australia, Ceylon, Egypt, Italy, France, and England, before returning to New York. Albert Goodwill Spalding, who was currently both the president of the Chicago National League Club and the owner of his lucrative sporting goods company, led the tour.

The celebration was a grand one with over two hundred and fifty people in attendance. Gene hated grandiose gatherings but his baseball and experiences in Hawaii had allowed him to make the cut. He was surprised anyone even knew who he was.

"I understand you were in Japan?" Spalding said as he approached Gene.

"Yes, sir. I was."

"I wish I could have gotten out there with the tour but the logistics of ocean passenger transport made it near impossible. I actually have a friend over there, a Japanese fellow, who has also played a vital role in developing the game in Japan. The two of you did, and I'm sure are still doing, great things. Any time I can sell more equipment, well, let's just say I'm a happy man. But make no mistake about it—I lost money on this tour! But the mission was accomplished nonetheless. We projected a more expansive American presence in the world. And you can't put a price on that!" Spalding noticed another group of people. "You'll excuse me!"

Off Spalding went, not even allowing Gene the opportunity of a formal introduction. Durante wondered what he was like in his younger days. He maneuvered his way over to a drink table where he picked up a glass of champagne.

"I hate these things."

Gene turned to see a dapper man with a trimmed mustache. He sported glasses without earpieces that pinched the bridge of his nose.

"Gatherings?" Gene clarified.

"Yes."

"I take it you're not originally from here, then? New York seems to be synonymous with large gatherings."

"I was born at 28 East 20th Street, my friend. New York is in my blood. But I also left it as I think most people should do for at least a time."

Gene, intrigued by the man, asked, "Where did you go?"

"I went to the Dakota Territory in '83 to hunt bison. Loved it so much I built a ranch there a year later. I must say, there's nothing quite like hunting on the banks of the Little Missouri. Have you ever been?"

"I have not," Gene admitted, fascinated by the man's vocal prowess.

"Spent three years there and then came back here, ran for the mayor of New York City, which I knew by the way was near impossible. I lost. I admit that. But I don't complain about it because complaining about a problem without proposing a solution is called whining. I've always said that. Perhaps I made some campaigning mistakes. But you know what, the only man who never makes mistakes is the man who never does anything."

"Wise words. I don't think I've ever met a New York cowboy politician."

"Don't forget former New York City Police Commissioner! However, I've decided to dedicate my time right now to writing. Last year I started a book, I'm calling it The Winning of the West. Naturally, it traces the history of the conquest of the American West."

"Naturally. Is there anything you don't do?"

"I try to do it all. Especially the things I am not particularly good at. Work hard at work worth doing."

"What do you do recreationally?"

"Boxing, tennis, hiking, rowing, polo, and horseback riding." The unreserved man smiled at his answer as the chairman began to make his introduction. "I think a speech is about to happen. Do you know the guest speaker? I respect him but sometimes I would like to skin him alive. You know what I mean?"

Gene was befuddled by the juxtaposition.

The man put out his hand. "A pleasure to meet you, Mister—"

"Gene Durante."

They shook hands as the man reciprocated, "Theodore Roosevelt."

Gene turned his attention to the stage where a guest speaker made his way center stage. He recognized him immediately. The man with a bushy mustache and an unruly whitened head of hair was the same man who wrote the novels *The Adventures of Tom Sawyer* and *Adventures of Huckleberry Finn*. Gene had read both, the latter being the more prominent of the two. Admittedly, he never really understood the acclaim.

Samuel Clemens, popularly known as Mark Twain, had twinkles in his merry eyes as his greatest ability, his weapon of words, was about to discharge.

"Though not a native, as intimated by the chairman, I have visited, a great many years ago, the Sandwich Islands—that peaceful land, that beautiful land, that far-off home of profound repose, and soft indolence, and dreamy solitude, where life is one long slumbrous Sabbath, the climate one long delicious summer day, and the good that die experience no change, for they but fall asleep in one heaven and wake up in another."

Gene knew immediately that this was going to be one of those long-winded speeches. He looked across the room to notice Roosevelt clearly feeling the same.

"And these boys have played base ball there! Base ball, which is the very symbol, the outward and visible expression of the drive, and push, and rush and struggle of the raging, tearing, booming nineteenth century! One cannot realize it, the place and the fact are so incongruous; it's like interrupting a funeral with a circus. Why, there's no legitimate point of contact, no possible kinship, between base ball and the Sandwich Islands; base ball is all fact, the Islands all sentiment. In base ball you've got to do everything just right, or you don't get there; in the islands you've got to do everything just wrong, or you can't stay there. You do it wrong to get it right, for if you do it right you get it wrong. There isn't a way to get it right, but to do it wrong, and the wronger you do it the righter it is. The natives illustrate this every day. They never mount a horse from the larboard side, they always mount him from the starboard; on the other hand, they never milk a cow on the starboard side, they always milk her on the larboard; it's why you see so many short people there—they've got their heads kicked off!"

Gene wondered how Mark Twain couldn't have known that the game was indeed played there before the tour; it wasn't as incongruous as he made it out to be. Gene listened as Twain droned on; that was only about a quarter of his speech.

Twain eventually concluded, "That is a service to sentiment; but they did the general world a practical service—a service to the great science of geography. Ah! Think of that! We don't talk enough about that—don't give it its value. Why, when these boys started out you couldn't see the equator at all; you could walk right over it and never know it was there. That is the kind of equator it was. Such an equator as that isn't any use to anybody; as for me, I would rather not have any equator at all than a dim thing like that, that you can't see. But that is all fixed now; you can see it now; you can't run over it now and not know it's there. And so I drink long life to the boys who ploughed a new equator round the globe, stealing bases on their bellies!"

The guests all toasted and cheered, complicit in the idea that baseball in the Hawaiian Islands or elsewhere had to be such an unlikely feat that any group who accomplished the deed should be celebrated.

Gene watched as Samuel Clemens made his rounds, shaking hands and making small talk. Eventually, they locked eyes. The American writer made his way towards Gene.

"I'm told you're the baseball coach from Japan who now teaches here in New York."

"I am," Gene answered unenthusiastically. "I also spent some time on the Hawaiian islands with Andrew Cartwright."

Twain's lip curled up into an insightful smirk. He grabbed Gene's hand to shake it and advanced himself up to his eardrum as if to surreptitiously drop truth itself into Gene's mind.

He whispered, "The human race has one really effective weapon, and that is laughter."

Twain patted Gene on the back and dispersed into the crowd. Durante stood still, choosing not to look back; instead he contemplated the magnitude of the evening. Was Mark Twain, the humorist, taking a jab at the very players he was honoring? Was it all an inside joke as they both knew the players had encountered several baseball-playing communities while abroad? Gene was perplexed to say the least.

Over the next few years, Durante watched Columbia's baseball team collapse and continue their losing ways. He also, however, watched the continual growth of American baseball.

He witnessed Rube Waddell pitch both games of a doubleheader for Milwaukee of the Western League. In game one, Waddell threw 17 innings in a 2-1 victory. His skipper Connie Mack promised him three days off to go fishing if he pitched the nightcap. In game two he took a one-hitter into the fifth inning and his team won 1-0 in a game shortened to five innings so that the Brewers could catch a train. He pitched a total of 22 innings in one day.

Gene was aghast when the Reds' captain Tommy Corcoran discovered a metal container under the third base coaching box, hiding an electrical device attached with wires in one of the earliest examples of sophisticated sign stealing.

He observed the evolving regulations as The National League Rules Committee decreed that all foul balls were to count as strike balls, except after two strikes.

On January 28, 1901, in Milwaukee, Wisconsin, he read how The American League of Professional Baseball Clubs formed.

He caught wind when Jimmy Hart of the Baltimore Orioles punched umpire John Haskell in the face.

And in 1903, he watched Jimmy Sebring take Cy Young deep, to become the first player to hit a home run in the first modern World Series. The Boston Americans went on to defeat the Pittsburgh Pirates, winning the series five games to three.

Gene Durante also experienced a new personal relationship bloom. He had been courting a fellow teacher at Columbia, and much to his pleasure, Florentia Ludwig, had taken an equal liking to him. The time they spent together made Gene feel something he had not felt in a very long time: the exciting passions of yearning and tenderness. He felt love.

Gene also learned that his friend William was visiting Boston. He thought he would make a weekend getaway of it to catch up with his former mentor. Gene hadn't seen William since that day on the bench where the older of the two announced he would be returning to America. Gene also wanted to take the opportunity to face his biggest fear: returning to the place he abandoned simply because he couldn't stand to face its reality. He was going to mourn; he was finally going to allow himself to grieve. Since abandoning his birthplace, he had grown strong and resilient and proved to himself that he could do anything on his own. Because of this, he was ready for companionship on the romantic level. He wanted to get married and couldn't wait to tell his friend William of the plan he had to propose.

While walking down the streets of New York City, on the way to the train, Gene noticed a man creeping out of the shadows of an alleyway. He heard the shot but didn't truly feel it at first. As he dropped to the concrete, blood infiltrating his white shirt, his mugger picked his pockets while unceasingly apologizing. Disoriented, Gene watched the attacker dart away.

He knew at the moment that he was going to die on that street. He found it odd that his thoughts weren't encompassed with images or memories of Florentia. Nor were they of William or John. Neither Valerie nor Rikuto. It certainly wasn't of Cartwright, Doc Adams, or Wheaton either. His last thoughts weren't even that of his mother.

Instead Gene recalled the fastball he was ready for, the one where he swung and connected.

The noise of the barrel meeting the ball rang out as the small spherical object sailed off into the azure sky.

The onlookers all stood in bewilderment. Gene stood too, in momentary disbelief. If there had been a fence, it would have gone over it, to the other side.

The pitcher followed the ball until he couldn't even see it anymore. At that point he just turned around to look at Gene, who had just blasted his best pitch into oblivion.

Gene started trotting and eventually picked up speed as he rounded the bases. The outfielders ran after the ball but had such a long distance to go that Gene was in no danger of being caught. He casually made his way home as the spectators cheered for him. He touched home plate and jogged over to his team's bench.

His teammates all congratulated him by patting his head or his shoulders. The cheering was uproarious, even more so than the moments before, far more vociferous than it actually had been those years ago. The cheering ascended, reaching a voluminous apex. And then, as if a film projector had tailed out, there was timeless silence.

Florentia Ludwig hadn't known she was pregnant when Gene Durante was shot and killed. Despite a successful childbirth, she hemorrhaged and died in the hospital. When the doctors asked, in her final moments, what she wished to name the child, the name that she had planned suddenly disappeared from memory. Instead, she could only remember how Gene once read her a poem.

The outlook wasn't brilliant for the Mudville nine that day;
the score stood four to two, with but one inning more to play.
And then when Cooney died at first, and Barrows did the same,
a sickly silence fell upon the patrons of the game.
A straggling few got up to go in deep despair. The rest
clung to that hope which springs eternal in the human breast;
they thought, if only Casey could get but a whack at that—
they'd put up even money, now, with Casey at the bat.

And so that's what she said.

"Casey."

It was in the hope that he too would get a chance to take a whack at life, to step up to the plate despite times being hard.

Casey at the Bat: A Ballad of the Republic Sung in the Year 1888. That was the full name of it. She recalled Gene saying that as she lay on his stomach.

"Casey Durante," she concluded.

Her newborn's name proved to be her last words.

Chapter 10

Degeneration of Man

"Our grandparents might have met!" Yuujin gasped.

Eugene couldn't help but smirk and shake his head at the enthusiasm.

"Doubt it," he retorted. "The world is an awfully big place."

"For as big as it is, it's also small. Our meeting has proved this."

"Maybe."

As Eugene said this, he suddenly became fixated on Yuujin's bruise once again. He was attempting to understand why; he had seen inhumane death and utter brutality in the war. He himself had killed. But this bruise was nevertheless disturbing him. He had been taking notice as the capillaries damaged by trauma, which caused localized bleeding into the surrounding tissue, had slowly formed on the face of the man. He supposed that was the thing about bruises; they were never very deep under the skin. That's why the bleeding caused visible discoloration. Healing would have to inevitably wait, as its only cure was time. It would wait until tissues absorbed the blood. Until that time, however, it was a reminder of that trauma.

"Eugene?" Yuujin's tone broke the trance.

"What?" he barked.

"Are you okay?"

Eugene nodded as the irony of that question bothered him endlessly. The prisoner of war was asking his oppressor if he was okay.

War was an endless fever dream, a succession of battles described best as intense and confusing. The twisted absurdity of it all rested in the fact that Eugene's heart told him all of this was justifiable. If there was ever a war that should be fought, this seemed like the one. He wondered, however, how many soldiers thought the exact same notion in previous armed conflicts.

Eugene wanted to apologize to Yuujin for striking him over a baseball team but there was something deep down, an internal reprimand, which began to override his desire.

He didn't like how he felt. He perceived himself dirty, a spoke in the wheel of subjugation. Fighting for the freedom of others would surely always have its bystanders, innocent or not, soldier or civilian. Was this simply a hard pill that needed to be swallowed?

Eugene suddenly recalled a poster he had seen one day on his way to play ball. It boldly sprawled the words **THIS IS THE ENEMY** on it while a drawing of a nefarious looking Japanese police officer carrying a dead naked Caucasian-looking woman over his shoulder was in full, colorized view. He remembered thinking the illustrated man looked like a rat, a vermin in uniform. His body language was more reminiscent of a gorilla than a person as he walked in a hulking, brutish manner. It suddenly clicked: that was the point. He was supposed to look savage. He was supposed to look bloodthirsty. He was supposed to look subhuman.

Eugene looked down at Yuujin. He saw none of those traits.

He gathered that this is what people did before they went to war against other people—they dehumanized them. In his case, he had watched it happen in real time and had fallen victim to its powerful persuasion.

Eugene pondered if one could ever truly do one's job in warfare while disbelieving the deliberate spreading of skewed information. He hoped so.

A reevaluation of morals was transpiring.

"This whole thing seems screwy sometimes, doesn't it?"

"Screwy?" Yuujin questioned.

"Ridiculous. Laughable. Unreasonable. Pick one."

"What does?"

"I don't know. Right and wrong; good and evil."

"Good is everything that is helpful, and bad is everything that is harmful."

"I don't think it's that simple. People take whatever is useful and convince others that it's good. We can justify anything as being good."

"So consequence is the key, you would say? Something has value, or doesn't, based on its outcomes?"

"You're getting too out there for me. I'm not as smart as you think I am. I'm a soldier. To me, to be good is to be noble. It's to be strong. To be powerful."

"And so you would say being bad is to be weak and cowardly? Timid and petty?"

Eugene began pacing and shaking his head, clearly in disagreement with his own analysis. "I come from the land of the free and the home of the brave. Do you understand what that means? There are people right now, Jewish people in Germany, enslaved as we speak in labor camps. That would continue if your side wins, by the way. And you might be next. Is it not noble to stop that?"

"It is."

"So you're fighting for the wrong side!"

"Your government knew about the camps before you entered the war. You were neutral. You entered this conflict because we attacked you. Not because of right and wrong."

"I don't control my government. None of us do. But I know my small part here is for the good of this world."

"I would agree."

"So why are you in that goddamn uniform!?"

"Our people, our governments, do not view freedom in the same way. Your democracy is captivated by the ideas of freedom and equality. The same desire as any slave. Perhaps by making everyone equal, you are making everyone a slave."

"Bullshit. What about you? How do you fit into all of this?"

"I am aware I have been a captive long before being a prisoner of war."

Eugene kicked over a small fractured stone.

"You're angry," Yuujin remarked.

"No shit. So what? Right and wrong is always inseparable from cultural values? Is that what you're saying? Again, it seems screwy."

"I guess it all comes down to this: do we judge people's actions as good or bad or do we judge people based on their intentions?"

"At the end of day, it doesn't even matter. We all go around and around, like we're all in some big blender trying to avoid the blades. Sooner or later though, we all get cut."

Yuujin thought about this before saying, "I think I am helping to break the mold right now."

Eugene looked at him skeptically before asking, "How so?"

"Right now, you are my oppressor. But I do not vilify you. I should be pessimistic and cynical. I should hate you. But I do not. To you, the capture of Japanese soldiers is a good thing. It is not good for my people or me. Still, I have no contempt for you or your people."

"Well, aren't you just a ray of sunshine."

"American sarcasm?"

"Yes."

"Ironic jokes. So odd."

"You don't have that?"

"We do, but it's different. My people would think you are talking literally."

"Never mind that, what is your point?"

"Revise our morals when needed. I think that's how we get through this."

"I think I'm done with this conversation."

The two remained awkwardly silent.

Eugene gazed out at nothing in particular, perhaps trying to make sense of the nonsensical world before him.

Yuujin focused on the collective remains that not so long ago formed a formidable palace. He felt consoled by the idea that if these tiny, insignificant wreckages were once again bonded, each piece of rubble would again have purpose and a function; beauty could be restored. He found it an interesting way to look at the world. Yuujin peered up to see Eugene, standing there a whole body with emotional shards shattered into oblivion. He too could be made whole. The entire world could in Yuujin's eyes.

"I met Joe DiMaggio once," uttered Eugene in nothing more than a whispered peep.

"Tell me," Yuujin quickly urged.

"In '43 I voluntarily joined the military. I guess I was influenced by Roosevelt's proclamation that suggested baseball should not suspend play during the war. And so I became a member of the Army's varsity baseball team to raise funds for the war effort and boost morale."

"You're a ball player?"

"Not a professional one. Anyway, he was stationed for a time at Atlantic City and was a physical education instructor. He also played ball for military teams and one day the team I was on played the team he was on."

"Did you meet him?"

Eugene thought for a moment as if recalling the encounter in real time before answering, "Yeah. I met him. One hell of a guy."

"You met Joltin' Joe!?"

"Ha! You know about that nickname? Yes, sir. Shook his hand and everything. The Yankee Clipper was everything you would imagine him to be and more."

"You are a baseball player and you met Joe DiMaggio. They should give you special privileges to keep you safe."

"That'll be the day," Eugene said under his breath.

"I was there, you know," Yuujin said vaguely.

"Where?"

"Tokyo in 1934."

Confused, and with a smidge of attitude, Eugene asked, "Am I supposed to know what that means?"

"That was the year the United States' baseball team played the Japanese baseball team. I was nine years old."

"You were at one of the games?"

"No. I was in the street as the American ballplayers made their way through town. The crowd was so big it was a mob. Five-hundred thousand people. "

Eugene's countenance was one of awe as he was barely able to spit out, "The All-Americans. That's what they called themselves. Right? The name of the team?"

"That's right. They were both tourists and ambassadors of good will. But most of all, they were ball players."

"Did you see any of them?"

"Yes. All of them. Lou Gehrig waved to me. Lefty Gomez smiled. Jimmie Foxx shook my hand. And of course—"

"—Babe Ruth!?"

"Yes. He was there, too."

"You saw Babe Ruth?"

"Yes."

"Did he talk to you? Wave? Did he acknowledge you in any way?"

"He winked," Yuujin answered.

"At you? He winked at you?"

"Yes."

"Are you sure?"

"Of course I am sure."

"It wasn't the person standing next to you? It was you?"

"It was to me."

"Holy shit! The Sultan of Swat winked at you. Do you realize what this means?"

"No. What does this mean?"

"I don't know, but it means something."

Yuujin smiled before continuing, "It gets better."

"It doesn't get better than having The Great Bambino wink at you."

"My sister, Sakura, was selected as one of the most beautiful waitresses in all of Tokyo."

"What does this have to do with Babe Ruth?"

"She was brought to the Garden Party of Marquis Okuma, the honorary president of Japanese baseball, to serve the American and Japanese baseball teams luncheon on the second day of their tour."

"Is that right?"

"Yes. She saw all of them."

"I'll be damned."

"I was very jealous of this."

"I would be too."

"But when my sister came home, she gave me a gift. It is my greatest possession."

"It's not."

"It is. A baseball."

"Autographed."

"By the entire All Americans baseball team."

Eugene flipped out and began stutteringly walking back and forth with no intention, his hands clasped onto his head. When he composed himself, he darted closer to Yuujin.

"You're telling me, you have a baseball signed by Babe Ruth and Lou Gehrig?"

"And Earl Averill, Charlie Gehringer, Connie Mack, Moe Berg and everyone else on the team."

"All on the same baseball."

"Yes."

He looked at the Japanese soldier in shock before coming to a revelation. "You're worth a fortune."

"I will never sell it."

"I wouldn't, either. I'd ask to be buried in the grave with the friggin' thing."

"The tour was very popular in Japan. The Americans played a total of eighteen games against the All-Nippon team."

"Was that like a Japanese all-star team?"

"Yes. It was all of our best players at the time. Tens of thousands of fans watched those games in arenas such as Meiji Jingu Stadium in Tokyo, Koshien Stadium in Kobe, and Yagiyama Baseball Field in Sendai."

"I'm guessing the Americans kicked ass," Eugene said confidently.

"They won all eighteen games."

"How did Ruth do?"

"Fourteen home runs."

"Wow. Legendary."

"The Japanese say, every time Babe Ruth came to bat, fans would wave both Japanese and American flags."

Eugene shook his head, dismayed, before saying, "That's crazy to think about now, isn't it? Since we're out here killing each other."

"Many people, only a few years ago, believed two nations who shared the game of baseball could never be true enemies."

"How wrong they were."

"Were they?"

The two men bored into each other, their eyes fixated on the others'. Much was said in the muted exchange and an understanding was wordlessly forged. Eugene looked away, breaking the spell. He asked, "What happened to that Japanese team?"

"They stayed together after the tour and formed the country's first professional baseball team at the end of that year. They called themselves the Great Tokyo baseball club."

"Not a bad name."

"The Japanese team traveled to the United States in 1935, playing against amateur, college, and Minor League teams."

"Good for them."

"The next year, they changed their name to the Tokyo Giants."

Eugene remembered this name. "Your favorite team."

"Yes. My favorite team."

Eugene smirked and said, "Who knows, maybe one day your favorite team and my favorite team will play each other."

"Maybe we will both be in the stands."

"Maybe."

Suddenly, they heard an approaching jeep. Eugene looked out to see the olive drab-colored Willys MB motoring towards them.

He stepped towards the vehicle that contained two men inside, the driver and a soldier in the backseat.

"Glad to see you guys looking so well!" the driver stated.

Before Eugene could speak, Lieutenant. Colonel Richard P. Ross stepped into his view and answered, "Same goes for you. You here for the POW?"

"Yes, sir."

"Good."

Ross turned to Eugene.

"Private First Class Durante—get the prisoner."

The driver looked and remarked, "Hey! Is that Eugene the Jeep? Good kid, that one."

"We like him just fine," Ross replied.

At first, Eugene didn't compute what was asked of him. A second later, he realized they were talking about the man he had been conversing with since taking the castle. He was a prisoner of war despite everything they had been through in that small amount of time. He could only conclude that in war, time worked differently.

"Yes, sir," he finally responded.

Eugene marched towards his Japanese hostage. His stomach twisted and turned and his legs felt rickety and unbalanced.

"Get up," he ordered.

Yuujin stood. "They are taking me away."

"Yes."

"I see. It is time. Thank you."

Eugene nodded and grabbed the captive's arm.

He whispered, "What's your name?"

"Yuujin. Yuujin Miyano."

"Eugene Durante. It was a pleasure to meet you."

He walked Yuujin towards the jeep, recalling their conversation about performances in the theater of war. If no one could tell that Eugene was frightened and acting in a way that every fiber of his being screamed was wrong, he deserved an Academy Award.

"He's a docile one. He won't give you any trouble," Eugene declared.

"Good to know," the soldier in the backseat answered. The soldier turned to Yuujin, who sat in the passenger seat, and added, "Doesn't mean this gun won't be pointed at your head for the entire ride to camp. Got that?"

The POW nodded and Eugene wondered if he would be judged by his intention to keep the Japanese soldier as safe as possible.

Yuujin wondered if Eugene would be disconcerted that he had decided not to look at his acquaintance again, for the American's own safety.

"He speaks some English too," Eugene said. "In case you need a translator in the camp."

"Thanks for the Intel," said the driver as he turned the wheel and pressed down on the jeep's accelerator.

And just like that, the two American soldiers drove off with their prisoner. Eugene watched the vehicle speed away until he felt a consoling pat on his shoulder. He looked to see his friend Loughran, who subsequently gave him a small but compelling nod before walking away.

Eugene turned to look at the destruction of Shuri Castle. In some odd way, he felt it was all that he had left of the man named Yuujin.

To Durante, their discourse was both eye-opening and much needed. But alas the scholarly and philosophical musings, which served as a great distraction, were over.

Eugene inspected his weapon, double-checked that it was properly loaded, and made his way towards Loughran and the other soldiers.

It was time to go back to war.

Chapter 11

Repatriation

On August 6th, 1945, the United States dropped an Atomic Bomb on Hiroshima. Three days later, on August 9th, they dropped a second on Nagasaki.

Japan subsequently surrendered on August 15th, 1945. The Japanese Instrument of Surrender documents were signed at Tokyo Bay on the deck of the American battleship USS Missouri on September 2nd, 1945, officially ending both World War II and the Second Sino-Japanese War.

The ship to Tokyo was cramped and smelled like rot and brine, sweat and infection. Many of the former prisoners had bathed in water before departing Okinawa, yet they still felt soiled and unclean. Yuujin surmised this was a commonality among most who were bound by battle.

He noticed many of the former soldiers clasped tightly onto urns as they bore the ashes of their fallen friends who died during imprisonment.

Japan was in full view. Yuujin had imagined what he would do first upon his return many times while in the POW camp. The first thought that came to mind was gyoza, the delicious Japanese dumpling that would often be stuffed with ground pork, cabbage, soy sauce, shiitake mushrooms, scallions, garlic, and ginger. He fantasized about their golden brown outsides, crisp when bitten into, and the warm juiciness inside. It was home, wrapped and pan-fried.

That's when he realized he should probably visit his family first.

The ship docked as eager passengers shuffled about in anticipation of disembarking. The boarding ramp descended and the gate opened. The men started to ardently depart.

Yuujin waited patiently, taking in the sights of those taking the steps from captivity to freedom by merely traversing over a narrow metal bridge. He thought back on his conversation with Eugene, about slavery and independence.

Yuujin stepped onto the ramp and crossed over, stepping foot on mainland Japan for the first time in a long time. He breathed in the tar-scented port air. He had never appreciated that smell before but he welcomed it now. It was time to go home.

His family home was just as he remembered it. The style was called *Kura-zukuri*, the traditional Japanese-looking exterior was present but it was made from more modern fire-resistant materials. His father had once told him that houses like these combined foreign culture with the type of house preferred by the samurai not so long ago.

Yuujin knocked, preparing himself for his return. He knew his presence would bring great joy to his family. He missed them dearly.

Yuujin knocked again in excitement, this time a little harder. He found himself smiling bigger than he ever remembered smiling. He placed his ear to the door. He heard nothing.

He stepped back and looked up towards the second floor. The house seemed as if it were in slumber. He looked around for familiar neighbors but found none currently outside.

Yuujin presumed they had all gone out. His welcoming would have to wait.

Two kimono-clad women wandered past Yuujin as he walked through the market stalls of an entertainment district. He turned to gaze at them and they did the same. He had almost forgotten what the face of a woman looked like.

He did not, however, forget the sight and smell of *gyoza*. He devoured the small rounded masses of steamed stuffed dough without even sitting.

Cars motored by and masses of people, mostly men in suits, scurried about. Bike riders sped by and buses soon followed. The streets were wide and people crossed them as vehicles hurried by, coming inches away from one another.

Some vehicles seemed out of place, however. It took Yuujin a moment to realize why but it soon came to him. The drab olive-colored jeeps, similar to the one that bustled him away from Eugene, were seemingly everywhere. American soldiers occupied Japan.

Yuujin was not sure why he didn't expect to see this, as he knew it inevitable. Nevertheless, the sight was surprising.

The recently dismissed prisoner of war made his way to the one spot that he knew would cheer him up: Korakuen Stadium, the home of the Tokyo Giants.

The field was not as he remembered it; the stadium was stockpiled with unexploded ammunition. Yuujin's heart skipped a beat at the combined sight of his favorite pastime melded with his greatest nightmare—all that was good merged with all that was bad. It made sense from a logical standpoint, he reasoned, as the stadium was sufficiently big and therefore a good place for storage, but the unexpectedness of it proved jarring.

He suddenly heard the innocent sounds of merriment and turned to see a few young Japanese boys rolling a ball to one another. It was a baseball. They were off in a corner that was not enshrined with projectiles for weaponry. They were smiling. They were happy. They were playing.

It made Yuujin feel as if hope was still alive and well.

"Clear all this out!" a loud bark resonated.

Yuujin turned to see a number of American soldiers enter the space. The one in the forefront was tall and trim, his presence undeniably powerful. His beige uniform blended in with the dirt of the stadium yet the man himself did not blend in at all. In fact it was quite the opposite; he stood out. A corncob pipe dangled from his mouth as he advanced on the territory.

"All of it!" the man continued. "It's time to reopen."

Yuujin walked towards the man and as he did, the American took notice.

"Will baseball resume soon?" Yuujin asked.

The man looked Yuujin up and down and responded, "Yes. I'm ordering this field to be cleared out immediately and I'm urging all of you to start playing baseball again. It's time for the world to turn around once more."

Yuujin felt a strange comfort in the man's strict tone.

"Were you a soldier?" the man asked.

"Yes. In Okinawa."

"You were captured?"

"Yes."

"Our boys treat you all right?"

Yuujin was not expecting the question but answered, "Yes. They were mostly kind."

"Good. You like baseball, I take it?"

"Yes. Very much."

"I used to play ball myself as a cadet at West Point. Fan of the Giants?"

"Very big fan. Eiji Sawamura is my favorite player."

"Is that the guy who struck out both Babe Ruth and Lou Gehrig?"

"Yes!"

"He must have been one hell of a talent to do that. Shame what happened."

Confusion appeared on Yuujin's face, which the American picked up on right away.

"You didn't hear? Last December a Japanese troop ship was torpedoed off the island of Formosa. Your man was on that ship. He was killed."

Yuujin's face plummeted as he muttered, "Killed by the creators of the game he loved."

"It is a cruel irony, no doubt about it. But I've come to think that ballplayers are like soldiers in that way. The old ones never die; they just fade away."

With that, the American marched off, leaving the stadium and Yuujin's field of vision. The words hung heavily as Yuujin contemplated the magnitude of their meaning. An American soldier passed by and asked, "Do you know who you were just talking to?"

Yuujin shook his head.

"That was General Douglas MacArthur."

It was a famous name that Yuujin had heard many times, especially as of late; General MacArthur led the Allied occupation of Japan.

Yuujin again stood in front of his family home. He walked up and knocked. He placed his ear against the door to see if he could hear any rumblings. He did.

The door opened, revealing a woman wearing a Western-inspired dress on the other side.

"Sakura!"

"Yuujin!"

The siblings entered a deep, long bow. They remained this way, in the doorway, for quite some time.

"I've missed you!" Yuujin declared.

"And I you. Come in!"

Yuujin made his way into the house, smiling, as everything seemed familiar.

"I was so worried about you when I found out you were in the camp."

"I'm fine and ready to start anew. Where are our parents?"

It was as if the air in the house vanished; a vacuum drew out both sound and joy. He watched her head descend in sorrow but before it did he saw the answer in her eyes.

"Sakura?"

She drew a deep breath. It was always her way of composing herself. She lifted her head up.

"They went to Hiroshima. To visit their friends."

Yuujin's eyes widened.

"They were going to bring them back here. They thought it would be safer. They never returned."

Yuujin collapsed onto the floor. The weight of the war, the casualties, the endless death, and his collective apprehensions were all set free in an agonizing scream of fear and loss. It was the type of scream one could never truly replicate. It was pain personified.

Sakura rushed over and, breaking with cultural habit, engaged in a rare act. She gripped her baby brother as tears rolled down her face. She knew that scream all too well. She'd heard it often in recent weeks. And she'd released one herself only a little over a month ago.

The two held their consoling embrace far longer than their greeting. Neither wished to let go, for letting go entailed some sort of acceptance; it signaled an emergence into the world of their new reality. And so they sat, clasping one another, for hours on end.

Chapter 12

The Echoing Eye of the Battered Beholder

The large green shrubs were vibrant and damp; the morning dew coupled with the rain from the night before caused water beads to drop from the vegetation onto the already mucky ground. Eugene unconcernedly pushed them aside to advance through the Japanese jungle. The flora had the propensity for beauty as much as it had the inclination to house danger.

"What do you think this place is like when it's not at war?" one soldier asked.

"Still the shithole that you see," another answered.

Eugene said nothing as a few cackled before the first soldier said, "I don't know. I kind of like nature. The landscape is pretty marvelous."

"Maybe. But the people, though. What the hell are you going to do about them?"

Eugene suddenly heard an unusual sound and stopped in his tracks while the soldiers ahead of him continued to advance. It was faint but he was sure it was something. He stared into a gap in the wilderness, transfixed on what he could only describe as a series of collective murmurs. He stepped off the footpath and hesitantly made his way into the abyss of undergrowth, raising his weapon and moving it side-to-side to scan for abnormalities.

"I can't with this guy! Durante, can you please tell him that this is no place to live, let alone vacation."

When no response was given, the patrol looked back to see Eugene was nowhere in sight.

Through the brush, Eugene noticed a bulge of bedrock protruding out of the earth. The whisperings were louder here. Eugene moved slowly and silently, each step deliberately heel first until the remainder of his foot, bit by bit, was secured on the ground.

He circumnavigated the cavernous den in an attempt to locate its entrance. He abruptly made out a weep but it was cut short as if someone suppressed the cry.

Eugene was coming upon the grotto's entrance; he could see it from the angle in which he positioned himself. He took a step to progress and stepped upon a broken branch. The cracking emanated and Eugene froze in his tracks. He slowly removed his foot from the disembodied tree arm and a softer noise echoed as a result.

There was complete silence from the cave. Eugene dared not move, hoping whoever was in that cavity chalked his blunder up to a passing animal. He looked around frantically; he detected no outside danger.

After he felt an appropriate amount of time had passed, Eugene continued to travel towards the mouth of the cave. His gun was at the ready as one foot slowly but continuously stepped in front of the other.

When he was directly in front of the opening, Eugene darted in, placing himself directly in the center of the ingress.

Numerous eyes stared at him. Their faces were mostly in the shadows of the darkness but their optical organs peered and pierced. Almost all of the gazes were fearful and terrified. Eugene knew at once these were not the faces of soldiers but of civilians. He had found a den of families hiding in secrecy.

Eugene stretched his hand out and soothingly said, "It's okay. Let me help you."

They did not budge from their positions.

"I can help you. Please. Surrender and we will keep you safe."

Eugene noticed a specific pair of eyes. The individual was making his way to the front of the group. There was something different about his eyes; they were grievous and grim, indignant and indoctrinated.

Eugene could see him holding something at his mid-section. As the solemn looking man stepped forward, Eugene saw that it was a grenade.

"Now we will die."

Eugene went to scream but nothing came out. Time seemingly slowed, as he was able to observe all the other eyes in the cave. They were more terror-stricken now than when they had first seen him. Almost all of them closed their eyes in their final moment, disallowing Eugene to see into their shivery souls. Even the steadfast man holding the bomb did so.

One pair of eyes, however, remained fixed on Eugene's. He was currently her only connection and presently he could say the same about her. She wasn't scared and perhaps this was what frightened Eugene the most. She had in mere moments reached the acceptance of her fate. Her glossy eyes were mournful for those next to her. They were mournful for all that were killed. They were mournful for the world. And yet, through her dark-colored pupils, there was hope—a hope for a future without her; a hope that others like her wouldn't suffer the same fate; there was even a small hope that the stranger before her would not perish along with her. All of that transmitted itself through nothing more than a sunken twinkle.

Eugene could hear the pin being removed from the grenade. His instinct was to jump back but he knew he could not break his connection with the young girl, the only one with opened eyes; it was all she had left.

His reciprocal stare was one of comprehension and appreciation. A comprehension that he knew there was no escape and an appreciation of her boldness, courage, and heroism for that very understanding. It was all that he could give that felt genuine; anything else would have been a lie.

Just as he could sense a mutual morbid gratefulness, he felt a forceful shove. Eugene was thrust into the air and landed seconds later onto the muddy ground. He looked up to see a fellow soldier. It was the one who kept saying how he hated this place. And then everything exploded.

Eugene awoke, panting and panicking. Sweat covered his body. He felt the bed sheets; they were drenched. He continued to gasp for air until he felt a soothing touch upon his leg.

From under the saturated covers came a voice. "You okay, baby?"

Soon a head popped up, a sight that always made Eugene serene.

"I'm sorry I woke you."

"Don't apologize," she said as she wrapped her arms around his torso. "Talk to me."

"It's fine."

"It's not. Talk to me."

He looked at her. He smiled at her persistence. He always did.

"When I was over there, there was this day where a group of us were sent to patrol up ahead. I heard something. Chatter. I went to investigate. Found a cave with Japanese people hiding in it. Then one man detonated a grenade...."

"Why would he do that?"

"Because they would rather die than surrender. Or at least he would. I suppose he made that decision for all of them." He took a deep sigh and concluded, "I shouldn't have said the word."

"What word?"

"Surrender. I said: surrender and we will keep you safe. That's when he decided to kill us all. I would have been dead, too, if it wasn't for another American soldier who intervened just at that moment. He pushed me out of the way."

A silence settled over him.

"Was he…?" she began.

Eugene sighed, "He lost both legs."

Eugene threw the sheets aside and leapt out of bed. He made his way to their small bathroom and turned on the faucet. He clutched onto the sink counter and dropped his head, the water forcefully running uninterrupted.

Eugene could feel her presence in the doorway.

"Sorry," Eugene said.

"You have nothing to apologize for."

"I'm being selfish. Your brother didn't get to come home."

"And yet the *Chicago Defender* declared that no bomber escorted by a Tuskegee Airman had ever been lost to enemy fire. It seems publicity knows no bounds."

Eugene stared in the mirror, his eyes peering into his own. Without warning, he felt his body being turned; he didn't resist. He found himself cocooned in a loving embrace as his head rested on her shoulder.

"Let me worry about ogling over those eyes."

Eugene felt supreme comfort in her words. He wanted to say so much to her in that moment but could only declare, "I love you, Hattie."

Lucky for him, it was all she ever wanted to hear.

"I love you, too. And you're the least selfish person I've ever met."

Chapter 13

The Burden of Sacrifice

Sakura frantically packed two small containers of rice as Yuujin walked downstairs. He was dressed in old weathered clothes. "Thank you," he said.

"It is just rice. We have to ration our belongings; there's a food shortage."

"Thank you for getting me the factory job."

"They were obliged to help repatriated soldiers."

"Are you okay?"

Sakura stopped what she was doing. It was evident that she was not okay. "I am fine," she answered.

"Sakura." He rarely addressed her by name. She lifted her head to him to meet his gentle gaze. "Talk to me," he urged. "Are you embarrassed about working?"

Judging by her face, he knew he was about to get an earful.

"Embarrassed? Why would I be? Because I am a woman?"

"It has not been our way."

"You don't know what our way has been. You've been gone." This stung Yuujin.

"Do you know why I haven't wed?" Sakura asked.

"No."

"Because I don't want to stop working."

"You don't have to."

"But I would be expected to. I have no interest in subservience or obedience or passiveness."

"You have always worked hard for your family."

"I will always work hard for those I love. But I find it a disgrace that our own government didn't even encourage us to enter the mobilization workforce when the war began out of cultural convention. Convention. I even hate the word itself. It wasn't until two years ago, only after we lost so many men, that women were allowed to work in a factory or join a volunteer labor corp. And here's the disadvantageous point—soon after being allowed, those who were capable, that is, women who were unmarried or able to leave school were required to go to work. We weren't even granted the allowance of choice."

"We are never granted the allowance of choice. Is it still not progress of a kind?"

"It is a double-edged sword. It is both favorable and unfavorable at the same time to work as a woman. Cultural constraints go against the very premise of us working for wages, especially in technological occupations. It is the reason why you, on your first day, will be making far more than me today. And yet I have worked for this company for two years. What happened to modernization? Isn't that what the Meiji Restoration and Taishō democracy was all about?"

Yuujin, emotionally deflated by his sister's passionate assessments, responded, "I am sorry. I did not know about the pay and the factory. By the looks of the streets, I think it's safe to say that we are no longer modernizing but westernizing. For better or worse."

"And what does that mean? We're going to start dropping nuclear bombs on the civilians of other countries?"

"I do not know," Yuujin admitted. "I apologize."

"It is not your fault. I just don't have our father to vent to any longer. I did not mean to take it out on you."

"Before I left, father told me that honor won in youth grows with age. Clearly, he had achieved this. I cannot say the same for myself but I can still try to be that for you. It would be my honor. Let me be your rock. Until, of course, you get a husband and can't work anymore."

Sakura's face turned red with fury as she sent him a glare that would make death tremble. She was greeted with the smile of a sibling attempting to hold back a laugh. His gag cracked her just a bit as she let out a begrudging chuckle through her anger.

Yuujin had treaded a tightrope and lived to see the other side.

Sakura and Yuujin went to work at the electrical factory. Their day was long and repetitive but Yuujin kept thinking how it was better than the battlefield. They used hand tools to wire, solder, insert parts and tubes into products, and provide final tests.

At lunchtime they ate their rice, talked to one another and some of the other workers who Sakura introduced, and soon went back to work.

The second half of the day was identical to the first. Of course, that could be seen as a good thing as no one was hurt on the job that day.

Sakura threw some vegetables in a boiling pot as Yuujin set the table.

"I can cook if you like," Yuujin declared.

"And ruin my soup? I think not," she responded facetiously. "You have some time before it's ready. You can do what you please."

"I was thinking of going through some of father's things."

She peered back at Yuujin and saw the nine-year-old boy she once handed a signed baseball to.

"Of course," Sakura responded.

It had been many years since Yuujin stood in the bedroom of his parents. He almost felt as if he was doing something wrong, betraying their privacy.

A large chest capped by other orderly belongings rested in the corner of their wardrobe. For whatever reason, it caught his eye. Yuujin carefully removed each item to get to the dull trunk that enchanted him. A thick layer of dust perched itself upon the black storage box as Yuujin dragged it out from its resting place.

He did not recall seeing the chest before and wondered what was in it. Yuujin attempted to blow the trunk clean, which he immediately regretted as collective tiny particles formed a cloud in the bedroom.

He unlatched and opened the chest. The very first item, slumbering on top of everything else, was his mother's wedding uchikake, the heavily embroidered kimono. Underneath that was his father's black kimono made from habutae silk that he had fashioned on the same ceremonious night.

Yuujin ran his fingers down the material as if touching his parents once more. He delicately placed the clothing aside and ventured again into the box.

What he saw surprised him—a sports magazine from 1927. On the cover, a tall black ballplayer shook hands with a Japanese ballplayer. With their free hand, they both held the knob of a baseball bat while the ends were secured on the ground. Yuujin gingerly opened the magazine. The American ballplayer on the cover was Biz Mackey and he was a part of a Negro League all-star squad that became the first pro team to play in Japan. Yuujin remembered hearing about this but he didn't recall the actual occurrence; he was two years old when the games were played. Did he attend one of them? Did his father? Why else would he have had the magazine? He did not know.

He flipped the pages to see something truly remarkable: Emperor Hirohito throwing a baseball while black players looked on. Yuujin wondered if any American president had done the same.

He would read the magazine cover to cover very shortly but his curiosity reared yet again. He went back into the chest.

Yuujin pulled out a medal with a crimped bow-like ribbon. It was his father's Yokohama Japan Victory Medal. The award was modest in size but Yuujin felt it was gargantuan. His father rarely spoke of the First World War; Yuujin now understood why.

Yuujin pulled out a series of papers. He recognized the upstanding calligraphy as his father's. He scanned the stationary and quickly realized what he held in his hand was his father's attempt at a memoir. Shocked, as he never heard mention of this, Yuujin excitedly decided to read what he could that evening. It didn't appear very long and was certainly incomplete.

Next was a neatly folded cloth. He slowly unwrapped it and as he did he could make out the circular red sun with the thick, symmetrical, sixteen red beams of symbolic sunrays emanating from it. It was the peace treaty war flag of the Imperial Japanese Army. However, once Yuujin fully unpacked the cloth, he found something curious at its center. In the middle of the stretched out flag, perfectly aligned in the red sun, was a small piece of square paper.

He picked up the napkin and could see a faint drawing on it. It appeared to be a diamond sketched in pencil. At each of the four points, a square was overlaid. Yuujin couldn't understand what it was or why his father had hidden it in an old flag.

"Dinner is ready!" Sakura yelled from downstairs.

"Okay! Thank you!" he answered.

He prudently placed the napkin back onto the flag and determined he would come back to his treasure trove of memories after dinner.

As he got up and walked over to the sports magazine, it suddenly dawned on him: the drawn diamond was a baseball diamond and the squares were bases. It was the crude sketch of a baseball field.

Chapter 14

The Dead Ends of Disillusion

Eugene jolted awake with a piercing scream. The howl cut through the early morning air, causing Hattie to convulse back into consciousness.

"Jesus goddamn Christ!" he said angrily, as if he had the power to control the thoughts, images, and scenarios that passed through his mind as he slept.

Hattie gently rubbed his leg and asked, "The cave dream again?"

"No," he answered. "A new one."

"You want to talk about it?"

"No."

"Maybe it will help if you did?"

"It didn't help when I told you about the cave dream, did it?"

"You haven't had that dream in a while. Maybe it did."

Eugene looked at Hattie with that reluctant glare that proved to be an admission of her correctness. He took a deep breath while swiping away a small puddle that had formed on his forehead.

"I was back at Sugar Loaf. The fight was over already. We'd won the hill. I was walking through the area, patrolling it, looking for survivors. The sky was gray and the landscape was muddy. I mean, beyond muddy; there was literally mud everywhere. But I couldn't see the ground because it was so littered with bodies. American bodies, Japanese bodies. All dead. The worst part was that most bodies weren't even connected. There were arms here, legs there. I walk over an incline and I see a graveyard of heads. All grinning at me like they know something I don't. They're not really heads I guess at this point, more like skulls because all the flesh has rotted away. They start laughing at me. I ask them why. One said, 'What are you doing over there?' Another one said, 'You belong with us!' and a third said, 'Don't worry. Soon enough.' Then they laughed again. That's when I see one I recognize. It's the head of a Japanese prisoner of war I met. His name was Yuujin. He wasn't a skull, he still had his skin, but—" Eugene paused.

"It's okay. You can tell me," she urged.

"Half his face was bruised something awful. This thick dark crimson discoloration."

"Did he say anything?"

"No. Just stared at me in silence while the others laughed around him. He felt broken and disenchanted; the youthful twinkle in his eye seemed long gone. Suddenly the muck turned to quicksand and the skulls began to sink, like they would be lost forever in the sands of time. All except Yuujin's. His was secure on solid ground but his bruise became more and more prevalent on his face. It started overcoming him. And then I woke up."

"Did he die? In real life?"

"I don't know. I don't think so. But I can't be sure."

Hattie was now rubbing his back. Eugene's breathing slowed and was less erratic.

"I don't suppose you want to go back to sleep, do you?" she asked.

"No. I'm going to put a pot of coffee on."

Eugene rolled out of bed and walked towards the kitchen before turning around and beholding his beauty sprawled out. The sheets barely covered her.

"If I could draw, I'd immortalize you. Oil on canvas."

"Is that so?"

"It is."

"Well, you better learn! I'm not going to look this good forever, you know."

Eugene half-grinned and remarked, "I'm not so sure about that. But if you're right, you're lucky I'm a quick learner."

"Is that right? Because you still haven't learned how to make my coffee!"

As Eugene rolled his eyes and headed towards the kitchen, they both simultaneously uttered, "One sugar. Cream. No milk!"

Eugene stepped out into the Harlem streets; it was quiet. He noticed a shop sign in a window. It was a Double-V. A soldier had told him what that meant: double victory—victory over Axis fascism overseas and victory over racism here at home.

During the war, hordes of African Americans migrated out of the South, eager to leave segregation and economic stagnation. Many came here.

Hattie had told him that going to New York was a welcomed farewell to the chain gangs, the cotton fields, and the torturous working hours. She said many viewed the move as something akin to going to a promised land.

Eugene always liked that about New York. It was a place of progress and hope, albeit small progresses and sometimes seemingly fleeting hopes.

Yet Eugene could feel the angst of the Harlem community when he walked down its streets. He didn't comprehend why, not fully, until he asked Hattie about it. She said that many of those who relocated had come face to face with the unfortunate surprise that New York was not the beacon of tolerance they had wished for. Hattie said her people were becoming disillusioned and angry as they realized their new promised land was also deficient. She said without deliverance they would come up against a familiar disappointment and a recognizable anger that their children were sure to inherit. She worried about this.

It seemed to be true, Eugene thought. Many of Harlem's residents were convinced the war effort would benefit their neighborhood in a big way. At the end of the day, however, many were denied entry to factory-level positions. The few jobs that did present themselves were, of course, not only the least desirable and lowest paying, but also the ones offering the least opportunity for advancement.

Hattie, however, did not reflect much of the frustration that was so palpable. She had found an opening in the war industry and was able to get clerical work. Her friends often told her that the only reason she did was because the heads of the company she worked for wanted to prevent contact with their white customers and coworkers in sales positions. But Hattie didn't care either way. She was working and even bought a war bond. Eugene knew there was some truth in what her friends told her and suspected deep down she knew it, too.

When Hattie was down and out, she would deflect the conversation away from herself and instead boast about her older sister who, unlike Hattie, was born down south. She received degrees in education and chemistry and taught at Dillard University. Hattie would say that if her sister could rise to such pre-eminence in the professional world, anyone could. Perhaps it was true.

Eugene felt honored to be with such a woman.

His parents, however, who he was traveling to visit, weren't quite as enthusiastic.

"What's the matter? You don't like bacon and eggs anymore?"

Eugene looked up at his father's semi-serious grin.

"We just sat down." Eugene retorted.

"He's teasing you," his mother, Margret, confirmed as she placed a pitcher of juice on the table.

Casey opened his morning paper while Eugene took a forkful of breakfast. "It's delicious," he remarked.

"Thank you, sweetheart."

From behind the paper, Casey asked, "What do you guys eat over there for breakfast? Bisquick?"

"Sometimes. Sometimes just bacon and eggs. Or cereal. Pretty much what everyone else eats."

"How is Hattie?" asked Margaret.

Eugene could see his father shaking his head from behind his paper.

"She's great," he said.

"Still working in clerical?" asked Casey.

"Yes."

"Good for her," he said. "At least she works."

"Are you being careful over there? I know there's a lot of crime."

"Margaret, our son just defeated the Axis powers, you think some street thugs are going to give him a problem?"

"Still, I worry."

"I'm fine. Honestly. I've never had an issue."

"Your room is always available if you want to move back in, dear."

"I'm fine. Thank you. We're very happy."

"I suppose that's all that matters," Margaret responded with a smile.

Casey took a sip of coffee and said, "A letter came for you."

Eugene's head darted up.

"Where is it?" he asked.

"I told the mailman to take it to Harlem since that's where you want to live now."

"He did not!" Margaret confirmed.

"Is it from..?"

"Yup," Casey confirmed.

"Where is it?"

"You can read it when you're done with your breakfast," his mother said.

"Living room table," his father answered.

Eugene darted up and bee-lined it to the living room. Margaret shot her husband a disapproving look, which he gleefully accepted.

Eugene saw the letter sitting solitarily on the table. He walked over and picked up the flat envelope that held his fate. He opened it and unfolded the letter. In the upper left hand corner rested the team's insignia. The word Dodgers, slightly tilted upwards, in blue script, caught his eye. A red outlined baseball whizzed past the team's name. Under it were the words, also in blue, GAMES AT EBBETS FIELD. To the right, in the center of the paper the letterhead read: BROOKLYN NATIONAL LEAGUE BASEBALL CLUB. Under it, the address: 215 MONTAGUE STREET. BROOKLYN 1. NEW YORK.

And then, of course, there was the letter itself.

Mr. Eugene Durante,
320 W. 54th Street
Unit 2D, N.Y.

Dear Eugene:

It is with great regret that I am writing to inform you The Brooklyn Dodgers have decided to rescind their contract offer due to the unfortunate wounds you incurred during your service. We very much lament having to give you such news after your incredible sacrifice to our beloved nation. I truly hope that you can find your place in this life and I wouldn't completely rule out other avenues of professional baseball just yet; great scouts and coaches are always hard to come by.

Thank you for your talents and for your duty.

Sincerely,

Walter F. O'Malley
Walter F. O'Malley, President

Eugene wasn't totally surprised yet the iota of hope that allowed him to believe he might read something to the contrary festered within him for some time. He put the letter down on the cloth-covered table.

Chin up he reminded himself. The thought of becoming a baseball player was every kid's dream. He found it a bitter pill to swallow to have that chapter of life close, especially because he was good enough before a bullet had entered his body.

For whatever reason, Eugene's mind propelled to a specific memory.

*Eugene looked at the stitched baseball in his hand; the word **Spalding** stamped across the cowhide. The other players were walking off the field but he felt compelled to stay despite having no reason to; the game was over. He looked out into the now empty stands wondering if one day they would be filled while he pitched for a professional team. He imagined their chants and their screams, their encouragements, and their heckles. He could hear the popping of the catcher's mitt after he threw a fastball. He could hear the whiff of a bat that didn't make contact. He could hear the zealous umpire scream, "Strike three!"*

"Do you always stick around to do nothing?"

Eugene, startled, turned around. Standing directly across from him was Joe DiMaggio.

"Mr. DiMaggio," he sputtered.

"You're Durante, right?"

"Yes, sir."

"You don't have to call me, sir. You have a good arm, Durante. And you hustle."

"Thank you."

"You looking to play professionally after the war?"

Eugene chuckled in a blushful sort of way and responded, "That would be a dream come true."

"I think you're good enough. If it was something you were serious about."

"I am!"

"Good. I'll see what I can do. Durante—you Italian?"

"I don't think so. At least my parents aren't."

"Odd. Durante is an Italian name. I think it means to endure or something along those lines. It reminds me of Dante. You know Dante?"

"The guy who wrote about his visit to Hell and his encounter with the Devil?"

"That's the one."

"I never read it."

"I suppose it doesn't matter; they say war is hell anyway." He continued to look at Eugene and said, *"You don't look Italian. Maybe somewhere in your history, though."*

"Now that I think of it, my mother might have mentioned my great-grandfather was Italian."

"No kiddin'? That makes us paisans! We have to look out for each other, kid. Sometimes our religion, some of our darker complexions, and let's be honest, an inability to speak great English make us seem a little unwanted compared to our Anglo Saxon Protestant brothers and sisters. That's why I try my best to conduct myself like a gentleman and role model not only on the field but off of it as well. A positive image is important for Italian-Americans. Hell, it's important for all Americans. You hear what I'm saying?"

"Absolutely, sir."

"How are you liking playing ball here?"

"I love it so far. How has your experience been?"

Joe DiMaggio looked at him, surprised by the question. After a humph, he answered, *"To be honest with you kid, I'm not exactly proud of my role in all of this. I'm living as comfortable a life as a soldier possibly can. Here I am playing ball against Major and Minor league players while others are dying overseas. I don't like it. The special privileges seemed nice at first but I don't know. What am I really doing? Tanning and drinking a lot? I think I'm the only soldier to ever gain weight during wartime."*

Eugene hesitantly asked, "You're not able to ask for a combat assignment?"

"I did. I was turned down. Prewar fame is an odd thing. I'm too valuable to risk yet they have no problem labeling my parents enemy aliens. Funny thing, isn't it?"

"Enemy aliens?"

"Yea. You didn't know? That's what you're labeled if you came from Germany, Japan, or Italy. My parents have to carry a photo ID booklet with them at all times. They're not allowed to travel outside a five-mile radius from their home without a permit. They even seized my pop's fishing boat."

"That's a thing?"

"Could be worse. Some are in internment camps. Imagine that. Confusing time, isn't it?"

"You can say that again."

DiMaggio looked up into the sun and said, "Play hard every day. It's the only way someone will notice you because every day a new person is watching. Always play your best."

"Thank you. I will."

"Keep doing what you're doing. It'll all work out for you. Good talk, kid."

Joltin' Joe turned around when Eugene asked, "Mr. DiMaggio?"

"Yeah?"

"Do you have any other advice for me?"

The ballplayer thought for a moment and then said, "Motivation is something nobody else can give you. Others can help motivate you, but basically it must come from you and it must be a constant desire to do your very best at all times and under any circumstances. That's all I got."

"Thank you."

"My pleasure. See you around."

Eugene wanted to say, "See you, too," but he didn't. He just watched the legend walk away from him until he disappeared in the descending darkness.

"Chin up."

The voice shattered the memory as Eugene found himself transported back into his parents' living room.

"We knew this might happen," his father continued.

"Yeah."

"I'm sorry you've been disillusioned, son."

"I'm not."

"Sure you are. Between your service and this letter, how could you not be?"

"Disillusioned people are bitter."

"Disillusioned people are wiser."

"But not happier."

"That may be true. But it's the most important lesson you can possibly learn."

"What is?"

"Life isn't always how you'd like it to be. And that's okay. You can go through life and you can do everything right and still end up on the bottom. Sometimes that's just the way it is."

"It's not right."

"I know. It's not. But maybe getting rid of those illusions, the ones that trick us into seeing false possibilities, at the end of the day, is a good thing. It lets us focus on what we can do instead of what we can't."

"I guess..."

"I know what you went through was hell. Believe me, I know. Your mother and I are here for you. We always will be."

"Thank you."

They both sat on the old living room chairs.

"You're serious with this girl, aren't you?"

"I am."

"So all that I told you about marrying within your own for your safety and peace of mind meant nothing?"

"I heard you. I just can't help what I feel and what I know."

"What do you know?"

"She's the one."

"Jesus Roosevelt Christ. What are you going to do? For work?"

"I don't know yet."

"Well, if you want a family you're going to have to figure it out."

"I will."

"And I'm not going to a wedding in Harlem so you can get that out of your head."

"I never said—"

"I know you didn't say you were going to get married in Harlem but I'm just telling you now—"

"—that we're going to get married."

Casey looked at his son, confused, and asked, "You love her but you don't want to marry her? She stood by your side while you were overseas and you're not even going to do right by her?"

Eugene always found it odd that his father could somehow have one opinion and then justify a completely contradictory opinion only moments later without ever feeling the least bit insincere.

Eugene answered, "I'm not saying we will never get married. I'm just saying maybe... not right now."

"Well, if you're not getting married, what are you doing?"

"Living life?"

"Son, this is what you do. You get married. You have children."

"I know. We're just not in a rush."

"Marriage is the best institution there is."

"I'm not saying it's not."

"And I'll tell you one thing and I know you don't want to hear it. When you look for a house, do it alone. You know those sons of bitches are going to take one look at Hattie and try to screw you. That's the federal government for ya. You don't believe me, do some research into the Home Owners' Loan Corporation or the Federal Housing Administration. Men like Hattie's brother fought for this country and mark my words, they won't even be able to get a home loan from the bank. Sometimes I think he's better off dead."

That last comment hit Eugene like a punch to the gut.

"This talk is obviously just between us," Casey said quietly. Eugene nodded.

"Whenever you're ready, get out of here. Get out of the city. Go live in the suburbs where the air is clean and people aren't on top of one another like rats in a cage. Do better for yourself. Get a house on a dead end block so you're off a main road, less traffic that way. Elevate your position in this life. Do the things…"

Casey's words trailed off. Then, he repeated them.

"Do the things."

This time he said it concretely as if they were his conclusion.

Eugene knew how his father completed the sentence in his head. *Do the things I could never do.*

There was a solemn silence in the room, as the two veterans reflected on a level most could never discern.

"You'd love her cooking," Eugene eventually said.

Casey looked at Eugene in an ambiguous way. Usually he was always able to tell the next thing out of his father's mouth, but this time he was stumped.

The gaze was both detached and impassive yet also probing. Eugene, however, couldn't tell if it was he who was being probed or if his father was penetrating and inquiring within his own mind, searching and sifting through thoughts.

"I'm sure I would."

Eugene immediately keyed into the word would. Was his father implying that he would indeed enjoy the food on a hypothetical level but would never get the chance because of societal bigotry and his own biased stubbornness?

Eugene did this often; he would dissect words and their emphasis to better understand those around him. It usually ended up superfluous because he rarely reached an objective truth in the words.

The room became quiet as both father and son retreated into their own intricate heads. Suddenly, Margaret popped her head in the room and declared, "There's still some breakfast left if either of you would like some. I can warm up your coffees on the stove."

Eugene and Casey looked at one another as if that was the first thing they both completely and unconditionally agreed upon.

Chapter 15

Memoirs of Keishi

Despite lasting for just under one year, Japan's victory over China over the control of Korea marked the emergence of Japan as a major world power and a force to be reckoned with; this was precisely the cultural environment I was brought up in.

Needless to say, I did not fit into the nationalistic mold of fortitude the way many of my peers did. That being said, I am not including this to reflect on the military and economic strength of our sovereign state. Though I did serve my country during The Great War, the truly important moments of my life took place just after those horrific but justified events. I have no desire to relive the days of battle despite my reservation that I may never truly outrun the dogs of war. My only desire is to relive the days of love and peace. Albeit such words are not commonplace in our society, instead of simply burying them in the eternal abyss of memory, I choose to commemorate them with the written word—the only sincere and individualistic outlet I may yet have.

I returned home a changed but eager man. If it were not for my parents, rational and resourceful dreamers in their own right, I might have succumbed to the depressing dark side of human nature. But alas, I found that my very being pointed towards the light; I wanted to find and explore the benevolence of man, outside of my family, that had eluded my community. I knew it existed because I saw it in the eyes of my parents.

Just before my deployment, I caught the Seattle Asahi, a baseball club composed of first-generation Japanese Americans, as they toured Japan competitively in 1914. Unfortunately, I missed them the second time around, last year, in 1918. If only Germany and the others would have surrendered a few months earlier.

The club was a bridge for me, an access point to an entirely new world; one that my father highly encouraged. He told me of his travels abroad and how such an odyssey helped shape the person he became.

In 1914, well into my medical studies, my father pulled those strings he always seemed to hold, and set up an opportunity where I met all of the players on the Asahi. At first this seemed childish to me as I was practically the same age, in some cases older, than most of these players. When I watched them play, however, and subsequently shook their hands, an American greeting they had adopted, it felt different than expected. I didn't look at them as young men simply playing sports. I saw the future leaders of Japanese society in America. Baseball seemed to serve as a vehicle and the boys appeared to know this.

I recognized then that something grander was occurring. This team acted as a link between the first and second generations of Japanese Americans. I felt as if part of me was outstretched and had the opportunity to place my fingertips on what was dubbed the land of opportunity.

At my father's behest, I showed them around. It was a surreal experience as people who looked just like me explored Japan as if they were tourists, which they indeed were despite being in their ancestral homeland.

I showed them the Itsukushima Shinto shrine, famous for its dramatic floating gate, which I explained we called a *torii*. When

I told them these entrances marked the transition from the mundane to the sacred, they remained respectful but I could tell they thought me superstitious. I was about to go on about how the three deities of Itsukushima Shrine were born when the goddess of the sun and her brother made a pledge on the Celestial Plane, but I hesitated. Would they not care about the jewel and sword used in the tale? I decided to skip to the end where I gave the common conclusion, "Since ancient times, these three have been revered and worshipped as deities that ensure the well-being of the imperial family, guard the nation, and protect seafarers."

I realized then that if these visitors did not look like me, I wouldn't have been embarrassed at all. I would have thought they simply couldn't understand because of cultural differences. But those familiar characteristics staring back at me made a profound difference.

We rode in jinrickshaws, viewed Mt. Fuji from the Gotemba train station, and visited Buddhist temples. I even took them by the newspaper offices of the Mainichi Shimbun and of course, the Shinbashi Railroad.

The students proved wise beyond their years. When I asked one what he liked so much about baseball, he replied, "We use the power of baseball as a way to fight prejudice and combat racist ideologies aimed at stigmatizing immigrants and their families."

And here I thought rounding the bases is what made it all worthwhile.

Looking back, I have to admit my father knew exactly what he was doing by giving me the honor of that exchange. He was opening my eyes to a world I had yet to explore. When the Asahi left, I perceived a never-before-felt void, as if I was supposed to accompany them back so they could show me their land as I had shown them mine. I felt a yearning. And so I planned to leave. But then, of course, Japan entered the war on the side of the Allies and my personal desires were put on hold.

I fought for my country with the seed of sightseeing implanted deep in my mind. In many ways, it kept me going.

I had grown into a man, my mother, Kayda, said upon my return. But my father had grown weary. I suppose year after year of hearing the tragic news that his friend's sons would never be coming home changed him. A worn countenance replaced his once jovial spirit. My father had entered his sixties during the beginning of the war and I remember being shocked to see his fading hair so whitened when I saw him for that first time again.

After the war, I eagerly planned my trip but became dismayed when my father dissuaded me as 1918 had brought into play another factor; there was a pandemic. Influenza was spreading and everyone was rightly concerned, though I was convinced that if a world war wasn't going to kill me, neither would a virus. Besides, I was young and thought myself strong.

There was not an individual on this planet that I respected more than my father. That is why it was so hard having that argument before I left. He pleaded for me to stay. I blustered that I needed to carve my own path. I had decided to go to America and nothing could stop me.

I, however, would not follow in the footsteps of those before me. I wished not to go to Boston like my father. Nor did I end up in Seattle like those students. Instead, I found myself in a city called Pasadena in Los Angeles, California.

Feeling that I had stitched enough wounds and wiped enough blood, I decided not to pursue any sort of medical profession in the States. Instead I took a job as a bellhop in a tourist hotel that was constructed shortly after the real estate boom of the 1880s. I landed in Pasadena at an interesting time, as the city had become something of a winter resort of wealthy Easterners. Many new neighborhoods and business districts were sprouting up, and along with that came infrastructure developments. More roads and transit connections had been created and I couldn't help but think of my father when I beheld the Atchison, Topeka and Santa Fe Railway. It was a modern powerhouse.

Looking back, I think I came to America for a few simple reasons. I wanted peace. I wanted baseball. And I wanted love. For a very short time, I found all three. I think these are the few reasons I am writing these memoirs that surely no one will ever read. May this act as a gentle reminder that such things are achievable, even when one finds oneself living at an inopportune moment in history.

I do not mean to say Japan was void of peace after the war. But after my experiences, I simply needed a change of scenery, as Americans like to say.

These lands provided me peace by virtue of being new. Harmony is something found in one's self and so to go to a place where you know not a soul provides a very rare fertility for the soil of tranquility to grow. Self-reflection led to self-criticism, which led to self-doubt, which led to self-punishment, which led to self-defense, which led to self-assurance, which lastly led back to self-love where inner peace was finally found. It proved to be the metamorphosis of individuality.

Baseball was far easier to access. The Los Angeles Angels were a Minor League Baseball team that played in the near-major Pacific Coast League. By the time I arrived, they had won five minor league titles and were an exciting group to watch.

Southern California also had a vibrant winter baseball season. As a matter of fact, many major league players often played with these semi-pro teams to keep their skills sharp and their wallets full.

You can say my relationship with baseball in California boiled down to one day; that day was January 26th, 1919.

The Pasadena Merchants and the Standard-Murphy Oil Company team were in the middle of a five-game series for the very illusory but completely coveted championship of Southern California when the unthinkable occurred.

Days prior, on January 18th, the city of Pasadena issued an order requiring flu masks be worn at all times in public. Obviously, I obliged. Shockingly, many people resisted. On the first business day after the ordinance fifty people were arrested and fined for not wearing their mask.

I realized then the stark contrast between American and Japanese cultures. My mother used to say, "The nail that sticks out gets hammered." I once overheard an American say, "The squeaky wheel gets the oil." What polar opposite views on life. America was founded on an insurrection and therefore disobedience in the face of maltreatment represented a sort of freedom. I had felt back home that individual freedoms took a backseat to the greater benefit of your family and country. In many ways, I still believe this.

I remember the players themselves were outraged and initially refused to wear the masks. I believe they even looked to move the game to another city. Alas, the game was played on the 26th and the players, fans, and even the canine mascot donned the cloth protection.

I was at that game. How could I not be? I felt I had to witness history. The game proved to be a good one, as the hitting seemed to be just as contagious as the ravaging virus. Pasadena tied it up, the score 9-9, with two runs in the bottom of the ninth. The game went 11 innings before the Standard-Murphy Oil Company finally claimed victory.

The outcome was superfluous compared to the surrealism of the imagery. There, in that odd time, on a dusty diamond in southern California, everyone came together to support a national pastime while supporting and protecting each other simultaneously. Looking back, I think it was the most profound day I ever had abroad. This may also have something to do with the fact that I met someone very special at that game. I have to come to the conclusion that my flu mask must have worked to my advantage, as she couldn't see half of my face!

The conversation started by luck as a foul ball came flying off the bat of former Detroit Tiger Art Griggs. I instinctually cowered to avert the pain as I saw the ball darting directly for me. I shuddered at the thought of impact, although it never came. I hesitantly opened one eye to see a hand in front of my face. In that hand was the baseball heading my way. I traced the appendage down to a woman on the wooden bleacher below me.

"Thanks," I said.

She looked at me like the coward I seemed to be. I wanted to tell her right then and there I fought valiantly in war but somehow I felt she wouldn't believe me. She slowly turned back around and handed the ball to the man she was sitting next to.

I didn't dare strike up the nerve to talk to the only woman in the stands that day. As fate would have it, however, I would soon come face-to-face with that fearless woman who should have been a third-baseman.

Four days after that game, Pasadena lifted its mask ordinance. The result was surprising; the city rejoiced as if being freed. A parade of cars honked their horns and people cheered. I watched a police officer on Colorado Boulevard throw his mask to the ground and burn it. This inspired others to do the same. Soon there was a bonfire in the streets amidst escalating cheers.

I stood there aghast, my mask securely in place. I remember thinking I just witnessed something truly peculiar.

"Animalistic, isn't it?"

I turned to see the woman who caught the foul ball. I don't know of too many love affairs that started with such a strident first line, but I suppose our partnering was never truly typical to begin with.

We started walking down the street together without any sort of formal invitation or request. Her name was Leticia and it turned out the man who sat next to her, who I presumed to be her husband, ended up being her brother.

I asked when her family came to California and she looked at me like the uneducated man I was.

I can recall so vividly the way she answered, "We were always here."

That was the first I learned of the Mexican-American war, the Conquest of California, and the term Californios. I soon came to realize it was a history not often talked about.

Leticia was a strong woman; this I greatly admired about her. She was also, once she let you in, an absolute bundle of joy. We would laugh for hours on end, discuss the world and our varying beliefs, and my favorite of all: cook our cuisines for one another. Her cooking skills were far superior to mine, of this I have no shame admitting.

On the only birthday that I spent in her presence, I woke up to something she called *chilaquiles*. She had cut corn tortillas into quarters and lightly fried them. Then she topped green salsa on mine and red on hers, teasing me that I couldn't handle the spice. On top of that went scrambled eggs and pulled chicken. On top of that cheese and cream. On the side was a healthy portion of *frijoles* or, as it was commonly known to non-Spanish speakers, refried beans. It was the best breakfast I ever ate in America. That evening I was presented with a soup called *Pozole*. Her version was a vegetable-based dish with hominy corn, herbs, and spices. She had stewed it overnight and when it was ready, she distributed lettuce, onions, radish, lime, and chili on top. As I took my first bite, Leticia told me the soup was traditionally used as a ritual sacrifice. I laughed. She did not. I stopped laughing. She started. This was usually how these things went on between us.

A couple days later, we took the stale tortillas and fried them in oil until they became golden and crunchy. In them went raw fish cured in fresh citrus juices. I was blown away by the assortment of flavors, never having tasted anything quite like it in my life.

Nothing ever went to waste at the hands of Leticia or her kin. While her family generally did not dislike me, her brother Francisco was not my biggest fan. I suspect that may have had something to do with the fact that I very much replaced him in escorting Leticia to baseball games, which I came to learn was more of her passion than his.

One day, as we sat in the stands, I jokingly said she should try out for third base.

She said she had tried to apply to no avail. At first I thought she was joking, her stone-cold visage not giving away her farce. But she wasn't. She had inquired about playing and they certainly didn't listen.

"It's hard to be the first," I said.

"I wouldn't be," was her response.

Leticia told me that in 1866 Vassar College in Poughkeepsie, New York had fielded the first women's baseball team. Over the next few years, a few dozen collegiate women's teams popped up across the country. By the 1870's, however, public backlash and bad press forced them to shut down the entire operation.

Still they, being a persistent group, found a way in. In 1875 two teams, dubbed The Blondes and The Brunettes, squared off against one another in Springfield, Illinois. Not only did they play, they were paid.

An all-black women's baseball team formed in 1883 Pennsylvania as well; they called themselves the Dolly Vardens.

Leticia told me of the Bloomer Girls, female clubs that traveled around the country playing against both men's and women's local teams. It was no sneaking suspicion that she longed to be a part of something like that.

I was always curious why that was her dream. I never did ask. Perhaps I feared that look she often gave me, the one where the answer must have been so obvious I was ridiculous for even asking.

I nagged her endlessly about trying out when opportunities arose but she was always hesitant. I think she felt a bond so strong to her family, she viewed such an endeavor as abandonment.

That's when I did the thing that, to this day, I wonder if I should have done. I wrote a letter to the All Star Ranger Girls, the only team I could find information on, and disguised my identity as a young woman looking to try out. There was no response for quite some time, but one day a letter came inviting me to La Junta, Colorado, where they were heading soon. It said they would see "what I got."

I showed the letter to Leticia, expecting a furious rage, but no such ire arose. Instead, she appeared, for the very first time, to be completely beside herself. Both an opportunity and a horrible choice presented itself. Did she want to follow her dreams or be there for her family? That night I told her to think about it as I left for my apartment. She grabbed and kissed me in a way I've never been kissed. Passion overflowed during that embrace. At her request, we pooled our resources that evening and booked a room in the very hotel I was working in. Soon thereafter we consummated our passion. I am not one to write such details on paper, but that experience was an act of ardor that I will never forget. I would have liked to hold onto that feeling forever. But as they say, all good things...

I never saw Leticia again. The next day she packed her bags and made her decision. She wrote a note in the middle of the night to her family and boarded a train to Colorado. Francisco had planned to wallop me until he saw my genuine surprise at her departure. I didn't think she would go in that way. I suppose it was the only way she could.

I thought my time in California would be miserable without my companion, but as it turned out I wouldn't be in America very much longer.

Later that year, I received a message from home. My father, the legendary Jin Miyano, had died from the influenza pandemic. I went back to Japan immediately.

Home hasn't been the same without the giant that was my father's grace and wisdom. I don't think I will ever stop regretting how we parted. My mother informs me that he was proud when I left, despite his disapproval. I don't know if I believe her, although I want to. In many ways I feel responsible for my father's passing. It weighs on my mind like an anchor, holding me in place as the feelings forever dig themselves into the bottom of my being. I don't know if it's true, if my presence here would have made a difference, but at least I would have been there for my family. I, too, abandoned them.

I often wonder what happened to Leticia. I hope she made it onto that team and barnstormed across the country, proving to herself and everyone around her that she had what it took.

As for me, I suppose I had my adventure and shall pick up where I left off. I have employment at the Red Cross station, which was set up in response to the pandemic. I suppose to atone for my childish haste, it only makes sense to dedicate myself to the medical profession. I will do so in honor of my father.

My biggest regret is still never saying goodbye. I never told him how much I appreciated him or his intelligence. I never told him I loved him. If I am to ever have a child of my own, I hope such a misfortune should never befall our family again.

I happened to meet a nurse today at the Red Cross station. I have to admit, I'm somewhat captivated. I have only her eyes to go off of, because of the cloth masks, but I'm wondering if sometimes that's all you need.

It's nice to know I have it in me to fall in love again.

The pandemic is over. It tragically took the lives of nearly a quarter of a million Japanese citizens. It infected five hundred million people around the globe—about a third of the world's population.

Many have said that baseball helped spread the second wave of virus, especially the 1918 World Series, when the Boston Red Sox defeated the Chicago Cubs. If people knew they would be responsible for the countless deaths of their own, I wonder if they would have changed their behavior. One could hope.

They say putting words on paper is a way of letting things go. I very much hope that to be true.

Chapter 16

Premonition at the Polo Grounds

Eugene stepped into his old bedroom. Everything within the four walls sat peacefully, undisturbed by time. Eugene half-expected layers of dust to be settled on top of the surfaces but quickly realized his mother would never allow such a thing to transpire.

He thought his parents sometimes still viewed him as the boy who once slept in this bed. He supposed they always would. Perhaps they kept it this way to make him feel comfortable if he ever needed to come back home, if something happened with Hattie. At times he felt they wished that to be the case.

The room was small but was filled with a wealth of memories from his childhood. Eugene walked up to his dresser and spotted a rectangular object reposing atop it. It was an old ticket to a baseball game he attended a few years back, when he was a teenager approaching the age of adulthood. The ticket was still in pristine condition and the writing on it clearly legible.

"The Giants"

New York Base Ball Club

Extends to

Eugene Durante

The Counting of Polo Grounds

Federal Tax   10c
Service Charge 15c
Total   25c

GOOD AT PRESS GATE ONLY

№ 845   *Non-Transferable*   *Horace C Stoncham*

SUBJECT TO CONDITIONS PRINTED ON REVERSE SIDE   *President*

Under all the lettering, in the background, in big rounded letters was the year: 1941.

Eugene recalled the day vividly as the ticket acted as a tangible connection to a game that survived only in memory.

Eugene gently took the ticket as his father handed it off to him.

"Don't lose this. You lose it, we can't get in. Got it?"

"I know how it works, pop," Eugene said with a sarcastic grin.

"Don't be a smart ass."

The subway car forcefully rocked back and forth, something no one on the train seemed to notice.

"I thought we were Yankee fans," said Eugene.

"We are. But I was able to get these Giant tickets. It's still a New York team. You root for your own, son."

"If the Giants were playing the Yankees today, would we be rooting for the Yankees?"

Casey grinned and answered, "Darn tootin' we would."

The double-decked ballpark was beautiful and grand, its fortitude a testament to steel and concrete. The father and son pair peered up at the magnificence of The Polo Grounds as a crowd was forming outside the gates.

"It looks like a bathtub," remarked Eugene.

"I was thinking more like a horseshoe," countered Casey.

They found their way to their seats and plopped down. Eugene beheld the grandstands as they extended to both sides of the clubhouse in centerfield. Casey took out a brown paper bag from his jacket pocket. He removed a tin-foil-wrapped treat and handed it to Eugene.

"Here," he said.

Casey then proceeded to take one out for himself. They unwrapped their packages and scrumptiously gazed at the peanut butter and jelly sandwiches within. Eugene took a big bite, causing some jelly to gush out of the sides and back onto the tinfoil.

"Not bad, huh?" asked Casey.

"Not bad at all," answered Eugene mid-chew. "Nice ballpark."

"Absolutely. It's no Yankee stadium but sill nothing to be scoffed at."

Eugene noticed a man shoot his father a dirty look, but Casey remained oblivious to the entire moment.

His father said, "I have a feeling something really special is gonna happen today at this game."

"You have a premonition?"

"What the hell is a premonition?"

"It's when you have a feeling about something in the future."

"Oh. Well then yeah, I have a premonition."

"What are you thinking? A perfect game?"

"That's pushing it. Maybe we should just hope for a victory."

The game started as The New York Giants took on the Boston Braves. For numerous innings they watched a pitching duel ensue along with some great defensive ath-

leticism. They cheered and booed along with the fans and clapped whenever a Brave hitter struck out.

In the seventh inning, with the score tied 1-1, Casey's premonition came true. Umpire Jocko Conlan waved his hands in the air and the playing ceased. Suddenly, a voice reverberated on the loudspeakers.

"I am speaking tonight from the White House in the presence of the Governing Board of the Pan American Union, the Canadian Minister, and their families."

Eugene turned to his father and asked, "What's going on?"

Casey held up his hand, encouraging Eugene to shush, while he whispered, "President Roosevelt is speaking."

"The pressing problems that confront us are military and naval problems. We cannot afford to approach them from the point of view of wishful thinkers or sentimentalists. What we face is cold, hard fact. The first and fundamental fact is that what started as a European war has developed, as the Nazis always intended it should develop, into a world war for world domination. Adolf Hitler never considered the domination of Europe as an end in itself. European conquest was but a step toward ultimate goals in all the other continents. It is unmistakably apparent to all of us that, unless the advance of Hitlerism is forcibly checked now, the Western Hemisphere will be within range of the Nazi weapons of destruction. For our own defense we have accordingly undertaken certain obviously necessary measures."

"Dad, what's going on?"
"Be quiet, son."

The piped-in speech continued, "I should like to be able to offer the hope that the shadow over the world might swiftly pass. I cannot. The facts compel my stating, with candor, that darker periods may lie ahead."

Eugene looked around; the fans all sat in silence, many perched on the very edges of their seats. They looked resolute and focused. Eugene felt as if he was the only one panicking.

"Your Government knows what terms Hitler, if victorious, would impose. They are, indeed, the only terms on which he would accept a so-called "negotiated" peace.

And, under those terms, Germany would literally parcel out the world—hoisting the swastika itself over vast territories and populations, and setting up puppet governments of its own choosing, wholly subject to the will and the policy of a conqueror.

"To the people of the Americas, a triumphant Hitler would say, as he said after the seizure of Austria, and as he said after Munich, and as he said after the seizure of Czechoslovakia: "I am now completely satisfied. This is the last territorial readjustment I will seek." And he would of course add: "All we want is peace, friendship, and profitable trade relations with you in the New World."

Eugene's thoughts immediately jumped to his own soldiering. Many of his friends couldn't wait to join a war as many of their fathers had done just decades ago. He, however, shuddered at the thought. He was not like his father, not tough in that sort of way. Suddenly, a certain man's name riveted his attention to the speech once again.

"Hitler's plan of world domination would be near its accomplishment today, were it not for two factors: One is the epic resistance of Britain, her colonies, and the great Dominions, fighting not only to maintain the existence of the Island of Britain, but also to hold the Near East and Africa. The *other is the magnificent defense of China, which will, I have reason to believe, increase in strength. All of these, together, are preventing the Axis from winning control of the seas by ships and aircraft. The Axis Powers can never achieve their objective of world domination unless they first obtain control of the seas. That is their supreme purpose today; and to achieve it, they must capture Great Britain."*

Eugene looked up at his father. He knew he could feel the presence of his stare, but Casey did not break his straightaway gaze.

"Some people seem to think that we are not attacked until bombs actually drop in the streets of New York or San Francisco or New Orleans or Chicago. But they are simply shutting their eyes to the lesson that we must learn from the fate of every Nation that the Nazis have conquered."

Eugene could see a dampness forming in the corner of his father's eyes. It was a sight he had never seen before.

"Nobody can foretell tonight just when the acts of the dictators will ripen into attack on this hemisphere and us. But we know enough by now to realize that it would be suicide to wait until they are in our front yard.

"When your enemy comes at you in a tank or a bombing plane, if you hold your fire until you see the whites of his eyes, you will never know what hit you. Our Bunker Hill of tomorrow may be several thousand miles from Boston.

"Anyone with an atlas, anyone with a reasonable knowledge of the sudden striking force of modern war, knows that it is stupid to wait until a probable enemy has gained a foothold from which to attack. Old-fashioned common sense calls for the use of a strategy that will prevent such an enemy from gaining a foothold in the first place."

Casey's tear freed itself from his eye and slowly slid down his shadowed cheek. He immediately realized it was the only time he gave in to his body's natural pain response in front of his son. His instinct was to wipe it away, but he chose not to. He chose to let Eugene see it and feel it, to see him steadfast in the face of fright.

"There are some timid ones among us who say that we must preserve peace at any price, lest we lose our liberties forever. To them I say this: never in the history of the world has a Nation lost its democracy by a successful struggle to defend its democracy. We must not be defeated by the fear of the very danger, which we are preparing to resist. Our freedom has shown its ability to survive war, but our freedom would never survive surrender. The only thing we have to fear is fear itself."

Eugene felt the very fear he was just told to not fear.

"Your Government has the right to expect of all citizens that they take part in the common work of our common defense, take loyal part from this moment forward."

Eugene suddenly felt the hand of his father enwrapped in his. The boy looked up but his father still did not make eye contact with him. He looked back towards the field as he could tell the speech was coming to its triumphant ending.

"Shall we now, with all our potential strength, hesitate to take every single measure necessary to maintain our American liberties? Our people and our Government will not hesitate to meet that challenge.

"As the President of a united and determined people, I say solemnly: We reassert the ancient American doctrine of freedom of the seas. We reassert the solidarity of the twenty-one American Republics and the Dominion of Canada in

the preservation of the independence of the hemisphere. We have pledged material support to the other democracies of the world—and we will fulfill that pledge.

"We in the Americas will decide for ourselves whether, and when, and where, our American interests are attacked or our security is threatened. We are placing our armed forces in strategic military position. We will not hesitate to use our armed forces to repel attack.

"We reassert our abiding faith in the vitality of our constitutional Republic as a perpetual home of freedom, of tolerance, and of devotion to the word of God.

"Therefore, with profound consciousness of my responsibilities to my countrymen and to my country's cause, I have tonight issued a proclamation that an unlimited national emergency exists and requires the strengthening of our defense to the extreme limit of our national power and authority.

"The Nation will expect all individuals and all groups to play their full parts, without stint, and without selfishness, and without doubt that our democracy will triumphantly survive.

"I repeat the words of the signers of the Declaration of Independence—that little band of patriots, fighting long ago against overwhelming odds, but certain, as we are now, of ultimate victory: 'With a firm reliance on the protection of Divine Providence, we mutually pledge to each other our lives, our fortunes, and our sacred honor.'"

The crowd reacted enthusiastically, cheering at the words from the President of the United States. Eugene watched his father clap but could not muster up the ability or desire to do so himself.

Soon enough the players were back at it and the game resumed. The forty-five minute address had scared the living daylights out of Eugene and he was sure it did the same to many others that day, even if they didn't show it.

The New York Giants beat the Braves by the score of 2-1.

Eugene spent the quiet subway ride back home fixated on those numbers. 2-1. He figured they might as well be the odds of him going to war. Or worse yet, he thought, the probability of him dying in war.

Eugene, still entranced by the ticket on his dresser, figured he beat the odds. It had been quite some time since he thought about that memory. He assumed that his mind must have hid it from him along with the pain and fear that was felt on that day. But he was glad he saw the ticket and relived the recollection. He was on the other side of it, still standing. He had come a long way to do so.

He stood back to break the gaze. It was time to move on.

Eugene made his way to the kitchen where his mother was cooking and his father was shining his shoes.

"I should be going," said Eugene.

"Already? I was just preparing supper," declared his mother.

Casey chimed in. "Margaret, you think he's not gonna eat? He says Hattie is a good cook, too. I'm sure she misses him."

"Oh, I know, it's just I wish we saw you more often."

Margaret went over and gave Eugene a big hug.

"You'll see me soon, I promise."

Casey placed his shoes on the floor and stood while extending his hand for a shake.

Eugene ignored the handshake gesture. Instead, he wrapped his arms around his father.

Taken by surprise, Casey didn't appear to know what to do with his hands until he came to his senses, with the help of an urging Margaret, and hugged his son back.

Eugene softly whispered in his father's ear, "Thanks, pop."

Chapter 17

Of Flowers, The Cherry Blossom; Of Men, The Warrior

Yuujin wiped a tear as he finished his father's abandoned memoir. It seemed as if a curse of unsatisfactory farewells had been cast upon his family. He hoped to one day break this apparent spell but then instantly felt averse to his wish with the fear that he just tempted fate. He shuddered at the thought of the universe making him sterile as a way to perversely grant him his desire.

He quickly shook the thoughts out of his head and focused on the greater epiphany: his father was far more connected to baseball than Yuujin could have possibly imagined. It truly was in his blood, as he so often exclaimed.

Yuujin couldn't help but hope that the reason his father stopped writing was because the memoir proved its usefulness in allowing him to let go. He was also happy to see that his father was genuinely in love with his mother as he was able to treasure another once again. Yuujin never related to the decree of pushing down one's feelings. He wished his father had been freer in expressing emotions with him.

Yet, he had no regrets in their relationship. To him, his father would always be a true champion, strong and staunch.

Yuujin felt neither strong nor staunch; his military experience ended in confiscation. Perhaps one day he would write a memoir of his own, describing his only real longing: to say goodbye to his parents. Perhaps it would even help.

Yuujin looked down into the chest and noticed one last mystery. He reached in and pulled out a white cloth mask. He sat in astonishment as he gripped his father's flu mask. He suddenly wondered if it were possible for it to still have any viral particles on it but was assured when he thought of his father's trustworthiness and accountability. Yuujin held in his hands the very thing that may have kept his father safe and alive. A veil that if discarded put one in grave danger. Yuujin retained his father's feasible ticket home and secure return. He clutched the inspiration for continuing a profession and guarded the item that kept him going long enough to eventually help create a son. As all this came full circle, Yuujin felt as if he was looking at a mold of his father's past.

"Thank you," he said, looking directly at the false face.

Yuujin carefully placed everything back into the chest, giving each item one last glance before he did. He placed the big black box back into hibernation in the corner of the wardrobe. Shutting its door, he left the past to rest in peace.

Yuujin sauntered through the hallway, observing the slightly run-down state of his home. It wasn't despicable but it wasn't admirable, either.

His room was simple, his belongings minimal. Yuujin walked straight to his dresser and opened a very specific drawer. A collection of clothing lay within. He began digging into the corner as if searching for a buried treasure. When he found it, his face lit up with excitement and he pulled out his prized possession.

His autographed baseball of The All Americans rested securely in his grasp. It made him think of Eugene and the look of disbelief on his face when he told him how he received it. Of course, it also made him think of Sakura and the day she handed it to him. Yuujin calculated that it had to be the happiest day of his life. He thought it curious how this one round object connected two complete strangers, enemies even in many ways, in such a profound way.

He sat down on the floor as he did when he was a boy and feasted his eyes upon the entirety of the ball.

Sakura was curled up on a worn chair, a post-dinner tradition she had developed years ago. Beside her, on a small table, was her steaming tea, held in a delicate cup that her mother had given her as a child. Picking up the heated tea and feeling its warmth was the closest she came to once again feeling that loving embrace only a mother could provide.

The cup's design featured heart-shaped leaves with purple and white tie-dyed blossoms. Her mother would often tell her such a flower was called Morning Glory and could only bloom in the cool, breezy mornings. Sakura was never saddened by the briefness of the meaning, but rather cherished it all the more. The flower grew to be her favorite and she believed it to be the best in all Japan, something she often argued against any who would say otherwise. These days, to look at the cup was to feel like a child again, innocent and wide-eyed.

Sakura flipped a page of Ineko Sata's *Tears of a Forewoman* as she read diligently. She had admired the writer, who had spoken up against the treatment of cigarette factory girls and defended striking workers seeking more humane working conditions. Sata wrote about the lives of ordinary working men and women, which connected deeply with Sakura.

She took a sip of tea without ever taking her eyes off the words. Enthralled, she darted through the page just as speedily as she did the previous one.

As Sakura went to blindly place her teacup down, she felt a presence behind her, hiding in the shadows. She instinctively jumped up, the teacup smashing onto the floor, as she turned to face the unknown.

Yuujin stood in the darkness.

"Yuujin! You scared me!"

She looked down at the shattered cup with an utter inability to accept what just transpired. Attempting to control her boiling anger, she added, "I still think I'm alone in this house sometimes."

Sakura went to pick up the broken pieces when she realized Yuujin still had not spoken.

"Yuujin? Is everything all right? It's not like *your* favorite cup was just destroyed."

Her brother stood stock-still, his head cast downwards towards his hand, in which he held his baseball.

"What is it?" asked Sakura, this time with a tinge of panic.

Yuujin looked up to observe the shattered porcelain, all the tiny pieces that were formerly whole. He noted that once something fractured into that many pieces, it was impossible to ever truly put it back together again. His eyes shifted back to his baseball.

"Yuujin! Say something! You're scaring me!"

Finally, as if needing to summon the strength first, he replied, "I looked at this ball thousands of times. I came home every day from school and headed straight to my room to behold my only gem. I surveyed it over and over and over again. But it wasn't until today that I realized all of these signatures look exactly the same. The names are all different but the hand that wrote them is not."

Yuujin looked up at his sister for an answer.

Sakura, trembling, attempted to harden her quivering lips.

Yuujin, in utter desperation, extended his hand with the ball in it and simply and emotionlessly asked, "Is it true?"

Sakura nodded her head and immediately confessed, "Yes."

Yuujin retracted his hand and observed the ball once more.

"I'm sorry! I tried so hard to get the autographs but I couldn't! I didn't want to disappoint you and father had already bought the ball. I didn't want to let the two of you down. I'm sorry, Yuujin."

He said nothing. After a few moments of tortured silence, Yuujin turned back and mechanically made his way upstairs. Sakura could hear him slump onto his bed and then heard nothing more. Crestfallen, she wistfully fell to her knees among the innumerable bits of cracked earthenware she knew could never be repaired.

Sakura awoke to a curtain of sunshine across her body as the glow of the light cocooned her in a warm protective wrap. Her lashes batted as she opened her eyes for the first time that day. She had no desire to get up, but like so many other mornings, did so anyway. She flung herself over the side of the bed and perched on the mattress for a moment. The daylight concentrated on her face as she basked in the dawn. She hoped it would provide enough regeneration for the day.

With her hand upon the doorframe, Sakura carefully peeked into her brother's room. The bed was vacant and made, the room empty.

The ruins in front of the worn chair were no longer present. Sakura rubbed her head trying to remember cleaning up the demolished cup but no such recollection arose. She headed to a cabinet and grabbed a sturdy ceramic mug. It was unpleasant in aesthetics but durable in practicality. As she went to make herself a cup of tea, Yuujin entered. She did not turn to face him.

Her brother took a few steps inside and stood erect with a box in hand.

With her back still to him, she asked, "Are you trying to scare me again? This time I might break the entire house and we'll be homeless. What would we do then?"

"Sakura," Yuujin said softly.

It was a tone not often uttered. His sister turned around to see him clasping onto the small box.

"What is that?"

He stepped forward and said, "I wanted to apologize for last night. I know how much that piece meant to you. Without ever trying to replace it, I hope you will accept this gift as atonement."

Sakura looked down at his outstretched arms and took the box from him. She placed it on a counter and proceeded to open it. Sakura unwrapped a beautiful porcelain teacup. Around its surface, a custom paint portrayed a vibrant blue fish swimming about. She tried not to smile, to no avail.

"The woman at the shop called it, 'Carp Ascending Waterfall.' She said it represented perseverance and strength. I figured we could use both right now."

Sakura looked up at her little brother. He was not the same as she last saw him; something was quite different. His face seemed to have matured overnight. He didn't appear worn but rather sophisticated. His posture seemed different too, somehow straighter. His eyes gleamed assuredness and great vigor while his words resounded courage.

"Thank you," Sakura said, looking back down at her new prized possession. She held it up and said, "Do you know the story behind this carp?"

"I do not."

"It is said that the carp fight their way upstream of the Yellow River, battling their way against the rapid currents. If they persevere and succeed, and few do, they reach the Dragon Gate and must leap the falls there. If they do this, they are transformed into mighty dragons. It has become a metaphor for success in life."

"I suppose I picked a good one then," Yuujin smiled.

"You did," she replied with a reciprocated grin.

"If you need me, I'll be in my room for a little while."

As Yuujin turned towards the staircase, Sakura added, "Brother—the story also represents perseverance in the military. Warriors used to eat carp before battle in an attempt to absorb their heroic qualities."

With a downtrodden expression, he replied, "I don't think that applies to me."

Yuujin began walking up the stairs when Sakura stiffened up her back and with great potency declared, "It does. Don't ever think otherwise, do you understand me?"

Taken a bit aback, Yuujin nodded.

"Fighting in war is strength," she continued. "Surviving a camp is perseverance. You are a warrior whether you realize it or not! This cup is as much yours as it is mine. You may use it whenever you like. But not after dinner. I like to read and drink tea then."

Yuujin couldn't help but openly laugh.

"What are you laughing at!?"

"When your rigor blooms it is powerful and hair-raising. Lucky for me, it is fleeting. I couldn't handle it otherwise. You are very forceful when you need to be. Thank you, Sakura. I love you."

Chapter 18

Opportunity Knocks but Once

It was as if it wanted to sparkle but couldn't muster the ability. The colorless gem appeared oddly oily unlike many of its pricey counterparts.

"Say, why is this one like this?" asked Eugene, attempting to sound as savvy as he could.

The jeweler walked over, looked at the piece, and answered, "That's a rough diamond."

"Is that bad?"

"It just means it hasn't been processed like the others."

"And why is that?"

"It was probably pulled too early, before it had time to fully develop."

"Like in the mines?"

"That's right."

"Sounds like my career," muttered Eugene under his breath.

The jeweler noticed the despondence in the veteran's eyes as he looked at the brilliant diamond rings around it.

"There's nothing wrong with the one you were looking at. It's just a little less refined and polished but it has many exceptional aspects nonetheless."

"Are we still talking about the ring? Or me?" countered Eugene.

"Look, you give Hattie that ring and she'll be the happiest person alive."

"Are you saying that as her cousin or the businessman trying to make a sale?"

The jeweler smiled, patted Eugene on the shoulder, and answered, "Both!"

Durante crouched down, looking more closely at the piece, before whispering, "She already has a diamond in the rough. She deserves one of these brilliant ones."

"What are we seeing again?" asked Hattie.

"Abbott and Costello in Hollywood! How have you never seen an Abbott and Costello movie!?"

"I've heard of them but I guess I just haven't gotten around to it. You know, too busy working!" She poked Eugene with her declaration as the two walked down the wet and glossy street.

"Well everyone deserves a break sometimes. Everyone needs a good laugh."

Hattie interlocked her arm in his and responded, "To be honest, I never went to the movies during the war. Somehow going to see a comedy when you and my brother and all the others were away just seemed wrong. I didn't want to laugh."

He kissed Hattie on the forehead and said, "I get that. But the conflict is over and if anyone can make you laugh again, it's these guys."

"I heard they were the highest paid entertainers in the world during the war."

"I believe it. You ever hear their "Who's on First?" routine?

"Nope."

"Oh my goodness. It's classic."

"Recite it for me!"

Eugene, feeling embarrassed at the mere thought of it, responded, "Ah, I'd mess it all up."

"I bet you could do it," she encouraged.

With the cinema in sight, Eugene saw his excuse.

"It's too long, we're already here."

"Saved this time, but don't think I'm going to forget about it!" The marquee of the theatre read:

Opening Night!

Kiss and Tell
Abbott and Costello in Hollywood

Eugene and Hattie stood on line to enter the building and could feel the instant encroachment of attention that came down upon them. The glaring eyes felt like a magnifying glass under the sun and its steady subjects felt the fire of the misguided zeal.

"Do you ever get used to it?" asked Hattie as she looked straight ahead.

"Nope," answered Eugene as he did the same. "It seems whether we're in my neighborhood or yours, people just can't seem to take their eyes off the most good-looking couple they ever did see."

A grin crossed Hattie's face and she poked Eugene again.

The laughs were in abundance as the crowd jubilantly watched the comedy duo do what they did best. Eugene peered over to his love from the corner of his eye. He observed her lips gradually curl as she smiled, her cheeks puffing out as a result. Moments later her lips separated and her mouth opened, allowing for a modest expression of mirth. This gave way to a full out chuckle. Soon a string of laughs exuded and Eugene felt deep relief knowing that he had taken her to something she found funny.

Relaxed, Eugene joined in on the revelry and the couple cracked up together for over an hour straight.

"What was your favorite part?" asked Eugene as they walked hand-in-hand down the damp street.

"The insomnia bit, of course! Maybe I should get one of those records and put a spell on you to sleep better at night."

"Maybe it might even work."

"What about you?"

"I liked when Abbott was scamming Costello with the barber lessons and the prank blade. Just when Costello thought he had it all figured out—"

"—it blew up in his face!"

"Literally."

Eugene slowed down under a lamppost.

"What's wrong, baby?" asked Hattie while examining her surroundings.

"I love you," Eugene asserted.

She smiled, grabbed his hands, and responded, "I love you, too. Is everything all right?"

"I feel—" he trailed off before he could continue.

"Go on," she urged.

"Broken. Like I was supposed to be this great thing and then life and the war got in the way and I can't go back to the way things were."

"Is this about the Dodgers not picking you up?"

"Part of it, yeah. But I also want to be more for you. I want us to be able to do whatever we want or go anywhere at any time. I want to give you everything and I feel like I have nothing to give."

Hattie squeezed his hands tight and said, "Listen to me. I don't need you to give me anything except who you are. When you're down I'm going to pick you up because I know you would do the same for me. Hell, you already have. We're in this together. You really think I'd have waited all that time, a bundle of nerves every day wondering where you were and if you were safe, if I wasn't in this? I love what's in here." She pointed to his heart. "And that hasn't changed since the day I met you. I don't expect it ever will. Now, get down on your knee and ask the damn question."

Shocked, Eugene stuttered, "W-what?"

"You heard me! I know you were in my cousin's jewelry store! Now hurry up before they change the damn laws and I feel like we're in the south!"

Eugene, apprehensive, said, "I don't have it."

"Why not!?"

"I was nervous to bring it out in public. It's back home."

Hattie grabbed his hand and the two bustled off into the dark, leaving the lamppost to illuminate nothing but an empty sidewalk.

The two crashed through their apartment door, their lips unable to withstand the hold they held on one another. Hattie's hands glided down his body as Eugene's sailed up hers.

They shuffled through the entrance. Eugene maneuvered them towards the kitchen area, their passion overflowing with every step they took.

"Turn around," Eugene said.

"You better get that ring before you tell me to bend over."

Eugene grabbed her shoulders and turned her around. Hattie beheld her transformed kitchen. A beautiful white tablecloth adorned her small round wooden table. A candle burned bright in its center. There were two place settings and a napkin above both plates.

"What is this?"

Eugene walked over to one of the chairs and pulled it out.

"Your seat, madam."

Hattie hesitatingly walked over. She sat as Eugene pushed her chair in.

"Who did this?"

"Some friends of yours. The movie was sort of a distraction. I guess the big surprise is ruined but the dinner part isn't!"

"You're cooking?" she balked.

"Yes, Hattie. Believe it or not—I can cook."

"With spices?"

"Would you relax? Sit back and take it easy."

Hattie did so and watched Eugene as he went to work in the kitchen.

As romantic music played in the background, Eugene placed an exquisite steak dinner in front of his admirer. Surrounding the beef was spinach with a lively green color, ru-by-red sliced tomatoes, and small potatoes garnished with a piece of rosemary, awaiting consumption.

"Eugene, this is too expensive. Is this the large end of the tenderloin?"

"Darn right it is," he said as he sat.

Hattie picked up her fork and knife and cut into her steak. She pulled her utensil back to reveal a pink color with hints of red.

"Medium rare, just how I like it. It's cooked perfectly," assured Hattie.

"Wait until you taste it."

She placed the thinly sliced piece into her mouth; its tenderness caused her to slide her head upwards as a statement of satisfaction.

"Good?" Eugene asked.

Hattie put her index finger up in the air to shush him so that she could enjoy the exquisiteness without interruption. She eventually finished chewing and swallowed. She looked back at him with amusement.

"What's that face?" Eugene grinned.

"This right here," she said, pointing to the steak, "this is your atonement for leaving me to go overseas. And don't think this is going to be a once in a blue moon type of thing! Now that I know you can do this, you can expect me to watch you labor in that kitchen while I sit comfortably here at this table watching you work."

"I don't know. All that sweat dripping down me from the burners might turn you on too much."

"Oh, you turn me on all right, but this piece of meat right here," she said as she forked the entire steak and lifted it up off the plate, "this is all I need to get me in a true frenzy."

"Watch out, I think your leg is about to spasm."

"Well then I better have a second bite."

"What's going to happen by the time you finish it?"

"I'll probably end up hiring you myself as a full time cook!"

They both laughed as Eugene concluded, "Enjoy it. God knows you deserve it."

Eugene poured steaming hot coffee into Hattie's cup and then his. He went to the refrigerator and pulled out two small glass bowls. He uncovered the clear wrapping and placed them on the table.

"I was going to say you shouldn't have gone to so much trouble but I think I'm just going to let you keep going," Hattie said in jest. "What do we have here?"

"Rice Bavarian Cream," answered Eugene.

"It looks delicious."

"Try it."

She took a spoonful and looked back up at him.

"Where'd you learn this!?"

With a chuckle, he responded, "My mother."

"I see."

"She coached me through it, to be honest."

"Does she know?"

"Know what?"

"What you plan to do tonight?"

"What am I planning to do tonight?"

"Eugene Durante! You think you're funny?"

"What!?"

"I will come over there and beat you with this spoon. Don't think I won't. I will."

"Eat your dessert and drink your coffee. You got your sugar and cream right here."

"You're lucky this is so delicious," she retorted.

Hattie poured a drop of cream into her coffee and grabbed the sugar bowl. She opened the lid and let out a strident scream.

"Bugs?" Eugene asked with sly elation.

The beaming beauty of the shimmering diamond ring sticking out of the sugar transfixed Hattie.

"Hattie Wright, will you marry me?"

Hattie looked over to see that Eugene had come around the table and taken the traditional knee.

"Baby, this is—how did you?"

"Go on, sweetheart."

Hattie took the gleaming gem out of the sugar and gazed into its impressive and graceful elegance and refinement.

Eugene helped the process along by sliding it onto her ring finger.

"Oh, my goodness," she uttered.

"Will you be my wife?"

Hattie looked down at Eugene, grabbed the back of his head, and kissed him. As she pulled away, she answered, "Yes. You know it."

She kissed him again, this time going down onto the floor with him. They rolled around along the floorboards as the coffee cooled and the dessert was abandoned.

Their discarded clothes created a trail leading directly to the bed. In it, Hattie and Eugene held each other in their arms. They were both aglow from perspiration.

"Your heart is beating pretty quickly," remarked Hattie.

"This is the best I've ever felt from my heart beating fast. I'll take it."

Hattie grinned and asked, "Do your parents know?"

"They do."

"What did they say?"

"Actually, it was kind of my dad's idea."

"No, it wasn't."

"He said I should do right by you. I couldn't disagree with him there."

"Wow. Didn't expect that."

"The world is just full of surprises, I suppose. I always knew, from the moment I laid eyes on you, that you were a once-in-a-lifetime opportunity. Someone like you is encountered only once by someone like me. I couldn't risk losing you forever. I had to act quickly and seize you up all for myself."

"That's funny, because I seem to recall me seizing you up!"

"Well, thank God one of us did!"

Hattie snuggled onto his chest and remarked, "I think this is my safe spot. I feel at peace here."

"I'll always protect you," Eugene said.

"I'll always protect you, too," Hattie stated.

"I know you will. Thank you."

Hattie took a deep breath and said, "I hope there's no caveat."

"Just a tiny one," Eugene admitted. She looked at him with enlarged eyes and he continued, "The ring is technically on lay-away. Your cousin let me take it for one day as a favor. I have to bring it back tomorrow until it's paid off."

Before he could turn to look at her, a pillow came smacking down across his face.

"I'm sorry," he said with a sincerity none could question.

Hattie's look went from exasperated to empathetic. She teasingly asked, "You couldn't wait to ask me, could you?"

"I couldn't."

The two kissed and fell back into the sultry confines of the covers.

Eugene awoke to an empty bed; Hattie had let him sleep in as she went to work. He couldn't help but feel ecstatic over the fact that he was engaged to the woman of his dreams. Last night was the best sleep he'd had since returning. He hoped the trend would continue.

The note on the refrigerator read:

"Good morning fiancé! All this sleeping late is going to end when we're married, right!? My ring is on the kitchen table. Don't lose it. I love you. See you tonight."

Eugene looked over to see the ring securely sitting in the middle of the table. He poured himself a cup of coffee and looked out the window. Their whole lives were ahead of them; all he had to do was not mess it up.

Eugene walked down the street to return the ring to the jeweler, Hattie's cousin.

"Did she say yes?"

"You know she did. Here it is. I'll be back as soon as I can to make my second payment. Keep it safe for me."

"You know I will. Congratulations."

The two hugged and patted each other on the back.

Eugene picked up a newspaper from an outdoor vendor and continued on home. Today he planned to look for a job.

Hattie walked in to the aroma of roasting chicken.

"It smells like I just died and went to heaven! Was I dreaming last night or did I find out my soon-to-be husband is a world class cook?"

Eugene peeked out and jested, "It was a dream. But I can make one or two things."

Hattie hung her coat on the rack and walked over to him.

"I need to get you an apron."

"I don't think so," he insisted before they kissed.

"What do we got tonight?"

"Chicken."

"Love it! Meat two nights in a row."

"I went through the paper looking for jobs today."

"As long as it doesn't interfere with your delicious cooking, I'm happy for you. Anything promising?"

"A couple of things. I think I'll do the interviews and see what happens."

Hattie walked over to him again and gave him a kiss before saying, "I'm so proud of you, baby."

"I love you. Clean up and shower and when you're done, dinner will be ready."

"How lucky am I!?" she cooed on her way to the bathroom.

Eugene and Hattie ate their delicious meal amidst laughter and love.

"They're not as good as your carrots with the syrup glaze, but they'll do," remarked Eugene.

"They're fantastic. I like how you cooked the peas and carrots along with the chicken. And the onions were a fine addition."

"The key ingredient, I think."

"Remind me to tell your momma she did one hell of a job teaching you these dishes."

"Didn't have much of a choice. I was the helper whether I wanted to be or not."

"No sisters."

"Exactly."

"You know I—"

There was a sudden knock on the door. Taken aback, the couple looked at one another.

"Were you expecting someone?" asked Eugene.

Hattie shook her head. They both stood and Eugene walked over to the door. He opened it. A tall, older man with a white mustache stood in the doorway.

"Are you Eugene Durante?"

"Yes. And who do I have the pleasure of speaking to?"

"My name is Ernie Mann. You weren't an easy person to find, Mr. Durante."

"I kinda like it that way. How can I help you, Mr. Mann?"

"I'm with the military. I suppose you can say their baseball division, at least for the time being. May I come in?"

Eugene's eyes lit up and he stuttered, "Of course."

Realizing he was in an old dirty undershirt, Eugene attempted to tuck himself in to look more presentable.

"I apologize if I disturbed you during your dinner," Ernie said as he noticed Hattie and the table.

"That's okay. This is my fiancée, Hattie. Hattie, this is Ernie Mann."

"How do you do, Mr. Mann?" asked Hattie.

"Very well, thank you. I'll make this short. The United States Army is looking for a way to keep thousands of its restless and heavily armed soldiers busy during this transitional period. The solution: we have repurposed *Stadion der Hitlerjugend,* the Hitler Youth Stadium. Just a short time ago, this building was used to house Nazi Party rallies. Now that we've acquired it, we've turned it, virtually overnight I might add, into a massive athletics apparatus. We've been hosting competitions in every sport imaginable. I believe this one might catch your attention, Mr. Durante: baseball."

Eugene looked back at Hattie before asking, "You want me to play baseball? With the troops?"

"That's right. You were a member of the Army's varsity baseball team to raise funds for the war effort and boost morale before seeing combat yourself. Is that not so, Mr. Durante?"

"Yes but—"

"—But you were injured and as a result were declined an offer to pitch for the Brooklyn Dodgers. Am I up to speed?"

Surprised by his bluntness and insight, Eugene responded, "Yes, sir."

"Good. You don't have to pitch, that's okay. Your team would play a three game exhibition series against a Japanese team. You'll be home for the first and third games and away for the second. If you accept, you'll be flown to Nuremberg tomorrow. It's a race against the weather, of course. But what good World Series isn't played in October? Perhaps you can even enjoy Oktoberfest. I hear it's peachy. Unfortunately, due to time, I need to know if you're in or out by the time I leave. And dare I say I'm leaving pretty soon. What do you say?"

Eugene ran his hand through his hair and looked back to Hattie, who nodded at him.

"I'm sorry you had to come all the way out here but I'm recently engaged and feel it's only right to move on with my life."

"I forgot to mention, you'd be compensated with a small but fair paycheck."

"He'll do it," stated Hattie with a tone of authority.

Eugene walked over to her and placed his hands in hers. "Baby, I just came home. I can't leave you again."

"Listen to me. Yesterday you said you felt like you were broken because you were supposed to be this great thing and then war got in the way and you can't go back to the way things were. This opportunity is a way of correcting all of that. This might be your final chance to play. How can you pass that up? I won't let you. Not on account of me. I'll be fine. I know how much this means to you. I want you to go. I want you to play. God knows you deserve it."

Eugene went to respond but all he could do was smile. He turned back to Ernie.

"I guess I'm going to Germany!"

"Good choice. I'll pick you up tomorrow outside this door at 7 a.m. sharp. Now, if you'll excuse me, I have to make my rounds." As he made his way to the door, he turned and said, "Oh, I've been told to mention that the teams are integrated. From the looks of it, I have a sneaking suspicion that you're not one to mind such a thing."

"Not one bit," answered Eugene.

"Imagine that. The Army's baseball team more forward-looking than Major League Baseball."

"I suspect that's going to change soon too, Mr. Mann," added Hattie.

"I suspect you're right. Good day. To the both of ya."

Mann exited as Eugene closed the door behind him. He slowly turned around to see Hattie about to burst. They jumped for joy and hollered while bouncing up and down.

"I'll pack your mitt!"

"I'll, I'll—I don't know what to do!"

"I do! Get over here and give me a kiss!"

Eugene complied and held Hattie in his arms.

"After I come back, I'm never letting you go."

"You better! Someone's gotta cook!"

As if a reminder, both of their heads darted towards the kitchen table to see their meal getting cold.

They simultaneously yelled, "The food!"

Chapter 19

Attenuate Shame, Restore Honor

Yuujin looked out of the downstairs window as he ate his breakfast. He appeared pensive and introspective.

"I thought you were going to visit your friend today?" asked Sakura. "Something on your mind?"

His concentration snapped and he turned to his sister with a smile. "I was just thinking."

"So, yes would be the appropriate answer. Something is on your mind."

"Not just one thing, but many. I don't know. Sort of a flood of thoughts, incomprehensible when together. I was trying to untangle them."

"You can talk to me."

"I know. Thank you."

"I'm very good at these things."

"What things?"

"Intelligent conversations."

Yuujin pointed to her stack of books and replied, "Judging from your readings, I do not doubt it."

"Do you disapprove of my literature?" she barked back.

"Not at all!"

"Good. I've been thinking this occupation by the Americans might even help us in the long run in achieving what we set out to accomplish but could not."

"A cruel irony, isn't it?"

"Indeed. Especially since they are the ones responsible for the deaths of our parents. They make it pretty hard for me not to hate them all."

"I try not to judge individuals by the actions of their government."

"I hope others will grant us the same benefit."

"I hope so, too."

"What's on your mind?"

"Honor and shame. The duality of that relationship that we live with always."

"Go on."

"Loyalty, courage, humility, forbearance, generosity, and self-control. We are taught that these are the pillars to uphold our honor."

"Sound principles or antiquated notions?"

"I think, for the most part, sound principles. In war, they tell us to be fearlessly heroic. By doing so, you sustain honor and eradicate shame."

"That code of conduct dates back to the 11th century."

"Yes. It does. But I've been thinking: what is so reprehensible about shame?"

Sakura's head notched sideways as she reflected upon this.

Yuujin continued, "Avoid shame at all costs! How many times have we heard that? I never really stopped to think: why?"

"I suppose, for better or worse, it's part of who we are. It's ingrained in our way of life. Our relationships are duty-based and therefore all our decisions are heavily affected by a sense of obligation. What other people think about us is more important than how we think about ourselves."

"Do you agree with this notion?"

"What do you think?" she retaliated with a hint of militancy. She reset herself and continued, "I admit it has its upsides and downsides, like everything in this world. I do believe altruism to be a noble practice."

"To make others happy is to not bring shame upon them. Something like that?"

"Something like that. You know I'm supposed to be the radical one in the family, right?"

"That's a funny thought in itself. To merely question something is to be radical."

"What's really on your mind? Do you feel shameful?"

"No. I do not. Not anymore. Not in the least. The other night, when you assured me I was a warrior, I believed you."

Sakura smiled and said, "I'm glad I could help. But what's wrong?"

"I started thinking about the relationship between a warrior's honor and the concept of shame. Needless to say, there is traditionally very little black and white in this marriage. As a soldier, I feel I did not fail in my obligations. Therefore, I do not shame myself."

"Good!"

"But my shame really has nothing to do with me. For us, shame exists when displayed through the lens of others. If eyes look upon me with negative feelings and accusations of failure, this is what constitutes shame. And in the ultimate irony, my own shame has nothing to do with me."

"You're right. Shame cannot be attenuated until you do what society wants you to."

"If I were falsely accused of a crime and proven innocent, my guilt would be removed but my shame would last as long as others remain suspicious and harbor negativity against me. True defeat is humiliation."

Sakura walked over and soothingly said, "Then let us make our own choice. Let us decide what is the honorable thing to do and let us declare which actions are dishonorable for us."

"I agree. But can this thinking work for our people? As you said, this mentality dates back centuries. I watched men in fighter planes purposely crash into Allied ships because surrender is taught to be the supreme dishonor. Not only that, troops, young men, volunteered for these missions both willingly and enthusiastically. They believed their actions restored honor to their families."

"We heard news of this. They said it was paramount patriotism."

"Of course they did."

"Do you think there's any truth in it? Do you think the honor of those families has been restored?"

"Oddly, yes. People act differently now towards those families. It's like a self-fulfilling prophecy."

"We can only do what we can. We can't control the thoughts of everyone. But if we have at it, we can chip away at beliefs bit by bit."

Sakura grabbed her brother's bowl and stacked it on top of hers as she headed towards the kitchen. Yuujin placed his arm against the wall and continued to look out.

"You want to know what I was thinking when you asked?"

"What?"

"I was speculating—when we attacked Pearl Harbor, did we shame all of our Japanese kin in America? I wonder what 'restore honor, avoid shame' looked like for them."

"It probably meant fighting against us, against their own."

"Could you blame them?"

"I don't know."

Yuujin looked back to behold Sakura, conflicted and sullen. "Don't be too hard on them. They were discriminated against by their fellow Americans and shot at by their fellow Japanese. They were soldiers without a country."

Sakura nodded and with a hint of optimism said, "Perhaps, in a strange way that was a freedom of sorts."

Yuujin smirked and replied, "Maybe it was." He looked at their clock, picked up his satchel, which was resting against the chair, and continued, "Well I better get going. I want to surprise Isao."

As Yuujin headed out, Sakura said, "Say hi for me. I haven't seen him since you two played about, bothering me as I tried to read."

"Will do. And Sakura?"

"Yes?"

"Thank you."

"That's what big sisters are for."

Yuujin's face lit up. He left with a new spring in his step.

Isao had been Yuujin's good friend through child-hood. His strongest memories of their accord always seemed to revolve around *kamishibai*—paper-theater.

When they were boys, there was an artist in town who made a meager living by selling candy. He would pull up on his bike and all the youths would eagerly surround him. Ironically, they were transfixed not by the sugary treats but by the small wooden stage he would set up on his bicycle. He had illustrated cards containing beautiful pictures and would narrate a riveting story of his own creation. The can-dy-man, as they used to refer to him, would go from town to town with his performance and returned every week to continue the serial saga. Isao and Yuujin would stand in sus-pense as they ate their candy and watched the performance.

Yuujin's parents called it poor-man's theater. He now thought, after experiencing what he had considered the rich-man's version, the theatre of war, that anyone who experienced both would no doubt prefer the one that be-stowed enjoyment and captivated the imagination.

Isao always wanted to grow to be an artist, much like those who practiced *kamishibai*. When he reached adoles-cence, Isao sustained a horrible injury to his leg in the facto-ry where he worked. This ailment was the sole reason for the deferment he received upon trying to join the Imperial Japanese Army. Street art must have still stirred his thoughts as Yuujin had heard that during the war Isao created his own paper-theatre and went to bomb-shelters and devastated neighborhoods to entertain not just children, but the adults as well.

Yuujin felt comfort in the hope that Isao's innocence was not eradicated; Japan could use all the inspiration and artistic healing it could summon.

The shack was just as Yuujin remembered. He hoped his friend, whom he had not seen since before the war, would be, too.

"Isao!? It's me—Yuujin! Are you home?" The old routine forced a nostalgic grin.

When there was no answer, he knocked on the door. "Isao! Stop drawing for a moment and come here!"

Isao's parents had both passed, one directly after the other, prior to the war. The memorial service was the last time Yuujin saw his friend. Yuujin slowly slid the door open. He peeked his head inside.

"Isao? Are you home?"

There was an emptiness to the reverberation of his voice, as if the space itself had grown eternally silent from abandonment.

Yuujin took off his shoes and entered the house, the sunlight illuminating the room through the opened door. It was not as he remembered it.

Drawings and papers overwhelmed the walls of the modest home. The art was stunningly beautiful. Excited, Yuujin walked up to the wall. Upon inspection, he realized the wall was a canvas for a single saga. Without a narrator, he would have to piece the story together himself, based solely on the images.

The serial presented the tale of a young boy playing about with friends and family. There were glorious drawings of flowers and all sorts of inventive creatures. The creatures were all friendly, even when they, too, cavorted. Yuujin surmised this was the boy's imagination at play.

The boy steadily grew and went to work, along with his critter companions, in a factory. One day, something went wrong with one of the machines and an accident caused the boy to fall upon the floor, grasping his leg. The colorful imaginings surrounded the youth and provided him with great comfort.

Yuujin smirked at the autobiographical nature of the story.

Later in the tale, he recalled the death of his parents. As the youth mourned, so too did the aging creatures.

The next picture featured a soldier saying goodbye as the protagonist, with tears strolling down his face, waved back. Yuujin's heart skipped a beat with the assumption that this was him.

As the cards on the wall went on, the once vibrant beasts became darker and duller, until finally in one picture, their entire demeanor changed and they resembled demons more than they did affectionate playmates.

They were no longer friends. The monsters tormented the young man, coercing him to do things he did not wish to. One creature slapped an armband around Isao. It was reminiscent of the badge of shame that Jews were forced to wear in Nazi Germany, only this one wasn't yellow; it was red.

Yuujin reached the end of the wall and with it, the final illustration.

The picture was an underwater landscape. A forest of ominous trees swayed beneath the water. Just above the water line, in the right-hand corner, at the very topic of the picture, one could see the fortitude of Mount Fuji. Isao walked without resistance towards the submerged thicket. There were neither demons nor playful creatures portrayed. Isao was completely alone.

Yuujin stepped back to try and interpret the conclusion, which soon hit him with the ferocity of an onslaught. The Sea of Trees. He drew a reimagining of the Sea of Trees, a moniker for *Aokigahara,* a forest on the northwestern flank of Mount Fuji. Here, it is said, the *yūrei* dwell, the mythological ghosts of the dead. A few locals had starting calling the woodlands *The Suicide Forest* because, for whatever reason, it was becoming an ideal spot to conduct such an act if and when the time was right.

He now understood why the house was empty.

Yuujin sat in contemplation.

"Can I get you something? Tea?" Sakura asked.

"No, thank you."

"We don't know that's where he went with absolute certainty."

"No, I suppose not. But the writing on the wall couldn't be clearer. That forest is vast. Most who don't wish to be found never are."

"I'm sorry, Yuujin."

"It seems this entire day has come full circle. Isao was ashamed of what we supported, who we supported. His demons could not let him forget it. He felt shame on a national level. Going to *Aokigahara* was his way of restoring his honor. It was the one place left where he felt he could walk alone in a final moment of peace."

"When you put it like that, it makes me feel more at ease."

"I wonder if that's the problem."

"How do you mean?"

"Years from now the Japanese will wear different clothing. We will engage in new activities for recreation. We might even rebel against our traditions."

"That doesn't sound so bad to me."

"Even if all that becomes true, I wonder whether it is truly possible to erode such an entrenched aspect of our society. Perhaps we will look and sound different but deep down we will always make decisions out of an obligation to bring honor to our families. I do not know if this is a good or bad thing."

Sakura lifted his chin up to meet her gaze and said, "For what it is worth, you have brought honor to this family."

Yuujin responded, "As have you."

"You have nothing to be ashamed of."

"I don't know if that's true."

"Okay. Let's suppose it's not. What do you propose we do to restore your sense of duty, to revitalize your honor? Maybe that's the missing piece. We offer no path to redemption outside of death. There must be something, something you can do that is positive and healthy that will provide you with the ability to once again recognize your integrity."

Yuujin nodded in agreement before saying, "Yes. Yes, you are right. But what?"

There was a sudden rapping upon their door; the siblings curiously looked at one another.

Yuujin stood and answered the door.

An aging man stood before him. There was a bicycle behind him.

"Yuujin Miyano?"

"Yes?"

"Special delivery," the lanky man continued. "This is for you."

The postman handed a letter to the veteran before nonchalantly turning around and hopping back on his pedal-driven vehicle.

Yuujin first noticed the stamp on the envelope; it was a saluting Japanese aviator.

"What is it?" Sakura urged.

Yuujin opened the envelope and began reading the letter as his sister watched intently. She observed bewilderment and trepidation cross his face.

A few moments later, as his hands descended, the letter dropped to the floor.

"What is it?" asked Sakura.

"It's the army."

"The army? What do they want!? You've already paid your debt!"

Yuujin hesitated, as if clarifying comprehension, before revealing, "They want me to play baseball."

"What?"

"They want me to play baseball against an American team."

"When?"

"Immediately."

"Immediately!? Where!?"

"Germany."

Chapter 20

The Quiet Hush That Precedes Pandemonium

He could see where the swastikas had been painted over. Eugene looked down at the field as he stood, suitcase still in hand, in the stands. The infield was finely crushed red brick while the outfield showcased its freshly mown grass. He had almost forgotten what it felt like, the sight of the green and the smell of the dirt. He imagined popping up after sliding foot first into second base. He envisioned standing on the mound and firing strike after strike, even though he knew his body could never allow for such a fantasy anymore.

He took a deep breath, noticing its appearance in the cold air. It was beginning to get brisk, which suited him just fine. In baseball, briskness indicated the time of year when everything was on the line. It was do or die and you better compete, otherwise the entire campaign, the entire year, all the battling back and struggling, was for naught.

It was eerily quiet out—eerie not because of anything frightening or nefarious, but because such silence brought Eugene back to the battlefield. The last time things were this hushed he was crouched atop a crest awaiting certain carnage.

273

He knew the comparison was exaggerated, but nevertheless, his nervous pause contributed to the anxious lull. In contrast, the din of New York's streets provided him with great comfort.

He surveyed the untouched field once more before turning around to leave and meet his teammates; he was to enter the world of the living once again.

Jin walked onto the field in glee. He dropped to his knees to feel the freshly cut strands of grass between his fingers. He took in the night's air as if the spirit of baseball itself could enter his body and rejuvenate his soul.

"Excited?" a voice asked, echoing in the empty stadium.

Yuujin popped up and turned to see who stood behind him. A Japanese man with a kind smile approached.

"What's your name?"

"Yuujin Miyano," he answered with a bow.

"Kenjiro Hoshino," the stranger retorted with the same greeting. "I will be managing your team."

"It is an honor to play. Thank you for the opportunity."

"The honor is mine. We have a bunch of good young men here. I'm trying to get acquainted with everyone. Have you played much baseball?"

"Only for fun. I am not a professional."

"But you enjoy the game?"

"I love the game."

"I can tell. That look upon your face when you saw the field was everything I needed to know.

"If you don't mind me asking, how did I end up on the list to be invited?"

"From what I understand, no one talked about baseball as much as you did. That's what people remembered most about you. They couldn't recall your name but we got it eventually. Naturally, you sounded like a good match."

"I am grateful."

"What position do you play?"

"I like to pitch."

"What do you throw?"

"A good curveball. A decent screwball."

"How's your fastball?"

"Not that fast."

Hoshino laughed. "Fear not. They say continuation is power. When you're not pitching, where can I put you?"

"Right field."

"Because the least amount of balls are hit there?"

"Precisely."

Tables and chairs were set up in the large clubhouse. A spread was on full display with many men already helping themselves to the buffet when Eugene walked in. It was an impressive first sight to behold.

"Hey! Is that the one they call Eugene the Jeep!?" someone called out. A sea of faces turned to see Eugene awkwardly standing in the doorway. He was the only one wearing a coat and the only one with his luggage.

"This guy is so hungry he didn't even stop at the hotel first!" another player called out.

Eugene's gawky countenance gave way to a smile. "I wanted to check out the field first," he answered.

"This guy! What? You think you're a professional ballplayer now?"

Soon a small group of players surrounded him; rounds of handshakes and introductions ensued.

When the preambles were complete, Eugene placed his belongings in the corner and hung his coat on a hook. As he walked towards the food table, a militaristic man in the second half of his life placed himself between Eugene and his destination. His worn face displayed lines of stress in a distinguished fashion and his posture might have been the most aligned of any man Durante had ever seen. He wasn't wearing a uniform but everything about him screamed general of the highest order.

"Son," he said in an authoritarian tone that still somehow bestowed warmth. "I'm Earl Vaughan. I'll be managing this team. We're happy to have you with us."

Eugene shook his superior's hand and answered, "Thank you for having me. What an experience."

"I've heard a lot of fine things about you. That's good. I also hear you're a hustler. That's what I like."

"Yes, sir. Unfortunately the pitching arm isn't what it used to be."

"I heard about that, too. Tough break. Sorry."

"It is what it is, sir."

"You have the speed to play center but we already have a star center fielder. Who knows, he might go pro one day. I'm not going to put you in right on account of your arm. I'm thinking left for you. Left fielders have to be smart. You seem pretty smart. How we handle situational plays will determine whether we sink or swim. Up for the task?"

"Yes, sir!" Eugene said with a certain degree of exuberance.

"I thought you might be. Speaking of situational plays, I have one for you right now." Vaughan lowered his voice and continued, "Don't make it obvious but do you see the inflated man behind me in the tweed suit with glasses?"

Eugene spotted the man, who stuck out like a sore thumb.

"He's a German reporter. He's covering the games. He speaks English but it's a little broken. You'll understand him. I want you to remember the war is over. We're all American ambassadors now. That's partly why we're here. You understand what I'm trying to say?"

"Loud and clear, sir."

"Good. Grab some grub and get a good night's sleep. Tomorrow is a big day. Drills first thing in the morning. The more we sweat in practice, the less we bleed in battle. I take it you agree?".

"Yes, sir. Thank you, sir."

Vaughan gently patted Eugene's shoulder and glided off.

The short rotund man stepped up to Durante, adjusted his glasses, and declared, "*Hallo!* I'm a reporter covering the games."

"It's very nice to meet you," Eugene responded, extending his hand.

The sportswriter seemed surprised by the gesture, responding only with a, "Oh!" before shaking it.

"What's your name?"

"Klaus Schmidt."

"I'm Eugene Durante. What can I do for you?"

"I'm trying to learn who is who and I was hoping I could ask you a few questions? About the games."

"It would be my pleasure, Herr Schmidt. Go ahead."

"Herr?" the reporter repeated in an impressed tone. "You know German?"

"No, no, only a few phrases I've heard in movies."

Eugene's words trailed off as he realized such characters were all Nazi villains.

"I see! What position do you play?"

"Well, I used to be a pitcher but some injuries make that a little hard right now. You'll most likely see me in left field."

"Starting?"

"I sure as hell hope so," he responded with a chuckle.

"I heard one of your teammates call you 'Eugene the Jeep.' Can you explain? Is that your nickname?"

"Yeah, I suppose it is. That one is a bit complicated," he remarked with a nervous laugh. "In America there's this comic strip called Popeye—"

"—The sailor man!"

"That's right! Well, there's this character called Eugene the Jeep. He's sort of a funny little alien who is able to move in and out spaces most people can't. Anyway, a lot of soldiers started calling the Willys MB light utility vehicle 'Eugene the Jeep' on account that it was small and could seemingly do it all, I mean the thing traveled through impossible terrains. Anyway, one day someone saw me in this Jeep and given my name, put two and two together; lo and behold I became Eugene the Jeep."

Klaus seemed as disappointed by this answer as Eugene seemed embarrassed.

The reporter continued, "Do you have a favorite baseball player?"

"I'd have to go with Joe DiMaggio. As fine a ball player and man as you'll ever meet. What about you, Klaus—you have a favorite?"

"When I was growing up, Lou Gehrig always fascinated me."

"The Iron Horse! Can't go wrong there."

"The son of German immigrants!"

"That's true."

"George Herman Ruth, also of German ancestry!"

"Also very true," responded Eugene with jest. "You guys produce good athletes."

Klaus composed himself and continued, "Will it be hard to play against people you were just at war with?"

Eugene didn't answer this question as quickly as the others. His demeanor hardened as his mind raced. During the whirlwind that was the last twenty-four hours, he'd barely had time to think about or process the notion. He ran his fingers through his hair and said, "The war is over. We're ambassadors of peace in a certain kind of way. I don't blame civilians for the decisions of their governments. I'd play ball with anyone."

A gleamingly delighted look came over the reporter and he concluded, "Thank you for your time, *Herr* Durante. Good luck with the games."

"Thank you. Good luck reporting!"

Klaus nodded and ambled off, searching for another story.

Durante grabbed a plate and proceeded to put various greens from a selection of salads, sliced cured meats, and freshly baked bread onto his dish. He turned to see a plethora of seating options. From the corner of his eye he swiftly noticed two lone gentlemen settled in the corner table. After a quick survey, Eugene confirmed they were the only black ballplayers in the room. He instinctively went to move towards the solitary diners when he felt someone grab his arm. The grip was substantial, prompting Eugene to remark, "Strong arm you got there."

"I noticed where you were about to head. All I hafta say is, I don't want any trouble. They deserve to be here as much as anyone. This whole thing is about post-war peace. I don't want anyone ruining that. No arguments, no fights. Got it?"

Eugene gently removed his teammate's arm and said, "I'm sorry, I didn't catch your name. I'm Eugene Durante."

"Jack Simmons," he answered firmly.

Eugene placed his arm on Simmons' shoulder and said, "Jack, I think you and I are going to be very good friends. I was about to go ask those gentlemen if they would mind if I sat with them. Care to join me?"

Jack, surprised by the response, nodded.

Eugene and Jack walked over and the two men looked up.

"Would you care for some company?" asked Eugene.

One of the sitting men looked at the other while they both noticed the room had suddenly gone silent, all attention focused on the four men.

"Unless we're disturbing you," cautiously countered Jack. "In which case we can go somewhere else."

"I like company," one of the veterans said.

"I like company too," the other added.

Eugene sat first. Jack followed suit.

"Eugene Durante," Eugene said, introducing himself.

"Walter Roberts."

"Benjamin Williams."

"Jack Simmons."

The four men simultaneously turned to look at the rest of the room. After a moment's interim, the room went back to normal.

"You the guy who had the deal with the Dodger's rescinded?" asked Walter.

"Sometimes I truly wonder how word spreads like wildfire," Eugene responded.

"Tough break," remarked Williams. "What positions do you guys play?"

"Left."

"I pitch," Jack said.

"Right," Williams added.

"Center field," Walter said. He looked at Eugene and Williams. "Looks like we'll be the holy trinity out there."

"So you're the star I heard about," Eugene jested while pointing towards Walter.

"I don't know about all that. Williams here has a cannon for an arm though, I'll tell you that."

"You guys know each other?" asked Jack.

"We played in the Negro League before the war," answered Williams.

Eugene and Jack looked at each other, impressed.

"Maybe the Dodgers will be offering you guys contracts soon," Eugene said, well aware of the color barrier in place.

"A black man playing for the Brooklyn Dodgers!?" Walter laughed. "Yeah, right."

Yuujin walked into the Japanese clubhouse, trailing his manager. The group was quiet; from the adjoining room one wouldn't even have known they were there. Most ate their food in silence.

One man resided in the corner of the room; he sat on a pillow with folded legs and hands. His upper body was erect yet his spine settled. He was meditating.

"Help yourself to some food," Hoshino said before trailing off.

Yuujin scanned the room but did not see any familiar faces. He meandered over to the buffet table and took a plate. He gathered his meal and walked to an empty table. He sat and proceeded to eat alone.

Yuujin was appreciative for both the food and the experience but couldn't help but feel the downtrodden energy of the room. He knew all too well what these men and their families had been through. He wanted to stand up and make a joke but he didn't know any, not any good ones anyway. His head descended back down to his dinner.

Without warning, a buzzing sound resounded through the confines of the four walls. It was a single string, a solitary note, but it rang out like a challenge to despondency itself.

Yuujin looked up to see a young man, roughly around the same age, with a shamisen, the three-stringed traditional Japanese instrument.

The reverberation demanded the attention of everyone in the room. The player, having achieved his goal in attracting an audience, let out another note, and then another. His fingers slowly glided across the strings. The echoing vibration seemed to have a symbiotic relationship to the musician; it was as if the music exuded out of his body and into the instrument and flowed out to all of the listeners only to suddenly reverse course and find its way back into his person.

Yuujin recalled his father once told him the secret to beautiful music rested not with the instrument but with the player. He suddenly understood the notion completely.

The melody started off slow but as soon as the young man knew he had them all captivated under his spell, he began to pick it up.

Yuujin could feel the spirited vigor of the room shift. Wanting to participate in some way, without being disrespectful, he looked around; he knew his singing would bring about sure disgrace but instead recalled the only instrument that had ever piqued his interest—*taiko* drums.

Of course, Yuujin didn't have the percussion instrument on hand; he did, however, have the surface of a table.

He began beating on the tabletop, creating a rhythm. A multitude of faces turned towards Yuujin, who was still unsure of how he'd be received.

"Yes!" yelled the *shamisen* player.

Yuujin's antics inspired others to do the same; soon the entire room was banging on the tables. Vitality surged as the marching-like pace suddenly motivated the former troops.

Kenjiro Hoshino grinned at the encouraging display by his players.

The harmonious sounds came to a resounding crescendo and the makeshift musicians all concluded simultaneously.

Seizing the opportunity, Hoshino exclaimed, "Ballplayers and apparent musicians! Tomorrow is the first of three. I see we have already experienced the necessary component of camaraderie. That is very good. In the afternoon we will forge some much-needed cohesion. As we coexist with nature instead of subjugating it, we too shall work with one another homogeneously, not against each other. We will learn how we think, how we act, and how we move. We will perform as one. And we will win. They no doubt think they have the advantage. They are not only the victors of the war but also victors of the vast majority of baseball games played between our peoples. It is said, appear weak when you are strong, and strong when you are weak. Let us use this to our advantage. They believe we will easily be defeated as the weaker team. Tomorrow, if they should see us before the game, display no signs of superiority. Go about your business humbly. If our game were not tomorrow, I would demand three hundred pitches from pitchers and one thousand swings from hitters at practice. But we do not have the luxury of such codified training; I do not wish to put you at a disadvantage from fatigue come game time. Instead, I have something else planned. I advise you all to now go to your beds and sleep with calmness for tomorrow we will unleash our ferocity."

Hoshino nodded in conclusion and exited the room. With that, everyone stood up and gathered their belongings. Yuujin finished the last few pieces of food he had left and threw his plate and utensils in the trash. He grabbed his things; on the way out he turned to once again notice the meditating man. He had neither flinched nor reacted to any of the commotion that had transpired. Impressed by his concentration, Yuujin smiled and assumed him to be the most remarkable player on the team.

Eugene couldn't sleep, as he lay motionless in his hotel bed. He had grown accustomed to a warm hand draped around his body. His head maneuvered to face the window. It suddenly dawned on him just how far he was once again from home.

His manager's words, which he repeated to the reporter, were not lost on him. He was an ambassador for peace. It was a real opportunity, not just a symbolic gesture, although he was sure many people saw it as just that. He reasoned that in some roundabout, indirect, and vague way, he was helping.

Before the war, on his first date with Hattie, someone spat at her feet to show their disrespect and disapproval. Upon returning from war, he saw someone do the same to an elderly Japanese woman walking across the street.

Eugene speculated that if people could see or even just hear about these two teams playing not against one another but with one another without alienation or animosity, surely they would understand we're not so different after all.

His idealistic thoughts darkened in the moonlight as an imposing shadow camouflaged his face. In his mind's eye, Eugene feared bigotry would be an ever-present enemy forever combating tolerance, fairness, and love. He worried that in its cunningness, it would consistently slither from one vulnerable group to another, seeking opportunities to strike and spread suspicion against any who were different in any way. Even when it seemed serene and subdued, being dissimilar would always set the stage for a spontaneous attack.

Eugene wanted to hit the man who spat at the woman he came to love. But she forbade him. In that moment he learned there was more than one way to fight and victory would be determined by society's collective ability to overcome the fatigue of the long and seemingly unending struggle. Eugene grew frightened at this prospect.

Still, he surmised, it would nonetheless always be a fight worth fighting.

Yuujin awoke to the sound of distant repeating thuds. His room was darkened, the moonlight providing little illumination. He quickly noticed the percussive pounding matched the rhythm of his heartbeat. Curious as to the source of the salvo, he threw his bed-sheets aside.

Yuujin found himself inside the long corridor leading out onto the field. From within the narrow confines of the passageway, he became well aware that the bursts blared just a little louder with every step he took.

The ball field was empty but fireworks fiercely ruptured over the stadium. Vibrant and grand, reddish-yellow explosions lit up the night sky and, as the sounds sped to catch up to the light, were quickly followed by deafening crashes. Yuujin marveled at the sight, hoping the celebratory ritual would prove to be for his team.

He presumed they were checking to see if everything was in working order for the upcoming games when the display entered a lull and another noise altogether could be heard, a far subtler buzzing. It sounded familiar but the veteran couldn't place it. He looked up and around in an attempt to locate the source to no avail.

The humming grew, like a perpetual ringing, until it felt as if Yuujin were next to clamor itself.

The sky suddenly filled with combustions and explosions. At first they appeared to be more fireworks but thick smoke clouds began forming around pleading tinges of light.

Without warning, just as the buzzing reached its climax, a white aircraft fighter stormed out of the veil; nationalistic red circles adorned its wings and fuselage as it boisterously soared over Allied-occupied Germany.

Yuujin anxiously traced its course to see it heading straight towards the ominously designed mouth of a shark. Its painted face had a red-tipped nose and its dark green body jolted towards its prey.

"The Warhawk," Yuujin murmured.

As the American and Japanese planes headed towards one another, a full-blown aerial battle swiftly materialized above. Gunfire belted, forcing the fighters to navigate in and out of the clouds.

Raucous applause erupted and Yuujin found the stadium's seats mystifyingly full. They cheered and rooted at the assault as fireworks continued to detonate.

Terrified, Yuujin's instincts told him to turn back towards the dugout, to safety. He ventured but promptly halted when he saw his teammates, attired in their baseball uniforms, aligned across the roofed structure, all with one knee on a dugout step. They each had a gun and each gun was cocked, awaiting only the simplest of orders.

Yuujin couldn't comprehend why his compatriots were aiming at him. He turned and saw the Americans mirror his countrymen. They too had their rifles pointed and they too wore their athletic apparel.

Finding himself in the middle of the pitcher's mound, Yuujin tried to speak but could not enunciate a single syllable. A shadow began forming around him, soon encircling him in blackness. He looked up to see a smoking plane plummeting straight down. His feet froze as if in cement. He turned to both sides for help but neither group budged.

Faceless players abruptly adorned the playing field, all pointing and laughing at Yuujin.

The encouraging fans lauded the event as the varying harmonies of hostility reached a crescendo. The former private, who once barely escaped the clutches of death in the caves below Shuri, looked up one last time and braced for the inevitable impact.

Yuujin awoke to the silence of his room. His chest convulsed up and down as beads of sweat dripped off his body. He took a deep breath. It was just a dream he reassured himself.

He smiled sarcastically, reflecting on how his nightmare, much like his path, was utterly unforeseen.

Life was not all what he expected it to be upon returning from service. It was harder and less rewarding than he had hoped. It was filled with more pain and anguish than he could have imagined. He viewed the upcoming games as his last chance for elation. What would happen after, he neither cared nor dared to think about. He deduced baseball was all he had left in the world aside from the love for his sister.

When one loves something, he pondered, one must put everything one has into it. Yuujin assured himself that he would give it everything he had; he would gather up every scrap of dogged determination in his resolve. His aspirations would remain unfettered throughout, no matter the score or the outlook. Willpower and steadfastness would be his constant companions, win or lose, in victory or failure. Whether or not such ambitions and dreams would manifest into triumph was an unknown that Yuujin willingly welcomed.

Eugene stepped out of the shower and grabbed a towel. Practice had gone well and his team was undeniably a good one.

The Americans had ended practice before the Japanese took the field; Eugene felt it odd that it seemed as if the organizers were going out of their way to make sure the two teams did not interact with one another prior to the games. If they were helping to heal, would it not make sense to meet and greet the other players? He supposed everyone was on edge about saying or doing the wrong things.

"Do you have a telephone here? I've been meaning to call my fiancée," said Eugene.

The kindly-looking receptionist behind the front desk answered, "We have a single wall phone right here in the lobby if that suits you, sir."

He looked around and spotted it. He turned back and remarked, "Fancy. Thank you!"

"Place your left foot straight in front of you while your right foot remains back at a forty-five degree angle. Your front leg should be bent, like a bow, while your knee and toes face the same direction."

Yuujin tried to imagine a bow but failed to see how his leg looked like one in its current state.

"Bend it slightly but not too much; you don't want too much pressure on the knee. You should be able to see the edge of your cleats if you are to look down."

Yuujin looked down to see cleats but questioned if what he saw were indeed the edges of them. He looked around to see if the other players were struggling in an equal manner.

"Your back leg should remain straight, like an arrow. Keep your body upright so that you are stable. Your feet should be parallel and about hip width apart from each other, so that your hips, knees and foot joints are in a straight line if one were to view you from above."

Yuujin suddenly thought back to that dark brown woodpecker with red-tipped feathers that he noticed moments before the bombardment of Shuri Castle. He wanted to believe that it survived the chaos as he did and very much hoped if it were to view him from above, it would see his hips, knees, and foot joints in a straight line.

"This is called the bow stance. Now, simply rotate your left heel and shift your weight, take a step forward with your back foot so that it is now the front leg and come back to another bow stance."

Yuujin moved as gracefully as he could, along with the other players gathered in centerfield as Kenjiro Hoshino led the exercise.

Their manager taught them a number of basic movements and eventually had them moving freely at their own pace.

"This is called Tai Chi. Some of you may know it. I studied this art while in China. I consider it meditation in motion. We have much to learn from it and I believe it applies nicely to baseball."

Hoshino adjusted a player's stance before returning to his speech.

"It is said that the soft and pliable will defeat the hard and strong. Force against force is without use, as neither side will move. Intelligence can act as a way to surprise our opponent. Tai Chi is, of course like all things, about balance and the constant flux between the hard and the soft. Once we surprise them and move them, it is time to take advantage of our leverage by using hardness to keep them down, rendering them soft."

Hoshino continually smashed fly balls to the outfield for practice. Yuujin raced after them while hearing his manager's philosophy from the batter's box.

"Your body must line up with the trajectory of the baseball coming your way. Impeccable alignment is key here. Align your weight and energy so that it is smoothly transferred into the land. The outfield grass is there to support you. Allow it to. Become your mitt. Become the ball. Become one with your body. All of this connects back down to the field beneath your feet. We catch the ball but the ground catches us as we direct ourselves harmoniously into that ground. You are transferring yourself, your energy, into the earth so that it can give back to you."

Japan's hurler fired fastball after fastball to Yuujin. Standing directly behind him was his manager.

"Tai Chi in its essence is a feeling. So is hitting. A fastball is too speedy to sit back and ponder whether or not you should swing. We cannot rely on pure logic for such a decision. A batter needs to become one with the ball in order to accurately have the will to act, the will to swing. We must learn to trust our instincts. All great hits are calculated guesses. Predict the outcome and your body shall will it into reality."

Yuujin smacked a sharp line drive into center field. His manager shot him an approving look.

"I miss you," Eugene declared.
"I miss you too, baby. What's wrong?"
"What do you mean?"

"I know that tone of voice. Something is upsetting you."

"I don't know. Maybe I should come back home. I feel like I finally came home only to—"

"—Hush!"

"Hush!?"

"That's right. Hush. The Eugene I know never stared fear in the face and backed down. It sounds to me that fear is starting to get the edge."

"Maybe you're right."

"I know I'm right. I also know you called me to hear me say it!"

"Hattie?"

"Yes?"

"I love you."

"There's my Eugene."

"How do you know me so well?"

"I guess that's what kindred souls are for. Now go out there and have fun. Enjoy yourself. You don't have to feel like the weight of the world is on your shoulders. Be you."

"I'll try."

"Good. Now hang up before we go bankrupt."

The Japanese players cleaned themselves up in the locker room as Coach Hoshino walked over to his most inexperienced player.

"Yuujin," he said.

Yuujin bowed out of respect and asked, "Yes?"

"You speak English. Is that correct?"

"Yes, sir."

"We have a German reporter here. He doesn't speak Japanese. I don't think our players know German. He knows some English. Can I bestow the duty of speaking for the players upon you?"

Yuujin bowed again and said, "It will be my honor. Thank you for entrusting me with such a task."

"I assume I don't have to tell you your words and actions reflect our team as a whole. Say nothing that would disrupt the harmony of our club. We also would not want to upset any fan watching. Never criticize your fellow players, coaches, or your team. Especially do not speak ill of the game of baseball itself. Do you understand?"

"I will speak with distinction and act with integrity."

"Thank you, Yuujin. Make us proud."

As Hoshino walked away, Yuujin felt a tremendous amount of pressure coupled with a modicum of anxiety rising within him. Before he could process it, however:

"*Hallo*! My name is Klaus Schmidt. I'm a reporter covering the game. I was hoping to ask you a few questions."

Feigning a smile and hiding his nerves, he answered, "It would be my honor."

"Your name is Yuujin Miyano. Is that correct?"

"Yes."

"Maybe you can just tell me a little bit about why you love baseball. How you view it. If you think it's important, things of that nature."

Yuujin's expression turned to complete seriousness as he answered, "Oh yes. Baseball is of the utmost importance. For me, it is something akin to a religious experience. That field out there is hallowed ground. The uniform we wear and the equipment we put on is nothing short of sacred. Baseball represents total devotion to an idea."

"Very nice! How did your practice go?"

"We were led fearlessly by Coach Kenjiro Hoshino. His tactics are a brilliant combination of traditional methods combined with more modern exercises. I think this will provide our team with the opportunity to play against the best of teams. We will obey him every step of the way."

"Do you think you can beat the Americans? They seem to have defeated the Japanese in most of the games played between countries."

Yuujin paused at the directness of the question. He thought carefully before responding.

"We learn little from victory, much from defeat. We have learned much from our opponent over the years and I think we are ready to play on even ground."

"That reminds me of a German saying: *Übung macht den Meister*—practice makes perfect!"

"I like this saying. We train for perfection and we learn most from the journey itself."

"What can we realistically expect from your team?"

"Intensity. Intensity always. We must demonstrate the fighting spirit."

"I look forward to watching you play. Thank you for your time, *Herr* Miyano. Good luck with the games."

"Thank you," Yuujin concluded with a bow.

As the jolly reporter trotted off, Yuujin turned to behold his pristine uniform. He would don number 14. This was chosen to honor his fallen hero, Eiji Sawamura, who died in battle. He planned to wear it with pride.

A ballplayer walked up to Yuujin and asked, "How was the reporter?"

Yuujin recognized him as the musician from the night before.

"Kind. Respectful. I enjoyed your playing."

"I enjoyed your percussion," he retorted.

"Sorry about that."

"Don't be. It was my favorite part."

"My name is Yuujin."

"Aito. Shortstop."

"It is a pleasure to meet you."

"Give me your attention," Hoshino demanded. "Our catcher, Yousuke, has offered to lead all of us in meditation."

"Oh, boy," Aito muttered under his breath.

Yuujin respectfully kneeled on the floor and folded his legs underneath his thighs, as did each and every player.

Yousuke said calmly, but with conviction, "It is my belief that we all need a moment of quiet before taking on any sort of encounter. I led meditation before battle just a few short months ago and it would be my honor to do it again, here with you. May the Buddha watch over us."

They all bowed their heads and clasped their hands as the contemplation and spiritual introspection commenced.

"Alright, everyone! Gather around!" barked Vaughan.

Eugene was buttoning up his jersey as his coach called for everyone's attention. He turned and looked in the mirror to see the beautifully stitched number 5 on his back; he had requested it in honor of Joe DiMaggio, who provided him with the motivation and inspiration to keep playing.

"Lord knows I'm no priest," Vaughan exclaimed. "But I am a fan of tradition. Now, while I fully expect to—" Vaughan looked around before continuing, "Is that reporter here? No? Good. While I fully expect to wash the floor with these bastards on the ball field like we did on the battlefield, I figure it can't do us any harm to partake in the ritual of prayer before the game. So let's get to it and take a knee."

The players, most of them grinning from ear to ear, huddled close and bent one knee to the ground while the other rested in a squatted position.

Eugene descended his head and absorbed the collective silence that preceded the prayer. In that moment, Eugene felt adequately composed and restrained. The unified inaction and quietness permitted him to audibly feel the thumping of his heart, something he hadn't experienced in such a way since the clash for the crest. It was a sensation best described as inner movement and outer stillness.

It was a juncture in time that he knew was as profound as it was short-lived. In just a few short moments it would be game time. He took a deep breath and exhaled his woes, exploiting the brief period in time for all that it was worth, for in just minutes the hush would be dispelled and replaced with certain chaos and pure pandemonium.

Chapter 21

Making Contact

Game One

"Good day and welcome to Baseball in Germany! My name is Curt Nelson and I'm alongside Jerry Elson. This is Armed Forces Radio and we are transmitting live from behind the American dugout. There are an awful lot of troops still stationed here in Germany and if they are unable to come to this repurposed stadium in Nuremberg, which I have to say is quite beautiful, we hope they can at least enjoy this transmission and root for their fellow countrymen."

"Well said, Curt. We have here an exhibition series of three games between an American team composed of enlisted and veteran military members and a Japanese team of a similar makeup. There are no fancy team names; the uniforms simply display *The Americans* and *The Japanese*. Now, let us just remind everyone that this is considered an exhibition because technically we already had our World Series here just a month ago."

"That's right, Jerry. A quick recap: a team of major and minor leaguers, representing the 71st Division of General

George Patton's Third Army, won the championship among German-based teams and went on to play the best team from France, which determined the champion of the European Theater of Operations."

"The opener was played on September 3rd, just one day after Japan surrendered to conclude the war."

"And in a surprising outcome, the French team, named the Overseas Invasion Service Expedition All-Stars—I think they need a better name if you ask me—won the series three games to two."

"The series proved to be so popular that the United States military decided to organize one more series before the weather became too cold to play."

"And it does feel like we're almost there. There's a brisk wind right now, that's for sure. It feels like championship baseball, doesn't it, Jerry?"

"It sure does. And it also looks like we're going to have a full stadium, once again putting those extra bleachers built by German POWs to good use. Despite the chilly weather, a warm sun is beating down on all in attendance. Vendors are still selling beer and Coke. G.I.'s are even munching on peanuts."

"It's great to see that sense of normalcy again. It almost feels like we're back home," said Curt.

"Almost," Jerry jested.

The majority of the American players seemed relaxed, even nonchalant as they meandered back and forth in the dugout and spit tobacco. Eugene, however, felt tense as he rotated his shoulders to be as stretched out as possible. He had been stretching continually as he was well aware he hadn't played competitively in some time and didn't want to blow a hamstring in the first game.

"They don't look very animated over there," remarked Billy.

Billy the Berserk was a nickname no one could forget. He was the team's third baseman and it was obvious upon meeting him that he had a flair for the wild. Outspoken and impulsive,

Eugene overheard him saying that he chose third base because it was the most exciting on account of the line drives constantly being scorched his way. Eugene suspected that as soon as Billy heard the position was nicknamed the hot corner, he wanted in. Billy said playing third was the closest thing to having bullets fly past you. Eugene questioned his sanity. Being from Cleveland, he chose number 29 to honor Ray Chapman, the only player to ever die from an injury received during a game. He was twenty-nine years old when he was hit in the head with a pitch while at bat. Billy was ever reverent whenever he mentioned this.

The Berserk may have been crazy but he made the men laugh, which Eugene supposed counted for something.

The Americans looked over to view the Japanese team who, compared to them, were quite orderly, sitting uniformly on their bench as their manager calmly spoke to them.

"The time has come," Hoshino stated. "I want to remind you not to concern yourselves with home runs. If they come, they come. But we play base to base. Work together. We are one team. Do not burden yourself with the responsibility of individual accomplishment. Move men over and drive them in. I say to you now, while you are up at the plate, if there's one thing to keep in mind it's this: make contact. Making contact is the primary goal of every at bat. Stand at the plate with your elbows close to your body and your feet not too far apart. Your swing should be sharp and even so that your bat meets the ball as it comes over the plate. Nothing can come from a strikeout, but if you put the ball in play, no matter how hard or softly hit, you put pressure on your opponent to make the play. There is always a chance when you make contact."

"Boys!" barked Vaughan.

The players turned to notice a bugle corps march onto the field. They all stepped up and out of the dugout, formed a single line, and placed their hats over their hearts. They unwaveringly turned their gaze to the Stars and Stripes that flew over the field as the Marching Brass commenced their rendition of the national anthem.

Eugene peeked over to notice the Japanese team had also stepped out of their dugout. They slightly bowed and kept their heads down.

When the Star Spangled Banner came to a triumphant end, the umpire screamed, "Play ball!"

The players receded into their respective dugouts. Eugene double-checked the lineup that was posted on the wall adjacent to the entrance that led back down into the locker room. He was batting third, playing left field. Being the home team, he grabbed his mitt and hustled out to take his position.

The Americans' dugout was located on the first base side, causing Eugene to run across the diamond, sprinting in good view of the Japanese dugout. He kept his eyes on left field as he bustled past the opposing team.

Yuujin held his bat in his hand, feeling its weight. He was slotted eighth in the lineup and decided to get as acquainted as he could with his wooden companion and took no notice of the ballplayers passing him by.

Eugene found his place in left field as his jog slowly came to a halt. He situated himself and looked out at his peer outfielders. He waved his glove towards them and Walter Roberts, the center fielder, waved back. Eugene looked straight ahead towards the infield. Jack Simmons was throwing his warm-up pitches as the Japanese leadoff hitter took practice swings, attempting to time Jack's fastball.

Eugene took the moment to appreciate the fact that he was about to play baseball. Life, he thought, was a funny thing.

"Ready," Jack called out from the mound.

The Japanese shortstop walked up to the plate. Aito took a few practice swings and settled into the batter's box.

Jack wound up and fired a strike to inaugurate the series as the fans cheered with enthusiasm.

The second pitch was high and a bit tight; Aito laid off it for the first ball of the at-bat.

Jack was a hard thrower; of this there was no doubt.

Eugene pounded his mitt in preparation, ready for a ball to come his way.

Jack hurled another fastball. It caught the outside corner of the plate as the umpire declared, "Strike two!"

Aito stepped out of the box and took a practice swing as Jack received the ball from his catcher.

"Put him away," Vaughan muttered from the dugout.

The fourth pitch landed just inches from where the previous pitch had crossed the plate. Aito carefully let it go and quickly looked back to the umpire for confirmation.

"Two balls, two strikes," the arbitrator declared.

"Let's go!" Eugene shouted from the outfield.

Jack Simmons reared back and fired a fastball directly down the middle. Aito swung and fouled the ball into the stands.

The next pitch attempted to jam him inside but the Japanese shortstop made weak contact and sent the ball squiggling into foul territory.

Jack and his catcher had the same thought; it was time to change it up.

The next pitch was a curveball.

Aito saw the pitch released and noticed the slight arc that was not present in the previous pitches. At first the ball appeared as if it might hit him, but then quickly rounded its way over the plate.

Aito swung, the barrel of his bat making good contact, as the ball was shot clear over the third baseman's head and into leftfield.

Eugene reacted instinctually, charging inwards. He didn't have a chance to catch it as the ball skipped numerous times before reaching him. He gloved it and reached into his mitt while looking at Aito reaching first.

Realizing the runner had no intention of testing his arm, Eugene relaxed and threw the ball to the shortstop, who had raced to the edge of the outfield as a cutoff man.

The first hit of the series had come from the first batter of the series.

Jack was caught off guard by the single and shook his head, looking disgustingly towards Aito, who elicited no response.

The second baseman was up next. Eiji was informally scouted as a speedy runner who made good contact.

Jack threw his fastball, which was a little high despite being the swiftest pitch he threw yet. Eiji took it for the first ball.

The second pitch was right down the middle for a strike, as was the third.

Jack assumed Eiji was looking for a curveball and shook off his catcher to ensure another fastball.

The fourth pitch was low but close and the batter fouled it off.

Jack discharged yet another fastball in the same location.

Eiji hit a weak ground ball on the third base line. Aito ran on contact and sprinted towards second base.

Billy the Berserk charged the ball as it slowly rolled towards him.

"First base!" the shortstop called out.

Billy gripped the ball with his bare hand and threw sidearm to first.

The ball settled into the first baseman's glove a hair before Eiji's foot hit the bag.

"Out!" the umpire declared.

Vaughan clapped from the dugout despite Aito reaching second base.

Jack had noticed a pattern from the first two batters. They both attempted to work deep into the count, often taking pitches right down the middle. They were trying to make him work.

The Japanese catcher strolled up to the plate. Yousuke was one of the older members of the team and had a larger frame than most of his teammates.

His feet nearly touched as he stood in the extreme back of the batter's box. He held his bat low, his bottom hand almost clutching the knob itself.

Jack wound up and let go.

Yousuke speedily moved his mighty frame forward as his bat came up. With a tremendous shift in weight, he made hard contact with the pitch, his body twisting as he followed through on the swing.

The ball was scorched in-between center and right field as it split past Roberts and Williams.

Before Roberts could even get to it, Aito had rounded third base and was heading home without the threat of being thrown out.

If Yousuke had been faster he might have attempted to stretch his hit into a double but his years had taught him to play these situations safely. He watched as Aito scored easily.

"Dammit!" Jack bellowed.

Yuujin wanted to scream and shout but maintained his calm composure. It was the first inning and his team was beating the Americans.

The very next pitch was a ground ball to Billy the Berserk. He threw it to the second baseman, who subsequently launched the ball to first to complete an around-the-horn double play.

As Jack yelled into his mitt, the Americans trotted off the field, towards their dugout.

Yuujin grabbed his glove and sprinted towards the outfield.

As Eugene cantered from left field to his dugout on the first base side, Yuujin made his way to right field from his dugout on the third base side.

The two converged around second base. Both looked straight ahead but as they passed one another they each caught a glimpse of the other from the corner of their eyes.

They did not stop moving but their entire demeanors changed. Eugene looked back to see number 14 moving farther and farther away from him. When he turned back around, Yuujin looked back to see number 5 blur into ambiguity.

"You look like you just saw a ghost," Benjamin Williams remarked.

What?" Eugene recouped and said, "I'm fine."

"You sure?"

"Yes. I'm sure."

Billy broke up the moment. "Hey guys, look at this. Look at their left fielder."

The Americans all peered out to see nothing abnormal about the man.

"What about him?" Jack asked.

"Anyone notice his number?"

The team collectively shook their heads.

"31," Billy remarked.

The players looked around as if they were supposed to know what he was attempting to say.

"So?" asked shortstop Arky Averill as he grabbed a bat to prepare to leadoff.

"So!?" Billy looked around at the blank stares in disgust. "He's their left fielder. When you're filling out a scorecard, what number is left field?"

"Seven," answered Williams.

"That's right. 7-31. His position and his number. 731. As in Unit 731. I bet he was a part of it."

"Billy what in God's name are you talking about?" second baseman Phil Chuisano queried.

"What? You guys haven't heard of Unit 731? War crimes and lethal human experimentation don't ring a bell?"

"The covert biological and chemical warfare unit of the Japanese," answered Jack.

"Thank you!" said Billy. "They were beyond sick. Amputating and re-attaching limbs to different parts of the body."

"Billy—" intervened Vaughan.

"Injecting people with piss or whatever they could get their Nip hands on."

"Billy!" roared Vaughan.

The manager had everyone's attention.

"This isn't the time or the place. We're here to play ball."

Eugene, who had remained silent, could hear Roberts whisper, "Is that true?" to Williams.

Billy stood up and looked his manager dead in the eyes before saying, "I...had a friend who was a prisoner of that unit."

"I understand, son. We all suffered loss. It's one of the few things connecting all of us together. Those who need to be punished will be. But it is not our responsibility nor our duty to do so. Do you understand?"

Billy nodded bitterly.

"Good. Now let's go. Arky, you're up."

As Averill stepped up the plate, Eugene could feel the energy in his dugout shift. Varying speculations were going through each player's head. No one was thinking about baseball.

The Japanese had called on Yoshio Hasegawa to pitch. He was touted as their ace and scouted as a possible future star for the Japanese Baseball League.

He held his mitt high over his face as he concealed the vast majority of the bottom half of his head, blockading any expression in shadow. His baseball cap was positioned slightly downwards, obscuring his forehead. Nothing was visible except his eyes, which were sharply focused as he received the sign from his catcher.

Arky hunched over the plate as he awaited the pitch. Hasegawa wound up and delivered an off-speed pitch to start the inning.

Averill swung but was way out in front of the ball, clearly not expecting that particular pitch to be thrown. He stepped out of the box and took a few practice swings to regain his composure as Hasegawa received the ball back and settled himself on the mound.

The next pitch was another breaking ball, dropping out of the zone as it headed towards the Americans' shortstop. Averill swung and chopped it foul.

Eugene positioned himself to stand next to Vaughan as they looked out at the game.

"He's going to bust him hard now," Vaughan remarked without breaking his gaze.

Hasegawa wound up and fired a fastball directly over the plate but parallel to Arky's front elbow. He swung fiercely but didn't connect.

The Japanese had struck out the first American they faced.

Arky sauntered back into the dugout as he muttered, "It wasn't even that fast."

Vaughan turned to Eugene and remarked, "It seems explosive after a couple of slower pitches. Like it has a little extra get-up. Be ready."

Eugene stepped out of the dugout and into the on-deck circle as Benjamin Williams treaded up to the plate.

He took a first-pitch fastball right down the middle.

"Strike one!" the umpire boasted.

He held up on the second pitch, a curveball in the dirt, allowing Hasegawa his first ball of the game.

Hasegawa stuck to his curveball as Williams scorched a line drive into the right field stands for a foul ball.

He, too, was behind in the count.

Eugene turned back to his manager and asked, "Fastball time?"

Vaughan looked up at him and smirked. "Not yet."

Hasegawa threw another curveball, again in the dirt to even the count at two balls and two strikes.

"Now," Vaughan stated.

Hasegawa fired and froze Williams, who couldn't get the bat off of his shoulders.

"Strike three!"

Eugene shot Vaughan a look of intrigue and turned to home plate. He strode to it with an unorthodox plan; he was going to look for a curveball and if he guessed right, he was going for it.

He gently kicked some dirt near his back foot, further securing his balance. As a lefty, he knew he had a good chance of pulling the ball and so he peered out into right field. The outline of the fielder seemed familiar as Eugene's heart felt like it skipped a beat.

He readied himself as Hasegawa received the signal of what pitch to throw. Eugene kept his eyes on his adversary's pitching hand.

Hasegawa's arms arrived up over his head before coming back down with an accompanying leg kick.

As the ball was released, Eugene followed its trajectory as it made its way towards him. Recognizing the spin, he knew it was a curveball.

The pitch broke off the outside corner of the plate and plummeted downwards.

Eugene identified it was not a strike but was committed. He threw his bat at the ball and made contact, his arms stretching out as far as they could.

The ball sprung off of his bat and catapulted over the second baseman's head.

Yuujin sprinted in to retrieve the bouncing baseball.

Eugene reached first base and stared out at the right fielder.

Yuujin threw the ball back into the infield.

The Americans clapped from the dugout as they had their first hit.

"Atta boy!" declared Vaughan.

Eugene took his lead off of first as their star center fielder and cleanup hitter Walter Roberts came up to bat.

Hasegawa started the at-bat off with an inside fastball.

"Ball," the umpire called.

Roberts remained in the box and was ready for the next pitch before Yousuke, the Japanese catcher, could even throw the ball back to Hasegawa.

The pitcher wound-up and propelled another fastball to Roberts.

The crack off the bat was deafening.

The fans rose as they watched the Japanese left fielder retreat deep into the outfield.

He hustled until he ran out of room and reached the wall. He placed his bare hand on the barrier for support as the ball plummeted down and into his glove for the final out of the inning.

"Dammit!" Roberts bellowed as he neared first.

The Japanese trotted off the field, having maintained their lead after the first inning had come to a close.

The Japanese left fielder who sported number 31, Shichirō Hirasawa, led off the top of the second inning.

Simmons turned to Billy with a subtle head nod before winding up. The pitch came in hard and fast and hit the batter square in the back. Shichirō writhed in pain before making his way down to first base.

The two teams visibly tensed up. Simmons stared down Shichirō as he jogged to the base but received no reciprocation.

Eugene shook his head in disagreement. He turned to his fellow outfielders who shot him an equally surprised look.

Itsuo, the third baseman, stepped up.

Jack went with a curveball and the batter swung downwards.

The baseball jolted off the bat and pounded the dirt in front of home plate. It bounced high in the air as Itsuo sped towards first base.

Jack ran in, awaiting the ball to come back down.

As he caught it, his catcher yelled, "First base!" due to the fact that Shichirō had already nearly reached second.

Jack hurled the ball to first base before Itsuo could reach it safely.

"Out!" the umpire announced.

The Japanese had a runner in scoring position with one man out.

"Come on, Ichiro!" Yuujin cheered as he nervously entered the on-deck circle.

Ichiro was a veteran ballplayer and a solid defensive first baseman. He had some pop in his day but most agreed his home run days were behind him. Still, he was considered a feared hitter and a difficult out.

Ichiro took a first-pitch fastball on the outside corner for a ball. The fans booed, judging it a strike from the stands.

The second pitch ran up and inside, causing Ichiro to throw his arms up to avoid getting hit as well.

"Come on, Jack! You got this!" encouraged Averill from shortstop.

The third pitch was perfectly placed on the outer half of the plate; Ichiro whipped his arms around and lined it foul.

Jack looked in and shook off his catcher.

Ichiro knew this meant the probability of another fastball just increased.

The pitch came in on the inner half of the plate. This time, Ichiro took it.

"Strike!"

The count was even at two and two.

Ichiro had a plan and that previous pitch was not ideal to execute his strategy.

Jack wound up and dropped a curveball.

Ichiro fell forward as his hips twitched. He whipped his arms around in an attempt to put as much barrel on the breaking ball as he could. As the pitch plunged, Ichiro changed the plane of his swing and connected. He sprayed the ball to the first baseman.

The American first baseman caught the routine ground ball as Shichirō advanced to third base. The out was made and the Japanese had another run just ninety feet away.

"Two outs!" Phil Chuisano reminded from second.

To say Yuujin was anxious would have been the understatement of the year. In fact, he felt jumpier now than he did when in his other uniform.

He kicked some dirt from the left side of the plate and established his stance. He perched over the plate like a crane awaiting opportunity, patiently preying on a pitch to snag.

Jack delivered his leg kick and slung a high fastball.

Yuujin's eyes lit up and he swung passionately but missed embarrassingly.

He twisted around from the force of his swing as he heard jeers from the crowd.

Jack's confidence rose as he beheld his way out of the inning.

"Shorten up that swing," Yuujin heard Hoshino order from the dugout.

Yuujin turned to his superior and nodded. He returned to the plate, taking a few half-swings in preparation.

Jack hurled a second fastball right down the middle of the plate.

Yuujin swung and missed again, although this time he was right on the pitch.

"Put this guy away, Jack," hooted Billy.

Jack quickly wound up and let loose another fastball.

Yuujin flicked his wrists with the sole goal of making contact.

The pitch was fouled straight back, above and beyond the catcher.

He was still alive.

Jack grinned as he received the baseball and resettled himself on the mound. He looked in to receive a sign from his catcher. Once done, he nodded in acceptance.

Jack, attempting to throw Yuujin for a loop, threw a curveball.

Yuujin flung himself at the pitch in an attempt to sustain his at-bat. He weakly fouled the pitch off as he clumsily stammered across the plate.

Jack went back to the high fastball and once again Yuujin was unable to lay off of it. This time, however, he fouled it opposite field, into the stands.

The fifth pitch was inside. Yuujin fouled that one off too.

The sixth pitch was farther inside. Yuujin miraculously laid off for the first ball of the encounter.

The seventh pitch was a curveball in the dirt for the second ball.

The eighth was a fastball that was smacked foul.

The ninth was a high fastball. It was the first Yuujin was able to take.

Yuujin had battled and worked the count full. He thought it highly unlikely that the pitcher would throw a curveball in this count and so he stood back and awaited his prediction.

Jack peered in and nodded at the pitch selection. The high-kicking right-hander swung his hands over his head as he initiated his preparatory movements. As he released the ball, he surreptitiously snapped his wrist.

Yuujin, not expecting the curveball, froze.

The ball broke down and away as the catcher shifted his body to block it. It bounced in the dirt and ricocheted off his glove as it scooted away.

"Run!"

Yuujin wasn't sure who said it or who the instruction was intended for but he dropped his bat and his head and bolted down the line when he noticed Shichirō break for home.

Jack Simmons ran home to cover the plate as Shichirō Hirasawa neared his destination.

The catcher slid, grabbed the ball, and threw a strike to Simmons. Jack caught the ball and brought his mitt down as Shichirō slid into home plate.

As the dust cleared, the umpire extended his arms to his sides and yelled, "Safe!"

Yuujin rounded first but stayed put as his team took a 2-0 lead. His countenance reflected utter seriousness but he was extremely jubilant behind it.

Shichirō unemotionally trotted into his dugout and was met with mild congratulations.

Yoshio Hasegawa, the Japanese pitcher, was up next and proved to be an easy out as Jack Simmons struck him out on three consecutive pitches.

As Yuujin made his way back to the dugout, he couldn't help but think that if he got injured in the very next inning he would still be tremendously proud of the small contribution he made to his team's minor but meaningful achievement. He could take this with him for the rest of his days.

The bottom of the second ended quickly but not without excitement as three consecutive American hitters scorched the ball into play, albeit right into the gloves of various defensemen.

Over the next two-and-a-half innings, everything stayed put; the score didn't change, and every time Yuujin and Eugene flipped roles they passed one another without consideration, without interaction.

That is, until the middle of the 5th inning.

"Strike three! Hirasawa goes down looking," exclaimed Curt Nelson.

"I don't think he was expecting that one as The Japanese strand one runner," added Jerry.

"Well this has been a little unexpected, I have to say. Four-and-a-half innings in, exactly halfway through the game, and The American bats have been relatively quiet."

"Agreed, Curt. Let's see if they change strategy going into the second half. Their pitcher, Jack Simmons, has settled in nicely. I'm sure he wouldn't mind a little offensive support."

"Certainly not. I think—" Curt cut himself short as he peered out onto the diamond. "That's funny," he remarked in an inquisitive tone. "There appears to be some sort of convergence around second base between one of the American players and one of the Japanese."

Eugene and Yuujin both slowed to a pause as they approached one another, finally confirming what they both suspected. They stood on opposite sides of second base.

"Hey," Yuujin uttered.

"Hey," Eugene retorted. "Your face looks better than the last time I saw you."

"All things heal." There was brief silence, filled only with a mutual deference, before he continued, "Nice hit in the first."

"It was alright. Nice way to work that count in the second."

"Connecting is hard. I was lucky to have walked."

"Luck is a funny thing, huh?"

"I would have to agree. Good luck."

"Same to you."

The two men started walking again, swapping their positions in relation to second base.

Yuujin turned around and added, "Eugene." Eugene looked back at him. "You're a good ball player," Yuujin stated.

"You're not so bad yourself, Yuujin."

With that, the two men continued on their way as ballplayers from both teams expressed puzzled looks.

"I'm not sure what that was about, Jerry," Curt continued.

"There wasn't any physical interaction between the two. It appeared civil but it was certainly not a sight we expected."

"Should we chalk it up to casual conversation?"

"I don't know, Curt. Sounds unlikely but that's what it looked like."

"Well I suppose a little casual competition never hurt anyone. Ribbing has been a part of organized sports for as long as I remember! They kept it courteous and that's all we can ask for."

Vaughan eyed Eugene as he entered the dugout and gratingly asked, "Friend of yours?"

Eugene placed his glove down and looked his manager dead in the eyes. "Not exactly, sir."

Sensing a complicated history, Vaughan simply shrugged and decided not to speak another word about it.

His teammates, after observing the exchange, followed suit.

In the bottom of the 8th inning, Eugene came to bat with one out and no one on base. He was one for three in his at-bats thus far. As he approached the plate, he could hear temperate hoots and hollers from the fans in the stands. He brushed it off and prepared himself.

Yoshio Hasegawa had been strong; he weaved in and out of any trouble he faced and continually came out unscathed. He projected more of the same.

The first pitch whizzed on by, high and outside. Eugene took it.

His mind had been galloping since that 5th inning occurrence. He suspected the opposing player was Yuujin but the confirmation of it somehow agitated him. This once uncluttered game now seemed substantially more personal, in a way he hadn't expected.

"Strike one!" announced the umpire.

Eugene was unfocused. He could feel the energy of his teammates shift since his encounter with Yuujin. He shook his head and attempted to put it back in the game.

The next pitch was a curve and Eugene made contact, though weakly.

A soft ground ball to the second baseman easily turned into the second out of the inning.

Eugene passively walked back to his dugout, put away his bat, and took a seat on the bench.

Crack!

Walter Roberts launched a deep fly ball to dead centerfield, the farthest part of the ballpark. The center fielder, after darting back, came to a halt and watched it soar clear over the fence.

The American players cheered, the first bit of elation they displayed since taking the field.

Roberts rounded the bases quickly and returned to his clapping colleagues; The Americans were finally on the scoreboard.

Hasegawa recomposed himself and turned his attention to the next batter, Billy the Berserk.

The American third baseman madly kicked the dirt near his back foot. He crouched into his batting stance and unflinchingly looked at his opponent without fear. His strategy was set in stone: lay off the breaking balls and await the fastball.

His plan worked the count to two balls and two strikes as he idly took all four pitches.

Hasegawa looked in and accepted the pitch selection from his catcher. He wound up and threw a fastball on the outside corner.

Billy connected and the ball bounded from his bat with potency.

Yuujin felt his heart jump as the red-stitched orb skyrocketed his way. He could tell immediately it was going to be close.

Billy dropped his bat and hustled towards first while looking at the escalating baseball.

Yuujin hurried towards the outfield wall. His trajectory put him on course to the very corner of right field where the foul pole stood firm, a sentry guarding over the difference of inches.

The American players all stood and peeked out of the dugout for a clear view.

Yuujin had reached the far wall as the ball had started to cascade. He jumped with all of his might and stretched out his gloved arm as far as it could conceivably elongate.

Billy watched as both the ball and Yuujin's glove disappeared over the opposite side.

Yuujin came back down onto his feet.

The players stood stock-still, awaiting some sort of verification.

Yuujin opened his glove to see an empty palm.

He shook his head as the umpire twirled his finger around, signaling a home run.

The crowd erupted in pandemonium as The Americans tied the game in the bottom of the 8th.

Billy the Berserk shouted in excitement as he rounded the bases. He was subsequently met with clamorous greetings as he headed back into the dugout.

Hasegawa displayed little reaction and simply set for the next at-bat.

Phil Chuisano popped up on the very first pitch, a high fly ball, behind the plate. The Japanese catcher removed his mask, settled under it, and made the easy play in foul territory.

They were headed into the 9th inning with a tied ball game.

Yuujin grasped the handle of his bat and gripped it with both hands. He was scheduled to lead off.

He stepped out of the dugout and took a few practice swings. He knew his function was to get on base. As he practiced his follow through, he looked up to lay his eyes upon his dream come true. There were fans in every seat, it was a tight ball game, and he was walking up to the plate to try and contribute in possibly the last inning of play. He made a mental photograph of the moment; a still shot that was to be preserved for the rest of his days. He knew then it was beyond the bounds of possibility to lose such a thing.

Jack Simmons had been coasting the second half of the game and returned to the mound to handle the 9th.

Yuujin planted himself, his knees nearly touching in a pigeon-toed position, as Jack received his catcher's signals.

The pitch barreled towards the middle of the plate. Yuujin reacted instinctively, his wrists maneuvering hastily. His swing was short but the barrel of his bat connected squarely with the ball.

Yuujin hit a scorching grounder up the middle. It flamed past the pitcher as it journeyed in the direction of second base.

Averill, the shortstop, and Chuisano, the second baseman, both dove for the ball but it shot past both fielders as it scampered into center field.

Yuujin had picked up his first hit.

"Walter!" Eugene called.

The center fielder picked up the rolling ball and looked to Eugene.

"First career hit!" he explained.

Walter Roberts nodded and tossed the ball in the vicinity of the Japanese dugout.

Coach Kenjiro Hoshino had to trot out of his way to recover and obtain the keepsake. He picked up the baseball with one hand while he raised the other in gratitude towards the center fielder.

Roberts tipped his cap and then refocused his attention to home plate.

Hoshino took the token back into the dugout as he rubbed the ball with two hands as if trying to keep it warm.

Yuujin kept his foot on first base for an unconventional amount of time. It was as if he didn't want to leave the bag now that he finally arrived at it. Or perhaps, he just didn't want to get picked off directly after his first hit.

The Japanese pitcher, Yoshio Hasegawa, stepped up to bat and Yuujin finally took a modest lead.

The first baseman and third baseman inched their way in, fully expecting a bunt, allowing Yuujin an extra step or two.

Jack wound up and fired a high fastball in an attempt to get Hasegawa to pop up any bunt attempt.

To everyone's surprise, the batter did not square up to bunt whatsoever. He took the pitch for the first ball of the count.

The corner infielders looked at one another and maintained their positions.

Yuujin sneaked in another step off of first and as Jack's leg came up, he liberated himself from the confines of first base. He was bound for second.

Hasegawa took the pitch, a fastball on the inside corner, when he saw Yuujin take off.

The catcher caught the ball as he sprung up from behind the plate. His throwing hand had already entered his mitt and clutched onto the ball as the umpire bellowed, "Strike!"

The catcher hurled the ball over Jack's head.

Averill hovered over second base as he seized the near perfect throw. He barely had to move his glove when Yuujin came sliding in.

Dirt kicked up around second base as Yuujin's hand touched the bag while Averill placed his glove on the base runner's body for the tag.

"Safe!" the umpire declared.

Averill, unhappy with the call, let out a protesting grunt before lobbing the ball back to Jack.

"Open your eyes, ump!" Vaughan snapped from the dugout.

Yuujin wiped down his uniform and took his lead off of second base.

Eugene couldn't help but grin from the outfield.

Hasegawa now squared up to bunt before Jack even entered his wind-up.

Simmons threw a curveball but Hasegawa was not fazed by the change. He caught the ball with his bat and expertly placed it on the first base side.

The American catcher burst out of his crouch but the bunt was executed too well.

Jack rushed towards the skipping ball as his counterpart ran for first. He reached the ball, grabbed it with his bare hand, and tossed it to first.

"Out!"

Yuujin reached third base safely as his teammate had sacrificed his at-bat for the greater chance to score a run.

The Japanese lineup turned around as their leadoff hitter strutted up.

Yuujin had observed that Aito was predominately a ground ball hitter. His best chance to score, however, other than a base hit, was for his team's shortstop to send a deep fly ball into the outfield.

Jack hurled a low fastball.

Aito figured the majority of pitches he was about to see would be low, an attempt to keep the ball on the ground. He observed the corner infielders were playing in. If he did hit it on the ground they would undoubtedly be coming home to try and get the runner out. He took a deep breath.

The second pitch was low and away and the third was so high the catcher had to stand to catch it.

Yuujin danced off third but retreated when he saw the American catcher direct his body towards him.

The next pitch wasn't close, either; Aito walked on four pitches, setting up an inning-ending double play scenario.

The corner infielders returned to their traditional positions while Averill and Chuisano now moved closer to second base.

With runners on first and third and one out, the Japanese second baseman settled into the batter's box.

Eiji had more bat control than his predecessor and it was lost on no one that Japan's best hitter loomed on deck. Eiji figured The Americans didn't want to load the bases with less than two outs to face Yousuke and thus calculated he would surely get a pitch to drive.

The first fastball tied him up as the umpire affirmed, "Strike one!"

Jack wound up and threw a curveball.

Eiji, not expecting an off-speed pitch, swung forcefully but was way out in front. He made no contact whatsoever.

With the count 0-2, Eiji shortened up in an attempt to stay alive.

Jack peered in and received his sign. He set.

Eiji was prepared for anything.

The pitch arrived and once again twisted its way to the plate.

Jack had done something he rarely did—he threw back-to-back curveballs.

Eiji recognized the pitch and sat back on it. He flicked his wrists, the plane of his bat perfectly aligning, and threw his hands with force.

He connected. The ball soared into right field as Benjamin Williams sprinted after it.

Yuujin retreated to third base for a possible tag up.

The ball sliced towards the short wall separating the fans from the players.

Williams was uncannily fast. His foot stepped over the foul line as he lifted his glove up.

As soon as Yuujin saw the ball enter Williams' glove, he dashed home.

Williams spun around and launched the baseball towards home plate.

The ball slung through the air on a seemingly perfect trajectory.

Yuujin ran with all he could muster. He kept his head down but as he approached his destination he could see Yousuke, who was on deck, throwing his hands down—a signal to slide because the play at the plate would be close.

Williams' throw reached the catcher on a fly though it was a bit offline, pulling him off of the plate.

Yuujin dove headfirst with outstretched hands as the catcher caught the ball and swung around to apply the tag.

Eugene watched anxiously from the outfield.

"Safe!"

Yuujin popped up and discreetly slapped Yousuke's hand on his way back to the dugout, an adopted Western gesture. He was beyond ecstatic but sportsmanship prevented him from showing the other team up as The Japanese retook the lead.

Simmons stuck with the fastball for the remainder of the inning, striking out Yousuke, employing five pitches to do so.

"Last licks, gentlemen!" reminded Vaughan as his team entered the dugout. "Let's get two and end this now."

"It's been a close game," remarked Curt.

"It sure has," noted Jerry. "We are heading into the bottom of the 9th with the score 3-2; The Japanese are up by a single run."

"It's primarily been a pitcher's duel. The big question is: can The Americans muster a comeback victory? We shall see. They have the bottom of their lineup coming up: 7, 8, and 9."

"It will be interesting to see if Earl Vaughan sticks with the pitcher Simmons, who is slated to bat third in the inning."

"I suppose he'll play that one by ear. I will say Simmons appears to be one of the better hitting pitchers out there. He has looked very comfortable at the plate despite having nothing to show for it."

"I see Yoshio Hasegawa is returning to the mound to finish what he started."

"I've been very impressed by this young man. He has shown resilience out there."

"So far he has outmatched Simmons. But this one is certainly far from over."

Yuujin watched nervously as Hasegawa took the American first baseman to task, striking him out on four pitches.

He felt assured knowing that the Japanese starter had lost neither his stuff nor his command.

Michael Sullivan, The American catcher, came to bat. He was huskier than most catchers but his agility and athleticism were bar none.

Hasegawa started him off with a breaking ball low and away.

Sullivan had a great eye, an asset to any hitting catcher. In his prime he would have been slotted in the middle of the line-up. Nowadays, however, he recognized his swing had slowed. Nonetheless, he maintained the potential to dispense damage.

The second pitch was a reproduction of the last and the American took it once again.

Sullivan would often boast of being a descendant of an Irish Gaelic clan. Any who met him would hear the tale of how his great-grandfather immigrated to the United States and became a member of the Dead Rabbits, the criminal street gang of Lower Manhattan. They would also, unquestionably, hear how proud he was to be American. He presented his loyalty via the removal of the 'O' from his original last name—O'Sullivan—as his family's desire to Americanize. Serving in the Second Great War was, in many ways, a dream come true for him. This exhibition series, though, was a pretty close second.

"Strike!"

Hasegawa dropped another curve to get back in the count.

Sullivan waited patiently; he was in no hurry to strike.

Hasegawa threw his first fastball of the at-bat but it got away from him and landed very high and outside.

Sullivan was in a hitter's count, three balls and one strike. He knew Hasegawa didn't want to walk him, thereby making it likely for the top of their lineup to get a shot at prolonging the inning.

Hasegawa set himself and consequently threw another curveball.

Sullivan could tell immediately it was not his best; the pitch didn't have much movement and settled right over the plate.

The American catcher valorously swung.

Yuujin witnessed the ball gust off of the bat as it soared into right field, into his terrain. He broke to his left as the ball speedily approached the grass; he knew he had very little time to react.

Yuujin lifted off of the ground and stretched his body as much as he could. He aimed his glove towards the incoming baseball.

He hit the ground harder than he imagined and quickly looked up. The ball was heading into the right field corner.

Sullivan rounded first base.

Yuujin popped up and ran towards the ball, which ricocheted off the outfield wall. The center fielder also dashed towards the ball but Yuujin knew he was still closer by a long shot.

Sullivan rounded second base.

Yuujin picked up the baseball with his bare hand and threw with all of his might to the cutoff man.

The ball bounced into the infield as Sullivan made it to third standing up.

The crowd cheered emphatically as The Americans now had the tying run ninety feet away and the winning run coming to bat.

Jack Simmons strolled up with a look of determination.

Hirasawa rubbed on the baseball for a better grip; if he were in any way rattled, no one could tell.

Yuujin walked with his head down as he rediscovered his spot in right field. He felt the pit in his stomach expand exponentially as he knew his antics could have just cost them the game. He told himself he should have not dove for the ball; he should have played it safer.

Jack was looking to make contact.

Hasegawa was going for the strikeout.

Yuujin readied himself when he noticed Coach Hoshino waving his corner outfielders inwards. He repositioned himself a few steps in; they would play shallow in case there was a play at the plate.

Jack swung and missed at the first pitch curveball.

Hasegawa set.

The second pitch was a fastball that caught Simmons by surprise. He swung, not wanting to miss his chance.

Yuujin watched as the pitch was scorched foul.

"Come on, Jack. You got this," Simmons muttered to himself.

With the count 0-2, Hasegawa knew he would go back to breaking balls and try to get Simmons to chase a pitch.

Simmons knew this, too. At this point, his only aim was to stay alive.

The next pitch wasn't close; Yousuke had to scoot to halt the ball from passing him as it bounced off of his chest protector.

Jack hoped Hasegawa would be hesitant to throw something like that again as a wild pitch would tie the game.

Hasegawa wound up.

Jack studiously braced for the pitch.

It was another off-speed pitch, but this one wasn't bouncing in the dirt. This one was going to catch some of the plate.

Jack swung without making great contact.

Yet the ball hopped off of his bat and wended to left field.

The Japanese left fielder, Shichirō Hirasawa, settled under the routine fly ball.

Sullivan trotted back to third base and prepared himself to tag up.

Hirasawa caught the ball for the second out in the inning as Sullivan broke from third and headed home. Hirasawa quickly transferred the ball to his throwing hand and discharged it.

To the Americans' surprise, the left fielder did not throw the ball home but to the third baseman, who then seamlessly pivoted to fire a strike towards the plate.

Sullivan slid feet first into home plate as he felt the catcher's glove make contact with his cleat.

Dirt kicked up, placing the catcher, runner, and umpire in a temporary cloud of obscurity.

When the veil of dust lifted, the umpire saw Yousuke presenting his clutched mitt with the baseball securely inside.

Both the teams and the fans anxiously awaited their fates.

Like a hammer with a clenched right fist, the umpire brought down his entire arm to parade the knockout blow.

"Out!"

Yoshio Hasegawa, in a rare display of emotion, swung his fist across his chest.

The Japanese had defeated The Americans in the first of three games.

Chapter 22

The Discipline of Fortitude

The piping hot water washed away the soiled stench of defeat. Eugene hadn't taken a shower this steamy in some time as his apartment's pipes never quite amped up to this level of heat. He hesitated to exit but knew stalls were limited and his teammates needed to clean up as well. He had to leave the transcendental chamber and return to reality.

Eugene walked into the locker room and sat on the bench in front of his assigned compartment.

He could hear Billy the Berserk talking to reporter Klaus Schmidt.

"Listen, they played good today. They were strong. But we're stronger. We got knocked down a little bit but we're going to get back up. We're going to bust ours to kick theirs. That's what we do. You know what I'm talkin' about, Klaus."

"Uh, yes. Any predictions for the next two games?"

"Mark my words, by the end of this series we are going to out-hustle, out-work, out-play, and outlast these guys. Just like we did in the Pacific. It'll be our blood and our sweat but at long last it will be their tears."

"Billy!"

The voice was acute and dominant. Everyone turned around to see Vaughan standing in the entranceway. "I think that's enough," he concluded.

Billy nodded his head like a wounded but ticked-off bear.

"Practice first thing in the morning. Maybe it will remind you gentlemen how to hit." Vaughan disappeared into the darkness of the corridor as Klaus stood uncomfortably in the middle of the uncommunicative room. He looked to Eugene for a friendly face but did not find one. He shuffled over nonetheless.

"May I ask you a few questions?"

"What for?" asked Eugene with a tinge of temper.

"So I can keep my job," Klaus answered with utter susceptibility.

Eugene looked up at the vulnerable man and said, "Of course. Shoot."

"Now that you've played your first game against Japan, what are your thoughts on the rest of the series?'

"They have a fine team with fine players. But so do we. They played hard and jumped out on top but we fought back. We had the winning run at the plate in the 9th and that's nothing to scoff at. It's going to be a battle these next two games for sure. I look forward to it."

"Are you happy with your performance today?"

"Not particularly. Even my hit in the first, it wasn't great contact."

"Is there anything that you experienced that was unexpected?"

He thought about Yuujin. Seeing him was unexpected and that was the understatement of his life.

"Yes," he answered. "Hasegawa had a very distinct style. He threw breaking balls when most Americans would have thrown fastballs, and fastballs when most Americans would have thrown something off-speed. It probably threw us for a little bit of a loop. But now we know. It will be interesting to see if that is something unique to Hasegawa or if it is a cultural baseball difference."

"Thank you, Eugene."

"Anytime, Klaus."

The reporter started to walk away when he swiftly turned back around.

"So sorry, one more question, yes?"

"Sure."

"In the middle of the 5th, there was an exchange between you and a Japanese player. It was their right fielder, Yuujin Miyano. Can you give us some insight into that?"

Eugene could feel the room shift from quiet to absolute silence. Many of his teammates turned around to hear his answer. Pressure cropped up and he suddenly felt uncomfortable.

All awaited his response.

"It was really nothing. This is baseball. It's not unheard of for players on opposing teams to interact. The war is over. This series isn't just about entertainment. It's also a sign of peace and goodwill," he faltered before concluding, "Someone once told me two nations who shared the game of baseball could never be true enemies. I guess we're out here trying to figure out if that's true."

With that, Eugene turned his back on Klaus and his teammates as he sat directly in front of his locker, seemingly staring off into space.

"Thank you," Klaus said to Eugene's back before leaving.

Klaus entered the Japanese locker room. It was equally as quiet as their counterparts but there existed an affirmative pervasive energy. The reporter searched for the only English-speaking player.

"*Hallo!* A word? For the paper?"

"Of course," Yuujin answered.

"Firstly, congratulations on today's victory."

"Thank you."

"I think many people were expecting your team to be a long shot. You came out of the gate strong and took the lead early. Can you tell us how you prepared yourselves and how you feel about your situation?"

"Sure. We came into this as one team with one mission. We may not know each other well but Coach Hoshino did a remarkable job of building us into a single unit. A job worth doing is worth doing together and that is how we approach the game. It is no secret that our strategy is simple. We put emphasis on placing runners on base and then advancing them into scoring position in a very deliberate and methodical way. Our aim is to manufacture as many runs as possible. It is helpful when someone like Yoshio Hasegawa is on the mound, holding the opposition to a limited amount of runs. If we continue this, we will be competitive in every game."

"Interesting!" Klaus said while furiously writing. "You scored the decisive run after leading off the 9th with a base hit. Tell us about that."

"I did what I could. First pitch fastball, he was trying to get ahead in the count. It caught a lot of the plate and I knew I might not see another opportunity to help my team. I was fortunate that their defenders were unable to get to it in time and from there I just attempted to advance from base to base before a third out."

"Great. I noticed an interaction with an American player—Eugene Durante. Can you tell us what was said?"

The Japanese right fielder suddenly became guarded. Attempting to mask his uneasiness, he answered, "Perhaps it would be more appropriate to ask him."

"I already did."

"Oh? What did he say?"

"He simply told me what happened. And I got a great quote, too." Klaus flipped through his tiny notebook. "He said, 'Someone once told me two nations who shared the game of baseball could never be true enemies.' I didn't ask specifically what was said as I didn't want to push him but I thought perhaps you could fill in the details."

"I see," Yuujin remarked. "Well, he broke the ice with a joke. The last time he saw me, I had a black eye. Actually he gave me the bruise. I don't blame him, of course; baseball is a passionate game."

Klaus suddenly realized there was a much bigger story. He felt torn between learning more and stopping Yuujin to let him know he came into this conversation unaware of their previous relationship.

Before he could even process what to do, Yuujin continued, "This was during the time I was his prisoner. The Americans had seized Shuri Castle and I was captured. Eugene Durante was put in charge of me at that time."

"Oh my," Klaus remarked as his eyes widened.

"What?" Yuujin asked, confused.

"I'm sorry. I didn't know that. When I said Eugene told me what happened, I meant that he told me that you two exchanged pleasantries near second base. He didn't mention you previously knew each other."

Yuujin appeared horrified. They both looked around, acutely aware that they were the only two who understood what they were saying.

"Do you want me to forget you said it?" asked Klaus.

Yuujin thought for a moment before responding, "No. It is the truth. There is no shame in it."

"How is it?" Jack asked, pointing to the marinated beef on all of their plates, as he sat at the same table as the night before, again with Eugene, Walter Roberts, and Benjamin Williams.

"It's delicious," Benjamin responded.

Jack settled into his seat and noted, "Tough game."

"Agreed," said Walter.

"I thought we were going to blow them out of the water, to be honest," Jack said.

"We underestimated them," Walter admitted.

"Close game though," said Jack. "We'll get right back in this thing. You okay, Eugene? You seem quiet."

"I'm fine," Eugene answered, taking a swig of water. "Just a little tired."

"What's your take on today?" asked Benjamin.

"I agree with Walter. We underestimated them." Eugene lowered his tone and added, "It didn't help that Billy said what he said at the start of the game. It threw our concentration."

There was a sudden uneasiness at their table.

"Well, what if it's true?" asked Jack.

"Seems like a stretch to me," said Walter. "As if he picked his position based on the number that's assigned for scorecards. And then picked his number in an attempt to throw it in our faces that he's a war criminal who somehow got away with it all. Sounds nuts to even say it out loud."

"You shouldn't have hit him," Eugene declared.

"What?" Jack questioned with a defensive tone.

"You shouldn't have plunked him," he reiterated.

"It slipped!"

Eugene turned his gaze directly to Jack, who couldn't look him in the eye.

"I don't know, it made sense at the time," Jack finally retorted. "And don't think it's lost on me that the game ended with me hitting a fly ball to him and then he threw out Sullivan; the revenge of the baseball gods or something. Hopefully their pitcher doesn't hit me back."

"They don't seem like the group to retaliate," Walter said.

"Then we don't have anything to worry about," Jack commented.

"They play differently than us. Like, the mentality is different or something," Eugene said.

Jack nodded, saying, "It's not just that. It's the way they sit on the bench, the way they react to a big play, the way they interact with one another, and us. When that left fielder got hit, it was as if he didn't care. He was just a cog in the wheel, like he was proud to get on base. The only emotion I saw was when Hasegawa won the game. Very different than what I'm used to."

"It is different," Benjamin chimed in. "Very different. Their outlook on the game is not the same as ours."

"Are you an expert in Japanese baseball, now?" Walter busted.

"I did my research," he resolutely answered. "You think I'm going up against an opposition while not trying to understand where they're coming from or how they think?"

"And what did you learn?" asked Jack.

"Sincerity is the end and the beginning of all things; without sincerity there would be nothing."

"What's that from?" asked Eugene.

"*The Doctrine of the Mean.*"

The three men quizzically looked at one another and then back at Benjamin Williams.

"What else ya got?" asked Walter.

"This idea of politeness is a cornerstone of their culture."

"You don't think they overdo it a bit, though?" Jack asked sarcastically.

"I don't think they do it out of a fear of offending good taste. To them, politeness is the outward manifestation of a sympathetic regard for the feelings of others. What we may consider an overkill of nicety, they would call a ceaseless search of the human mind for the beautiful. If you think about it that way, politeness, for them, nearly approaches the status of love."

Once again, the three men stared at their comrade, impressed with his words.

"What are you, some kind of genius or something?" Jack finally asked.

"No. I just have a photographic memory."

"And what was that from?" asked Walter.

"Inazō Nitobe's *Bushido: The Soul of Japan.*"

"You read Japanese?" asked Jack.

"No. The book is in English," Williams responded in a tone mocking the obviousness of his answer.

Jack looked back and forth at his three conversationalists and said, "Wait. Let me get this straight. You're telling me that the reason these guys act the way they do—is because they love me?"

Yuujin found his coach on the darkened baseball field. The elder stood behind home plate and solitarily looked out, as if watching an invisible game play out.

Not wanting to disturb him, the young right fielder silently turned around and headed back inside.

"It's a glorious night," remarked Kenjiro Hoshino.

Yuujin stopped in his tracks and looked back to see if his coach was talking to him.

Hoshino didn't break his fixed state but Yuujin realized there was no one else that he could be speaking to.

"You're a good player," Hoshino continued. "All heart."

Yuujin, starting to walk towards his coach, answered, "Thank you. You bring the best out in me."

"I suppose you are wondering what I'm doing out here."

"Strategizing for the second game, no doubt."

Hoshino chuckled and responded, "Now that would actually be productive."

"What are you doing, then? If you don't mind me asking."

"Reflecting," Hoshino answered.

"Ah. Would you like me to leave you be?"

"No. Despite being solitary in life, I do enjoy occasional company."

"Then, I will stay."

The two looked out into the night.

Hoshino remained calm and motionless while Yuujin felt antsy, unaware of what to say or do.

Hoshino eventually broke the meditative glare and said, "I've missed baseball very much. Today reminded me just how much I miss coaching."

"You don't coach anymore?" asked Yuujin.

"No. I do not."

"You should. You are very good at it."

"To coach again in Japan would be to once more feel the sting of dishonor."

Yuujin hesitated before asking, "What happened?"

"I taught schoolboys on the verge of manhood. Three years ago, on graduation night, a handful of my students were seen smoking and drinking at a local restaurant. They were all obviously underage. It was reported. As you know, the group bears responsibility for individual indiscretions. The school was disgraced. I resigned and the team immediately withdrew from our upcoming tournament. The guilty students fell to their knees and begged the forgiveness of the other players. I never went back."

"From shame?"

"Yes. From shame."

"I sympathize with you, Coach Hoshino. Shame is a powerful force."

"That it is."

"Regardless, it is my hope that you find your way back to baseball. You are a great asset to any student of the game. Despite feeling disgraced, you have truly helped me find my own sense of honor. If there is ever a way I can help you reclaim yours, I would jump at the opportunity."

Hoshino, for the first time in the conversation, looked at Yuujin. He nodded in delight and admiration.

"Thank you, Yuujin. Your words bring me peace." Hoshino's body loosened as if a weight had been lifted. "I believe you came out here tonight for a reason as well. Perhaps to reflect, also. I shall leave you to it. Goodnight, Yuujin."

"Goodnight, coach."

Hoshino began walking towards the dugout when he stopped and turned around. "Yuujin?"

"Yes?"

With a noble smile, Hoshino concluded, "Your parents must be very proud." He then walked down the two steps and disappeared through the corridor.

Yuujin stood stationary in front of home plate, yearning for his manager's hallowed words to be true.

Chapter 23

Keep Swinging

Game Two

"Welcome to the second of this three game exhibition series! I'm Curt Nelson and I'm alongside Jerry Elson. This is Armed Forces Radio and we are transmitting live from behind the American dugout!"

"And we have an interesting development today, don't we?"

"We sure do! Front page of today's local paper has quite the story. Or at least so I'm told! Remember that peculiar occurrence that took place around second base between an American player and a Japanese player? Well, it turns out there's a history between these two."

"That's right, Curt. The American player was left fielder Eugene Durante. The Japanese player was right fielder Yuujin Miyano. Just to recap, in the middle of the 5th inning of the first game these two players converged around second base and appeared to have some words. We noted that there was nothing overly hostile about the encounter but it did stick out, at least enough for us to mention it on air."

"Correct. As it turns out, these two individuals have a past. In May of this year, during the Battle of Okinawa, American forces captured Shuri Castle where the Imperial Japanese Army had set up its headquarters. Our valiant left fielder was present for this victory. And so was, you guessed it, Yuujin Miyano."

"Yuujin was taken prisoner by the Americans and was actually placed under the careful watch of Eugene Durante until a transport eventually came to haul him away to a POW camp."

"And so we have an interesting dynamic in play, Jerry. Not only do we have the obvious; winners and losers of war playing against one another, but on a more personal level we have a captive playing against his captor."

"Talk about drama! I can only imagine what the players are saying amongst themselves!"

"Did he mistreat you?" asked Itsuo in the Japanese dugout. Multiple players had surrounded Yuujin.

"There are legal routes you can go," added Eiji.

"Everything is fine. He did not harm me in any way."

"I thought he punched you in the face?" countered Ichiro.

"He did. It was a moment of passion. We became," Yuujin paused, thinking of the right word before deciding on, "acquaintances afterwards. I have no ill will."

"You're my goddamn hero," remarked Billy the Berserk. The American players had reacted similarly towards Eugene in their dugout.

"Talk about serendipity," said Phil Chuisano.

"What's it like playing against him?" asked Sullivan.

"Did he give you trouble?" asked Billy.

"No," quickly answered Eugene.

"I was their prisoner."

Everyone looked to see who made the statement. There, on the far end of the bench, sat Arky Averill, who would be leading off again

"I was a tank crewman during the early days of the war. About ten of us were captured in the Philippines. We were beaten routinely. We were starved. We were abused. They made us work in mines and war-related factories. Six of us made it back out. It was like the Geneva Conventions meant jack shit. If I'd been you, Eugene, I would've shot that Jap bastard in the back of his head the moment after he thought he wasn't going to die."

An eerie hush fell over the players.

Averill continued, "I know these people. They're cruel. There won't be an apology for it, either. You'll see; mark my words. I'll never forgive them. And neither should you."

With that, Averill grabbed his bat and stalked out.

"You heard him," Billy roared. "This one's for Arky and his fallen four!"

The dugout broke out in animated exuberance.

Eugene, however, sat in silence. He was both disturbed by what Arky had been through and disoriented at the thought that Yuujin's good-naturedness was the cause of the current animosity towards their opponents.

This had indeed become more than just a game, but not in the way he expected nor in the way he hoped.

Vaughan emerged from the corridor and entered the dugout.

"You boys look excited! I like that. Let's turn that drive into line drives and score some runs!"

The stadium was packed once again.

Arky Averill marched up to the plate. Tora Haku, who did not make an appearance in the first game, was on the mound for The Japanese.

Coach Hoshino had observed that Haku was neither a good fielder nor a good hitter; he was, however, the fastest thrower on the team and possessed accuracy.

The Americans hovered around the top of the dugout, appearing both anxious and restless.

Averill settled in at the box.

The umpire placed his hand down, signaling all were ready.

Haku wound up.

The first pitch of the second game barreled in for a strike.

The crowd cheered.

Averill took half of a practice swing and readied himself.

The second pitch was off-speed and outside; Arky took it.

"One ball, one strike," the umpire remarked.

Haku went back to the fastball and Averill sent it right up the middle of the diamond for a scorching single.

He hustled to first base and rounded the bag as the ball came in to the cutoff man; The Americans cheered.

Benjamin Williams came to the plate next, hoping to follow up Arky's base hit with one of his own.

Haku threw two consecutive balls; Williams took both of them.

"Let's go, Benny!" Billy screamed from the dugout.

Tora Haku wound up and delivered.

Williams connected and the ball sizzled over the head of the third baseman and headed down the left field line.

Shichirō Hirasawa, the Japanese left fielder, sprinted towards the bouncing baseball as Averill rounded second and Williams rounded first.

The ball kicked about in the corner when Hirasawa reached and grabbed it with his bare hand.

The ball arrived at the cutoff man as Averill rounded third but quickly put the brakes on.

The Americans had runners on second and third with no one out in the top of the first inning.

Eugene strolled up, still distressed over the happenings in the press and in the dugout. He also knew he had a job to do. He was presented with a great opportunity and he didn't intend to squander it.

The fans seemingly cheered louder for him than last time, something he was not expecting.

"Forget Eugene the Jeep! We got Durante the Detainer!" Billy barked.

Eugene could hear the laughter as he concentrated on the upcoming pitch.

Haku wound up and fired a first-pitch fastball. Eugene, harnessing anger and disgust, took a big swing—and connected.

The ball shot high up in the air. Everyone followed its trajectory as their collective chins ascended and then descended as they watched it fall into the mitt of the third baseman.

"Dammit!" shouted Eugene as he hustled back to the dugout.

As he went to take a step downwards, Billy grabbed his arm. Eugene looked up, surprised.

"Hey. Don't worry about that one. We're going to pick you up."

With that, Billy stepped up and into the on-deck circle as Walter Roberts vacated the area and headed to the plate.

Eugene felt strange from the response. Billy had a newfound bond with his team, a bond forged in the fires of revenge and retribution. They had found, or perhaps even created, a common enemy on the field. Eugene entertained the possibility that he was overthinking everything, yet the prospect that he wasn't stirred great concern.

The belting off the bat broke Eugene from his contemplative trance. He looked up to see Roberts rounding fist. His eyeline darted home as he watched Averill and Williams score. Roberts landed on second base.

Supportive cries erupted from every direction as The Americans took an early 2-0 lead.

Billy advanced to the plate while loudly supporting his teammate standing on second.

The man who was nicknamed The Berserk wasted no time in attempting to progress the assembly line of offense.

He swung at the first pitch from Tora Haku and served it into right field.

Roberts took off as Billy made contact, knowing it would fall in. He hastened to third and rounded the base without a misstep.

Yuujin snagged the ball and, predicting he had no shot to catch the speedy Roberts, threw it in to the cutoff man to hold Billy to a single.

Roberts crossed the plate as Billy continued to elate. "Tora Tora Tora!" he roared. "We have our own lightning attack!"

The Japanese catcher called for time and sprinted towards the mound to calm his pitcher.

"You okay?" asked Yousuke.

"Yes," answered Haku.

"Don't let the outside forces get to you. We must keep calm in the face of adversity. Yes?"

"I will."

"Good. We need to stop the bleeding. Low and inside. Let's get a double play and get out of this now."

Haku nodded and Yousuke retreated behind the plate.

Phil Chuisano was up next.

"Let's go, Philly," Billy boomed from first.

The first pitch was located just where they wanted it. Chuisano swung and hit a line drive towards the Japanese shortstop. Aito caught it on a single bounce, threw to the second baseman Eiji, who in turn flung the ball to Ichiro at first to complete the inning-ending double play.

Billy trotted back to the dugout clapping his hands.

"Let's go! One-two-three! We got this!"

Eugene spotted Yuujin jogging in and decided to wait until he passed second to head out; he had little desire to encounter the Japanese right fielder.

Wally Traynor took the mound for The Americans. He had patrolled first base in the first game, a position that Jack Simmons now played.

He was not as hard throwing as Simmons but Vaughan had been impressed with his accuracy and decided to hand him the ball with what he hoped would be a bounce back game.

Yuujin was slightly promoted, as he was now hitting 7th in the batting order. Ichiro moved up to 6th and Itsuo moved down to 8th.

Hoshino marched up and down as his players prepared.

"It's only three runs. We can easily get those back. When we are knocked down, we don't give up—we keep swinging."

Traynor's command was indeed impressive as he was able to hit the very corner of the plate at will, leaving the Japanese hitters baffled and off-balance.

Aito flew out to centerfield; Eiji to right field, and Yousuke ripped a line drive directly at Simmons, who nabbed the ball on a fly to send the Japanese down in order in the bottom of the inning.

Eugene noticed Yuujin running towards the outfield as soon as the last out was made. He decided to make his way across the outfield grass instead of traveling directly towards the dugout, thereby avoiding unwanted contact.

WHAM!

Sullivan launched a deep fly ball. The right fielder, Hirasawa, could only watch as it soared over his head and subsequently the wall; The Americans added another run to the scoreboard.

The fans cheered as Sullivan took his time running the bases.

"The Americans brought the bats tonight, didn't they, Jerry?"

"They absolutely did! Four runs and it's only the second inning. I bet the ending of game one left a bad taste in their mouths as they are out for blood here in the rematch."

POP!

Benjamin Williams smashed a breaking ball with two outs in the second with Traynor on first.

Traynor took off but soon slowed to a jog as he watched the ball disappear over the right field wall for another home run.

Eugene observed from the on-deck circle. He slapped the hands of Traynor and then Williams as they happily made their way back to their dugout and their teammates.

The deafening delight continued as Eugene walked up to the plate with two outs and no one on.

He took the first pitch inside as the stadium cooled from its celebratory fervor.

Eugene sent the second pitch blistering over first base and into the right field stands for a high-velocity first strike.

The third pitch was Haku's third straight fastball. Eugene somehow managed to sear this one with even more intensity than his previous one. He watched the ball escalate towards left field as he dropped his bat to run but quickly realized it was curving foul.

"Good contact!" yelled Billy. "Keep swinging, Eugene!"

Haku went to his curveball and duped Durante. He swung extremely early, not connecting whatsoever.

Eugene had struck out to end the inning.

Yuujin swung two bats for practice as he watched Ichiro foul off the first two pitches he saw.

He looked to left field to notice Eugene. He wondered if his American counterpart felt betrayed at all by the article. He wanted to tell him it was not his intention and the entire thing started off as a misunderstanding. He sensed Eugene was off; he could tell by his two at-bats and his body language in the outfield. He also noticed he had gone out of his way to ignore him.

"Strike three!" the umpire shouted.

Yuujin placed the bats down and headed back to the dugout as their half inning of offense had come to another quick close.

The Americans tacked on another run in the third, making the score 6-0.

Yuujin stepped up to lead off the bottom of the 3rd. Selective boos could be heard from the stands, which Yuujin disregarded. He dug in.

The first pitch was up and in, causing the batter to scatter out of the way. A sprinkle of cheers broke out.

Yuujin made his way back into the batter's box. He dug in deeper and harder.

Traynor wound up and delivered.

The pitch was again inside, but this time in the strike zone.

Prepared, he swung and lined a hard single over Simmons.

He rounded first and quickly receded when Williams came up throwing.

He had given The Japanese their first hit.

Traynor worked in and out of trouble, eventually forcing Eiji to pop out to Averill with two outs and two on.

The one-sided onslaught continued. By the time the fifth inning concluded, The Americans had taken a 9-0 lead.

Yuujin came up for his second at bat in the sixth.

Traynor had been, for the most part, cruising. The Japanese continued swinging but kept grounding and popping out.

Yuujin, feeling rather confident from his previous at-bat, fouled the first pitch fastball straight back.

Eugene took note of the quick transformation. In an extremely short amount of time, Yuujin had become a hitter desperately trying to make contact, to one who jumped out aggressively. Self-assurance and tenacity were key to becoming a great hitter. In that moment, Eugene wondered where those qualities had gone in his own approach.

His reflections were quelled when Yuujin served the ball into the outfield. It was a clean hit; clear over Billy's grasp.

Eugene charged in.

Yuujin sprinted to first, keeping an eye on the ball and Eugene's proximity to it.

Eugene approached the ball and from the corner of his eye saw the runner round first.

Yuujin was attempting to stretch his single into a double.

Eugene gloved the ball, quickly reached into his mitt, and came up throwing. He hurled it towards second, putting so much energy into the throw that he belly flopped onto the grass after releasing the ball.

Yuujin could tell it was a good throw. He could also tell it was coming in to his left of second base. He slid, attempting to hug the outside half of the bag.

Chuisano came up with the catch, which bounced just once before he secured it. Phil swung around to apply the tag as his glove came down hard on Yuujin's hand. They both looked to the umpire.

"Safe!"

"Yuujin Miyano has just turned a single into a double with pure hustle," Jerry Elson noted.

"And to up the stakes, it was Eugene Durante, his alleged rival, who came up with the throw from left field," added Curt.

"Say what you want, but this young Japanese player is no pushover. We saw that long at-bat of his in the first game where he worked the count, along with a single when the pressure was on. Today he is two for two and The Japanese don't have many hits outside of his."

"He does look confident out there, unlike the rest of his team who appears to have deflated."

"Down nine runs can do that to a team, Curt."

"No doubt. Overall, The Americans seem far more prepared this time around."

Traynor quickly regrouped, retiring the side without Yuujin advancing from second.

Yuujin hustled back to his dugout, something all of The Americans took notice of.

Eugene roped Haku's pitch to left field. He dropped his bat and ran to first.

Hirasawa ran in, attempting to track the free-falling ball. He extended his body and his outstretched arm in a desperate attempt to make the catch.

Eugene approached the bag as he witnessed the Japanese left fielder dive. The ball situated itself in the very top of the webbing and stayed put as Hirasawa hit the ground.

Eugene, dismayed, stopped in his tracks and simply put his hands on his waist as if pondering his inability to catch a break. He watched the Japanese amble off the field and shook his head. He felt a mitt suddenly slap his backside.

"Don't let it get to ya. We're going to need that bat in the third game."

Eugene turned to see it was Jack, who had already taken first.

By the time the eighth inning rolled around, The Americans had a dominating lead; it was 12-0. The Japanese ballplayers had grown weary and disheartened, their trots onto and off the field slowed and their fight declawed.

The Americans were four outs away from evening up the series when Yuujin came up for what all assumed would be his final at-bat of the game with two outs and no one on. He was once again met with a shower of hisses.

Traynor was still going strong. He watched as the young ballplayer strolled up. Miyano was the only hitter in the game to have more than one knock off him.

Yuujin took the first pitch for a ball, slightly outside.

Eugene cleared his mind the best he could as he took a step inwards; he didn't want a repeat of Yuujin's double.

The second pitch was high.

"Two balls, no strikes," the umpire stated.

Yuujin watched the next pitch pour in for a strike.

The fourth pitch crossed directly over the border of the plate. Yuujin went to swing but held up as he meticulously followed the ball into the catcher's mitt. He looked back to await the umpire's call.

"Just outside," the adjudicator claimed.

"Oh come on!" bellowed Billy from third. "You don't want to go home?"

Traynor grinned at his teammate's comments as he received the ball back. The count was 3-1.

Traynor deviated from his norm by throwing an off-speed pitch with three balls in the count. Yuujin swung and missed badly, way out in front.

"Full count!" the umpire reminded.

Traynor fired a fastball directly down the middle of the plate and Yuujin weakly fouled it down the first base line.

The seventh pitch was another fastball that resulted in another foul ball.

The eighth was high but Yuujin swung anyway, sending it back, over the catcher's reach.

Yuujin straightened out the next pitch but still sent it into the left field stands.

The tenth pitch of the at-bat was low. Yuujin lunged down and threw his bat at the ball, making weak contact and sending it rambling foul.

"This kid doesn't give up!" Curt declared.

"This will be the eleventh pitch of the at-bat. Once again, the 3-2—fouled again!"

"He has probably swung at a few balls but he's stayed alive."

"Traynor looks understandably irritated. He's just four outs away from shutting the door on these guys and their seven hole hitter is giving him a hard time," Jerry announced.

"Another foul ball! That's twelve pitches. He just keeps swinging! He absolutely refuses to give up despite knowing there's no way his team can pull off a comeback at this point."

"Here comes lucky thirteen."

Yuujin watched the ball zoom in; he calculated it would be another borderline pitch. Continuing to protect the plate, he swung, barely connecting.

The ball dribbled upwards, staying inside of the white foul line.

Traynor pounced off the mound.

Yuujin broke for first.

"Traynor is running towards the ball as Miyano is busting it down the line with momentum," Jerry broadcasted.

"Traynor picks up the ball. He throws to first. It's going to be close!"

"And Miyano is…out! Oh, just got him by a hair!"

Curt added, "That was closer than I thought it was going to be off the bat."

"It sure was. Miyano gave them a run for their money on that play."

"The eighth inning has come to a close as The Americans are just decimating their opponent today with a 12-0 lead."

"Ironically, Eugene Durante is the only American player without a hit."

Yuujin Miyano once again hurried back to his dugout, once again drawing the respectful attention of The Americans.

"That kid's crazy," muttered Billy as he trotted in.

The American manager awaited his hurler.

"You good for one more?" asked Vaughan.

"I should be. As long as that Miyano doesn't come up again," Traynor responded.

Chuisano turned to Eugene and asked, "How the hell were you able to keep that guy still?"

The Americans did not add to their already secure cushion of a lead in the top of the ninth.

Traynor returned in the bottom of the inning to conclude the game.

He proved to be visibly fatigued, both in body language and accuracy as he walked the first two batters of the inning, who were the 8th and 9th hitters.

"Let's go Aito!" Yuujin hollered.

The Japanese shortstop jumped on the first pitch and hit a sharp line drive between short and third for a base hit.

Itsuo held up on third, allowing the bases to be loaded for Eiji.

"Time!" yelled Sullivan.

The umpire granted the request and the catcher made his way to Traynor.

"Tired?" asked Sullivan.

"A little," sighed Traynor.

"Coach doesn't want to waste another arm with such a big lead. Sorry to put you in that sacrificial role."

"Eh, I'm used to it."

"Don't overthink it. Let 'em have it and let 'em put the ball in play. They will get themselves out eventually. No more free passes."

"Got it."

Sullivan encouragingly slapped Traynor on the stomach and headed back.

Traynor followed the advice and no longer attempted to hit the corners of the plate.

Eiji fouled the first pitch back and then popped the second one up to Jack Simmons, who made the play for the first out of the inning.

"There we go!" yelled Billy. "Two more outs and we go home, boys!"

Yousuke trekked to the plate.

Traynor knew their most powerful hitter would give his fatigued fastball a ride but hoped it would fall into a mitt. It didn't.

Yousuke scalded the ball into the outfield, splitting Williams and Roberts. As the ball bounced off of the wall, two Japanese base runners had already crossed the plate. Roberts eventually recovered the ball and fired it in. Yousuke halted at second as the third runner scored without a throw.

Traynor annoyingly clapped his glove open and closed, a signal that he wanted the ball back as soon as possible.

Reo Hirabayashi, their cleanup hitter and center fielder, marched up to the plate.

Reo had been a prisoner of war under the British in Burma. He was one of the few Japanese soldiers to become famous only after reaching an internment camp. Upon being drafted, and all through the battles on the Burma front, Reo carried a secret, hidden in an airtight can. This secret ultimately made its way to the camp where it was finally revealed and put to use. The mystery turned out to be rice-malt yeast.

Reo was a trained sake brewer before the war. While being imprisoned, he encouraged the cooks and food suppliers to set aside some rice each day and once a month he concocted the glorious flavor, bouquet, and color of traditional sake. Many told him they only kept their spirits up due to the anticipation of drinking something so comforting.

Now, Reo kept the Japanese team's inconceivable hope alive by shooting a base hit to center field. Yousuke moved up to third and stayed put.

"Let's turn two and end this!" encouraged Averill.

Eugene took a step in as Shichirō Hirasawa walked up to the plate. He knew Yousuke was not a fast runner and if the ball came to him on a fly, he could end the game with a good throw.

Hirasawa worked the count to 2-2.

Traynor threw his first breaking ball since Sullivan had come out for the pep talk.

Hirasawa connected and Eugene recognized right away that his intuition had been correct. He ran in and planted himself under the ball as Yousuke retreated back to third, ready to tag up.

Eugene made the play and came up throwing.

Yousuke broke from third to only then immediately stop and stammer back to the bag as Eugene's strong throw made it all the way to Sullivan without a bounce.

"Two outs!" shouted Roberts from centerfield.

Ichiro approached the plate but Traynor's eyes darted not to him, but to the lanky hitter entering the on-deck circle.

Yuujin picked up the practice bat and combined it with his to give weight to his practice swings. He noticed a number of

American players were eyeing him. At first he did not understand but soon grasped the idea that he had somehow become a feared hitter in the eyes of his competitors.

Ichiro took a first-pitch ball. The crowd was now standing on its feet in expectation.

Traynor's second pitch was straight and as fast as he could muster.

Ichiro made good contact and the ball soared into the outfield.

Yuujin and Eugene simultaneously turned their heads to behold the outcome.

Walter Roberts glided to his left, his trot smooth and seemingly effortless, and caught the ball for the last out of the game.

Traynor pumped his fist and soon shook the hand of Sullivan.

The Americans had evened up the series at a game apiece.

Chapter 24

Sanctuary Between The White Lines

The Japanese locker room was quiet. Klaus Schmidt could feel the palpable demoralization as he trudged through changing athletes.

Yuujin heard him approaching and stood up to fulfill his media duty.

"Tough loss," Klaus remarked in a near whisper.

Yuujin nodded his head.

"I'm supposed to ask you a few questions."

"I understand."

"Okay," Klaus responded nervously. "Today was obviously not an easy day for your team. What do you think went wrong?"

"The Americans came out swinging and never stopped. They were determined and rigorous in their approach. When one falls behind, it becomes harder to mount a comeback. I am, however, very proud of my team's performance in the last inning. We maintained our fighting spirit despite insurmountable odds. Through that journey, I believe we became stronger today."

"This fighting spirit you mentioned was exhibited most of all in you. I noticed this 'intensity always,' as you once put it, was embodied by you today. Do you consider yourself the leader of this team?"

Yuujin looked around, admiring his teammates, and shook his head.

"No, not at all. Coach Hoshino is our leader and veteran players like Yousuke, Shichirō, and Ichiro are the true team leaders. I am just trying to contribute."

"What is your prediction for the final game?"

"Firstly, playing two games has been an honor and a blessing for me. Playing another only furthers that reverence. I expect a good game, a close game, and a competitive game."

"I hope that to be the case. One final question. Have you learned anything about baseball from this experience?"

Yuujin reflected upon the question for a moment before answering, "Baseball is life and life is baseball. Every time we get a hit we are closer to home. Every time we reach home we score a run. Every run inches us towards our ultimate goal of achieving victory. This is life. Success is not achieved through a once in a lifetime grand event but rather through a culmination of singular moments. To borrow a phrase, it's the little things. It's what makes baseball, and life, beautiful."

Klaus smiled at Yuujin's answer as he speedily wrote in his pad.

"Thank you, Yuujin. That was superb."

The American locker room was rambunctious, except for Eugene, who sat on the changing bench slowly buttoning his shirt, lost in thought. He wasn't aware of the reporter approaching.

"Hallo," said the calming accented voice.

Eugene slowly turned around to see Klaus standing over him.

"Congratulations on your victory," said the reporter.

"Wish I could have contributed. Only player in the lineup today that didn't get a hit. Guess I had stuff on my mind."

Eugene's accusatory tone stabbed Klaus.

"I am sorry about the story. It was, in a way, a misunderstanding."

"How is that?"

"I told Yuujin you had told me about your interaction at second base. He assumed you'd told me everything and then started to talk about his experiences in the war in relation to you. I told him I wouldn't print it. He said there was no shame in it."

"Sounds like our buddy, Yuujin," Eugene remarked as he stood up. "Listen, Klaus, today isn't the day for me. Go talk to the other players, the ones that helped the team win. I'm of no interest to your story."

Deterred, Schmidt nodded and said, "Of course. Thank you anyway."

Eugene fastened the last button on his shirt as he heard Billy shout, "Santa Klaus! Come over here, it's a celebration. I have a present for you. I want to introduce you to my good friend Arky Averill, who has quite the story. You're going to love it."

A pit formed in Eugene's stomach as he picked up his bag and exited the room.

"What's wrong? I know that tone," Hattie said.

"I don't know."

"Did you lose again?"

"No. We won today."

"So what is it?"

"I don't know."

"Yes, you do."

After a long pause, Eugene said, "The team won. I lost."

"What do you mean?"

"Do you remember that dream I had? About the heads on Sugar Loaf?"

"I do."

"Do you remember the one person who was alive at the end? The one I punched?"

"He's there, in Germany?" she inferred.

"Yea."

"Did you talk to him?"

"Briefly. It's kind of a long story."

"We don't have time for long stories so give me what you're feeling in a nutshell."

"Well, I feel like in some weird way the war isn't over. It just transitioned from the battlefield to the baseball field."

"I see."

"At least in war I didn't have to think like this, I only had to try and stay alive. This somehow seems harder."

"Well you just remember who you are and where you came from. You're not like the others. All you can do is be you."

"Yeah. I guess"

"That thing I know you're facing will always be there. It doesn't matter if you're on the battlefield or the ball field. It's pervasive. We know that better than most."

"You do. Not me."

"Are you not my other half?"

Eugene couldn't help but smile at the love radiating from the other end of the phone. "You know something, baby?"

"What?"

"You're my savior."

"Best believe it. Now let's hang up so my engagement ring payments aren't interrupted.   "

"Love you, Hattie."

"I love you, Eugene."

Yuujin looked up at the stars as he once again found himself standing in front of home plate in the empty ballpark.

"This is becoming tradition."

Yuujin turned to see Coach Hoshino walking towards him.

"Another beautiful night," Yuujin remarked.

"Not something I expected you to say after such a crushing defeat."

"It is an honor to play this game, win or lose."

Hoshino reached Yuujin and responded, "That is true. Come for the stars?"

"I was trying to find the three stars."

"Ah yes, the familial symbol of three. The child holding up the parents, where it is said consciousness itself can be seen."

"It always relieved me to look up and see it. But I can't seem to find it tonight."

"You were, in many ways, that child today, Yuujin. Holding up our team."

"I just did what I could."

"Of course."

They both looked up at the vast blanket of twinkling lights shining through the darkness.

"What brings you out tonight?" asked Yuujin

"You."

"Me?"

"Yes. I wanted to talk to you."

"How did you know where to find me?"

"Where else would you be?" he asked with a grin. "I came to check on you. Outside complications can be distracting to a ballplayer."

"I try to focus on the game."

"I saw that. You managed well."

"Do you have advice for such occasions?"

"I do. Tai Chi."

"Energy."

"That's right. Think of distractions as additional players on the field. Confront them. Use their energy to your advantage. Incorporate that into the game. When we change our relationship to distractions they become distractions no longer."

"They become fuel."

"Precisely. Can you handle that?"

"I can."

"Good. You're getting the ball in game three."

Yuujin swiveled around to face his manager and asked, "I'm pitching?"

"That's right. That is your dream, isn't it? To pitch in a professional game?"

"Yes, but—"

"No but—it is done."

"I won't disappoint you."

"I know. The only disadvantage to doing so is the tradition of pitchers hitting ninth."

"Nine hole hitters are only last the first time around. Then they might as well function as leadoff hitters."

"Very wise. Let me ask you, do you know who Jiddu Krishnamurti is?"

Yuujin shook his head.

"He is an Indian philosopher. I heard him speak on one of his tours not so long ago. He said, 'Tradition becomes our security, and when the mind is secure it is in decay.'"

The words confused Yuujin, who asked, "What does this mean?"

"It means you are both pitching and batting second. Good night, Yuujin."

As Coach Hoshino walked away, Yuujin felt paralyzed. He couldn't even summon the words to thank his manager; he just watched him withdraw from the field.

Yuujin suddenly felt the weight of such a responsibility. The deciding game would very much depend on his performance. He was utterly terrified.

He turned to leave and jolted in alarm, stunned to find Eugene standing directly in front of him.

"Sorry! I didn't mean to startle you," Eugene said quietly.

"I am sorry. I didn't hear you. I've been taking up the field long enough."

Yuujin started walking away when Eugene remarked, "Gorgeous night. Isn't it?"

"It is," he answered as he slowed.

"I never apologized for hitting you. It was wrong of me. I'm sorry."

"Water under the bridge, as you say."

Eugene chuckled without amusement and responded, "I'm glad. I have to admit I'm surprised you are as good as you are. You're a true ballplayer."

"I flap around like a fish out of water."

"Maybe a little. But it doesn't really matter how you look doing it. It's all about the results. You have heart. That's the most important thing."

"Why did you ignore me earlier, coming on and off the field?"

Eugene just shook his head and said, "I really don't know. I don't have a good answer for you. I guess I was scared in some way."

"Scared?"

"Sure. Maybe ticked off at the article Schmidt wrote and the attention it was getting."

"It was not my intention—"

"I know. No need to apologize. It just seems like the world is watching and listening, and I know it's not, but many are and I didn't know how to act or react. Christ, it sounds childish when I say it out loud."

"You have nothing to be uneasy about. You are honorable and true. It has been a blessing to play against you."

"Thanks." Eugene looked at his counterpart in true candor and said, "You know, I can't tell you how much it meant just to see your face, to know that you were alive. I thought about you from time to time since the war ended. I barely knew you and yet our encounter, though brief, really stuck in my head."

"It was the best conversation I've ever had," Yuujin noted.

"I think it was mine too! Hey, you still have that ball? With all those signatures?"

"Actually, it turned out that my sister forged the signatures all those years ago when she couldn't get them from the players. I never noticed until I came home."

Eugene's body reacted in physical pain as he took a deep breath. "That hurts."

"It did."

"What did you do with it?"

"I kept it."

"To torture yourself?"

"It is still my most prized possession."

"How do you figure?"

"It represents how far my sister was willing to go to bring a bit of joy to her baby brother. That is worth more than any autograph of a stranger."

"Well said." They stood quietly for a moment, then Eugene continued, "But it still hurts like hell, doesn't it?"

"Very much so."

They both laughed.

"I'm sorry about the boos and some of the pettiness going on. And for Billy's comments. And Jack hitting your left fielder. What's his deal anyway?"

"Shichirō?"

"Yeah. Some of the boys have it in their head that he was part of something pretty bad."

"I'm sure many soldiers were. But I can't see Shichirō being involved."

"Why is that?"

"He was part of the proletarian movement. I believe he's a filmmaker. From what I understand he works in nuance and subtlety since our government cracked down pretty hard on proletarian artists and organizers. I doubt the movement is even still alive. Shichirō has had friends tortured to death by police for bringing to light the hardships many people faced and the ways they were exploited. Shichirō was made to publicly denounce his socialist beliefs or choose death."

"Well, I'm certainly no fan of socialism, but I have to admit that hardly seems fair."

"That's life."

"I suppose it is. Doesn't make it right, though."

"Pining for another philosophical conversation about right and wrong?" Yuujin excitedly asked.

"Absolutely not. Maybe some other time, though."

"I very much hope there will be another time."

"How about we shake on it then?" Eugene asked as he extended his hand. "It sort of makes it an unofficial but binding agreement."

Yuujin took a step and reciprocated by grasping Eugene's hand.

"To another time."

The handshake was firm yet friendly. They were both aware of the weight of the moment, how long this act of solidarity took to coalesce.

When their hands parted, the disconnection was felt in the core of both men.

"See you around, Yuujin," Eugene said as he started walking away.

"See you."

As Eugene looked to his dugout, he heard Yuujin call after him, "I'm starting next game."

"No shit," Eugene curiously said. "Congratulations. Go easy on me, will ya?"

Yuujin grinned and answered, "No promises."

"There never are."

Yuujin took this in; it hit harder than he thought it would.

Eugene continued, "Anything else you want to tell me before I head back or you just want me to keep turning back around?"

Yuujin chuckled and thought to himself. "Actually, yes."

"What is it now?"

"I have an idea."

The American locker room was loose and jovial. Eugene confidently stood in front of his station as he buttoned up his jersey. He kept looking towards the entranceway.

Eventually, Klaus entered and Eugene pounced.

"Klaus!" he called out.

The reporter turned to see the American outfielder walking towards him. A few Americans took notice as well.

"I'm sorry about last time. With everything going on, I just wasn't in the mood."

"Completely understandable, Mr. Durante."

"But if it's alright with you—I'd like to make a statement. Maybe something for your paper that you can publish when this series is over after today."

"Surely! That would be great!" he said as he grabbed his pencil and pad.

"Okay. I want you to ask me why I love baseball."

"Sure. Why do you love baseball?"

Eugene suddenly felt fretful. He fought to ignore it and compose himself.

"Take your time," Klaus gently said.

"Thanks Klaus. You know something—you're a great guy."

The reporter appeared amused at the expressed tenderness. There was a hint of a smile, and then he repeated, "So, why do you like baseball?"

"Because baseball is the ultimate metaphor for the human experience."

"Go on."

A few players turned to watch the interview as the room became quiet.

"In both life and baseball decisions are made. Some turn out good, others turn out not so good."

Eugene and Billy made brief eye contact before Durante turned back to Klaus.

"When I was a kid, my mother took me with her to go shopping and this one time I grabbed a little decoration off the shelf. It must have been shiny or something, I don't know. When we got home, my mother noticed what I had in my hand and asked where it came from. Believe me when I say she grabbed my hand so fast and marched me right back to that store and made me apologize and give the adornment back. I was caught stealing. Ironically, in my first game for the Army I was also caught stealing, although in a much different way. I got caught stealing third with two outs to ruin a perfectly good inning. I'm sorry; I know I'm rambling here. What I'm trying to say is: these things happen in both baseball and life. But the thing that's most important is our chance to redeem our mistakes. I returned that toy when I was a child and I hit the game winning double the same day I was caught stealing."

Eugene wiped the manifested nerves from his brow. The entire team was now solemn and attuned to his words.

"There's a sanctuary between these white lines. It's a place where the outside world shouldn't matter. It should be a haven for devotion and rapport, solidarity and understanding. In many ways, the ballpark needs to be a last stand, our refuge, a fortress or garrison that defends these ideals."

Eugene peeked over at Walter and Williams.

"There's a devil in this diamond. Of that, there's no doubt. We need to cleanse it. I know I'm not the one who should even be saying this, but I'm not seeing anyone else say it. These words are not meant to be self-serving or righteous. I apologize if they come off that way. I'm saying what I'm saying because I have a friend over there on the other side. His name is Yuujin Miyano. He's an incredibly talented and kind human being. He is not my enemy and I am not his, even though there was a time where I viewed him as such."

Eugene took a deep breath.

"In both baseball and life, there is redemption. It allows us to transform, move on, and do so together. I feel like many, myself included, have forgotten its power and importance. Without it we will all fall into a deep dark hole with no way out. So I implore all of us, when things get increasingly dim— seek redemption."

Chapter 25

Redemption

Game Three

"Welcome everyone to the rubber game of this three game exhibition series! I'm sure you know us by now—I'm Curt Nelson and I'm alongside Jerry Elson. This is Armed Forces Radio and we are transmitting live from behind the American dugout. What kind of game do you predict, Jerry?"

"It's hard to tell. We saw a pitching duel in game one and an absolute blow out in game two. I think if this is to be a high-scoring game, The Americans have it in the bag. If it's low-scoring, however, it could be anyone's game."

Eugene securely tied up his cleats as his team flooded into the dugout. He looked out to see another packed stadium as he embraced the cool breeze that blew his way. He looked across to see Yuujin on the lip of his dugout. His friend nodded in readiness and Eugene reciprocated.

"The Americans are going back to Jack Simmons to take the mound while the Japanese will be testing a new pitcher," said Jerry.

"That's right. And it's someone who's caused some buzz in the first two games. They are—"

"Hold up a moment, Curt. There appears to be something going on down there."

"You're right. It appears one American player and one Japanese player are taking the field."

Yuujin trotted out to right center field while Eugene made his way to left center field.

The players on both benches, taken by surprise, looked out to see their teammates. The crowd's commotion subdued as countless fingers pointed to the unexpected sight.

Yuujin found a spot that seemed right and he looked out to see Eugene established as well. He looked to his glove, where a baseball rested. He took the ball out of the mitt and gripped it.

Eugene could feel the nervous anticipation in the stadium. He looked around, viewing a myriad of gazing eyes. Then he took a deep breath and looked to his friend.

Yuujin's feet and shoulders lined up to his target. His elbow retracted back as his hips opened up. His body torqued and his throwing arm extended. The ball departed from his fingertips and Yuujin followed through, his arm decelerating soon afterwards.

Eugene watched the ball arc into the air. He followed its trajectory and never let it out of his sight, his eyes fixed on its flight plan. He brought his glove up in preparation.

The baseball nestled into the pocket of Eugene's mitt. He closed his glove immediately after the ball made contact with it and the moment seemed to freeze in history.

Yuujin and Eugene suddenly heard nothing; all speech and sound evanesced. Both players experienced an unexplainable slowing of time; the fans were suddenly hypnotized, the blades of grass in the outfield ceased to sway; all outside perceptions and impressions did not exist. There was simply a throw and a catch.

And then, just as suddenly as it came, the moment passed; Eugene quickly used his second hand to secure the catch.

He looked down at the ball, taking in the solemn gravity of such a simple action.

Eugene clutched onto the ball and lobbed it into the sky. Yuu-jin viewed reverence, affection, and goodwill land into his glove.

The two continued their catch as a bubble formed around the pair; the focus of the entire stadium remained transfixed.

After numerous back and forth throws, Eugene called out, "Warmed up?"

"Yes. I'm warm. You?"

"I'm good," answered Eugene as he sent one final throw to his ally.

Yuujin caught the ball and the two ran in towards one an-other. They convened in dead center field.

"Thank you," Eugene said.

"Thank *you,*" Yuujin relayed.

Eugene and Yuujin shook hands in front of the overflowing crowd. The grip soon transitioned into a hug. They patted each other's backs and as the stadium observed, it felt as if it were the world that was watching.

The two players separated and Yuujin jogged in towards his team. He tossed his mitt to a teammate in his dugout and made his way to his team's on-deck circle. Eugene shuffled to left field to await his teammates.

"Well I'll be damned," muttered Vaughan. He looked back towards his silent and baffled team and ordered, "Okay, I guess this is it! Let's go out there and give 'em a game to remember!"

The players quickly catapulted onto the field.

"Well that was certainly something!" Curt remarked.

"That's an understatement! I believe it's safe to say we just witnessed a symbolic fraternity between nations. A sort of reuni-fication, if you will."

"Beautifully put. It was quite the sight, wasn't it, Jerry?"

"It certainly was."

"It was also perfectly appropriate that it was Yuujin Miyano and Eugene Durante making such a statement. These two have a storied history that we have been following here. It just goes to show you that if these two, with their experiences with one another, can overcome it all, there may be hope for us yet."

"Well said, Curt. The teams are almost ready to commence here and it is now do or die for both of these clubs. The winner of today's game will be the winner of the series. It's sure to be a pressure cooker."

Jack Simmons tossed a few warm ups and then signaled his readiness.

Aito walked up to the plate. He kicked some dirt near his cleats and settled in.

Jack looked at Sullivan's dancing fingers to get the sign.

He wound up and fired as the conclusive game commenced.

"Strike one!"

The fans cheered as Aito stepped out of the box. Seconds later he stepped back in and leaned into his stance.

Jack's next pitch was scorched up the middle; Chuisano and Averill barely budged as they immediately recognized they had no chance.

Aito rounded first and stayed put as Roberts threw the ball in from centerfield.

Yuujin strolled up to the plate and unexpectedly heard vociferous applause. Hiding his smile, he put his head down and settled in.

Jack delivered the pitch as Aito broke for second base.

Yuujin recognized the straight and fast pitch and judged it to be in the strike zone. He swung swiftly.

A line drive shot into the outfield as Yuujin took off.

Eugene didn't have to move a foot as the ball voyaged directly into his glove; Aito hastily retreated back to first. Upon catching it, Eugene motioned his mitt to Yuujin, who could only shrug as he headed back to his dugout. The crowd cheered in appreciation of the irony.

"One down!" yelled Billy.

"Let's turn two!" added Traynor, playing first base as he did in the opening game.

Chuisano and Averill moved into double-play depth as Yousuke came up to bat.

The first pitch was an outside breaking ball.

Jack went back to a fastball but the second pitch whizzed inside.

"Two balls, no strikes," announced the umpire.

Yousuke focused and held his bat steady.

They both knew a fastball was coming.

The third pitch caught the plate and Yousuke connected.

Benjamin Williams took off simultaneously. He bolted towards the ball, which looked to be headed into the right field corner.

Williams strode like a skipping rock across water. He inched closer and closer to the ball, seemingly traveling double the speed of most right fielders. If he were on another team, he would most assuredly be their center fielder.

Aito retreated back to first when he realized Williams was in range.

With neither a dive nor a jump, Williams reached the searing ball and held his glove up. He made the catch nearing the corner of the field, still on the run.

Aito dabbed first with his foot and tagged up, rushing towards second base.

Williams twisted around and came up throwing.

His arm unleashed an absolute bullet as he essentially threw a strike to second base.

Averill caught the ball on a fly and dropped his mitt to apply the tag as Aito slid.

"Out!" yelled the umpire.

The crowd cheered. Jack pointed to his right fielder in appreciation as The Americans made their way off the field.

Eugene checked the lineup posted on the dugout wall once more. He was still batting third. He felt indebted to his manager for sticking by him despite not getting a single hit in the previous game.

Yuujin took the mound and began his warm-ups. A culmination of dreams and desires were about to transition into actuality.

Eugene placed one foot up, over the lip of the dugout as he parked himself next to Vaughan.

"Thanks, coach."

Vaughan turned to look at him with intrigued eyes.

"What the hell for?"

"Keeping me slotted in the three hole."

"Thank yourself. You were the only one without a hit last game. This was the best way to protect you," he slyly answered.

Eugene laughed.

"Your friend out there doesn't look like he throws very hard," Vaughan remarked.

"Something tells me he'll find a way to figure it out."

Arky Averill stood at the plate.

Yuujin brought his arms over his head and stopped. After a few painstakingly slow seconds, he speedily kicked his leg and finished his delivery, discharging a first-pitch strike.

Vaughan looked at Eugene and declared, "Unconventional."

"Sounds about right."

Yuujin's delivery made Averill uncomfortable as his timing was thrown off. The second pitch was a curveball and Averill swung and missed.

"Back to the fastball or another breaking pitch?" asked Vaughan with the tone of a test.

"Breaking," answered Eugene.

Yuujin fired a high fastball and Averill angrily swung at it.

Vaughan and Eugene looked at one another in fascination.

Averill muttered to himself on his way back to the dugout. "Don't worry about that one, Arky!" Billy protested. "We'll figure that windup out."

The star of the top of the first inning, Benjamin Williams, walked up to the plate as Eugene advanced onto the on-deck circle.

"Let's go, Benny!" Roberts bellowed from the dugout, grabbing his bat in case a man should get on.

Yuujin brought his hands over his head and once again stopped, although this time very briefly. He quickly finished his delivery and threw a curveball.

Williams, fooled by the ramped up wind up, swung but was way out in front of the pitch.

Vaughan snickered from the dugout as Williams refocused.

Yuujin brought his hands over his head and paused, this time for what seemed like an eternity. When he unfroze, his physical articulation did not accelerate but remained drowsily lackadaisical. The ball, however, jumped out of his hand and crossed the plate, catching Williams by surprise.

"Strike two!"

"Was this guy a magician during the war or what?" Chuisano decried.

"That pitch was probably eighty miles per hour but I bet it looked like ninety," added Traynor as he sat on the edge of the bench.

Williams practiced his swing and dug back into the box.

Yuujin repeated the exact same delivery with identical timing but this time instead of a fastball, a nasty curveball left his hand.

Williams was frozen as he watched the ball twist into the strike zone.

"Strike three!"

Williams walked away before the umpire could even complete the utterance.

"Hey, Durante!" Vaughan barked. Eugene turned around to hear the other half. "Good friggin' luck."

Eugene took his time walking to the plate.

The fans suddenly stood on their feet and applauded. An appreciative clap soon gave way to an all out roar.

When Eugene reached the plate he removed his hat. "Take your hat off and wave, Yuujin," he encouraged.

"They're yelling for you," he retorted.

"No. They're yelling for us."

Eugene and Yuujin simultaneously twirled their hats in the air amidst the thundering hurrah.

The supportive yells did not subside despite Eugene digging into the batter's box.

Yuujin dispatched the quick version of his delivery and threw a strike over the heart of the plate. Eugene watched it sail into the catcher's mitt.

"Strike one!"

The ovation simmered back down as Yuujin received the ball back.

Eugene took a second pitch, this one outside.

"One ball, one strike."

Eugene stepped out of the box and hoped Yuujin was enjoying the moment as much as he was. He looked out at his supportive brethren and soaked in the energy of his final game.

Eugene settled himself back in.

Yuujin wound up as Eugene concentrated.

Another breaking ball came his way, curving inside on the southpaw.

Eugene swung; the sweet spot of the bat linked up to the ball in perfect hitting harmony. The baseball sprung off the bat and catapulted into deep right field.

In terms of distance there was no doubt. The ball, however, twisted as it approached the foul pole.

Both teams rose, anxiously awaiting the outcome as Eugene stiffly stood at the plate as if he were just another spectator.

The ball bounced off the pole with a booming buzz and ricocheted back onto the outfield grass.

Eugene dropped his bat and started his trot. He sneaked a peek to Yuujin, who, shaking his head, frustratingly grinned at Durante.

The fans cheered the loudest yet as Eugene slowly rounded each base, redeeming himself for his abysmal performance the game before. His instinct was to take his time and savor the moment, but he also understood the unwritten rules of baseball did not take kindly to any degree of grandstanding.

The gusts of the fans' glee propelled Eugene around third base. He eyed home and felt a strange and sudden forlornness. Despite the fact that when one places their foot on home plate it is the acme of the base rounding experience, it is also the moment when it is all over. The adrenaline slowly deescalates and from that point on it all starts anew. That was, Eugene surmised, the beauty of the game.

Durante slowed his brisk walk as he approached the 17-inch plate. Knowing the euphoria was about to come to a hasty end, Eugene decided to meet what could be the last home run he would ever hit head-on.

He confidently stepped on the five-sided slab of white rubber as his run was simultaneously counted in the score box. In that moment, Eugene became aware of something he always knew but never thought about. Home plate was the only base on ground level. It was secure and impregnable. No matter how hard you slid into it, it stayed precisely where it was. At that juncture, with his foot still on the plate, Eugene decisively understood why they called it home.

Hattie flashed in his mind, just before he removed his foot from the plate.

Eugene had reached home in more ways than one.

Yuujin forced Roberts to ground out to third to end the inning and the two teams flipped positions on the field.

Jack wasn't as sharp as he was in the first game but battled nonetheless; he got through the first four innings without giving up a run.

In that time, Yuujin sailed through the American lineup as no runner reached base after Eugene's home run.

"Well, we're heading into the top of the 5th inning with a one-run game," Curt said.

"We sure are. Yuujin Miyano has been impressive but the big question is: can he keep it going? Simmons has had trouble finding the plate at times but keeps finding a way to get out of it."

"His velocity isn't where it was in the first game."

"I have to tell you, Curt, I was expecting a few more runs in this game by now."

"Agreed. After the last outing, such a low-scoring affair seems inconceivable."

"It also feels like this game is flying by."

"If only we could revel in baseball a little while longer."

Jack Simmons took the mound once more as the 5th inning opened.

The veteran outfielder Shichirō Hirasawa stepped up to the plate to lead things off.

The first fastball Shichirō saw was roped into left field.

Eugene recognized he could not get to the ball in time and ran to it as fast as he could to try to hold Shichirō to a single.

The ball bounced in fair territory and proceeded to roll straight up the foul line, past Eugene, who hustled after it.

Shichirō cruised into second base with ease. The throw eventually came in to Arky, who had jogged into the outfield to receive it.

Billy and Traynor inched up in their respective positions, in tune with their opponent's style of play.

Ichiro squared up to bunt before Jack could even release the ball.

It was executed beautifully as the Japanese first baseman sent the ball directly to the American first baseman.

Traynor caught the skipping ball as Shichirō ran to third. Traynor ran to his left and tagged the rapidly moving Ichiro for the first out of the inning.

The Japanese had once again proved exceedingly efficient at small ball.

With a runner on third and one out, Eiji, their second baseman, had a chance to help his team tie the game.

Eiji took a first-pitch ball.

Coach Hoshino leaned in to Yuujin and said, "If this were five years ago, I'd put the squeeze play on. Shichirō was speedy. He has lost a step or two. We all do."

Eiji took the second pitch, this time for a strike.

"Eiji handles the bat very well," remarked Yuujin. "He could lay down a good one."

Hoshino smirked and responded, "He could. But that would be an emotional decision. This game is one of probability."

"That is true. But they wouldn't expect it. Not from us."

"Strategy is a fickle science."

"I'm starting to think it is an art."

The two exchanged a knowing glance.

Jack fired a high fastball; Eiji swung and popped it high up in the air.

"I got it!" yelled Billy as he moved into foul territory.

Having plenty of room, Billy made the easy out.

"One more and we're out of this!" encouraged Chuisano.

Simmons, however, let the next batter, Itsuo, get away on a five pitch walk. He had runners at the corners with two outs.

The American catcher walked out to the mound as Yoshio Hasegawa, the nine-hole hitter, walked up to the plate.

"This is their weakest hitter by far," Sullivan remarked. "Three fast ones and we're home free."

"Got it," answered Jack.

Sullivan jogged back to reclaim his position behind the plate.

Jack worked from the stretch, a more compact pitching delivery, as a means to limit a runner's ability to steal.

Yoshio took the first pitch.

"Strike one!"

Jack confidently repeated what he had just executed and Yoshio swung and missed.

"No balls, two strikes," the umpire said.

Yoshio dug in as Jack set. A third fastball charged the plate. It was slightly higher than the previous two but maintained the same velocity.

Yoshio swung and connected.

The runners took off upon contact.

The blooper was hit weakly but dropped in for a single between third base and left field.

Shichirō Hirasawa crossed the plate to tie the game as Itsuo advanced to second.

"Dammit!" yelled Simmons from the mound.

"That's okay! You got this, Jack. One more and we're out of it," encouraged Traynor from first.

The lineup flipped as Aito, the leadoff hitter, approached the plate. He had scorched a single in his first at bat and now looked to give his team the lead.

Jack threw a curveball to the hitter's surprise. Aito swung and missed, way out in front of the ball.

More surprisingly, Jack threw a second curveball.

Once again, Aito swung and missed, his anxiousness blatantly being taken advantage of.

Aito stepped out and gathered himself. The mind games of baseball proved rampant and rife as the leadoff hitter tried to gauge whether or not Simmons would dare throw a third breaking pitch, something he did not do often. His best pitch was still his fastball. Aito knew that Jack knew that he knew this. Was that part of the deception?

Aito stepped back in, not knowing what to expect. At this point, he just picked a pitch and sat on it. He told himself to await a fastball.

Jack quickly swung his hands over his head and kicked his leg.

Aito's eyes lit up as he saw the ball coming in. He swung.

Jack had dropped a third curveball and for the third straight time, Aito had swung and feebly missed.

Jack's extended inning in the top of the fifth was foiled by Yuujin's fast-paced outing in the bottom of the inning. He made quick work of the lineup.

"You okay?" asked Vaughan.

Jack nodded and said, "I'm good right now but I don't know if I can finish this one."

"Don't worry about that. Just give us what you can. I'm keeping my eye on you. You're doing a hell of a job."

"Thanks, coach."

Jack walked back out to the mound as the sixth inning commenced.

Yuujin was to lead off. He was profoundly aware that they had entered the second half of the last game but tried not to concern himself with anything other than the moment.

The pitching counterparts were ready. Jack went into his delivery as Yuujin anticipated a first-pitch fastball.

Yuujin guessed right and a blistering line drive withdrew from his bat.

Traynor reacted instinctively. He threw his mitt up as his feet left the dirt. He leapt through the air, keeping his eyes on the searing baseball.

Traynor hit the ground hard on his crash back down but could feel a weighted object in his glove. That, plus the cheers from the stands, let him know he had made an impressive play. He came back up and held his mitt in the air to signal the catch before throwing the ball back to the pitcher.

"Nice play!" Jack pronounced.

"Are they given' out gold gloves for this thing!?" Billy the Berserk shouted from across the diamond.

Jack turned his attention to Yousuke, the Japanese slugger.

A first pitch curveball thumped in the dirt.

Jack threw another curveball, this one outside.

Yousuke determined Jack was running out of gas and was turning to calculated tricks and ruses to compensate.

Jack went back to his fastball and Yousuke smacked a single into center field.

"That's okay, Jack!" encouraged Billy. "Double play and we're out of this thing."

Reo Hirabayashi dug in with a plan, albeit an unorthodox one; he planned to sit on a curveball. Reo had noticed Jack was throwing more breaking balls and they weren't as sharp or located as well as his fastball.

Jack knew the opposition was on to him. He was trying to pull another rabbit out of the hat but when he reached down into it, he felt nothing left.

Jack's first pitch was a fastball with little velocity, which Reo took.

"Strike one!"

Sullivan knew he couldn't throw another one like that without paying the price. He put down the signal for a curveball.

Jack nodded at the sign and went into his windup.

Reo gently rotated his wrists and with them, the bat.

The pitch came in with little movement and hung.

The batter made hard contact. The ball soared deep into left-centerfield.

Both Williams and Roberts dashed towards it. Before either could reach the track, however, the ball disappeared over the wall.

The Japanese dugout clapped in excitement as Reo rounded the bases. He had given his team a 3-1 lead.

Sullivan went out to calm his visibly angry pitcher as Reo crossed the plate.

"Two more then we'll get back in this, yeah?"

"Yeah," Jack grunted.

"Come on, we scored a dozen runs last game. Our guys aren't going to let us down. They'll pick us up. Let's just get out of this."

Jack, using just fastballs, retired the next two batters, though each hit the ball exceedingly hard.

Jack exhaustingly collapsed onto the bench as his teammates came around and patted his legs and shoulders. He reared his head back knowing he gave his team his all, wondering if that would prove enough.

Yuujin's team had provided him with a two run lead and it was his job to keep it .

The American catcher led off the inning for the offense.

Yuujin brought his arms over his head and stopped. After his routine pause, he kicked his leg and completed his delivery.

The first pitch was low and outside.

Sullivan remained in the box, barely moving a muscle; he was ready for the next pitch before Yuujin even retrieved the ball.

Yuujin wound up and propelled a high fastball.

Sullivan's eyes lit up.

With a swift smack, the catcher slapped the ball into the outfield.

It was hit hard and split Reo and Yoshio in the outfield; both players attempted to cut the ball off so that it did not roll to the wall.

Sullivan rounded first base as Reo got to the ball. Sullivan didn't have the greatest speed and the center fielder was quite aware.

The throw came in strong but a little offline. Aito had to come off the bag to grab the ball; he tried to swing back and tag Sullivan's leg as the slide commenced.

"Safe!"

After fetching the ball, Yuujin calmly turned his attention to the next batter, Jack Simmons.

"Whatcha think?" Vaughan asked while looking at Eugene. "Should I give them a taste of their own medicine?"

"Small ball?"

Yea."

"Can Jack bunt well?"

"Don't know."

"Can Sullivan get to third on time?"

"Don't know."

Eugene answered with widened eyes.

Vaughan concluded, "Ah, what the hell."

He stood on the top step of the dugout and started relaying a series of encoded gestures to the batter.

When the sequence was over, Eugene asked, "Is this the right strategic move?"

Vaughan chuckled and answered, "I have a feeling. Sometimes you just gotta follow your gut, kid."

Yuujin threw a curveball and Jack squared around to bunt, much to the defense's surprise.

Simmons managed to nudge the ball to the first base side of the plate, ensuring safe passage for Sullivan.

Yousuke sprung up and scurried towards the ball. He picked it up and released a bullet to the chest of Ichiro at first base.

Not being a particularly quick runner, Jack was out by a couple of steps.

He trotted back to the dugout and was greeted with encouragement over a job well done.

Yuujin had a runner on third base with one out. He knew The Americans would no doubt attempt anything to bring home that run.

Arky Averill stepped up, looking to drive in Sullivan.

The Japanese outfielders maneuvered forward a step or two in an attempt to better their chances of getting Sullivan out if there was to be a play at the plate.

A tumbling curveball dropped in for the first strike of the at-bat.

Yuujin deceptively wound up and next executed a prime screwball. He watched as it shifted from left to right from his perspective. It broke in the opposite direction of his previous curveball, throwing off the batter's eyeline.

Averill spoiled the pitch, barely making contact.

Yuujin had Arky where he wanted him, no balls and two strikes.

Yousuke would normally inform a pitcher to bounce some off-speed pitches in this situation to try and get the batter to chase, but with a runner at third, he hesitated risking a wild pitch.

The third pitch fastball was high and Averill took it for the first ball.

"One ball, two strikes," the umpire reminded.

Yuujin nodded in agreement with Yousuke and entered his delivery.

Averill, with utter focus, saw the incoming pitch break down and in. He swung at the screwball and made contact.

The moderately struck ground ball scooted directly between Itsuo and Aito, as if it could see exactly where it needed to go in order to avoid the shortstop and third baseman and reach the outfield.

Sullivan crossed home plate without breaking a sweat as Averill clapped his hands in elation.

Yuujin reminded himself to keep composed; his team was still up by a run.

Benjamin Williams took advantage of a first pitch fastball and walloped it into the outfield for a clean base hit.

Averill stopped at second as The Americans yearned for a two-out rally.

Eugene was 1-2 on the day with a homerun and a strikeout. He dug in as Yuujin faced true pressure for the first time in the game.

The first-pitch curveball twisted in for a first-pitch strike.

Eugene could feel the crowd; he knew they wanted something exciting. He could only hope to deliver them what they craved.

Yuujin switched to a well-placed fastball on the outside corner and Eugene fouled it off into the left field seats.

Yousuke called for the screwball.

The pitch moved down and away from the lefty hitter and Eugene took it.

"Ball," the umpire stated. "One ball, two strikes."

Eugene was impressed that Yuujin wasn't afraid to throw any pitch in any count. It made it hard to guess what was coming.

Yuujin brought his arms over his head, stopped, and dispatched.

Eugene observed the ball coming in; he deduced it was going to be borderline and committed himself to swing. The pitch broke down and away at the last minute; Yuujin had gone back to the screwball.

Eugene did his best to adjust; he told himself he just needed to make contact at that point. With his eyes fixated on the dropping ball, Durante connected.

The speedy runners took off on contact as Eugene shot a routine ground ball towards third base. Itsuo placed himself behind the bag to retrieve the ball.

The ball, sharply hit, struck the corner of third base and shot up into the air. The bizarre occurrence caught the third baseman off-guard, as he was suddenly no longer tracking the ball's path. The baseball eventually dropped in front of the short-stop but all the runners were already safely at their destination.

"Wow! Talk about a bad break, Curt!"

"You're telling me—first the seeing-eye single by Averill and now this. What are the chances? Miyano looked like he was about to get out of the inning with minimal damage but now The Americans have the bases loaded with arguably their best hitter up at the plate."

"That's right. Walter Roberts has not had a hit in this game and would sure like to correct that."

"He sure would, Jerry. And this is also a great test for Yuujin Miyano. Some might call it on-the-job training but it is also on-the-job courage."

"Baptism by fire is what it is, Curt. Baptism by fire."

Roberts kissed his bat. It was a tradition he enacted only in the most tense of situations; he didn't want to overuse its power and charm. An ex-girlfriend once told him too much of anything was a bad thing—love included.

Yuujin wiped some sweat from his forehead and leaned in to receive the sign.

Yousuke called for a screwball.

Yuujin nodded and entered the stretch.

The pitch danced down and in and Roberts swung and missed.

Yousuke called for the same pitch in the same location.

Yuujin once again nodded.

Roberts recognized the pitch this go around but the movement was so impressive he could only foul it off.

Yousuke snuck a peek at Roberts' eyes, as he believed he could see into a person's soul by doing so. What he saw was a man eager to constantly prove himself, a man accustomed to the hustle and bustle of life. He had seen fire and was not scared of it. As a matter of fact, he relished it. Life had continually thrown curveballs at him but he did not falter. He would protect the plate like he protected everything else in his life. His eyes were that of a baseball warrior. It made him hard to trick and a difficult out. Yousuke combined this with what he knew of his own pitcher. He knew Roberts wanted the fastball. He knew the fastball was Yuujin's weakest pitch. He knew the screwball seemed ideal but Roberts was not a man often fooled twice—let alone three times.

Yousuke threw down two fingers.

Yuujin nodded.

The curveball dodged away from Roberts, who swung and connected with the ball when it had nearly reached the dirt.

It shot off the bat and traveled weakly over the diamond, in-between first base and right field.

Ichiro ran backwards as Yoshio galloped inwards. The base runners were on the move and the fans waited breathlessly on their feet.

It soon became clear that the right fielder was way too far to make the catch. The first baseman was the only hope for The Japanese to come out of the inning unscathed.

With his glove's palm facing upwards and his wrist tucked close in to his waist, the baseball remarkably dropped into Ichiro's glove.

Yuujin punched his fist through the air; he had gotten out of it with his team's lead still intact.

Jack trotted onto the field but did not go to the mound; instead he took to first base. Traynor, who manned that position all game, made his way to the mound. He had held The Japanese at bay in game two and his manager needed him to do it again for three innings. He was up to the task.

While not as sharp as his previous outing, Traynor kept his opponents off the scoreboard in the top of the 7th.

Yuujin circled the mound, endeavoring to match his pitching counterpart. Hoshino was aware Yuujin had never ventured this far into a start before; his arm was neither trained for it nor was it acclimated to the stamina needed for such a feat. He kept an attentive eye on his starter.

The Berserk led off. His feet were shoulder-width and his knees bent slightly. He kept his bat above his head, both hands tightly gripping it.

Yuujin entered his prolonged windup.

A curveball cuddled in.

"Strike!"

Yousuke threw down the signal for a fastball.

Billy took the second pitch outside, noting it had lost velocity.

Yousuke had the same observation, well aware that Yuujin had a below-average fastball to begin with.

Billy timed the third pitch curveball perfectly and hit a rocket. Unfortunately for him, it was directly at center fielder Reo Hirabayashi, who did not have to move a step to make the play.

Chuisano came up with the intention of putting the ball in play but never got the chance as Yuujin threw four consecutive pitches out of the strike zone.

As Chuisano made his way to first, Yousuke made his way to the mound.

"You're scared," he stated.

"I lost the plate," Yuujin responded.

"You lost the plate because you are trying to nibble."

"The first out was a loud out."

"Yet an out nonetheless. We can't afford to give them free base runners. They must earn it. Understood?"

Yuujin nodded at his catcher.

Traynor stood with an open stance, his front foot rested further from home plate than his back foot. He liked being open to the pitcher as he found that he could get a better read on the ball using both of his eyes.

Yuujin threw back-to-back screwballs for balls.

Traynor stood patiently waiting for a heater.

A curveball dropped in for the first strike.

Yousuke called for a screwball in an attempt to get the batter to pound the ball into the ground for a double play.

Yuujin's pitch bounced in the dirt, requiring quick instincts and footwork from the veteran catcher to keep the ball in front of him.

"Three balls, one strike," the umpire stated.

Traynor had himself a hitter's count and hadn't even moved his bat from his shoulders.

Yuujin removed his hat and ran his fingers through his hair before placing the cap back on. He looked in to receive the sign. He nodded.

A slow curve found the plate and Traynor realized he might never see his desired fastball.

He swung and connected, swatting the ball over the third baseman's head in fair territory.

Chuisano rounded second as Shichirō Hirasawa chased down the ball as it caromed off the left field wall.

Traynor pulled into second as Chuisano slid into third. The ball came in to the cutoff man as The Americans suddenly had runners on second and third with one out.

Yuujin's head fell at the outcome. However, he quickly recalled a memory, one where his mother told him to keep his head up in times of despair. One must look frustration and inadequacy in the face if one is to defeat it.

The words resounded in his mind and Yuujin stood tall at the mound. He was prepared for whatever was to come.

Sullivan took a first-pitch fastball for strike one.

Yousuke enjoyed calling pitches when other catchers were up at the plate. He considered them to often be the most strategic players on the diamond and always found it a worthwhile challenge to get into their heads.

Yuujin was surprised to see Yousuke call for another fastball but didn't dare shake off his superior.

Sullivan smashed the pitch foul, grinning at himself. He had gotten the pitch he wanted but not the one he was expecting.

Yousuke called for the screwball and Yuujin wound up, trying to muster something a little more, the extra strength that pitchers summon on special occasions.

The screwball was the same velocity as his depleted fastball; it darted down and inched inwards as it broke.

Sullivan swung, missing the ball completely for the second out.

Hoshino and the few non-playing ballplayers eagerly clapped, as they were an out away from getting out of the inning.

Yuujin took a deep breath. He had to reset himself to start another at-bat.

Jack Simmons sauntered up. He had observed that Yuujin liked to get either a first-pitch fastball or curveball over the plate to leverage the count in his favor early on. Jack's plan was therefore to be aggressive.

Yuujin threw a first pitch screwball and Simmons swung and missed.

Yousuke and Yuujin were attempting to execute something unexpected but ingeniously effective.

Jack took the second pitch, also a screwball, for a ball.

He subsequently swatted a curveball foul.

The fourth pitch was another curveball away.

The fifth was a high fastball that Jack didn't bite at; the count was full.

Yuujin rubbed the ball to get a better grip.

Yousuke called for a curve.

Simmons readied himself.

Yuujin brought his arms over his head and stopped. The hiatus was the longest of the game thus far. He suddenly kicked his leg and threw the pitch.

In that millisecond, Jack guessed that he was getting a fastball, the type that a pitcher throws when he has nothing left. The delayed wind-up was meant to put him in a dreamy state, to catch him dozing and sneak a fastball in as a surprise.

Jack watched the ball as it trudged to the plate. At about the halfway mark in its journey, Simmons noticed topspin; he had guessed wrong. A curveball was coming his way. He had buckled and froze, but figured it would still land high and inside for the fourth ball.

The ball moved vertically with no horizontal break. Yousuke barely had to move his mitt as the ball scraped the very border of the strike zone.

Jack's head turned back to the umpire as he dropped his bat and took a step towards first base.

"Strike three!!"

Jack contorted his body in anger as he shouted, "Oh come on! That was a goddamn ball and you know it! Inside! It was inside!"

The umpire said nothing in response. Frustrated, Jack picked up his bat and headed towards the dugout as the Japanese fielders jogged in.

The seventh inning had come to a close.

Traynor cavorted in and out of trouble in the top of the eighth as he gave up a leadoff walk but then got the next two batters to fly out to right field.

As the American pitcher attempted to close the door on the inning, Hoshino approached Yousuke.

"What do you think?" the manager asked.

"He's tired."

"I can see that. He's moving around the mound a lot."

"He's not completely wild out there yet but his throwing velocity has decreased. He's taking more and more time in-between pitches to regroup."

"Think he can last for one more?"

Yousuke thought on this and glimpsed over at his starter, situated on the other end of the bench. Yuujin was nearly panting; he was clearly fatigued.

"One more. But have someone ready to go. I don't know if he'll make it through."

Hoshino nodded and responded, "Make sure he doesn't drop that elbow. He's not used to the weariness on his body. Once his mechanics go, it's all over."

Yousuke nodded but the sound of contact drew his attention.

Traynor got his competitor to ground to second for the final out.

Hoshino looked at Yuujin, who on cue stood up, put his hat back on, and proceeded to exit the dugout.

Yuujin walked to the mound much slower than before. He was preserving an energy that both he and his opponents knew he needed.

Arky Averill led off the bottom of the 8th inning with a scorching one-hopper to the second baseman. Eiji made a clean play and threw to Ichiro for the first out.

Benjamin Williams, the American right fielder, settled in.

After two straight balls, he lined a curveball towards shortstop.

Aito backhanded the ball but when he went to come up with the throw, the ball fumbled out of his hand and landed back on the ground. He went to recover but Williams' speed was so great a throw wasn't even warranted.

Aito, embarrassed, threw the ball back to Yuujin, who noticed the humiliation on the shortstop.

"Don't worry," Yuujin assured. "We'll get us out of this."

The sentiment struck Aito as Yuujin turned back to the mound.

Eugene marched up with an opportunity; he was the go-ahead run. He reminded himself not to do too much, not to overthink it. After all, no one trying to hit a home run usually hits a home run.

Eugene couldn't imagine he would see a fastball and he had already taken Yuujin's curveball deep in his first at-bat. He had struck out on the screwball and hit a lucky single off of it, too. It seemed the safe guess.

Yousuke knew all this was going through Eugene's head. Yet, he knew it was still their best bet.

Yuujin brought his arms over his head. As he stopped, he gazed into Eugene's eyes and winked. He quickly kicked his leg and delivered the pitch.

Eugene, thrown off by this act, felt like Yuujin knew something he did not.

A screwball with little movement came barreling towards the plate.

Eugene swung over the pitch and dabbled it out in front of the plate. Yousuke sprung up and made his way to the rolling object. He picked it up with his bare hand, spun around, and fired a strike to Ichiro at first base.

"Out!"

Williams had reached second base on the play.

Eugene trotted back to the dugout attempting to conceal his smile. Yuujin used the oldest trick in the book and it worked. He was sure he had learned it from an American.

Walter Roberts took Yuujin's first pitch curveball and pulled it into left field for a base hit.

Shichirō caught the ball on a single bounce as it was hit hard. He came up throwing, knowing Williams was a fast runner.

When Roberts saw the throw was going home, he rounded first and kicked it into high gear.

Williams rounded third but held up; he swiftly retreated back.

Yousuke received the accurate throw at home and thought about throwing to second in an extremely unlikely attempt to get Roberts but did otherwise.

Roberts slid into second and sleekly popped up as The Americans had two runners in scoring position with two outs.

Yousuke called for time and walked out to the mound.

"What do you want to do?" Yousuke asked.

"Get them out," Yuujin responded.

"Me, too. We have a base open. We can intentionally walk the next guy if you feel confident you won't walk Chuisano with the bases loaded."

"Is that honorable?"

"It's strategic. He's hit you hard even if he has nothing to show for it. Chuisano hasn't, even though you walked him last time."

Yuujin thought for a moment and then asked, "What do you think?"

Yousuke looked Yuujin straight in the eye and questioned, "Can you still get it over the plate?"

"Yes," he responded without question.

"Okay. Let's walk him."

Yousuke went behind home plate but never crouched down. Instead, he reached his ungloved hand straight out.

"Are you kiddin' me?" Billy responded at the sight.

Yuujin lobbed a pitch to his catcher's hand.

Yousuke stepped over and caught the ball.

"Ball," the umpire said.

"You're going to walk me to load the bases?" Billy taunted.

Yuujin threw ball two.

"Chuisano is not going to like that. He takes these things very personally."

Yousuke did not respond to The Berserk but instead caught ball three.

"What if I just lunged across the plate and clobbered this slow pitch over the wall? I can do that. Better not miss."

Yuujin softly tossed another outside pitch. Billy brought his hands back and stepped forward. He motioned towards the ball but let it go for the intentional walk to be completed.

"Big mistake," Billy boasted as he made his way to first base.

Phil Chuisano had the bases loaded with two outs. He took a deep breath in; he did not want to squander the opportunity.

Yuujin threw a fastball for strike one, a risky plan of action that paid off.

He reverted to the curveball but it missed low and away.

Yousuke called for another fastball.

The pitch came up and in and Chuisano let it go, despite his eyes lighting up. That idea didn't pan out as desired and Yousuke next called for a screwball.

The pitch darted down and in but Chuisano didn't bite as the ball crossed the plate too low to be a strike.

"Three balls, one strike," the umpire announced.

Chuisano had a hitter's count and everyone knew it. Yuujin had no wiggle room. He would have to throw a strike.

Yousuke threw down the sign for another screwball, much to Yuujin's surprise. While his poker face would never show it, Yuujin, for the first time ever, had the instinct to shake off his pitcher. It was, of course, a mere thought, one he would never put into action.

Yuujin nodded and set.

Chuisano swung and missed at the pitch.

The batter softly hit the top of his head with his bat and muttered, "Come on Chuisano, don't flip your wig now."

He knew he had swung at ball four.

With a full count and the bases loaded, the entire inning, and very possibly the entire game, came down to the next pitch.

Yuujin circled the mound as he wiped his forehead with his forearm. He placed his hat back on and stepped on the rubber. He was gasping for air out of exertion and his body ached. It was a type of soreness he had never felt, not even in the army. His legs, hips, and torso were drained of energy.

Yuujin looked in. Yousuke threw down the signal for a fastball.

Yuujin nodded, knowing that there was a good chance this pitch would be all arm, a phrase he had come to learn that referred to a pitcher that only has the strength of his throwing arm left.

Yuujin brought his arms over his head. He stopped only for a mere moment before he kicked his leg and delivered the pitch.

With his legs giving way, he could tell he had a limited ability to push off of the rubber. Still, he assembled all the strength he had left and put it all into this one pitch.

The fastball must have been the fastest pitch Yuujin threw all day. It was slightly elevated but in the center of the plate. Incidentally, that was right in Chuisano's wheelhouse.

The second baseman's mouth watered at the sight and he swung with intensity.

Chuisano's bat caught a piece of it but Yousuke captured the foul tip in his glove.

"Strike three!!"

Yuujin was too tired to react and simply walked off the mound.

The ninth inning of the final game was about to commence.

Eugene too trotted slowly, though not from tiredness; he was more than aware he was about to play the last inning of his life and wanted to appreciate it in all of its glory.

Traynor warmed up as the position players tossed a practice ball to keep their arms warm and their form ripe.

Walter Roberts caught a throw from Williams. He turned to face Eugene.

"Hey, Durante!" Roberts called out.

Eugene opened and closed his glove to indicate he was ready for the throw.

"It's been an honor," Roberts stated.

Eugene smiled and responded, "The honor was all mine, my friend."

Roberts tossed Eugene the ball. He caught it, reveling in that unique sound of popping leather.

The Japanese were due to send up their 8, 9, and 1 hitters. Yuujin hoped to be gifted with one final at-bat; all he needed was one teammate to reach base.

Soon the practice balls were thrown in and Traynor signaled he was ready.

Itsuo, the third baseman, tapped home plate with his bat and proceeded into his stance.

Traynor took a deep breath and looked in for the signal. When he received it, he set and entered his windup.

Itsuo predicted a first pitch fastball and moments later, was proved right. He swung; the barrel of the bat met the ball in the sweetest of spots. The ball seethed right back to the pitcher.

Traynor wasn't speedy enough to react; the expeditious ball struck him directly in the face.

A spray of blood spurted onto the mound as Traynor fell to the ground, grabbing his face. The ball trickled away as Itsuo hustled down the first base line.

Traynor instinctively attempted to get up and retrieve the ball but stumbled back down, losing his glove in the process.

He looked down to see blood on his hands.

"No!" he shouted. "James! James! Wake up!!"

Traynor started clawing at the dirt on the mound as if trying to dig it up.

"Come on, James!" he screamed.

Traynor found himself back on the battlefield. In front of him a motionless friend was sprawled out across the dirt. Traynor had dug himself a makeshift trench for protection and dragged his friend into it. He flipped the body over and desperately attempted cardiopulmonary resuscitation.

As he engaged in chest compressions, he looked up to see a sea of Japanese faces confusingly staring at him.

"You killed my friend!"

He looked down to see his friend's blood on his hands.

Without warning, he felt Sullivan's comforting and secure arms around his body.

Snapping out of it, Traynor dazedly looked up to see Vaughan and a medical examiner above him. He wasn't sure when they had come and how much time had elapsed. He looked down to see trickles of blood on the ground and on his uniform. He couldn't feel parts of his face.

"How bad is it, doc?" he begged. "Am I going to make it?" he pleaded.

"Everything is okay," he heard a soothing voice say. "You were struck by a baseball. You're playing a game."

Easing out of his flashback, Traynor looked around with a fresh but muddled perspective.

"I think my nose is broke," he solemnly noted.

"Can't get much worse than what it looked like before," he heard Sullivan say with a snicker.

"You'll be fine, son," the doctor insisted. "Help me lift him," he instructed.

Traynor was brought to his feet.

"Good game," Vaughan stated.

"Who's going to pitch?" Traynor asked, still in a mental fog, while wiping blood from his face.

Vaughan answered, "We'll get it from here, don't you worry."

Vaughan patted Traynor on the square of his back as the doctor and an assistant helped carry him off the field.

The fans rose in appreciation and clapped as the pitcher was hauled off. Just before reaching the dugout, Traynor took his hat off and raised it in the air. The crowd erupted louder. Traynor smiled without truly knowing why before putting his cap back on. It was what ballplayers did. After the ritualistic act, he disappeared into the dugout corridor.

"What now?" Sullivan asked while the infielders and their manager were huddled on the mound.

Eugene, looking down at the grass, felt horrible about Traynor; the thought of not seeing this series through at the last moment seemed like a cruel fate. He looked up to shockingly see Vaughan from the mound pointing at him. Vaughan was waving him in.

Eugene jogged towards the assemblage wondering what defensive replacements were about to transpire. He reached the mound to find his manager rubbing a baseball.

"What's the plan?" Eugene asked.

Vaughan said nothing but instead looked down at the ball and then out at the stands. Eventually, he answered, "Think you got one inning left in that bum arm of yours?"

Eugene could see Vaughan grinning. "Me? Are you sure?"

"Positive. I'll get the kid who hasn't seen any action and put him in left field and pray no one hits anything to him." Vaughan tossed the ball to Eugene. "Have fun."

Vaughan walked off the mound and pointed to an eager-looking youth on the bench.

"Gomez! Left field!"

Gomez ran out with an enthusiastic hustle.

"Funny, "Sullivan remarked, "I never noticed him before."

"Is he even eighteen?" Arky asked.

"Must have just turned of age and enlisted in the last days of the war," Sullivan said before turning his attention to Eugene. "What do you throw?"

"Fastball. Slider. Changeup."

"What the hell is a changeup?"

"It's an offspee—"

"—Kidding. I've heard of it. Never caught one before, though. Might be fun. Let's get you warmed up."

Eugene looked at the mound like an old friend who had been out of touch for quite some time.

"Here goes nothing," he muttered.

Yoshio Hasegawa entered the batter's box as Eugene blew on his hands. Sullivan threw down a single digit and Eugene nodded.

His delivery was fluid; his arms came up over his head as his leg kicked upwards. He pushed himself off of the rubber and threw the ball as fast as he could.

Sullivan watched it sail over his head and he shot up to retrieve the wild pitch as Itsuo ran to second.

A stunned yet amused Sullivan walked the ball back to Eugene and said, "You know you're supposed to aim for my glove, right?"

"Shut up. Had to loosen the rust."

Yoshio squared around to bunt before Eugene even entered his delivery, which was no surprise to Sullivan, who had called for a high fastball in anticipation of this tactic.

Eugene's pitch was perfectly placed; Yoshio moved his bat upwards and connected.

The ball popped up and Sullivan hopped to attention and threw away his facemask. Settling under it in the mere moments of its hang time, Sullivan made the catch for the first out.

"There you go!" Sullivan said as he lobbed the ball back to Eugene.

Aito moved up to hit as Yuujin entered the on-deck circle.

Yousuke walked over to his manager and asked, "Who are we sending out in the bottom of the inning?"

Hoshino thought before responding, "Yuujin."

"Yuujin? He has nothing left."

Hoshino turned to his catcher and replied, "He has heart."

Eugene checked the runner and afterward looked to the plate. With a wrist snap, he threw a first pitch slider that drifted into the strike zone.

"Strike one!"

Curious, Sullivan wanted to see the changeup and so put down the appropriate sign.

Eugene set and delivered.

The pitch came in about ten miles per hour slower than his fastball and Aito could do nothing but foul it off.

Sullivan nodded as if entertained.

Eugene was surprised his arm felt as good as it did. He knew it wouldn't be too long before that feeling ceased but rejoiced in the meantime. He was on the mound again, a feat he never thought possible.

He peered in to get the signal.

Sullivan wanted a fastball.

Eugene agreed. He wound up and fired.

The fastball was a bit high and outside but Aito swung and missed.

"Yea! Atta boy!" Billy cheered from third base.

Eugene could feel the surge of the strikeout rejuvenate him. He caught the ball and circled the mound. He adjusted his hat, stepped on the rubber, and looked up to face what he envisioned to be his next victim.

When Eugene saw his face, however, he realized he had forgotten Yuujin was due up.

Yuujin had a grin on his face but Eugene's countenance was of complete seriousness.

He threw a low slider to start off the at-bat. Yuujin took it.
"Ball."

Eugene set and flung a fastball that caught the outside corner.
"Strike!"

Impressed with the giddy-up of the last pitch, Sullivan called for more of the same.

Eugene wound up.

Yuujin, not wanting another fastball to go by, swung but missed what was essentially the exact same pitch.

"One ball, two strikes," the umpire stated.

Yuujin went into defensive mode as making any sort of contact became imperative.

Eugene entered his delivery and heaved a changeup.

Yuujin was thrown off by the speed and froze.

Sullivan caught the ball aligned just below Yuujin's knees. He stealthily brought his glove up in an attempt to frame it as a strike.

Yuujin snapped his head back to see the call.

The umpire shook his head and assured, "Ball."

Boos burst from the countless umpires in the stands that disagreed with the call.

Eugene and Sullivan agreed to go back to the slider.

As the pitch glided out of the strike zone, Yuujin swung and weakly fouled it off.

Sullivan called for it again.

Eugene kicked his leg and propelled the baseball.

The pitch slithered down and in; Yuujin took it.

"Ball three."

Knowing Sullivan, Eugene discerned exactly what his catcher was about to call: high heat.

A moment later, he proved to be a prophet.

Eugene set.

Yuujin awaited the pitch with focused precision.

Eugene wound up.

Yuujin stilled his body.

The pitch was exactly where Sullivan wanted it—nearly eye level and center.

Yuujin swung and fouled it straight back.

Eugene peered in. Sullivan called for another fastball but Eugene shook him off.

Yuujin knew the majority of time a pitcher shakes his catcher off he intends to throw a fastball.

Eugene wanted the changeup. He had hoped between the change of speed and the unorthodox pitch selection after shaking off his catcher, Yuujin wouldn't expect it.

He set and delivered.

Yuujin was taken aback by the off-speed pitch but could not afford to go down looking. He threw his bat at the ball as he lunged forward, barely making contact.

The ball spurted foul.

Eugene shook his head in annoyance although he was not in the least bit surprised. His arm was beginning to tighten up. In that moment, he decided this contest would not end by deception. He would give Yuujin his best and if he played his cards right it would be the last pitch of his career.

Sullivan, as if sensing this, threw down one finger.

Eugene propelled his arms over his head as his leg kicked in the air. He gathered as much strength as he could summon and reared back.

Yuujin barely noticed the ball as it wondrously sped to its destination. Protecting the plate, he offered but swung directly through it.

Eugene had struck out his counterpart. He bounced off the mound with a smile and a pounce. He surmised it was one hell of a way to go out.

Yuujin, on the other hand, was disappointed as he walked back to the dugout. He was met with strangely yearning eyes from his manager and catcher.

"What?" he perplexingly asked.

"The game is yours to win or lose," Hoshino stated. "In the end, we go with our best."

Yuujin glared at his manager in disbelief before stepping down into the dugout to replace his bat with his mitt.

"Well. This is it, Jerry. We're heading to the bottom of the ninth inning with The Japanese holding on to a single run lead."

"It's been a great series and a superb rubber game. Despite the low scoring affair, this outing has been pretty exciting!"

"Agreed. Both teams have had to work out of troublesome situations numerous times and the balance of the game could have shifted in anyone's favor."

"The Americans have the bottom of the lineup coming up and leading off for them is a player we've not seen as of yet."

"That's right. Orlando Gomez will lead it off. He came into the game after the unfortunate Traynor incident."

"Gomez is just shy of nineteen years old."

"He looks it too!"

While looking at a sheet of paper, Jerry noted, "I see here he's a first generation American but his father was no stranger to the game, either; he played for the Havana Baseball Club in Cuba and even managed after retiring as a player."

"It's funny how baseball is so cross-generational and multi-cultural, isn't it?"

"Indeed, Curt. And now—my gosh I don't believe my eyes—it looks as if Kenjiro Hoshino has asked Yuujin Miyano to try to close this one out."

"A surprising move. It appeared Miyano emptied the tank at the end of last inning. He has to be running on fumes at this point."

"Starting pitchers are no strangers to going the distance but we can't forget, this isn't Major League Baseball. I hope nothing unfortunate happens to his arm as he looks to be a young bright star of the game."

Gomez kicked some dirt out of the batter's box as Yuujin set himself. The pitcher couldn't help but feel a connection to the batter as mere days ago Miyano was considered the childlike novice on the field. He noted how quickly that had changed.

"Let's go baby-face!" yelled Billy from the dugout.

Yuujin brought his arms over his head and stopped before kicking his leg and administering the pitch.

Gomez, who had grown accustomed to seizing rare opportunities whenever they were presented, saw the low velocity fastball and swung.

The ball was subsequently bombarded into the right field stands, albeit foul. The surge of strength surprised all who viewed the small-framed individual.

"Hey, that's not bad power," remarked Chuisano.

"Straighten that out, kid!" Roberts added.

Yuujin gathered the signal; it was one Yousuke had not presented previously, which was no shock to Yuujin as the pitch selection duo briefly discussed strategy before the inning.

He entered his windup and released a high arching pitch that couldn't have been faster than forty miles per hour.

The pitch domed from above Gomez's head to the middle of the plate.

The ambitious hitter swung but missed badly and jeers of amusement could be heard from the fans.

"What is this!? Softball!?" Averill barked.

Yousuke thought about going back to the fastball, which would feel accelerated by comparison, but Gomez's reaction to the first pitch of the at-bat lingered in his mind.

Yuujin received the sign and nodded.

Gomez kept his hands tucked near his armpits as the ball was released. As the pitch came in, they extended upwards and outwards in anticipation to hit the ball.

It was another off-speed low-velocity trick pitch. Gomez recognized this and let it go but the ball descended into the middle of the plate.

"Strike three!"

Gomez arched his back in frustration; he had waited for a chance to contribute and got junk pitches he couldn't possibly have expected.

He marched back to the dugout as Sullivan strode up.

Yuujin was two outs away from beating the American players.

Sullivan swung with fury at the first pitch he saw, which was another off-speed lob.

Upon swinging through it, he muttered to himself, "Goddammit!"

The next pitch was the same and Sullivan swung again, this time making contact.

It popped high up in the air.

"Got it!" yelled Yuujin as the ball hovered directly above him.

In an abnormal play, Yuujin made the catch for the second out.

"I can't believe this shit," Billy remarked from the bench.

As Sullivan entered the dugout, he snarled, "It's like a god-damn rainbow, that pitch!"

Jack Simmons knew full well the game rested in his hands; it was his job to keep it going and pass the baton.

Yuujin stuck to the aptly descried rainbow pitch as there was no reason not to.

Jack took the first one low for a ball. He stepped out of the box and reminded himself not to try too much, not to force anything.

The next pitch arched above his head before coming back down. He swung and connected, serving it into left field.

The American dugout clapped in unison as Simmons reached first with a base hit to keep the inning alive.

New life was inhaled into the collective team spirit as their lineup turned over.

Arky Averill dug into the dirt near his back foot before crouching down into his stance.

The rainbow pitch landed outside to start the at-bat.

Yousuke called for a fastball and Yuujin nodded.

The jump in velocity seemed tremendous but the pitch was nevertheless inside.

Arky didn't think his opponent would go back to the fast-ball and he was right. The third pitch had the trademark trajectory and he swung against his better judgment.

Yuujin was two strikes away.

Another rainbow pitch sunk out of the strike zone and Arky demonstrated self-control.

"Three balls, one strike," the umpire noted.

Yuujin had allowed Averill to enter the ultimate hitter's count.

Yousuke knew the following batters had pop and if there was ever a time to go back to the fastball it would be here and now, despite Averill's probable anticipation of it.

Yuujin brought his arms over his head. A long interlude commenced. He languidly kicked his leg and fired.

Averill got his fastball, which jumped out of the pitcher's arm. He swung and connected.

The ball flew into the left field stands.

The count was full.

Yuujin was going back to the off-speed; of this he was sure.

Once confirmed, he entered his windup, which he quickened.

Averill instinctively assumed a fastball was coming because of the hastened delivery.

To his surprise, the slow pitch ballooned towards the plate and froze him. The ball, however, never tumbled downwards and stayed above his head.

"Ball four! Take your base!"

Averill made his way to first, and Jack to second. Yuujin peered out at the American on-deck circle as Eugene walked into it. He knew right there and then the fates would have it no other way. The two were destined to meet at such a pivotal moment.

"Hey!"

Yousuke broke Yuujin's concentration. The pitcher hadn't even noticed his partner had made his way out to the mound.

"This doesn't have to end with him," the catcher said as if reading his mind. "Williams can end the game either way. Don't lose him. We're one out away and they're one big hit away. Got it?"

"Got it," Yuujin answered in truth.

Yousuke retreated back.

Williams took a first pitch fastball for a strike. He regrouped by stepping out.

Eugene held two bats in his hand for practice while feeling a knot form in the pit of his stomach. He had always craved the spotlight when it came to a big moment in the game.

Williams took a slow second pitch for a ball low and away.

"Throw me that again," Williams whispered in confidence.

In that moment, Eugene did not desire the limelight of notoriety. He hoped Williams would end it here, one way or another. He felt that, strangely, it was a win either way. Either his country or his friend would be the victor. He couldn't think of a better pickle to be in. He simply didn't want to be the one to make that determination.

Yuujin wound up and tossed his rainbow pitch.

Williams carefully followed its trajectory and swung without losing sight of the ball and its arc.

The American right fielder smashed the baseball.

Simmons and Averill took off on contact.

Eugene watched the smacked ball fall in front of the center fielder.

Reo Hirabayashi caught the ball on one hop and came up throwing.

Simmons rounded third.

The throw was perfectly aligned and reached Yousuke without ever touching the ground as Jack halted and receded.

Yousuke fired to third to try and get Jack but he was back in safely.

The full house rose in expectation.

"Well, I'll be, Curt. Of course it would come down to this."

"It seems almost destined, doesn't it? Here we are in the bottom of the ninth inning. Bases loaded. Two outs. And it all comes down to a matchup between Eugene Durante and Yuujin Miyano."

"Can you think of a more appropriate sendoff?"

"I certainly could not, Jerry. I suppose before any celebration starts I would just like to say this experience, broadcasting these games for the United States Military alongside you, has been an honor and a privilege. And I wouldn't want to do it with anyone else."

"Curt, I feel the same way. Thank you for having me."

"And now our attention turns to a moment we have all been waiting for but couldn't possibly predict."

"I think we should throw the curveball and screwball back into the mix," Yuujin told Yousuke, who had come to quickly check on his pitcher.

"I don't know if your arm can take it. You're probably half-way to three hundred pitches."

"If my arm falls off have the paramedics sew it back on."

There was no jest in his comment, simply determination and obstinacy.

"Okay. Let's do it. Start him off with a curveball and let's see what happens from there."

Yuujin nodded.

Eugene felt chills reverberating through his body. The hairs on the back of his neck stood up in full attention and the knot in the pit of his stomach widened tenfold in sheer seconds.

Every fan was on their feet and the weight of the world war seemed to hang in the delicate balance of a bat-and-ball pastime.

The arms came over Yuujin's head and he stopped. The interlude was palpable. He kicked his leg and threw.

The curveball coiled into the catcher's glove near the outside of the plate.

"Ball," the umpire exclaimed.

Yuujin thought he had the strike but didn't get the call. He inhaled as he got the ball back.

Yousuke threw down the sign for a fastball.

Yuujin wound up and discharged the ball.

It sped inside and Eugene took the borderline pitch.

"Ball two!"

Yuujin was suddenly in a heap of trouble. He wiped his brow and recomposed himself.

Eugene watched the rainbow pitch loft into the strike zone.

"Strike one!"

Eugene stepped out and took a practice swing. He gathered himself and stepped back in.

Yousuke called for another trick pitch.

Eugene followed the baseball as it started off over his head. It quickly plummeted down; he swung.

The ball nearly reached the dirt and Eugene couldn't follow the ball's path with his bat in time. He swung and missed.

Yuujin had fought back and evened the count at two and two.

Yousuke wanted to go back to the curveball.

Eugene didn't expect a pitch with forward spin but felt it was too close to the plate to take. He lunged and swung, spoiling the pitch foul.

The count remained even.

Yuujin didn't want the count to go full and understood this to be the reason why Yousuke was calling for another fastball.

Yuujin brought his arms over his head, stopped briefly, kicked his leg, then speedily dispatched.

The fastball was high in the zone.

Eugene swung.

Yuujin felt as if his breath was expunged in that split second.

Eugene fouled the pitch straight back.

Yousuke threw down a sign.

Yuujin wound up.

Eugene stood in expectancy.

The rainbow pitch once again flung over the head of the batter and tumbled down.

The pitch seemed identical to the one Eugene had swung and missed at, but he couldn't predict if the ball was going to drop to the dirt again.

He swung and once again tried to adjust the plane of his bat to meet the ball.

Eugene barely made contact, scrambling it foul.

Yousuke called for the same pitch.

Yuujin delivered.

The baseball sailed over Eugene's head but didn't arch downward until late into its orbit.

Eugene's eyes lit up and he lifted his front foot to gather as much power as he could.

As the ball hung in the air, Eugene forced himself to lay off. The pitch eventually dived down and into the catcher's mitt around Eugene's elbows. He snapped back to hear the call.

"Ball three."

The clamorous crowd somehow reached a decibel level not thought possible and the stands shook from the excited stomping soldiers.

Eugene and Yuujin each took a breath and readied themselves. Yousuke called for a fastball.

Yuujin nodded and Eugene narrowed his field of vision in concentration.

Yuujin swung his arms over his head.

He stopped.

He waited.

Eugene waited.

The players waited.

Each overwrought G.I. fan waited.

Yuujin kicked his leg one final time and let go, freeing himself of both the baseball and the burden.

The weight of the game's load now shifted solely to Eugene.

In the end, there was no trickery or deception; the ball journeyed straight and true. It was everything Yuujin had left, for better or for worse.

Eugene had never been the type to let things go and had no intention of watching anything pass by him, in life or in baseball.

And so, he took his chance and his opportunity and forced his wooden club to leave his shoulders and act.

A flash of light ruptured in refraction as Klaus Schmidt captured the image on his camera from the front row of the stands. The reporter instantly knew that whatever was to follow bore no meaning on the significance of the moment or the experience of such nationalistic redemption.

Eugene's bat broke on contact. Splinters of wood scattered around home plate. His initial reaction was to look down to make sure no one was hurt.

Something about the shared silence, however, forced him to look up. He saw the left fielder running back as fast as he could.

Yuujin immediately turned to observe the outcome.

Eugene took a step towards first, the only ingrained reaction for a batter to have.

They mutually watched the outfielder reach the wall. He put his bare hand up to avoid crashing into it. It soon became apparent that he was planning to time a jump.

The ball was on course to barely clear the fence. The left fielder jumped into the air, his glove reaching over the wall.

In a moment of the pure unknown, Yuujin's and Eugene's eyes darted for one another. Within each other they found reconciliation. They felt accord. And they formed harmony. In that singular instant of time, a certain kind of devil was exorcised from their diamond.

Eugene and Yuujin looked back out, at the far reaches of the makeshift baseball field.

They astonishingly watched in unison as both the ball and the glove disappeared over the great baseball barrier. Much like how Spalding once drifted into the magic of that Boston night; how Sana expired into the enchanting and uncanny obscurity of blackness; how Joe DiMaggio mythically disappeared in the descending darkness; they too, that ball and that glove, marvelously dissolved from the desirable divination of the diamond, from the very mystique of baseball itself.

Epilogue

1992

A light rain pelted the overpass of Naha Airport.

A familiar but aged couple stood hand-in-hand outside the terminal where recent arrivals could be picked up.

"You said the driving was arranged?" asked Hattie.

"That's right. A town car," answered Eugene.

"Fancy," she lightheartedly added.

"I'm sure it'll be here soon."

Eugene looked over to see a fellow man of his generation, dressed in the uniform of an infantry regiment of the United States Army.

"Still fits," Eugene called out.

The Japanese-American stranger turned to see the couple and smiled.

"Yes. It does. Had to shed ten pounds before it did, though."

"Going to the event?" Eugene asked.

"I am. You too?"

Eugene nodded, "Yup."

"Have you ever been here? To Okinawa?"

The smallest of smiles etched itself across Eugene's face and he responded, "Not since '45." With a nod at the veteran, he added, "What regiment?"

"The 442nd."

"The most decorated unit for its size in U.S. military history, if I'm not mistaken."

The former soldier grinned and remarked, "You are not."

"The unit was composed almost entirely of second-generation American soldiers of Japanese ancestry, correct?"

"Correct. My parents came here when they were a young couple."

"Were they…" Eugene trailed off and the man looked at him as if beckoning him to continue. "Were they forced to a relocation center during the war?"

The older man nodded his head and answered, "While I was overseas fighting, they were in an internment camp."

"Contemptible," was the only thing Eugene could think to say.

"I never thought I would see the day of a formal apology coupled with reparations but then a few years ago it happened. I'm thankful for that."

Eugene could feel Hattie's hand clench up in a tight squeeze.

"As you should be. Enjoy the ceremony," Eugene concluded.

"You as well."

A black car pulled up and a prim and proper looking woman exited the vehicle with a sign that read *DURANTE*.

Eugene and Hattie waved and the driver promptly opened the back door to let them in while taking their luggage.

Eugene turned once more to the stately veteran and gestured a farewell with the tipping of his head.

He entered the car and turned immediately to his wife.

"Are you okay?"

"I dealt with you being a Yankee fan during the 80s. I'll be fine."

The two held each other's gaze until Hattie rested her head on her husband's shoulder. She raised her hand to behold her wedding ring.

"I love this ring," she nostalgically noted.

"Me, too. That's why it took me nearly a year to pay off."

"Who would have thought playing baseball would help."

"Certainly not me."

"I guess I knew what I was doing when I sent you over there to Germany."

"I think Truman said the same thing."

Hattie shot Eugene a look.

"Kidding. You always know what you're doing, honey."

He patted her shoulder and she nestled into him.

"I wouldn't get too comfortable, darling; it's only about a ten minute ride."

As the car ascended into the district of the city of Naha, the rain began to cease and sunlight shoved itself out from behind the clouds.

Eugene looked out the window as the roads bent and turned until he saw it: the gleaming reconstruction of Shuri Castle.

Eugene and Hattie walked up to the imperial site; journalists, veterans, and suits of all kinds were present. They admired the resplendent red castle.

"It's beautiful," remarked Hattie.

"By the time I got to it, it was already destroyed."

A voice behind them said, "It's as impressive as I said it was, isn't it?"

Eugene and Hattie turned around to see Yuujin, sporting a suit and tie. His smile was requited and the two old-timers hurriedly clung onto one another. The embrace was tight and lengthy; it was the hug of unification and kinship. Of loyalty and respect. It was a hug of an anticipated alliance and consummate celebration. It was a hug that commemorated the memories of an era bygone.

They held each other a moment longer and then patted each other's backs.

"Look at you!" Eugene exclaimed. "You don't look a day over fifty."

"Maybe, but I feel my age," he replied before turning to Hattie. "It is so nice to see you again."

They wrapped their arms around one another as Hattie remarked, "I can't believe it's been fifteen years since you were in New York."

"I know! I can't believe I finally got you two to Japan! It's been a lifelong ambition of mine."

"Oh, that's what happens when you have kids," Eugene countered.

"How are they?"

"Claude is great. Married with kids. And Julia is an engineer at NASA."

"Don't know where she gets her smarts from," Hattie added.

"Obviously you," Eugene countered.

A woman in a green cocktail dress, which perfectly matched her eyes, made her way over to the trio. Her blonde hair was fashioned in a blunt bob hairstyle with bangs and her wrist was adorned with a beautiful green jade in gold-over-sterling bracelet.

"Guys, I would like to introduce you to my wife," Yuujin excitedly said. "Eugene, Hattie, this is Harley."

Hattie and Eugene appeared baffled.

"You didn't tell us you got married!" Eugene pronounced as he extended his hand.

Harley shook it and then Hattie's and said, "It's a pleasure to meet you both. Yuujin has spoken very highly of you."

"We got married just last year. Although I do have to point out I've been pursuing her for quite some time!"

"I was a hard woman to pin down, no doubt about it."

"Harley studied horticulture at the University of Edinburgh and then came here and worked at Kyū-Furukawa Gardens in Kita, Tokyo for many years."

"Impressive!" Hattie remarked.

"I just retired last year," Harley said. "Making a little room in my life for more personal milestones. When I met Yuujin, I just fell in love with his poetry and by extension, his soul. He's truly one of a kind."

"I didn't know you wrote poetry," Eugene jabbed as if offended.

"Only recently, and I don't share it often," he answered abashedly. "Oh, look! The ceremony is starting!"

The two couples walked up closer to where the ribbon cutting was to take place. A small stage was assembled with a podium and a man in a black suit with a white shirt and red tie took to it.

"Greetings everyone! Thank you all for coming! Before we proceed with what we're all here to do, I thought it would be pertinent to give a little backstory of this historic site. This magnificent royal palace was first built in the 15th century, although expansions and updates continued throughout the years, coupling the stylistic elements from the imperial architecture of the Ming Dynasty with structures uniquely Ryukyuan."

Eugene looked over to notice Yuujin had vanished.

"The castle was designed with two throne rooms for the king. One so he could see his kingdom and the other so he could view his court. It was here, in this castle, that some of our most sacred ceremonies were performed. This all came to a halt in 1879 when the Empire of Japan declared the kingdom abolished and the islands annexed.

"Then, of course, in 1945, the Empire of Japan made Okinawa the site of its last stand, and Shuri Castle was destroyed in the fighting. In addition to human life: artifacts, artworks and other records of Okinawan history and culture were lost during that period.

Many have said Okinawa's postwar period could never truly end until Shuri Castle was rebuilt. Of course, that was no easy feat considering the financial, logistical, and political hurdles. But here we are. Awakening to that very dream becoming reality.

"We have proudly used traditional materials and methods to rebuild our important structure. The lumber comes from the forests of the Kunigami area of northern Okinawa! The terracotta roof tiles were constructed from the ancient pottery district of Tsuboya! Artists trained in prewar knowledge, in prewar tradition, contributed to the painting and lacquer work.

"Shuri Castle once represented power, strength, and honor; it does so again, now with the added symbol of being able to rise up once more! This reconstruction finally exemplifies and epitomizes our government's readiness and willingness to honor the responsibilities that accompany sovereignty.

"Today is a great day for our people. It is a great day for Okinawa. It is a revival of our identity and culture and a revitalization of our livelihoods and well-being.

"I thank you all for being here and without further ado, I present to you Yuujin Miyano, a veteran and former private in the Imperial Japanese Army who was stationed right here on the morning of May 25th, 1945, when Shuri Castle was bombarded."

Polite but passionate applause erupted from those gathered.

"Mr. Miyano, you may cut the ribbon."

Yuujin was handed a pair of scissors. He slowly approached the narrow strip of material and gazed up at the newly renovated castle. He had spent his life talking about the glory and beauty of a place that once was. And now, before his eyes, he was witness to the very thing he had hoped to see accomplished in his lifetime.

He cut the ribbon, an effective symbol of a new beginning in his estimation, and the crowd once again applauded.

Bows, handshakes and gestures of gratitude and excitement commenced before people flooded into the newly renovated site.

"Thank you for inviting me," Eugene said.

"I could think of no other guest of honor. It seemed appropriate," Yuujin responded.

The two veterans found themselves separated from their wives and exploring the restored Seiden, the largest wooden building in the prefecture. They examined painting recreations and wooden plaques conveying imperial calligraphy.

"It's amazing," Eugene remarked. "Is this how you remember it?"

"Actually, it looks better."

Eugene laughed and continued, "Your wife seems like a lovely person. I wish you all the happiness, Yuujin. You deserve it."

"I aspire to be the example of love set by you and Hattie. I will never forget my trip to New York. You were most gracious hosts."

"I'm just glad you got to see the Yankees kick ass."

"Very good team."

"Historically, yes. But as of late, I don't know. They better get something going soon or they're going to lose some fans. We're due for a dynasty."

"I'm sure they will improve soon."

"Still waiting for my favorite team to play your favorite team."

"Now that would be a sight to behold."

"Well, it better happen soon. We're getting up there," Eugene gnarled.

"We're in our late sixties; we have plenty of time."

"I hope you're right, my friend."

They stopped in front of a gilded royal throne.

Eugene added, "I think you should sit in it."

"I think they would kick me out. Don't forget, I'm not a true Okinawan despite having family who lived here. Come, I want to see the North and South halls. They flank our current position. I hear they were turned into galleries displaying the few surviving treasures of Ryukyuan heritage we have left."

"You still speak like a soldier."

"Some habits…"

Yuujin and Eugene entered the courtyard to see a performance of music and dance, the artists donning the court robes of their ancestors.

"This place feels alive! What's going on here?" Eugene asked.

"Reenactments of court ceremonies. A tradition that hasn't taken place in over one-hundred years."

"Wow. How do they know what to do?"

"Scholars from the Okinawa Prefectural University of the Arts conducted extensive research to find out. We are in everyone's debt who helped us meet this goal."

"The more things change, the more they stay the same."

"A truer proverb has never been said."

Eugene suddenly felt a shooting sensation in his lower back.

"Hey, can we sit for a second?"

"Of course, there's a bench over there. Are you alright?"

"I'm dandy."

Eugene and Yuujin sat on a stone bench looking at the prodigious resurrection of the rich traditions of high Ryukyuan Kingdom culture. Yuujin took a deep breath of appreciation. He noticed Eugene seemed fixed on a certain spot.

"What are you looking at?"

"Over there," Eugene answered while pointing to a vacant area. "Do you recall what happened there?"

A happy expression suddenly crossed his face and he answered, "That's where you punched me."

"I was going to say that's where we had our conversations but yeah, that too. You're never going to give that up, are you?"

Yuujin shrugged and said, "I never held on to it."

The two allowed for a lull in conversation to just enjoy their surroundings.

"I like this country already," Eugene remarked. "You value traditions and things of the past. Back home, I just feel like everything is changing before my eyes. Like I can't keep up."

"Something tells me you'll always be able to keep up. You're Eugene the Jeep."

Eugene chortled and said, "Haven't heard that one in a long time. I hated it right up until Billy called me Durante the Detainer. He was such an ass."

"Do you ever hear from him? Or the rest of the crew?"

"I heard Billy died of a heart attack a few years back. And no, I never really stayed in touch with anyone for very long. Jack Simmons and Walter Roberts for a little but I haven't spoken to them in years."

"I only had the pleasure of keeping in contact with Coach Hoshino."

"Still alive?"

"No. Cancer."

"Life can be a real bitch, can't she?"

"I don't think so. Every moment is one to treasure."

"You would say that. How's your sister?"

"Happy," Yuujin answered with a look of joy.

"Good. Married?"

"No. It is not legal for her to be."

Eugene appeared confused before realizing the implication of his assertion.

"Well, things are changing, like I said. Hopefully one day soon."

"Hopefully," Yuujin agreed.

After another interlude, Eugene continued, "I know I've told you this, but I was so proud of you. Playing ten seasons for Nippon Professional Baseball. I couldn't watch the games and I had no idea what was happening over there but goddamn, it was like I was there with you."

"You were. I felt you."

They smiled at each other and Eugene patted his friend's leg.

"Thank you, Yuujin."

"For what?"

"Everything. Every word. Every thought. Every bit of encouragement I ever needed whether you knew I needed it or not. Sometimes I feel I could use your wisdom on a daily basis."

"What's on your mind?"

"I know you're getting all excited over the thought of having another philosophical conversation."

"We haven't had a good one in a while. Long distance calls are too expensive."

"That they are. Well, as things change and such, I guess sometimes I just feel like one of those displaced animals whose habitat was destroyed from cutting down a rainforest. I don't know why I feel like that. I'm healthy, I have a wonderful family, and I'm retired. But it's like this nagging constant in the back of my mind."

"What do you feel displaced from?"

"Who I was. Does that make sense? The world of my upbringing? I don't know. I suppose if I boil it down, I'm really asking where's my place in all of this? In today's world, what does it mean to be a man?"

"You haven't figured that out yet? You've been one for so long," Yuujin jested.

"I thought I did. But I don't know."

"I'm only joking. It is not an easy question. I am sure it is no surprise to you that many of my own peers have never viewed me as prototypically male."

"Get out of town," Eugene deadpanned.

"I hate emotional pain. I'm not aggressive by nature, especially towards women, and I view them as equals. I'm gentle. And I am not bound by other people's perceptions of manliness."

"So you don't care what people think? That sounds pretty masculine."

"Masculinity and manliness are not one and the same."

"Good point. We all have those traits. You know, my father taught me to suck it up and stay strong. I can't say I haven't benefited from that over my life."

"Perseverance is important. But so is being a whole person. We should not suppress our own natures."

"It's sort of unnatural, right?"

"Indeed. I think being a man is not really so different than being a woman. All we can do on the individual level is try and keep bettering ourselves."

"I don't know. My father also told me being a man meant to protect, provide, and procreate. That's what being a man meant for him."

"I think they are still applicable."

"I was a soldier in World War II. I protected my country and by extension my family. I'm not saying war is a necessary component to act out our ability to protect but I don't know what it's replaced with."

"It's replaced with standing up for people who are outnumbered and outmatched. Not just with fists but with words. Words seem to be our new battlefield."

"Yeah, problem is I'm not as good with them as you are. I think sometimes I'm better off on the front line. There was a simplicity in it."

"Maybe part of being a man means being able to adapt."

"Maybe. What about to provide? I spent my life providing for my family. I now come to the realization that they really don't need me anymore. Which is good, that's a good thing; I know it means I did my job, but what I'm saying is that it feels like there's empty space where that duty once was."

Eugene sighed. Yuujin could tell he was forming another thought.

"Maybe that's why we're so obsessed with achievement, you know; because without it we feel useless. Are we cared about because we're truly loved or are we cared about because we fulfill this role of provider in the world? And once that role is completed, well, then we're just forgotten. I don't mean to sound bleak, Yuujin, I'm just talking out loud."

"It's all understandable. I don't know if it's true, though. I think we are both cared about by the people who surround us. Our relationship is proof of that. Claude and Julia may not need you for financial support but your children will always need your guidance, even when they think they don't. Everyone goes through hard times. Hearing from an elder that has gone through it all is of the utmost importance."

"Emotional support. I get that. And the last one? Procreate?"

"You can still try," Yuujin joked with a nudge.

"Yeah, if at first you don't succeed..." Eugene chuckled.

"I don't have any children but I certainly don't feel less of a man for it. I procreate my time to friends and family. I generate words and produce a legacy through my poetry. You did everything you could for your kids. While that mission is never truly over, the main objective was met with astounding success. I know this because I met them."

"Thank you, Yuujin. Speaking about it, I think this has a lot to do with purpose, as if purpose and what it means to be a man are intrinsically linked. In youth, my service was my purpose. In adulthood, it was my family. Now, I'm a senior citizen and I don't know what I'm supposed to be doing. I need a task. A problem to solve."

"How about the world economic situation?"

They laughed and Eugene commented, "Above my pay grade."

"I know you'll find your way, your purpose. Be open with yourself and others. I can attest to your ability to embrace diversity in all forms."

"You know, speaking of diversity, I met a man at the airport today, a Japanese-American who is here somewhere right now. He said his parents were relocated to an internment camp because of their ethnicity when we were fighting each other. Joe DiMaggio once told me the same thing."

"Your country apologized for this."

"They did, nearly half a century later. My point is, I wonder when we will stop scapegoating people, when we will no longer need to take out our collective frustrations out on a certain kind of people."

"On those in a weakened position. Minorities of any kind."

"Exactly. I bemoan how I thought about you guys entering the war and how I only later realized how wrong I was."

"Propaganda is a powerful tool."

"It is. I just hope that all hate can stay behind us now. It must be very frustrating to take a step back after taking one forward."

"If the Berlin Wall can fall, anything is possible."

"True."

"There's a quote by an American scientist I particularly enjoy. 'If a human disagrees with you, let him live. In a hundred billion galaxies, you will not find another.' I think this is profound."

"I think you're profound, Yuujin Miyano."

"Had enough philosophy?"

"I have."

"Shall we do the thing we came to do?"

"Let's! I need to get to my luggage."

The flaming crimson-coral sun, still slightly above the horizon, gleamed brilliantly. Eugene and Yuujin both appreciated the sight for completely different reasons; for one it was a reminder and appreciation of the past while for the other it was an astonishment of a new experience. As the sun continued to gradually descend, a glorious red hue dispersed to the West and onto the land and nearby ocean. It was a moment frozen in time, or so Eugene and Yuujin wished.

The baseball entered Eugene's mitt against the beautiful setting. "Not as much pop as you used to have," the American poked.

"I'm going easy. Don't want to hurt your hand," the Japanese man countered.

Yuujin turned to look at what he was protecting: Shuri Castle; it was finally the true cardinal symbol of strength he always viewed it to be.

Eugene threw to Yuujin, their dress jackets scattered on the ground next to them.

"Still got some velocity yourself," Yuujin remarked.

"Anything has more velocity than that Eephus pitch you threw that game."

"My rainbow pitch!"

"Whatever you want to call it!"

"I had nothing left!"

"Still, you persisted."

"We both did."

They cheerfully exchanged the baseball back and forth, forging the conviction that much could be set right and the playing field leveled, by virtue of something as simple as a catch between two human beings.

The ball glided through the air, silhouetted as it was positioned against the backdrop of the falling sun before being secured.

Eugene looked at the ball in his mitt. Sprawled across the recently purchased baseball was the name *Spalding.*

"What do you think?" Yuujin asked.

Eugene looked around, taking in his surroundings as the bright star illuminated him in more ways than one.

"Spectacular."

In 2004 the New York Yankees
finally played an exhibition game
against the Yomiuri Giants.

The Yankees won 6-2.

In 2023, Team USA met the
Japanese national baseball team
for the very first time during the
World Baseball Classic
at the championship game.

Japan won their record-extending
third title after defeating
the defending champions 3–2.

ABOUT THE AUTHOR

GREGORY CIOFFI

Gregory Cioffi (SAG-AFTRA, AEA) is an actor, director, and writer. His works have been published in various literary magazines; many of which have been archived in numerous libraries including Yale University's Beinecke Collection (Rare Books and Manuscript Library). His poem *Confined But Commemorating*, written about Memorial Day during the pandemic, won third place in the Nassau County Poet Laureate Society Poetry Contest. Greg's film *The Museum of Lost Things* won awards at The Long Island International Film Expo, Global Shorts, and The Madrid International Film Festival. Be on the lookout for his next film, *The Concertgoer*, which is currently on the festival circuit. Greg is an Adjunct Professor of English at Long Island University, an Associate Professor of Literature & Composition at Post University, and he also teaches Creative Writing, Poetry, and Basic Acting at Nassau Community College.

for more information, visit
www.gandeproductions.com

CHECK OUT OTHER GREAT READS FROM
HENRY GRAY PUBLISHING

THE MAN FROM BELIZE by Steven Kobrin

Life-saving heart surgeon Dr. Kent Stirling lives in paradise, dividing his time between two medical practices in the exotic Yucatan. Deeply in love with the woman of his dreams, he has everything a man could desire... until enemies from his secret past as a government hitman convene to eliminate him, including a death-dealing assassin known as the Viper.

THE LAST STAGE by Bruce Scivally

Dying in his small Los Angeles bungalow, with his Jewish wife, Josephine, whom he calls Sadie, at his side, famed lawman Wyatt Earp imagines an ending more befitting a man of his reputation: returning to his mining claims in a small desert town, tying up loose ends with Sadie, and – after he strikes gold – confronting a quartet of robbers in a showdown.

VEIL OF SEDUCTION by Emily Dinova

1922. Lorelei Alba, a fiercely independent and ambitious woman, is determined to break into the male-dominated world of investigative journalism by doing the unimaginable – infiltrating Morning Falls Asylum, the gothic hospital to which "troublesome" women are dispatched, never to be seen again. Once there, she meets the darkly handsome and enigmatic Doctor Roman Dreugue, who claims to have found the cure for insanity. But Lorelei's instincts tell her something is terribly wrong, even as her curiosity pulls her deeper into Roman's intimate and isolated world of intrigue.

THE UNDERSTUDY by Charlie Peters

"Tell your boss that I have one of his employees." With those words a kidnapping plot begins in the middle of a high-stakes corporate merger. But the kidnappers' plans don't unfold—they unravel.

"If you're thinking of committing the perfect crime, read Charlie Peters' elegant new thriller first. Find out just how many ways perfection can go wrong." – Dan Hearn, author of *Bad August*

For more info visit HenryGrayPublishing.com

...AND ENJOY OUR NEW RELEASES!

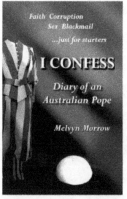

I CONFESS: DIARY OF AN AUSTRALIAN POPE
by Melvyn Morrow

"When I became pope, almost the first word the Curia taught me was 'ricatto'—blackmail."
- Pope John XXIV

From acclaimed playwright Melvyn Morrow comes this engrossing tale of an Australian cardinal who has, through extraordinary circumstances, become pope. His personal diary reveals the inner workings of the Vatican and—when he realizes his tenure may be short and begins enacting sweeping reforms—the centuries-old system in place to make sure that the status quo is maintained—at any cost. It's like an Agatha Christie mystery set in the Vatican, where the most powerful person is powerless in the face of opposing forces both within and without his inner circle.

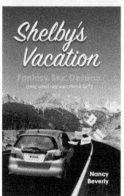

SHELBY'S VACATION by Nancy Beverly

Fantasy. Sex. Despair. (Hey, what are vacations for?)

Shelby sets out from L.A. on a much-needed vacation to mend her heart from her latest unrequited crush. By happenstance, she ends up at a rustic mountain resort where she meets the manager, Carol, who has her own memories of the past inhibiting her ability to create a real relationship in the present. Their casual vacation encounter turns into something more profound than either of them bargained for, as each learns what holds them back from living and loving.

"This is an uplifting and romantic novel about the power of love to heal hearts and minds."
- Elizabeth Sims, author of the award-winning
Lillian Byrd crime series

TOO MUCH IN THE SON by Charlie Peters
Leo Malone. Running from his past. Running into trouble.

In Martinique, Leo Malone meets Taylor Hoffman, a young man who could be his identical twin. Whey they run afoul of a local gangster, Taylor is murdered and Leo assumes his identity to sneak safely out of the country and back to Los Angeles. But when Taylor's estranged parents meet Leo at the airport, mistaking him for their son, Leo's best-laid plans spiral out of control.

Full of surprising twists and turns, **Too Much in the Son** is part Agatha Christie, part Elmore Leonard, with a dash of David Mamet and served with a Larry David chaser, examining the lies, intrigue and violence that make an unexpected family.

YOU'LL FIND FUN WITH

PAPA ROCK'S WORD SEARCH *BOOKS*

PAPA ROCK'S HORROR MOVIES WORD SEARCH
by Rock Scivally

Sharpen your stakes—er, pencils—to solve these unique puzzles designed for anyone who loves classic horror films from the first Frankenstein film in 1910 to the giant bug movies of the 1950s.

If you grew up watching scary movies presented by a local horror host, or collected plastic model kits of monsters or read monster magazines, then this is the Word Search book for you!

PAPA ROCK'S SON OF HORROR MOVIES WORD SEARCH
by Rock Scivally

The 1960s. The 1970s. Two decades that encapsulated a shift in screen horror, from Dracula, Frankenstein, the Wolfman, and giant insects, to Blacula, Dr. Phibes, Regan, Damien, Carrie, a killer baby, and a rat named Ben. Pick up your pens, your pencils, or your blood-red highlighters and literally find all your horror film favorites from 1960 to 1979 within these pages. Happy Haunting!

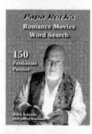

PAPA ROCK'S ROMANCE MOVIES WORD SEARCH
by Rock Scivally and Jeffrey Breslauer

Here are Word Searches for 150 classic Romance movies made between 1921 and 1999, from the tragedy of *Camille* to the comedy of *Notting Hill,* with stops in-between for *Gone With the Wind, Casablanca, Roman Holiday, Breakfast at Tiffany's, The Way We Were, When Harry Met Sally, Jerry Maguire,* and *Titanic,* among many others. Just remember—if this book closes before you've finished working a puzzle, you'll regret it, maybe not today, maybe not tomorrow, but soon and for the rest of your life.

PAPA ROCK'S WESTERN MOVIES WORD SEARCH
by Rock Scivally

Westerns have been an enduring genre in American cinema from the very beginning. There have been serious Westerns, comedy Westerns, epic Westerns, and art-house Westerns. And you'll find examples of all of them in PAPA ROCK'S WESTERN MOVIES WORD SEARCH book. Within these pages are 150 Word Searches based on classic Western movies, including *The Searchers, The Westerner, Stagecoach, My Darling Clementine, Gunfight at the O.K. Corral, Rio Bravo, The Good, the Bad, and the Ugly, Dances With Wolves, Unforgiven,* and many more.

If you enjoyed reading
The Devil in the Diamond
*and think others will, too, please leave a
review on the website of your
favorite bookseller*